ONE DEAD COOKIE

This Large Print Book carries the
Seal of Approval of N.A.V.H.

ONE DEAD COOKIE

VIRGINIA LOWELL

WHEELER PUBLISHING
A part of Gale, Cengage Learning

GALE
CENGAGE Learning·

Farmington Hills, Mich • San Francisco • New York • Waterville, Maine
Meriden, Conn • Mason, Ohio • Chicago

BRUTON MEMORIAL LIBRARY
302 McLENDON STREET
PLANT CITY, FLORIDA 33563

GALE
CENGAGE Learning®

Copyright © 2013 by Penguin Group (USA) Inc.
A Cookie Cutter Shop Mystery.
Wheeler Publishing, a part of Gale, Cengage Learning.

ALL RIGHTS RESERVED
This is a work of fiction. Names, characters, places, and incidents either are the product of the author's imagination or are used fictitiously, and any resemblance to actual persons, living or dead, business establishments, events or locales is entirely coincidental. The publisher does not have any control over and does not assume any responsibility for author or third-party websites or their content.
The recipes contained in this book are to be followed exactly as written. The publisher is not responsible for your specific health or allergy needs that may require medical supervision. The publisher is not responsible for any adverse reactions to the recipes contained in this book.
Wheeler Publishing Large Print Cozy Mystery.
The text of this Large Print edition is unabridged.
Other aspects of the book may vary from the original edition.
Set in 16 pt. Plantin.

LIBRARY OF CONGRESS CATALOGING-IN-PUBLICATION DATA

Lowell, Virginia.
　　One dead cookie / by Virginia Lowell. — Large Print edition.
　　　pages cm. — (A Cookie Cutter Shop Mystery) (Wheeler Publishing Large Print Cozy Mystery)
　　ISBN 978-1-4104-6800-0 (softcover) — ISBN 1-4104-6800-3 (softcover)
　　1. Bakeries—Fiction. 2. Cookies—Fiction. 3. Murder—Investigation—Fiction. 4. Large type books. I. Title.
　　PS3612.O888O54 2014
　　813'.6—dc23
　　　　　　　　　　　　　　　　　　　　　　　2013051114

Published in 2014 by arrangement with The Berkley Publishing Group, a member of Penguin Group (USA) LLC, a Penguin Random House Company

Printed in the United States of America
1 2 3 4 5　　　18 17 16 15 14

BRUTON MEMORIAL LIBRARY
302 McLENDON STREET
PLANT CITY, FLORIDA 33563

*In memory of my mother and her
bookcases filled with mysteries*

$25.99

ACKNOWLEDGMENTS

Writing this series has brought so many extraordinary people into my life. I am grateful to the members of the National Cookie Cutter Collectors Club for their tireless enthusiasm and the depth of their cookie-cutter knowledge, which they share generously. Many, many thanks to the wonderful and creative writers at www.killer characters.com. As always, I want to thank my editor, Michelle Vega, who is a joy to work with, and the talented folks at Berkley Prime Crime. I am indebted to Jean Wohlers, whose luscious cutout cookie recipe, slightly altered, appears in this book — although I must admit that her cookies taste better than mine. And to Sherry Ladig, a special thanks for her discerning eye and for teaching me, just in time, that "combining lemon extract and rosewater in one cookie is like putting two divas on stage at the same time."

CHAPTER ONE

Olivia Greyson could feel his eyes watching her. She knew what was going on, and she refused to be duped. Olivia concentrated on the cardboard box next to her on the sofa. The contents glowed in the soft light from the lamp on the side table. Olivia lifted one of the objects, a shiny aluminum butterfly shape, possibly the last cookie cutter her friend Clarisse Chamberlain had purchased. A few weeks later, she'd been murdered.

That's when the manipulative little guy pulled out the big guns. He whimpered.

"Oh, honestly," Olivia said, her exasperation tinged with guilt. "You make it sound like I've locked you in prison with no food or water. I know we ran out of your treats. I'm sorry, but I just don't have time to go out and find a store that's open this time of night."

Olivia's rescue Yorkshire terrier, Spunky, sat on top of the Queen Anne desk, which

9

Olivia had placed under the front window of her second-story apartment. It was Spunky's favorite spot in the living room. He had a clear view of the entire room, including the television, and he could look out the window onto the Chatterley Heights town square.

Spunky dropped his head onto his paws as if all hope had fled.

"Nice try, Spunks. I told you, Maddie promised to pick up a box of your favorite goodies on her way to the store tomorrow morning. That's the best I can —"

With sudden, renewed energy, Spunky jumped up and peered out the window, his ears perked. He stood on his hind legs, front paws tapping on the glass, and growled.

"What is it, Spunky?" Olivia hurried to the window and squinted into the darkness beyond her porch light. She couldn't see her own front door, which was also the door to The Gingerbread House, the store Olivia owned and operated with her best friend since age ten, Maddie Briggs. If someone was trying to break in . . . Olivia looked around for her cell phone, then remembered she'd left it in her bedroom to charge. She'd have to use the kitchen phone.

Spunky started yapping. His nails scraped on the window as if he wanted to jump out

10

and chase something . . . or someone. Olivia doused the living room lights and rejoined her guard dog. All she saw was darkness, but Spunky kept up his fierce warning. His attention focused on the right side of the park. Streetlamps provided some light for the sidewalks around the square, but not much beyond. The businesses that lined the square showed up in outline. Most of them used porch lights at night, but not much more than sixty-watt bulbs. Chatterley Heights considered itself safe from big-city crime, despite evidence to the contrary.

Olivia couldn't see anything suspicious outside. She wondered if it was worth calling 911 because Spunky saw something he didn't like. He didn't like squirrels or chipmunks or cats or most other dogs. At that moment, Spunky lost interest. He dropped to all fours and yawned. Olivia hoped the excitement had distracted him from his obsession with his missing treats. Just in case, she turned on Animal Planet before returning to her box of cookie cutters.

Olivia settled on her sofa and picked up the butterfly cookie cutter that had reminded her of Clarisse Chamberlain. Olivia still missed their long talks. Clarisse had been both friend and business mentor to

11

her. It was due to Clarisse's encouragement that Olivia had mustered the courage to open The Gingerbread House. For that alone, Olivia felt deeply grateful. Working in The Gingerbread House, helping customers select sugar sprinkles or icing colors, baking and decorating cookies with Maddie: all of it made Olivia's heart smile even when her feet ached.

Clarisse Chamberlain had amassed an impressive and valuable cookie cutter collection, which she'd bequeathed to Olivia. The box next to her on the sofa and the ones on the living room floor were only a small part of that collection. Clarisse would have been delighted to know that her beloved cutters would be featured at the upcoming engagement party for Maddie and her fiancé, Lucas Ashford, owner of Heights Hardware, right next door.

In happier times, Olivia and Clarisse had once explored a huge flea market a few miles from Chatterley Heights. One vendor had been selling off his deceased mother's substantial cookie cutter collection, much of which dated back to the 1980s and '90s. The cutters were interesting but not terribly valuable. With a sudden gasp, Clarisse had grabbed a simple, well-used butterfly shape and held it in the palm of her hand. "My mother had a cutter exactly like this," she'd said. "It was her favorite. I couldn't find it among her things after her death." Olivia now held that very cutter in the palm of her own hand. She smoothed her fingertip over a dent in the wing, remembering Clarisse's delight that the piece was worn, which meant it had been loved. Olivia placed it on her coffee table.

Spunky, now bored with the animal channel, eyed the butterfly cookie cutter on the coffee table, his ears perked with interest. He must have decided it was either a treat or a toy, because he hopped off his perch on the desk, trotted over to the coffee table, and jumped up. He sniffed the butterfly's wing and wagged his fluffy tail.

Olivia knew what that meant. Spunky had decided the butterfly was a doggie toy. "Hey," Olivia said. "Not everything in this apartment belongs to you, kiddo."

Spunky, naturally, dismissed his mistress's statement as illogical and tried to capture the entire butterfly in his teeth. When that proved awkward, he nudged the cutter off the table with his nose and leaped down after it. Olivia followed, but not fast enough. Spunky caught the hemmed edge of the butterfly wing between his teeth and pranced toward the kitchen.

"This is a sneaky way to get some extra dog food, isn't it?" Olivia followed Spunky into the kitchen. As she reached into his bag of dry food, the phone rang. Olivia glanced at her clock. Midnight. The phone had come with the house, and Olivia had gotten a new answering machine installed with caller ID. It hadn't taken long to discover that only telemarketers called her home number, so she usually left the answering machine unplugged. Her cell was in her bedroom, turned off and plugged into its charger. She figured the call was probably from Maddie, who never paid attention to the time when she wanted to talk.

"Maddie can wait until tomorrow morning," Olivia explained to Spunky, who never took his liquid brown eyes off the kibbles in his mistress's hand. "You and I need to finish selecting the cutters to use for this ever-expanding extravaganza she insists on hosting."

On the other hand, what if it's an emergency? As Olivia reached for the receiver, the phone went silent.

Olivia dropped some of the dry food into Spunky's bowl and poured herself a glass of merlot. Before she could wedge the cork back into the bottle, the phone rang again.

14

Olivia took a small sip of wine and answered.

"I assume you are engrossed in party planning?"

"Hi, Maddie. Did you know it's past midnight? And that it's my turn to open the store tomorrow morning, bright and early?" Olivia watched Spunky dive into his late snack with reckless abandon.

"Have you been drinking merlot without me? Hang on, I'll be right over."

"Oh no, you won't," Olivia said. "We agreed. This is my gift to you, since you won't accept anything that costs actual money. I'm making special cookies and a magnificent cookie cake for your engagement party, using original recipes and Clarisse's cutters."

A long and distinctly audible sigh traveled across the phone line. "It's not that I don't trust you, Livie, but . . ."

"What, you think I'm not creative enough to come up with a couple new cookie recipes? Hold that thought. I want to get my cell from the bedroom. I'll call you right back."

Olivia retrieved her cell and speed-dialed Maddie, who said, "Don't be silly. If we were talking casseroles, then yes, I can't see you creating anything remotely edible. But cookies? No problem. It's just that . . . well, you know me. I don't want to miss the fun. Couldn't I be your helper? Pretty please with pink petal dust on top?"

"I wonder . . . ," Olivia murmured as she thought, *Petals . . . petals make me think of flowers and* —

"You'll let me help?" Maddie asked.

"You just did." Olivia envisioned a pyramid made of daisy-shaped cookies with a bouquet of fresh flowers on top. Maddie and Lucas's party would be held in the extravagant garden behind the upscale Bon Vivant restaurant, so the theme was . . . "Perfect," Olivia said.

"Come on, Livie. I could just help you bake. You'd hardly notice I was there."

"Impossible. See you in the store tomorrow."

"Poop head," Maddie said. "Anyway, that isn't why I called. And don't hang up, you'll want to hear this."

"Hmm?" Olivia walked back into the living room and used her remote to mute the television. On Animal Planet, lions were hunting down antelopes. At least, Olivia thought they were antelopes. She cringed, but Spunky, who'd made fast work of the kibbles and had returned to his earlier post, looked fascinated, in a predatory sort of

16

way. Holding her cell to her ear, Olivia nestled on the sofa along with the box of cookie cutters.

"I hope you're listening, Livie, because you'll want to know this. It involves Binnie Sloan."

"Uh-oh, what has our intrepid pseudo-reporter immortalized in print this time?" Binnie Sloan published the local newspaper, *The Weekly Chatter,* which consisted mostly of gossip.

"A rumor," Maddie said. "At least that's what Binnie claims. I'm guessing she made it up. She hinted in her blog that you and Del had a parting of the ways and no longer speak to each other."

"Really? I wonder when that happened. You'd think I'd remember." Olivia began to rummage through a box of cutters, hunting for flower shapes.

"Binnie was vague on that point," Maddie said, "but apparently a huge fight was involved, unforgivable insults were exchanged, and irreconcilable differences ensued. She did refer to your tendency to stick your nose into Del's professional business and that he's sick of it."

"Was that a quote from Del?" Olivia found a tulip cookie cutter and started a pile of garden-themed shapes on her coffee table.

"Binnie implied that she'd spoken with Del, so I'm guessing he said no such thing. It doesn't even sound like him. Del is a pretty easygoing guy, plus I doubt he'd give Binnie an interview under any circumstances."

Olivia knew from personal experience that Del could get testy on occasion, but only about something important. Like her safety . . . and her apparent disregard for it. That was an issue they continued to work on, but Del had shown no signs of extreme frustration with Olivia or their relationship. Quite the opposite, in fact. "Well, thanks for the update," Olivia said. "I don't intend to fret, and I'm sure Del won't either. And now I need to get back to . . . well, you'll just have to wait and see."

"But wait! There's more!" Whenever Maddie mimicked a late-night infomercial, it meant she'd kept the juiciest news for last.

"Of course there is," Olivia said.

"I hear weary resignation in your voice, Livie. However, you need to hear this; it's weird."

"Is this another invention from Binnie's strange mind?" Olivia removed three cutters from her box. She'd netted a six-petaled flower, a bunny, and an Eiffel Tower shape. The flower worked, and the bunny was gar-

18

denish, in a cute yet destructive way. The Eiffel Tower went back into the box.

"Binnie swears up and down in her blog that this rumor came anonymously through email." Maddie's normally bubbly tone had quieted. "If I had access to that email, I could probably track the source, but Binnie claims she deleted it to protect her source from exposure.

"Here's the scoop: Del has become interested in 'a pretty, younger woman' who works part-time in The Gingerbread House. You are furious. You are threatening to fire your pretty, younger, part-time employee. At least Binnie didn't publish Jennifer's name, address, and phone number."

"This is disturbing." Olivia abandoned her one-handed cookie cutter search and curled her legs underneath her on the sofa. "Everyone knows the only young woman we've hired lately is Jennifer Elsworth. I doubt the poor woman has been in town for more than a few days. I've gotten in Binnie's way more than once, so I can understand her going after me. I don't care what nonsense she makes up about my life, but I won't have her dragging our employees into her nasty little fantasies."

"Binnie is clever, in a sneaky, conniving kind of way," Maddie said, "but why would she take revenge on you through an innocent bystander? You and Del will just ignore her insults, as long as they aren't illegal. But Binnie doesn't know Jennifer. What if she has a violent temper . . . or a boyfriend with a violent temper? Or what if she sues Binnie for slander or something? Wait, I'm starting to enjoy this."

"It's libel, not slander, and anyway, it takes only a few minutes to get on Binnie's bad side," Olivia said. "Maybe Jennifer insulted Nedra."

"Possible," Maddie said. "Binnie loves that strange niece of hers. Jennifer is pretty and personable, and Ned is Ned. She's emaciated, rarely speaks, points her camera at you when you're emptying the garbage. . . . I'll stop there."

"I suppose we don't know Jennifer very well, either," Olivia said. "She's great with customers, and she knows a fair amount about cookie cutters and making decorated cookies. Which is why we — or more accurately, you — hired her without references. Have you talked with her about this rumor of Binnie's?"

"You bet I did." Maddie sounded as close to angry as Olivia had ever heard. "I told Jennifer that the best way to handle Binnie Sloan is to ignore anything she says or does. That drives her crazy. I said, 'Don't let Binnie get to you. If someone is rude enough to repeat what she blogged about you, just roll your eyes and snort in derision.' I had to demonstrate that for her, so we ended up laughing. I offered to help her sue Binnie, but she shrugged and said it wasn't important. So I think she's okay for now."

Olivia checked her watch. "Gotta go, Maddie. I've got some creative baking to do if you want those special cookies for your engagement bash. I'm opening the store tomorrow. I'll have a talk with Jennifer when she comes in to work. I don't really know much about her. Not that I'm worried Del might really be interested in her."

"Livie, are you really mad at me for hiring Jennifer without consulting you? Do you think I screwed up and hired a heartless home wrecker?"

"I didn't say that," Olivia said. "She's a bit hard to read, that's all I mean."

"Hard to read like, maybe, a sociopathic killer?"

"Good night, Maddie."

CHAPTER TWO

A short burst of church bells in the distance roused Olivia from a dreamless sleep, but not enough to awaken her. She found them soothing. When the bells pealed a second time, Olivia wished they would stop clanging and let her . . . Wait, what day was it? Was she snoozing through Maddie's engagement party? Had she remembered to deliver the cookie cake? Had she even *started* the cookie cake?

When Spunky launched into his ferocious protector-of-the-house bark, Olivia shot upright and realized at once that she wasn't in bed. She'd fallen asleep scrunched into a fetal position next to the box of cookie cutters that took up half her sofa. She still wore the jeans and raggedy sweatshirt she'd changed into after a quick supper. She must have wilted from sheer exhaustion, because she'd left the television on. A tiger chased a herd of zebras, their cries muted to faint murmurs. Olivia rooted for the zebras. She'd also left her living room windows open and the lights on. *Way to save energy, Livie.*

The chimes rang again, but this time Olivia recognized them as her front doorbell. Spunky growled through bared teeth, ready to take on whatever evil creature threatened his territory, his food, and his Olivia.

"Hush, Spunky. I'm sure there's a rational explanation." Olivia checked her watch. Five a.m. Apparently, the Dixie Cups were also up early and, according to Olivia's cell phone, were off to the Chapel of Love with the intention of getting married. Maddie was forever changing Olivia's ringtone. She grabbed her cell and flipped it open before the Dixie Cups could repeat their matrimonial plans. As Olivia prepared a curt greeting for her caller, someone pounded on the front door of her house. It couldn't be Maddie; she had keys to both the front door and the foyer door, which opened into The Gingerbread House.

"Doesn't anybody sleep anymore?" Olivia hadn't intended her lament to be quite so loud. A familiar laugh drifted through the open front window, which faced the town square. *Del?* She stumbled toward the window.

An equally familiar voice chirped from the cell phone in Olivia's hand. "We can sleep when we're too old to party." Maddie sounded altogether too alert. "You'll be fine, Livie. You just need a cookie."

Olivia peered downward through her living room window screen, but the porch hid the front door. "Del? Is that you?" Del Jenkins, sheriff of Chatterley Heights, left the porch and appeared as a shadowy figure on the lawn. He looked up at Olivia's window and waved.

"Did you say Del is with you?" Maddie's voice asked from the cell phone in Olivia's hand.

Del disappeared. In a few seconds, he pounded on the front door, as if Olivia could possibly forget he was out there. "Hey, Livie, let me in. It's cold." She was grateful there were no neighbors to awaken. At night, Olivia's Queen Anne was the only occupied building around the town square's perimeter.

Del Jenkins might be Olivia's "special friend" — to use her mother's quaint phrase — but that didn't mean he could simply show up before dawn without warning. Unless . . . Maddie and Del were trying to get

24

hold of her at five a.m. For Maddie, this wasn't so unusual. But both at the same time? What were the odds?

Olivia grabbed her keys and ran downstairs with a yapping Yorkie racing ahead of her. When she reached the foyer, she grabbed Spunky to keep him from leaping into the predawn darkness. With a wiggling dog under one arm, Olivia fumbled with the lock and deadbolt for the front door. As soon as the door cracked opened, Del slid through.

"I was sure glad to see you at the window, Livie. When you didn't answer your doorbell, I got worried." Del wore his full sheriff's uniform. When he removed his hat, his straight sandy hair fell forward, covering one eye. His visible eye, red-rimmed and puffy, told Olivia how little sleep he'd had.

"Worried? What's happening? Please don't tell me there's been another murder." Olivia squeezed Spunky too hard, and he yelped.

Del gave her a brief, mirthless smile. "No murder, nothing like that. It's all under control now. Sorry I overreacted, it's just that . . ." Del ran his fingers through his hair, a gesture Olivia recognized.

"If it's all over, come on upstairs for a cup of coffee." Olivia locked and bolted the front and foyer doors and climbed the stairs to her apartment. Del followed, once he'd tested all the doors to make sure they were securely locked.

"Thanks, I could use a caffeine infusion," Del said. "Cody is trying to finish up some crime-scene coursework in DC, so I'm covering his duties. It's been slow and tedious, but not exactly exhausting . . . until the last few hours, that is."

Olivia locked her apartment door behind them before releasing her grip on Spunky. She was convinced he knew how to open an unlocked door. The poor guy had started life in a puppy mill, where he was neglected and mistreated, leaving him with one front paw turned slightly inward. Not that it slowed him down. In fact, the injured paw only seemed to bother him when he was angling for an extra treat.

Olivia led the way to her kitchen, where she measured Italian roast into Mr. Coffee's basket. "You look awful," she said to Del. "I meant that in a kind and concerned way," she added while she filled the coffeepot with fresh water.

"Thanks."

Olivia pressed the machine's on button, almost tripping over Spunky as he circled her feet, using mental telepathy to transmit the word "treat" to her brain. Spunky gave her a stern yap.

"You've already been fed," Olivia reminded him.

"Gee," Del said, "and I was hoping for a cookie."

"Men." Olivia scrounged a plate and two clean cups from her dishwasher.

Del tossed his hat on the kitchen counter, shed his uniform jacket, and slumped onto a chair. "I tried your cell, but it went right to voice mail."

"I was probably talking to Maddie." Olivia's cell phone lay on the living room table, where she'd tossed it when Del arrived. "Oops," she said. "I hung up on her."

Del stood and reached for his hat. "Go ahead and call her. I really should get back to the station."

"Oh no you don't. Sit." When Olivia pressed hard on Del's shoulder, he didn't resist. "Come on, Del, you practically wore out my doorbell, pounded on my door, demanded to be let in, declared yourself worried about me . . . this all before dawn, mind you." The coffee hadn't finished dripping, but Olivia sloshed some into a cup. She plunked it down in front of Del. "Explain yourself."

Del took a long gulp of coffee, nearly draining the cup. "This is not for public

27

consumption," he said.

"That goes without saying." Olivia refilled his cup and reunited Mr. Coffee with his pot.

"There's been a break-in at Lady Chatterley's."

Olivia stifled a giggle; Del's curt statement sounded like a line from a racy mystery spoof. However, Lady Chatterley's Clothing Boutique for Elegant Ladies was a perfectly respectable, upscale shop on West Park Street, a prime location on the busy town square. "Was anyone hurt?"

"It was night, so the store was empty," Del said. "They never keep more than a few hundred dollars in cash on hand, and it gets locked in the safe at closing. We're not entirely sure when the break-in occurred. The manager called us."

"Lola goes to work in the middle of the night? What dedication."

Del laughed. "What really happened is even more amusing. Lola got a call at about four a.m. from Ida, the waitress at Pete's Diner. Ida went in to work early to make some . . . I don't know, muffins or something. She thought she saw movement at Lady Chatterley's' front door, so she dug out her binoculars and had a look. The front door was open and swinging in the wind.

Ida thought that was odd, called the store, got no answer, and so on."

"Sounds like Ida." Olivia sipped her coffee and thought back to Spunky's behavior the night before. "You know, I might be able to help pinpoint the time of the break-in."

Del's eyebrows shot up. "Tell me."

"To be more accurate," Olivia said, "it was Spunky. He was fussing about not getting his treats, and then he suddenly began yapping out the front window. I doubt he heard anything, but he was wiggling around on the desk. I think he saw some movement outside. He was upset enough to forget about treats, so I'd say it was serious."

"When was this?"

"Around midnight," Olivia said, "maybe a bit later. I went to look out the window, but I don't have Spunky's remarkable vision. After a bit, he got bored and settled down. That's all I've got."

"It helps, thanks." Del jotted some notes on a small pad.

"Was anything taken?"

"Lola didn't think so," Del said. "The intruder took a hammer to the safe, but he didn't get into it. Anyway, we think it was a hammer."

"A hammer? Isn't that a bit odd? There must be more effective ways to get into a safe." Olivia fixed herself half a cup of coffee with cream and sugar.

"It isn't that easy," Del said. "Lady Chatterley's has state-of-the-art protection. Given the prices they charge, a thief might assume they keep lots of cash on hand. Especially if that thief was, say, an addict who was thinking more about his next fix than the most efficient way to break into a safe."

Del lifted his cup with both hands and frowned at its contents. Olivia knew that look. Either it was time to run some vinegar through her Mr. Coffee machine to dissolve the crud, or Del was bothered by some aspect of the break-in. "What are you thinking?" she asked. "Pretend I'm Cody."

"That's a stretch," Del said, laughing. "And I mean that literally. You are tall, but not six foot three."

"I was hoping for: 'You're much more attractive, Livie,' but never mind. Your deputy is out of town; talk to me. Don't make me guess." Olivia tried hard not to inject herself into Del's police work, and normally that was easy. She didn't care how many speeding tickets he handed out in the course of the day. But a robbery attempt in Chatterley Heights, town of her birth? She took that personally.

"So, got any cookies?" Del gave her a grin that felt like a hug.

"When have I not kept cookies stashed away for the odd dropper-in?"

"Odd?"

"As in charming and fun." Olivia reached for a covered cake pan on top of her refrigerator. "These are fresh. I'm experimenting with recipes for Maddie and Lucas's party."

"I go for the old standbys myself," Del said. "I've never figured out what's in them, but I know what I like."

"Well, if these cookies are awful, I'd rather hear it from you than from the hungry and disappointed hordes at Maddie's party on Saturday. My reputation is at stake. I'm convinced Maddie doesn't believe I can pull off this baking feat without her help. I'm having doubts myself."

Del reached into the pan and selected a lion shape decorated with burgundy fur and a purple dragée eye. "I did a quick assessment and determined he's the biggest and fiercest cookie."

"I expected no less." Olivia poured the last of the coffee into his cup, rinsed the pot and basket, and added more grounds and water. When she pushed the start button and turned around, Del was chewing the lion's head. He had a puzzled expression on his face.

"Are you thinking about the break-in again?" Olivia asked.

"Um, not really." Del wedged the remains of his cookie on his saucer.

"I see," Olivia said. "You hate the cookie."

"I don't hate it exactly." Del avoided Olivia's eyes.

"It's okay, I'm a grown-up baker. I can take it," Olivia said. "But time's a-wasting, and I need feedback. What is it about the cookie that makes it unappealing? Taste? Texture? Its very existence?"

"I wouldn't call it unappealing exactly. All right, Livie, in the interests of scientific analysis and as long as you won't take it personally." Del took a small bite of the offending cookie and closed his eyes. "It's a bit . . . I don't know, maybe . . . understated? Your cookies are usually so rich and buttery or spicy or whatever the right terms are. They have a lot of flavor. I can't stop eating them. This one is . . ." Del cast a furtive glance at the kitchen door, his only escape. "Well, it's bland. It doesn't have much flavor. And the texture is weird."

Del watched her so warily that Olivia had to laugh. "To be honest, you confirmed my suspicions. For some reason I thought it would be a good idea to try making more healthy cutout cookies. So I replaced some of the butter with the low cholesterol fake stuff. That changed the texture, and not for the better. Also, I used too much, so I had to keep adding flour to get it to roll out, which made it drier and less tasty. I would have rolled it out in confectioners' sugar, but I was trying to limit the sugar content. So thank you, Del. Now I don't need to inflict my experiment on anyone else." Olivia confiscated the remainder of his lion and dropped it into the garbage can. The remaining cookies suffered the same fate. Finally, Olivia brought a small box to the table. "These are the old standbys you remember," she said. "Something to cleanse the palate."

Del opened the box and selected the top cookie, a simple pink daisy shape with a red outline around the petals. He took a substantial bite and sighed. Reaching across the table, Del covered Olivia's hand with his own. "Cookies," he said, "are not meant to be healthy."

"Words of great depth and wisdom," Olivia said. "Now back to the break-in at Lady Chatterley's. I have a question. They sell a lot of expensive clothing in that store. I know Chatterley Heights is a small town, and maybe I'm jaded from living in a big

33

city, but I'd expect a store as sophisticated as Lady Chatterley's to have a good alarm system."

"They do," Del said, shaking his head. "Like I said, state-of-the-art. That's what bothers me. Lola closed up yesterday, and she swears she set the alarm system, as always. But it was deactivated. That took some know-how."

"So why would someone skilled enough to deactivate an alarm system bash at a safe with a hammer?"

"Exactly," Del said. "It's possible the thief wasn't good enough to crack the safe, so he got frustrated."

"And took it out on the safe?"

"An entertaining image," Del said, "but unlikely. We don't yet know for sure that he — assuming it's a he — used an actual hammer, though the dents look like a hammerhead. But who brings a hammer along for a break-in? There are quieter ways to break and enter, and this guy sure knew what he was doing when it came to deactivating an alarm." Del stood up and reached for his uniform jacket.

"Maybe there were two thieves?"

Del paused a second before shaking his head. "One smart and skilled and the other dumb and violent? Only in the movies." He glanced at the kitchen clock. "Gotta go. I'm supposed to be on duty at the station by six, which was eight minutes ago."

With a tired Spunky under her arm, Olivia followed Del down the stairs and unlocked the front door for him. Del gave Olivia a quick kiss, and said, "I'll let you know when we catch the guy. Meanwhile, keep your eyes open and be careful. The Gingerbread House could become a target, too. I hope Cody gets back soon; I can't be everywhere at once."

"You don't need to stand guard over me." Olivia heard the testiness in her own voice and tried to tone it down. "We have plenty of staff on duty all day, and Spunky will raise the roof if he hears anyone in the house at night."

"Okay, point taken." Del stepped onto the porch. He hesitated, then spun around to face Olivia. Folding her in his arms, he rubbed his cheek against her hair. "I can't help it. I worry. So sue me," he said lightly. He kissed the tip of her nose and left.

Olivia watched him walk away and whispered, "Me, too."

CHAPTER THREE

The sun had barely risen when del left her apartment, and Olivia already had a plan. She had nearly three hours before The Gingerbread House officially opened at nine a.m. She'd need to shower and dress for work, and it would take about half an hour to prepare the store for opening. That left a couple hours of free time.

Wearing the same clothes she'd worn when she fell asleep on the sofa, Olivia took Spunky on a brisk early morning run through the park. After twenty minutes, Spunky was tired enough to curl up for a morning nap. Olivia took a quick shower and changed into chocolate brown linen slacks and a light matching sweater.

When she reentered her living room, keys in hand, Spunky lifted one eyelid and closed it at once. He didn't protest as Olivia quietly locked him inside her apartment. She thought about taking Spunky downstairs to the store's sales area, where he held court during the day. With an intruder on the loose, however, that might not be the safest place to leave a small dog alone. Of course, if he'd realized a car ride was on Olivia's agenda, the wily little Yorkie would have found a way to sneak out with her. Guile was his middle name.

Olivia had a creative cookie challenge to tackle, and it would require her full concentration. She had volunteered to provide decorated cookies for Maddie's afternoon-long, blowout engagement party, to which everyone in the town of Chatterley Heights plus the surrounding area considered themselves invited. Maddie and her future husband, Lucas Ashford, had planned a quiet, private, no-frills wedding, so the engagement party was both a celebration and their gift to their hometown. Olivia was helping Maddie plan the party, which would be held in the ever-expanding garden behind the Bon Vivant restaurant on the north edge of town.

Providing dozens and dozens of decorated cookies for the many guests to snack on was a huge feat in itself. However, Maddie also wanted a cake made of cookies. She envisioned something gloriously original, gorgeous, and, of course, yummy. Naturally,

Olivia wanted to create such a gift for her best friend. The cookie cake was Maddie's one request for a wedding gift, to be served at the engagement party. Olivia had four more days to accomplish the entire assignment, while doing her part to keep The Gingerbread House running smoothly. Her imagination, usually so attuned to anything cookie-related, had overloaded and shut down.

Now that Olivia wasn't running with an energetic dog, the morning air felt chilly. She walked briskly to the side street where she parked the used PT Cruiser with which she was not-so-secretly in love. She told herself that her affection arose from the car's practical design, which allowed her to transport numerous covered cake pans filled with iced cookies to themed events. But she had to admit that her heart stirred every time she saw the elaborate painting she had commissioned to advertise The Gingerbread House. A fanciful depiction of a yellow-and-purple Victorian house, festooned with silver and copper cookie cutters, decorated the hood. Across the doors, ornate lettering spelled "The Gingerbread House," and grinning gingerbread men and women somersaulted all over the car's trunk. Definitely not her most practical expenditure.

However, her ride got noticed.

The scent of cinnamon welcomed Olivia when she opened the PT Cruiser's door. Simply sitting inside ought to have triggered an idea for Maddie's cookie cake, but Olivia had tried it several times without success. She needed visual stimulation. She turned her key in the ignition and drove off without a destination in mind. Her car pointed north, so north she went.

Ever since Frederick P. Chatterley first wandered onto the stretch of land that became Chatterley Heights about two hundred and fifty years earlier, the town's wealthier inhabitants had clustered north of the town square. No one knew why. The land wasn't more arable, nor were the views particularly stunning. Frederick P. was not a get-up-and-go sort of town founder. His sole desire was to get up on his trusty steed and go to the home of his mistress of the moment, and the north end of town had been the closest he could get to her without moving in next door. Eventually the Chatterley family built a mansion on the site of Frederick P.'s original house.

Olivia drove through the historic section of town, now solidly middle class, and across the northern boundary of Chatterley Heights. Unlike so many small towns, Chatterley Heights had experienced minimal suburban sprawl. Olivia soon reached a sparsely populated area. Only one new business had chosen to locate beyond the north edge of town — the Bon Vivant restaurant, an upscale establishment that took pains to meld into the countryside. Olivia and Del had shared a number of tasty meals at Bon Vivant, often featuring previously unimagined varieties of pizza accompanied by excellent merlot. As she drove past the restaurant, Olivia smiled at the memory of those times. She and Del always tried to snag a table by the window so they could enjoy the restaurant's elaborate garden, showcased against lush rolling hills in the distance.

Olivia saw no approaching cars through her rearview mirror, so she lifted her foot off the accelerator and drifted to a halt. She'd remembered reading in the town's otherwise irritating newspaper, *The Weekly Chatter,* about Bon Vivant's ever-more-ambitious plans for its garden. Olivia was fairly certain the article had called the renovation "over-the-top frou-frou."

Bon Vivant had begun with a modest garden, which seemed to double in size each time Olivia returned to the restaurant. Maddie and Lucas had chosen the setting for

40

their engagement party because they thought it might be large enough to accommodate their guests, as long as those guests spread themselves throughout the grounds.

A garden sounded like the perfect place to awaken Olivia's cookie creativity. She felt her initial idea for the cookies wasn't unique enough. Flower and bunny shapes were fine for a spring store event, but Olivia wanted a less predictable theme. To be honest, she hoped to present Maddie with a cookie creation she wouldn't have thought of herself. If that was possible.

It was six forty a.m. when Olivia pulled into the parking lot, and Bon Vivant was open for breakfast. She slipped into a light jacket she kept in the car, just in case. The morning air was chilly for late April, and she didn't want to shiver her way through the gardens. The parking lot held three cars. Olivia walked around to the rear of the restaurant, where she found the patio seating area empty. She went inside, ordered a cup of coffee, and obtained permission to wander through the garden.

Olivia paused on the patio to sip her coffee and take in the view. Bon Vivant had added a few small trees since the last time she and Del had dined there. She couldn't identify them, but at least they didn't obscure the lush hills in the distance. Not yet, anyway. Curving paths divided the expanding garden into sections, each with a different theme. Beyond the garden stretched several acres of undeveloped land. Olivia wondered if Bon Vivant owned any or all of it. Given the restaurant's popularity, she suspected it was doing well financially, despite the hefty prices.

A light breeze carried a sweet scent that reminded Olivia of her idea to incorporate real flowers into the cookie cake design. She followed the scent to a large patch of lily of the valley. Olivia was fairly certain that lilies of the valley were poisonous. Not the party theme she had in mind. She wished she'd thought to bring a plant identification guide, one with lots of color photos.

Olivia wandered at random, allowing whim and fragrance to guide her. She came to a garden filled with wildflowers organized in rows. The small patch flourished due to care and an automated watering system. Not a single weed poked through the displays. The effect was stunning, yet Olivia found herself uninspired. She wished for a bit less perfection. Her favorite cookie cutters always had dents or scratches or those tiny variations that indicated they were handmade.

Once again the Dixie Cups musically expressed their imminent wedding plans, in case the event had slipped Olivia's mind. She fumbled for her cell. "I'm all for fun," Olivia said, "but this is getting old."

"What? Not even a 'Hi, Maddie, friend of my childhood, it's great to hear from you?' I might be having a serious premarital crisis, you know. Or even better, maybe I found a dead body in the kitchen."

"Uh-huh." Olivia instantly regretted her cynical tone. Ebullience was Maddie's normal state, and wedding pressures had ramped it up to levels intolerable to ordinary humans. "Sorry," Olivia said. "I'm feeling pressed for time, which makes me cranky. What's up?"

"Oh, Livie, I'm so excited. Aunt Sadie finished my dress, and it is unbelievably, incredibly, gloriously stunning. The embroidery is fabulously . . . well, I'm running out of adjectives or whatever they're called."

"Adverbs."

Maddie laughed. "Anyway, I tried the dress on, and wow. The embroidered flowers are Aunt Sadie's best work ever. They're done mostly in shades of purple, but she added some reddish embroidery floss that's close to the color of my hair. The bodice is a bit loose. I guess I've been running around so much, I lost some weight. Aunt Sadie offered to take it in, but I told her to leave it. A few cookies, and I'll be back to normal." Maddie's generous curves were legendary, as was her wild red hair. "And speaking of cookies . . ."

"No, you can't take over the cookie baking for your own engagement party," Olivia said. "And stop worrying. Everything is under control."

"Livie, I can always tell when you're lying. Besides, I'm calling from the Gingerbread House kitchen, and I see no signs of furious baking, no creative design ideas, no unique ingredients. . . . Need I say more?"

"Snoop. I am not ready to admit defeat." *Although it's starting to feel tempting.*

"Livie, don't think of it as giving up. Think of it as saving your best friend's engagement party from cookie-less disaster."

"I think I've just been insulted."

"Look," Maddie said, "how about a compromise? I know you'll come up with a plan — you are, of course, the queen of planning — but you have too much going on at once. And you need a design idea, like, yesterday. I know how you get when you're feeling too pressured. So let me help with the baking. You'll be able to think better, it'll be fun, and together we can get the baking done in

44

half the time it would take you alone."

"Probably less than half the time," Olivia said.

"So that's a yes?"

"Well, I guess I —"

"Yippee! Oops, sorry about the decibel level."

Olivia felt a surge of relief. "I get to come up with the ideas, though."

"I promise you are free to ignore all my brilliant suggestions," Maddie said. "I can't wait to get started. Only don't feel pressured by that."

"Quit while you're ahead," Olivia said, laughing. "I'll go commune with nature and see if it triggers a brilliant cookie idea. Since you're already at the store and bursting with nervous energy, you can open. So there."

"Done," Maddie said. "Go commune."

Olivia switched her ringtone to vibrate and looked around for a promising direction to try next. Numerous gardens fanned out before her, forming a large semicircle divided by curving paths. To her left, Olivia saw flowering shrubs and trees shading wooden benches. The scene looked inviting, a good place to sit and ponder the enormity of her creative baking task and the woefully inadequate amount of time left to accomplish it. Instead, Olivia turned to her right, a sunny area with small, low patches of greenery dotted with bits of color. Bland, yet pleasant. Olivia's watch told her she had well over an hour before Maddie might need her at The Gingerbread House. She decided to explore the few remaining gardens before settling on a tree-shaded bench to wait for a tasty idea to pop into her head.

The fully risen sun warmed Olivia as she followed a winding path between two patches of bushy green plants. She picked a stiff leaf from one of the plants and bent it in half. It released a rich lemony fragrance. She couldn't find a marker to identify the plants, so she used her cell phone camera for a close-up of the leaves and sent the photo to her computer. She put the leaf in the pocket of her linen pants, hoping it wouldn't stain.

Olivia strolled past several plots filled with culinary herbs, many of which she recognized, such as Greek oregano with its fuzzy leaves. Oregano made her think of pizza, which caused a tummy rumble. She'd raced out of the house without eating. She thought the small plants with tiny leaves might be thyme, and the large grayish leaves on the next batch of plants had to be sage. The last garden held lavender, which Olivia recognized from her mother's herb garden. It would be lovely later in the season, with its long stems and spiky flowers. This early in the spring, the plants hadn't reached the bud stage. Olivia wondered if Bon Vivant harvested their lavender, as her mother did. Olivia knew the buds dried into fragrant potpourri, which she doubted Bon Vivant would go to the trouble of creating. The restaurant must be using the buds for cooking. Olivia picked one fragrant stalk.

A young couple emerged from Bon Vivant carrying coffee cups. The woman pointed toward the flower gardens, and the two of them headed in Olivia's direction. A server held the door open for a second couple and led them to a table on the patio. Feeling guilty about the lavender stalk in her hand, Olivia escaped to the shade. The copse of trees wasn't large, but it felt like a dense forest. When planting the young flowering trees, Bon Vivant had chosen to preserve several older, larger trees.

Olivia chose a bench under an old oak, well hidden from the restaurant. She checked her cell, which she'd left on vibrate, and saw with relief that she had no messages. She had about twenty minutes to relax and hope for culinary inspiration to descend.

Olivia squeezed a lavender leaf between

her fingertips and breathed in the sharp sweetness. Her mother would undoubtedly take one whiff, go into an otherworldly state, and discover a new path to universal peace. Olivia wasn't a trance sort of person, but she let her mind wander. It led her to potpourri. She didn't actually like potpourri. She closed her eyes and tried to focus on the use of lavender in baking. Instead, she remembered the organic, lavender-scented spray cleaner her mother insisted on using to clean the kitchen counter.

A shout in the distance told Olivia she wouldn't enjoy her solitude for much longer. She needed an idea, and she needed it now. To purge the scent of lavender cleanser from her stubborn mind, Olivia dug the folded lemony leaf from her pocket and held it to her nostrils. Heavenly. Lemon-scented cleanser, now that was a product she could — *Enough with the cleansers, Livie. Think about cookies.*

A childhood memory flashed into Olivia's mind. The scene came back to her so clearly, she could remember the aromas. Her mother, Ellie, did nothing in a tentative way. When she tackled an activity, she did so with every fiber of her ethereal being. Olivia's lifelong love affair with decorated cookies and cookie cutters had begun when her mother had gone through her baking phase.

At age nine, Olivia had still wanted time with her mother, so she spent every possible moment in the kitchen, sometimes at the expense of homework. Her mild-mannered, intellectual father had expressed concern, in his distracted way. Her mother, however, insisted that school should never get in the way of a child's education. Cookie cutters illustrated history, Ellie had said. While they mixed, rolled, and cut out shapes from the dough, Ellie told stories about fairs in medieval England, where maidens would devour cookies shaped like men, hoping to summon bridegrooms.

Ellie's teachings had included information about edible and poisonous plants. She'd insisted her daughter learn to recognize the difference between the two. Olivia had forgotten most of the details, but she'd retained one fragrant lesson about edible plants. Her mother had a habit of leaping from one topic to another through an obscure route. She'd been explaining meringue powder, composed mostly of dried egg whites and used in royal icing. Without a moment's pause, she had launched into a tutorial on everything meringue, including meringue cookies. Olivia remembered feeling dizzy as her mother twirled around the kitchen, collecting baking ingredients. At one point, Ellie opened a high cupboard and selected a jar of lavender buds she'd harvested and dried the previous summer.

Olivia was surprised by how precisely the conversation replayed in her mind. Ellie had opened the jar of dried lavender and breathed in the scent, closing her eyes in ecstasy. "So luscious. Smell this, Livie," she'd said, holding the jar under her daughter's nose.

Olivia had wrinkled her nose at the sharp smell. "Ugh. Too strong."

"Such a sensitive child," Ellie said. "That's a good thing, Livie, and don't let anyone tell you different."

"Um, okay." Olivia had no idea what her mother was talking about, but she was always willing to resist any opinions that clashed with her own.

"And now, my child, prepare to be amazed and astonished." Ellie whipped up a light dough, added lavender buds, and dropped it by small spoonfuls onto a baking pan. A gentle lavender fragrance sweetened the kitchen air as the cookies baked. When Ellie removed the pan from the oven, Olivia saw pale lavender nuggets that looked too pretty to eat. Her mother let them cool on a rack before popping one into her mouth whole.

"Utterly delicious," Ellie said with a happy sigh. "These are meringues, Livie. Try one."

"Are you sure?"

"It's a taste experience you will never forget," Ellie said.

Olivia picked up a meringue and sniffed it. Definitely lavender, but more pleasant than the buds her mother had waved under her nose. The cookie felt firm, yet light as air. Following Ellie's example, she tossed the morsel into her mouth.

"That's my girl," Ellie said.

As the meringue dissolved in her mouth, Olivia experienced an explosion of sweet perfume that snaked up her nostrils. "Wow," she said. "That was . . . Wow."

Ellie giggled like a child as she reached for another meringue. Olivia's hand was close behind. Between them they finished off half the pan, yet the cookies had been so light that Olivia felt she'd eaten nothing more than scented air.

The generic ring of a nearby cell phone startled Olivia back to the present. She smiled at the lavender wand in her left hand. It no longer irritated her. In fact, she felt downright friendly toward the tiny purple buds the lavender plants would soon produce; they had given her part of the answer to her dilemma about flavors for the cookies she'd promised to create for Maddie's engagement blowout.

Sadie Briggs, Maddie's aunt and a skilled seamstress, had designed Maddie's wedding gown. The dress was pale yellow satin with tiny lavender buttons down the back of the bodice. Aunt Sadie embroidered beautifully and she had decorated the dress with tiny flowers. According to Maddie, the flowers were lavender to deep purple. So lavender-flavored sugar cookies would be perfect for the engagement party.

Since Maddie's wedding dress was yellow satin, lemon sugar cookies seemed the logical choice for a second flavor. Not terribly original. Olivia sniffed the leaf she had stuffed in her pocket. It was still fragrant and definitely lemony. If she could identify the plant, maybe she could include it in a cookie recipe. Assuming it tasted as good as it smelled and wasn't poisonous, that is. She'd need an organic source for both herbs. Maybe the restaurant would have . . .

Once again, a generic ringtone disrupted the peaceful setting. The sound came from behind Olivia's bench. This time a quiet voice answered on the first ring. Olivia decided it was time to leave. Too many distractions. As she reached toward her empty coffee cup, the disembodied voice spoke in a low, brusque whisper. There was a hard edge to the voice that sent a chill through Olivia. She guessed the speaker was a man, but it was hard to tell. A very angry woman might sound as harsh.

Instinctively, Olivia sank down on the bench seat, out of sight. She felt a bit silly, not to mention uncomfortable, and she doubted there was any real danger. On the other hand, an encounter with an irritable stranger wasn't her idea of an ideal start to her day.

After a minute or so of silence, Olivia began to relax. Perhaps the stranger had wandered farther away. Olivia checked her watch; she'd need to leave soon if she wanted to arrive at The Gingerbread House not long after opening. She prided herself on being available to customers during working hours, if at all possible. Olivia slid her two herb samples into her pants pocket and retrieved her empty coffee cup.

"Are you crazy? What were you thinking?" The words were whispered, but even so, the anger came through. After a pause, Olivia heard the voice again, but the only phrases she could make out were "People around . . . Meet me . . ." and, after a few moments, "stupid thing to do." Olivia thought she heard the crunch of footsteps

53

on undergrowth . . . then silence. She waited until it felt safe to peek over the back of the bench. She saw nothing and heard only the scurrying of small animals and a male mourning dove cooing for a mate. Olivia wished good luck to the lonely dove as she hurried back into the sunshine.

A sweet buttery scent greeted Olivia as she entered The Gingerbread House. Maddie must have just taken a freshly baked sheet of cutout sugar cookies from the oven. Olivia was glad she'd stopped for a light breakfast at Bon Vivant before heading to the store. Otherwise, she'd be tempted to down a dozen or so of those cookies.

On the sales floor, a middle-aged woman listened with rapt attention to the store's newest sales clerk, Jennifer Elsworth. With her honey brown hair and clear green eyes, Jennifer was an attractive young woman. Though quiet and serious, her impressive knowledge of vintage cookie cutters and baking more than compensated for her lack of animation. Jennifer gave Olivia a quick nod of acknowledgment but kept her attention focused on her customer. Olivia approved. Jennifer had shown up at the store two days earlier looking for a job, and Maddie had interviewed her. To demonstrate her knowledge and sales prowess, Jennifer had walked up to a customer who was "just looking" and skillfully convinced her to purchase several vintage cutters. Maddie had hired her on the spot.

Jennifer hadn't yet discussed her background or why she had moved to Chatterley Heights. In fact, Jennifer had shared nothing about herself, which made Olivia uneasy. Maybe it was time to create a job application form. She hadn't seen a need before now. They'd hired only one permanent part-time employee, Bertha Binkman, who had spent forty years as the Chamberlain family housekeeper. Because of Olivia's friendship with Clarisse Chamberlain, she knew Bertha well and trusted her implicitly. Not that Jennifer seemed untrustworthy; quite the opposite. And they did need help in the store.

The kitchen door opened, and Maddie breezed through carrying a tray loaded with decorated cookies. She offered their customer first choice. With a guilty grimace, the woman took two. Jennifer declined.

"Welcome, stranger," Maddie said as she carried the tray over to Olivia. "Did you get any breakfast? I can offer you a pizza-shaped cookie with fondant pepperoni."

Among the various foods shapes, Maddie

had indeed included several cookie wedges decorated with pepperoni-like circles of fondant. Olivia selected a cookie "slice," telling herself that one scrambled egg did not constitute a full breakfast. She bit off the narrow end, almost expecting it to taste spicy. It didn't.

"There's something disturbing about cardamom-flavored pizza," Olivia said.

"I'll take that as a compliment." Maddie deposited the cookie tray next to the coffee urn they always kept filled for the public. "Not many customers so far, but we'll get more business once word spreads around town that fresh cookies have appeared. Come on, let's talk while we can. Jennifer has everything under control. She is a marvel."

Olivia followed Maddie into the kitchen, where their own Mr. Coffee was spitting out the last drops of a fresh pot. Maddie poured two cups while Olivia dug to the back of the stuffed refrigerator for the cream and sugar. "There must be eight batches of cookie dough in here," Olivia said. "You've been working."

"Lo these many hours," Maddie said. "Our customers expect cookies every day, and I figured you had your hands full. I'll freeze enough cookies for a week or more once I get all that dough cut, rolled, and baked. Then I can help you with the cookies for the party. How did your brainstorming go?"

Olivia finished her cookie, remembering the voice she'd heard from the bench among the trees behind the Bon Vivant restaurant.

"I gather it wasn't productive?" Maddie doctored her coffee with cream and sugar and danced it back to the worktable without spilling a drop. "If you're still hungry, I put aside a few cookies for us. We need our strength." She pointed toward a small plate.

"My brainstorming was a total success. More or less." Olivia selected a magenta bunny cookie from the table and tasted its ear. She wasn't really hungry, but that rarely stopped her from eating a cookie. "I came up with a couple of cookie ideas which are, if I may say so, worthy of you."

"Good to know." When Olivia didn't elaborate, Maddie asked, "So are you planning to share your ideas with me, your obedient co-baker? Livie? You seem distracted. Don't tell me there's been another murder in poor, dwindling Chatterley Heights. There's no other explanation for your failure to spill your brilliant baking ideas and bask in my admiring gratitude."

"Sometimes you're scary," Olivia said.

"That was a compliment, in case you wondered. Actually, I was thinking about a conversation I overheard . . . well, half a conversation. I'm probably making a big deal out of nothing, but . . ." She repeated for Maddie, as precisely as she could remember, the angry whispered words she'd heard.

Maddie frowned in quiet thought for so long that Olivia began to worry she'd made the incident sound more sinister than it probably was. "I suppose there are numerous perfectly innocent explanations," she said. "A marital spat, for instance. Bickering spouses can be brutal to each other," Olivia remembered her own marriage as it broke down. Although she couldn't recall even Ryan, her ex-husband, using quite so harsh a tone with her, or her with him. Sarcasm was Ryan's personal favorite way to get his point across. "I missed most of the conversation," Olivia said, "and I might have misinterpreted what I did hear."

"Or you heard right, and you are a witness to half a criminal conversation. Remember, someone broke into Lady Chatterley's last night."

Olivia poured herself a cup of fresh coffee, added cream, and reached for the sugar.

"From what Del told me, nothing was taken."

Maddie perked up. "What else did Del tell you? And no stinting on the details."

Oops. Olivia had promised Del she would keep mum about anything he shared with her about ongoing investigations. Once again, she had failed. "Look Maddie, I can't tell you everything Del says to me. He trusts me . . . more or less. I don't want to mess that up."

Maddie didn't protest. In fact, she was suspiciously silent.

"Maddie? You have that look on your face. You've already heard all the details of the break-in, haven't you? Did you bug my apartment?"

"Don't be silly, Livie. I am but a simple baker; I have no idea how to bug an apartment. Lucas would know, but I would never involve him in such a nefarious scheme. No, I'm simply amused by your city ways."

"City ways? What the . . . ? Oh. There are no secrets in small towns, right?"

"Right." Maddie's generous mouth curved in a smug grin. Even the curly mass of red hair that piled on top of her head seemed to puff up with self-satisfaction. "Plus, my friend Lola is the top manager at Lady Chatterley's, remember? She told me every detail about the break-in, including the weird fact that someone expertly dismantled the store's state-of-the-art alarm system only to bash the safe with a hammer. So incompetent."

"And, as you said, weird. It might explain why nothing was taken. Maybe the intruder only wanted cash and got angry when he couldn't find any." Olivia relaxed. After all, Del understood the relentless power of the small town rumor mill better than she did. Juicy information always zipped through Chatterley Heights faster than a professionally set wildfire; Del wouldn't assume she'd lit the match. Would he?

"It makes me think the intruder was a man. I doubt a woman could resist carting off a selection of expensive dresses." Maddie emptied a bowl of cookie dough onto the rolling mat. "What if there were two burglars? Maybe the voice you heard in the Bon Vivant garden was one of them checking in with his partner in crime. Maybe one turned off the burglar alarm and left, and the other was supposed to steal the money, only he couldn't get into the safe. That would explain the anger you heard. Plus, if —"

"Whoa, that's a whole lot of speculation," Olivia said.

"You never let me have any fun." Maddie glanced up at the clock over the sink. "The hordes will descend soon to devour our free cookies. I'd better start baking and decorating for later." She gathered her icing ingredients: meringue powder, confectioners' sugar, lemon extract, and a handful of tiny bottles of gel food coloring.

"I'll help Jennifer work the sales floor." Olivia wiped cookie crumbs into the garbage can before she deposited the plates in the dishwasher. "By the way, how is she working out?"

"Great! That girl knows her cookie cutters. Bertha says she connects well with the customers." Maddie washed her hands, which meant she was ready to begin measuring ingredients into the mixing bowl.

"Does she seem a bit distant to you?" Olivia asked. "Has she shared much about her background? I'm wondering why I've never met her before, even at Cookie Cutter Collectors Club meetings."

"Livie, you are so suspicious. Jennifer isn't actually from Chatterley Heights. She grew up in Twiterton, but she left as a child. She's been living in DC, wanted to be in a small town, remembered this area with fondness, and so on. That's about all I know. She isn't talkative, which I can appreciate because it allows me to talk more. She's a steady worker, knowledgeable . . . really, what's not to like? I get tired of high school girls who would rather text on their cell phones than wait on customers. Not that I wasn't exactly the same at their age, except for not having a cell phone." Maddie measured lemon extract into the mixing bowl. "Begone," she said. "I am about to transform these simple ingredients into the miraculous substance known as royal icing." She lowered the beaters into the bowl.

As the mixer began to whir, Olivia closed the kitchen door behind her and scanned the sales floor, one of her most favorite places on earth. She counted four customers wandering among the tables of cookie cutter displays. Three more had commandeered the coffee table for an intense discussion that required nearness to cookies. Across the floor, a young couple watched, clearly entranced, as Jennifer explained the many and mysterious attachments for a large red mixer that had gone unsold since The Gingerbread House first opened its doors. No one so much as glanced at Olivia as she tidied the display of baking equipment.

Olivia's back was to the sales floor when she heard a staccato *clip-clip* behind her, followed by a sound that made her think of castanets. "Mom?"

"So clever of you, Livie. How did you know?"

Olivia turned to see her petite mother, Ellie, dressed in a shiny lavender top, slim black pants, and charcoal suede shoes tied with black laces. Her long gray hair hung over one shoulder in a braid, and a gray suede fedora tilted rakishly atop her head. "Wow," Olivia said. "You look amazing. Are those sequins?"

"My little costume enhancement." Ellie smoothed her fingers across several rows of deep purple sequins sewn around the neck of her lavender top. As she spun in a pirouette to show off the entire effect, her feet made a clicking sound.

"Hey, are those tap shoes? This is so unfair. You wouldn't let me take tap dance lessons when I was a kid."

"I'm sorry about that, dear," Ellie said. "I was a teensy bit afraid you would get your feet tangled up and lose your balance. I was only thinking of your safety."

"Well, Mom, I am eight inches taller than you are. It's easier to stay balanced when you're so close to the ground."

"Ouch," Ellie said, grinning up at her five-foot-seven-inch daughter.

"Okay, that was mean of me. How about a cookie?" Olivia made a silent promise to accept her clumsiness, inherited from her late father, and to celebrate the fact that she could reach high shelves.

"Apology accepted," Ellie said. "And normally I'd love a cookie, but I'm on the run. I didn't even have time to take off my tap shoes after my lesson, and I'm already late for my League of Women Voters meeting, which I'm supposed to chair. I merely stopped by to offer you my help with the baking for Maddie's lovely yet ambitious engagement party. My kitchen is at your disposal. So much easier to keep Maddie in the dark about your cookie plans, and it would be such fun to bake with you again."

"Mom, that would be perfect. I've already agreed to let Maddie help, but I'd rather she didn't know about my experimental failures. Can you really fit baking sessions into your schedule? Don't you have activities planned for every hour of every day?"

"You're exaggerating just a bit, Livie," Ellie said with an indulgent smile. "You got that from your father, along with a tiny tendency toward sarcasm. Although I do realize you are stressed at the moment, which always —"

"Mom? The League of Women Voters?"

Olivia pointed to the Hansel and Gretel clock on the wall, a gift from her mother to celebrate The Gingerbread House's grand opening. The clock face depicted an intricate view of the inside of the witch's house, complete with children and oven. The visual detail made it difficult to read the time accurately. "According to Hansel and Gretel," Olivia said, "either you are due at your meeting right now, or you're up to thirteen minutes late."

"Oh good, I still have time. We usually drink coffee and eat doughnuts for at least twenty minutes before calling the meeting to order. No one will miss me until the doughnuts are gone." Ellie glanced toward the cookie tray, still blocked by the two intense women. "Maybe I'll have that cookie, after all. For strength, you know." She tap-danced the few feet to the table, which startled the women into jumping aside. Ellie snagged two cookies and tap-danced back to Olivia. "That was fun."

"I'm torn between pride and embarrassment," Olivia said.

"Thank you." Ellie bit the tail off a bright red cardinal with dark red sprinkles. "When can you come to the house for a baking session? I'd skip my yoga class this afternoon, but I'll need it after the league meeting.

After that, I'm free. Maybe you could come for dinner? Allan would love to see you, and I'm sure Jason could join us once he finishes his shift at the garage."

"Jason would skip transplant surgery for a free home-cooked meal." Olivia's string bean of a brother could lose weight eating six meals a day. "I promised to help Maddie decorate cookies for the store tomorrow, but I could probably get there by seven. You can start dinner without me. I'd feel responsible if Jason passed out from hunger."

"I'll feed Jason while I'm cooking dinner, and he can eat a second meal with the rest of us. That should hold him till breakfast. Allan is consumed by yet another new Internet business he's developing, so he won't linger at the table. Honestly, I think that man is happy only when he's starting up a business. Once it's humming along nicely, he gets bored and sells it."

"He seems to be good at it," Olivia said.

"That he is." Ellie finished her second cookie, and said, "Gotta tap-dance away. See you sevenish." But she didn't move. She stared at the sales counter with a thoughtful expression.

Olivia followed her gaze and saw their new clerk, Jennifer, pushing a large box across the counter toward the young couple to whom she'd been demonstrating the wonders of the fancy red mixer. Olivia had come to think of that mixer as her worst-ever business decision. She checked the shelf the mixer had dominated for so long. It wasn't there.

"I don't believe it," Olivia said. "Did Jennifer actually sell that red mixer?"

"I watched her box it up and run the credit card," Ellie said. "But I keep wondering . . ."

Olivia felt a flicker of anxiety. "What? What are you wondering? Because if that credit card is bogus, I'm out a lot of —"

"Take a deep breath, Livie."

"But —"

"I was only wondering about Jennifer. Does she have family around here? She reminds me of someone, but I can't think who."

"Maddie hired her," Olivia said. "All I know is she recently moved here from DC, and she has a great deal of knowledge about cookie cutters and baking. And she sold the red mixer, which makes her a goddess in my eyes."

"Understandable, dear. Anyway, I'm now officially late, no matter how we interpret the Hansel and Gretel clock." Munching on a cookie, Ellie tap-danced toward the front door. She wove flawlessly around display tables and two of the customers. When she reached the front of the store, she tapped around to face Olivia, blew her a kiss, and danced backward out the door.

The customers followed Ellie's performance in startled silence. As the door closed behind her mother, all five faces turned toward Olivia. Their reactions ranged from puzzlement to outright amusement. One customer giggled.

Olivia shrugged. "I've never seen that woman before in my life."

CHAPTER FOUR

Promptly at seven p.m., Olivia arrived at the front door of her childhood home. Spunky wiggled in her arms, eager to be back on his own four paws. He recognized the Greyson-Meyers house and yapped with excitement. Olivia had recently begun taking her little Yorkie with her when she visited her family and friends. He didn't do well with long periods of apartment arrest, and he was a popular guest. In fact, Olivia had received more invitations than usual lately. The reason, she suspected, was Spunky's adorable nature, not hers. It was no accident that Spunky had survived so long on the streets of Baltimore after escaping from the puppy mill. The little con artist could really turn on the charm.

Jason, Olivia's brother, opened the door holding a half-eaten ham sandwich. "Hey Olive Oyl, you're on time. And you brought my buddy. Hey, Spunks." Jason tore a piece of ham from his sandwich and fed it to Spunky.

"He isn't starving, you know," Olivia said. "You don't have to share your dinner with him."

"Mom already fixed me some ham and potatoes, but she didn't think you'd be here on time, so she made me a sandwich to help tide me over. Come on in. Mom's in the kitchen. We ran out of ham, so she's cooking some chicken thing." Jason usually teased and taunted Olivia, but maybe his recent breakup with his troubled girlfriend had forced him to grow up a bit.

"Hey, I hear Del finally dumped you for a younger woman."

Or maybe not. "I'm going to ignore that," Olivia said.

Jason chortled as he stuffed the remainder of his sandwich into his mouth.

Olivia sniffed the air as she entered the kitchen. "Yum! You're making lemon chicken." She scrunched next to her mother to smell the aroma as the oven door opened. "I love lemon chicken. I'm so glad Jason ate all the ham."

"I knew you would be, Livie." Ellie basted the chicken breasts and reset the timer for ten minutes. "I used fresh Greek oregano from the garden, too. Such a satisfying fragrance."

"Speaking of which . . ." Olivia set her package of herbs on the kitchen counter.

"Something from Bon Vivant? Are you implying that my cooking isn't good enough for you?" Ellie opened the bag and removed two small packets.

"Lavender buds and lemon verbena leaves," Olivia said. "Both organic, dried from last season. I didn't know if you'd dried either one. I was in the Bon Vivant garden this morning, so I asked if I could buy some of their supply. Only don't tell anyone. The manager said they barely have enough for their own use until the new crops are ready. Especially the lemon verbena, which they use a lot."

Ellie handed four plates to Olivia, a silent order to set the table. "I hope they explained that lemon verbena really should be dried and crushed before it's used in cooking. The fresh leaves are tough. If they are cut into pieces, I imagine they could do some damage to the esophagus. Something you might want to remember in relation to your investigative work."

"I'll keep that in mind."

Ellie lifted a large bowl of tabbouleh from the refrigerator and placed it on the table.

"I suppose the parsley and mint came

from your garden, too?" Olivia might have sounded a bit irritable, but really, her mother could make her feel inadequate with no more than a gentle smile . . . which was precisely what Ellie offered her, along with a handful of silverware.

"We'll give the chicken a few more minutes before calling the boys to dinner," Ellie said. "That gives you just enough time to tell me why you've brought lavender and lemon verbena with you. Such interesting ingredients. I'm assuming they have something to do with our cookie-baking session this evening?"

Olivia explained her ideas for the special cookies she wanted to create for Maddie's engagement party. "Don't tell Allan and Jason," Olivia said. "I want it to be a secret, if that's possible anywhere within the town limits."

"I'm very good at secrets," Ellie said. "Besides, even if we explained our cookie experimentation to Allan and Jason, they wouldn't retain the information. Nor would it occur to either of them to mention the idea to anyone else. Trust me."

As if he'd heard his name, Jason appeared at the kitchen entrance. "Is dinner ready yet? I'm starving. So is Allan."

"You can't be starving," Olivia said. "You

just ate a whole ham and a sack of potatoes."

"Did not. Anyway, that was, like, half an hour ago. I don't have excess fat to keep me going, like you do." Jason retreated before his sister could whack him with a pot-holder, the only weapon at hand.

As Ellie brought butter, salt, and pepper to the table, Jason returned to the kitchen with his stepfather, Allan Meyers, who rubbed his hands together when he saw the lemon chicken. Jason snatched a warm roll and downed it in two bites. Ellie watched her son with a tolerant smile. Olivia rolled her eyes.

Allan curled a strong arm around his wife's waist and pulled her to him. "Ellie, you are the best cook ever to breathe air." As he planted a kiss on Ellie's lips, a pink flush spread across her cheeks. In so many ways, Allan Meyers was the polar opposite of Olivia's gentle, introverted father, who had died of pancreatic cancer when she was a teenager. A well-known ornithologist, he had fit the stereotype of the distracted academic. In contrast, Allan, a businessman, exuded outgoing friendliness and energy. The two men were physical opposites, as well. Olivia's father had been tall and thin, while Allan was beefy and only a couple inches taller than Olivia.

Jason commandeered the chicken, took the two biggest pieces, and stationed the platter near his own plate.

"Jason, I think your mother and sister might be hungry, too," Allan said.

"Hm?" Jason had stuffed a second roll in his mouth as he reached for the bowl of tabbouleh. "Oh sorry," he mumbled as he passed the chicken to Ellie.

Olivia gave up the notion that her brother had matured. She'd seen his caring side when his girlfriend had been suspected of murder, but apparently that wouldn't be surfacing on a regular basis.

"So, Livie," Allan said, "what's this I hear about a rift between you and Del?"

Ellie gave her husband a stern look. "Allan, you know that isn't true. Binnie Sloan made it up, as she always does. Really, you need to spend less time starting all those Internet businesses and more time observing your surroundings."

Allan grinned at her. "I was teasing," he said. "Just trying to liven up the conversation."

"Jerk," Ellie said. It was the strongest insult she ever used.

"Sorry, honey, couldn't help myself. You are right, observing my surroundings is important, and it's also good business practice. But really, Livie, why is Binnie going after you right now, with Maddie and Lucas's nuptials coming up? She won't win new readers that way. A little gossip is fine, but Binnie needs to focus more on events that bring people together, make them feel part of the community."

"Who knows?" Olivia said as she helped herself to a heaping serving of tabbouleh. She rarely feasted on such wonderful home-cooked food. "Binnie isn't what you'd call a savvy businesswoman."

Jason had already cleaned his plate and begun to reload with seconds of everything. "Binnie is weird," he said. "Even Struts got upset about that last post, the one about your cookies. I was in her office when she called Binnie and balled her out. Struts can really swear. She's the best boss ever." Jason's chicken-filled fork was halfway to his mouth when he added, "But don't worry. Binnie told Struts that post was already gone, that it was only up for a few minutes. So you've got friends, Livie. For some reason."

"Wait, what post? What are you talking about?" Olivia noticed her mother was pushing her food around her plate. "Mom?" Ellie's expression reminded Olivia of the time in seventh grade when a jealous classmate's mother had spread a rumor about Olivia. She'd insisted Olivia got good grades only because her scholarly father did her homework for her. Ellie had intervened, though Olivia had never found out how. The classmate ceased hostilities, and her mother publicly disavowed the rumor.

Allan turned his laser gaze on his wife. "Ellie, did you . . . ? That's my girl!"

Ellie straightened her spine and lifted her chin. "No one messes with my family," she said. "I'm normally dispassionate and non-judgmental about the unfortunate behavior of others, even Binnie Sloan, but I'm afraid I'd missed three yoga classes in a row. Two is clearly my limit. I must remember that in future."

"Mom, if you managed to silence Binnie for even a few minutes, I salute you," Olivia said. "Only please tell me what her blog was about, okay? I'm dissolving here."

"Just a moment," Ellie said. She opened a cupboard and took out an unopened bottle of cabernet sauvignon and four glasses. It was unusual for her to offer wine for dinner at home. She wasn't a teetotaler; it simply didn't occur to her.

"I'm not angry, Mom," Olivia watched her mother pop the cork. "Is it that bad?"

"A glass of red wine with dinner is good

for one's health." Ellie half filled each wine glass. "Besides," she said with her signature serene smile, "I'm rather proud of myself. I do so hate to give up on anyone, but I'd given up on Binnie. I'd begun to think her beyond the reach even of the universe and its —"

"Sweetheart," Allan said, "you are torturing your daughter."

"Oh." Ellie took a sip of wine. "Well, if I must. . . . Binnie wrote on her unfortunate blog that some unnamed customer found dog fur in one of the cookies you and Maddie put out this morning. Which is ridiculous, of course. You would have heard about it right away. Besides, everyone knows that terriers have hair, rather than fur. Although I suppose hair can look like fur. . . ."

"I'll sue her," Olivia said. "She could ruin my business with lies like that. If the health department heard —"

"I know, dear, which is precisely why I warned Binnie that she would find herself on the losing end of a very expensive lawsuit if she did not instantly remove her accusation. And she did. Quickly, I might add. I watched it disappear, and I checked several times to be certain she didn't post it again.

"You see, I was sure Binnie had made up the entire story by herself. Not that I'm naive enough to believe no one else in Chatterley Heights would say such a thing, small towns being what they are and, well, people being who they are, but . . . Don't glare, Livie, it will give you a headache. I'm convinced Binnie made that story up because it's what she has done so many, many times before, and, sadly, people rarely change." Ellie took a substantial gulp of her wine. "More tabbouleh, anyone?"

No one spoke. Allan beamed at his wife, and Jason's mouth hung open . . . in amazement, for once, rather than hunger. "Great job, Mom," Jason said. "I can't wait to tell Struts and the guys at the garage. Can we have dessert now?"

"I'm impressed," Olivia said. "It's rare for Binnie to back down. Threats usually energize her. Would you really have filed a lawsuit if she hadn't removed that post?"

"You bet I would." Ellie nodded so hard that a long lock of wavy hair flipped forward over her shoulder. "I had Mr. Willard's number in front of me, in case Binnie didn't cooperate. Mr. Willard seems so gentle and civil, for a lawyer, and his advanced age does rather lull folks into a false sense of ease when he questions them."

Mr. Willard was also Olivia's attorney, and she had observed him in action. Binnie would never have known what hit her.

Jason picked up his fork and used it to salute his mother. "Now, about that dessert?"

"You take after your father," Ellie said as she opened the refrigerator. "He could eat all day and never gain an ounce. It's a trait I particularly dislike in a person." She centered a key lime pie on the table and handed Olivia the pie server. "I ran out of time, so this pie came from the Chatterley Café." Ellie began to clear the empty plates. "Their key lime is better than mine, and anyway, I think cookies are more fun to make than pie. Don't tell anyone I said that."

Olivia cut a small wedge for her tiny mother and a slightly larger one for herself. She passed the pie pan to Allan, who took an average slice. Jason began to eat the remaining pie right out of the pan. Olivia paused after her first delectable bite, and asked, "Mom, when you tap-danced your way through the store today, you said my new sales clerk reminded you of someone. Did you ever figure out who?"

Ellie put down her fork and frowned. "No, Livie, and it's been driving me crazy. I've lived in Chatterley Heights my whole life. I know everyone's name, the names of their children, their grandchildren, their ex-spouses . . . but I don't have any recollection of your new clerk. What was her name again?"

"Jennifer Elsworth."

"Jennie? I recognized her," Jason said with his mouth full of key lime pie. His family members stared at him, which didn't appear to faze him. As his fork aimed toward the pie, Olivia slid the pan away. "Hey!" Jason's long arm shot toward the pan, but Olivia whisked it beyond his reach.

Allan pushed back his chair. "Great dinner, Ellie. I've got work to do, so I'll leave all of you to chat about, um, whatever." Spunky perked up his ears and watched Allan with huge, hopeful eyes. "Want to come along, little guy?" Allan asked. Spunky flapped his tail against the floor.

"Sorry, Livie," Allan said. "I started stocking one of my desk drawers with doggie treats for when you're out of town and Spunky stays with us. I guess he remembers."

"Trust me, he will never forget. Go ahead, Spunks. Maybe I'll let the nice man keep you forever." Olivia was only slightly hurt when Spunky reacted to her threat by leaping to all fours and bounding over to Allan.

Allan gave his wife a peck on the cheek

and headed down the hallway to his home office with Spunky trotting close behind.

"You're excused," Ellie said to his retreating back. "Poor Allan, he gets so bored talking about anything but business."

"Okay, Jason, we need details," Olivia said. "No more pie until you tell us how you recognized Jennifer."

"Geez. All right, but don't blame me if I pass out from hunger." Jason pushed back his chair and stretched out his legs. "I don't remember her last name, but Elsworth doesn't sound familiar."

"But how come you know her and we don't?"

"I didn't meet her in Chatterley Heights," Jason said. "I'm pretty sure she grew up in Twiterton. I only met her once, but I do remember it was at a football game, an away game at Twiterton High. That was the year I played on the football team, my junior year, remember?"

"I wasn't here," Olivia said.

Ellie reached across the table and patted her son's hand. "I was very proud of you, dear."

"Thanks, Mom, but I sucked at football. I was okay at basketball, but football is for guys who get fed enough."

"You can have the pie back when you tell

81

us everything you know about Jennifer," Olivia said.

Jason groaned. "I hardly know anything except she was cute and kind of shy. She was dating my friend, Kevin, the Chatterley Heights quarterback. He never said how they met. I was with my girlfriend that night. She had her license, plus her parents' car, so we hung out after the game. Jennie didn't say much."

"If she didn't say much, why would you remember her?" Olivia asked.

"Like I said, she was cute. Also, Kevin was being sort of a jerk, so I felt bad for her. I never saw her again after that."

"What did she look like then?"

"She was a blonde," Jason said, "and she had a good figure. Kind of quiet, like I said."

"Did Kevin and Jennifer break up? Is that why you never saw her again?" Olivia found herself more and more curious about her reserved clerk with so much cookie cutter expertise.

Jason shrugged. "Maybe, I don't know."

"Kevin didn't tell you?"

"Well, I sort of never spoke to Kevin again."

"Why not?" Olivia felt uneasy about pushing Jason. He seemed uncomfortable, and she wondered if more had happened that evening than he wanted to reveal.

When Jason didn't respond, Ellie said, "That was a difficult time for your brother, Livie."

"It's okay, Mom." Jason hunched over the table and stared at his intertwined fingers. "I was a little out of control back then. That night the four of us sneaked off after the game. Kevin and I were supposed to go back on the bus with the team. Instead, we got hold of a bottle of vodka and —"

"How did you — ?"

"It doesn't matter, okay, Livie? We got some, that's all. We drank until the bottle was empty, and then my girlfriend drove us home. And, yeah, I know we shouldn't have been on the road, but my girlfriend only had a couple sips. She was on a diet or something. Jennie passed out, though. We carried her to her house and sort of propped her up on the porch. Then we rang the doorbell and ran, so we wouldn't get caught. We all got home safe, only Kevin got really sick, so his parents figured out what had happened, and we got into trouble. The coach kicked Kevin and me off the team. Kevin blamed me because . . . well, it doesn't matter."

Ellie squeezed Jason's forearm and said, "Don't leave Livie thinking you or Charlene provided the alcohol, dear."

Jason heaved a long sigh. "Yeah, okay, it was Jennie who brought the bottle. She stole it from her mother. She said there was plenty more and her mom wouldn't notice. Kevin lied to his parents and said I brought it, but I told Mom the truth, and she told Kevin's mom."

"Mom? She believed you, and not her own son?" Olivia asked.

"I'm afraid so, dear. Some mothers are able to see their children clearly, yet still love them."

"Anyway," Jason said, "Kevin and I stopped speaking to each other, and I never saw or heard about Jennie until I recognized her in the store."

"Did she recognize you?" Olivia asked.

"She didn't seem to," Jason said with a shake of his head. "You know, there is one reason I remember Jennie, besides how cute she was. She said she didn't have a dad, and her mom was . . . I think she said her mom was on drugs. I remember thinking I was luckier than Jennie. I didn't have a dad anymore, but I had a mom who cared enough to notice my existence at least."

"Thank you, dear," Ellie said. "I think."

Jason snickered, and the mood lightened. "Hey, that took a lot of energy," he said.

"Some key lime pie might help me get my strength back."

Olivia shoved the pie pan toward him. "Thanks for telling me all that, Jason. I think it explains a lot." She could understand Jennifer's reticence, given her tough childhood. "Do you happen to remember how old Jennie was?"

Jason opened a mouth filled with pie, and said, "Nope, but she seemed about our age. Anyway, she wasn't a kid."

"Don't talk with your mouth full, Jason." There was a touch of pride in Ellie's stern voice.

Excited and exhausted, Olivia slumped on a kitchen chair in her childhood kitchen to watch her mother slide a sheet of round cutout cookies into the oven. She and Ellie had spent nearly three hours experimenting with recipes for decorated cookies to serve at Maddie's engagement party. After they'd finished mixing the batches, they'd begun to roll and cut the dough. Soon they would be able to taste the results.

"Mom, how can you keep standing on your feet for so long?" Olivia asked. "I mean, aside from the fact that you are practically weightless."

"Tai chi," Ellie said as she set the oven

timer. "And calisthenics, of course. I'm afraid my weightlessness is pure myth. I gained a pound over the winter, after I worked so hard last summer to get back to ninety-nine pounds."

"A pound, wow. You must need a whole new wardrobe after packing all that weight on your little body."

"Livie, dear, sarcasm is not your most attractive quality. When one is four foot eleven, an extra pound can be quite cumbersome."

"Uh-huh." Olivia stretched her arms over her head. She'd developed a kink in her back from working at the kitchen's low counters, designed for her mother's diminutive stature.

"How about a glass of lemonade while we wait for the cookies to bake?" Ellie opened a cupboard and selected two tall glasses.

"How about a glass of wine instead?"

Ellie hesitated only a moment before exchanging the tumblers for two wine glasses, which she brought to the table, along with the merlot from dinner. "For medicinal purposes," Ellie said. "Today I ran in the morning, followed by a kung fu class at noon, and then I tap-danced until the league meeting. Between you and me, I'm a bit achy. In a good way, of course."

"Of course." Olivia divided the remaining wine between their glasses. "Mom, can I ask you something? It's about what Jason told me earlier. I'll understand if you'd rather not say anything. I'm asking because Jennifer does work for The Gingerbread House now, and I need to know if I can trust her."

"And you are curious, as well," Ellie said. "You were always so curious, even as a tiny —"

"The timer for the cookies is going off in three minutes, Mom."

"Have I mentioned how impatient you've always been?"

"Not since yesterday."

"I'll wait a bit, then. Now you asked about Jennie. . . ." Ellie took a slow sip of her merlot. "I really don't know much about her. I tried to investigate a bit after Jason's experience, but information was hard to come by."

"I don't think I've ever heard you say that before," Olivia said.

"No one is perfect," Ellie said. "You know, it's odd how little contact we here in Chatterley Heights have with a town that's only ten miles down the road. I suppose it's because our two school systems draw children from different areas. Twiterton has become something of a bedroom community for DC, so the families tend to be wealthier. They are attracted to more urban sorts of leisure activities, I imagine. I do know a few of the women who live there, but you must have met many more than I have. I'm sure they come to The Gingerbread House. There's nothing else like it anywhere nearby."

"I get lots of business from Twiterton, but they don't stick around to chat," Olivia said.

"I suppose not. Well, I never did learn a great deal about Jennie. I don't remember her last name, but it wasn't Elsworth. She might be married now."

"I guess she could be using a married name," Olivia said, "though she didn't mention a husband. Or a divorce."

"After the episode Jason described to you," Ellie said, "we mostly talked about Charlene, his girlfriend. Jennie's name came up only in passing. Jason did mention that Jennie said she'd lost another family member. A sibling, I think." Ellie started as the timer dinged. She peeked into the oven, and said, "Done to perfection. They smell delicious." She put the cookie sheet on a cooling rack and slid another batch into the oven.

"So on top of having a mom on drugs and

no dad, Jennifer lost a sibling. No wonder she doesn't discuss her past," Olivia said as she lifted the cookies off the sheet with a spatula and slid them onto another cooling rack. "You know, Mom, it would be easier and quicker to cool the cookies if you'd line your cookie sheets with parchment paper, plus you wouldn't have to scrub the sheets so hard to clean them."

"So you keep telling me, Livie, but I can't help thinking what a waste of resources that would be."

"Mom, we're talking about art here. Decorated cookies are worth a few wasted resources." The cookies needed to cool a few minutes before they were ready for tasting. This first batch contained lavender oil and a scattering of lavender buds. They looked gorgeous, but beauty was only half the battle. If they weren't melt-in-the-mouth delicious, it was back to the recipe board for Olivia. With only three days left before the party, Olivia was feeling the pressure. At least she had a starting place. It was the second batch she was really worried about, since she had no idea what finely ground lemon verbena tasted like. She'd added a touch of lemon extract to the recipe, but not too much. Her worry was that lemon cutout cookies were so common. For Maddie's engagement party, they would have to be special.

Olivia reunited with her glass of merlot. "I wonder if Elsworth is just a name Jennifer made up or if she really was — or still is — married. And why wouldn't she be open about her ties to this area? Jennifer told Maddie that she moved away from Twiterton as a child, but Jason met her as a teenager. If she was a junior in high school, she would have been sixteen or seventeen."

"You won't let up on that poor girl, will you?"

"Mom, aren't you the least bit curious about why Jennifer returned to this area and won't reveal who she really is?"

"Well, maybe she wanted to come home but isn't ready to deal with the sadness in her past," Ellie said. "Either way, I think we should respect her privacy." When the timer dinged, Ellie hopped up to put another batch of cookies in the oven. "I'm out of cookie sheets. I'll clean one while you wield the cutter."

Olivia rolled the lavender dough one last time and cut as many cookies as she could, using her mother's biscuit cutter. After the cookies went into the oven, she sacrificed the last remnants of the lavender batch. As she rolled and cut a first batch of lemon verbena cookie shapes, Olivia asked herself why she was so curious about her new clerk. She had no complaints about Jennifer's work. She was respectful, attentive to the customers, knowledgeable about cutters and virtually everything else in the store . . . and yet so secretive. That bothered Olivia. Why would Jennifer return to this particular area of Maryland, secure a job near, yet not in, her hometown, and keep her identity under wraps? Why had Jennifer lied about the age at which she'd left Twiterton? And why, out of all the possibilities in Chatterley Heights, had she sought a job at The Gingerbread House? Olivia felt her skin prickle with foreboding. She couldn't help worrying that her little store was about to become the epicenter of a category four hurricane.

CHAPTER FIVE

On Wednesday morning, with only three days left before Maddie and Lucas's engagement party, Olivia tried to quell her panic as she gazed out the window of Pete's Diner and watched the early morning sun awaken the town square. Her table afforded a view of the statue of Frederick P. Chatterley, accidental founder of Chatterley Heights, and his ever-patient horse. She wondered what it said about Frederick P. that, after two hundred and fifty years of trying, he still hadn't managed to mount his steed.

"You gonna drink that coffee or just smell it?" Ida, Pete's senior waitress in more ways than one, raised thin, gray eyebrows at the full cup of cold coffee Olivia held in both hands. "Must be nice having time to waste. Some of us have to work." Ida had spent fifty of her sixty working years as a cook, waitress, and manager at Pete's Diner. She usually wore an old uniform and a hairnet, and she treated all customers with equal disdain. No one ever complained. At least not more than once.

"What? Oh, Ida, you startled me." Olivia spilled a few drops of coffee, which she dabbed with her napkin. "I was just enjoying the sunrise and feeling glad that spring is here."

"Spring will be gone before you get that cup emptied," Ida said. "Here, let me do that. Lord knows I've got experience." She pulled a damp rag from one of her uniform pockets and mopped the table clean. "Hand over the cup, I'll get you some fresh coffee. When's your mother getting here?"

Olivia's watch read 6:52 a.m. "In about eight minutes, give or take."

"Good." Ida said. "Ellie'll liven up the place. I suppose you want me to drag over more chairs, like I've got nothing else to do. How many?"

Olivia counted on her fingers as she listed. "Mom, Allan, and Jason, that's three. Mr. Willard and Bertha make five. But not Maddie. She's opening the store. And Del, of course." Sheriff Del Jenkins and Olivia were, as *The Weekly Chatter* had often described them until recently, an item. For both of them, free time was hard to come by, so they invited each other to informal gatherings whenever possible.

"Forget about seeing your boyfriend," Ida said. She poked an escaped lock of iron gray hair back under her hairnet, which she wore while cooking. When she switched to waitressing, she never bothered to remove it. "Don't tell me you didn't hear what happened? I swear, all those years living in Baltimore drove the small town right out of you."

Olivia felt her face and hands chill as the blood retreated to her thudding heart. "What happened? Is Del . . . is he okay?"

To Olivia's surprise, Ida laughed. "Well, he ain't a crime statistic. Not yet, anyway. Though the more he hangs around you —"

"What happened?" Olivia was too worried to keep the impatience out of her voice.

"Okay, keep your bobby socks on," Ida said. "The sheriff is just fine. Can't say the same for that bank teller fellow, what's-his-name. You know, the one who's got a pretty cousin working over at Lady Chatterley's?"

"Lola? But I thought her connection to the Chatterley Heights National Bank was through her husband. He's a vice president."

Ida sighed and rolled her eyes heavenward, creasing her forehead with wrinkles. "How do you think Lola's cousin got his teller job and then got promoted to head teller so fast? Anyway, every morning he gets to the bank early to count all the money or something, and then he lets the other tellers in when they arrive. Only this morning, someone was waiting for him." Ida deepened her voice for dramatic effect. "Soon as he unlocked the front door, somebody knocked him senseless and dragged him inside. That's all I know." With a shrug of her thin shoulders, Ida scraped a chair across the floor and shoved it under Olivia's table. "Get the rest of the story out of that boyfriend of yours," Ida said, "and then tell me. You owe me."

"This must have just happened," Olivia said.

"Yep," Ida said. "The sheriff called about ten minutes ago."

"So Del told you all those details?"

"Of course not." Ida's tone implied Livie was one pancake short of a stack. "I got my ways." Shaking her head at the ignorance of youth, Ida headed for another table.

Feeling rattled, Olivia stared out the diner window and noticed a man and a woman entering the park grounds from the southwest corner of the town square. She couldn't see the couple clearly, but given the woman's animated gesticulation, Olivia wondered if she might be her mother, Ellie. If so, the man would be Olivia's stepfather. Good. Ellie would probably know every last detail about what happened at the bank. Or if she didn't, she'd know whom to call.

As the couple cut diagonally through the park, Olivia realized the woman was too tall to be her mother. The woman stepped into the sunlight, and Olivia recognized the shoulder-length sandy hair of her childhood friend, Stacey Harald. Stacey's ex-husband, Wade, walked alongside, shoulders hunched forward and eyes focused on the grass under his feet. According to Olivia's watch, it was five minutes to seven, an unusual time for two rancorously divorced individuals to be out for a chilly stroll in the park.

"Those two have been going at it for days." Ida plunked a clean cup in front of Olivia and filled it with steaming coffee. She slid the cream and sugar closer, and said, "I know how much you like this stuff. One of these days it'll catch up with you. You'll end up round as one of them fancy cookies you're always making."

"Thanks for your concern," Olivia said. "What did you mean by 'going at it'? Stacey and Wade, I mean. They haven't gotten back together, have they?" Olivia watched as Stacey halted, planted her fists on her hips, and appeared to deliver a harsh lecture to

Wade's stiff back.

"Ha! Not a chance," Ida said. A half smile dispersed a wave of wrinkles across the left side of her cheek. "Stacey's too tough for that. She never should have married that drunken hothead, let alone have two kids with him. Lord knows what he's gotten himself into now. Probably lost his job at the garage again."

Olivia tore herself away from the drama unfolding in the park and forced her attention back to her cookie ideas for the engagement party. She'd jotted down the two recipes she and her mother had tried out the night before, one for lavender cookies and the other lemon. Neither was quite right. The lavender cookies were lovely, but to Olivia they'd tasted overwhelmingly . . . well, lavender. Maybe she should cut down on the lavender and add a bit more lemon or some vanilla to mellow the flavor. She thought about using vanilla royal icing and sprinkling lavender sugar on top, for a sweet hint of flavor. The lemon verbena cookies posed a tougher problem. She and her mother both loved the lemony flavor, but the cookies were an odd greenish color. Maybe if she dyed the cookie dough. . . .

Olivia was so engrossed in her vision of perfect cookies that she started when the diner door opened. Her petite mother floated in, followed by Olivia's hearty stepfather. Allan wore a suit and tie as if he were attending a breakfast meeting to discuss business. Her younger brother, Jason, wore his oil-stained work jeans and a light jacket over his T-shirt. He poked his head inside and surveyed the diner as if he needed reassurance before entering. When Ida passed by bearing a tray of cholesterol-laden breakfasts, Jason appeared convinced.

"Livie dear, what a good idea to meet at Pete's," Ellie said. "Such tasty, old-fashioned breakfasts. I'm so hungry I could eat three of them." She slipped off a form-fitting sweater-coat the color of ripe raspberries to reveal a comfortably loose dusty rose outfit with a mandarin collar.

"Ooh, nice." Olivia ran her fingertips over the silky fabric of her mother's sleeve. "What are those thingies down the front of your jacket?"

"They are called buttons, dear."

"I guessed that, but —"

"They're toad-and-ball buttons," Allan said, looking pleased with himself.

Ellie bestowed an indulgent smile upon her husband. "Close, sweetheart, so very close. But I think you meant *frog*-and-ball buttons."

"Can we order?" Jason asked. "I know we're waiting for some other folks, but I'm starving."

Ellie scanned her menu as Ida delivered coffee. "I intend to order instantly," she said. "I need fortification as we finish our planning for the engagement party. I have a tai chi class at eight thirty. I can order for Bertha and Mr. Willard."

"Don't bother, I know what they like," Ida said. "Those two old love birds eat here nearly every morning. Bertha has oatmeal and fruit, and Mr. Willard always orders pancakes, sausage, eggs, and a blueberry muffin, but I don't know where he puts them."

As usual, Ida didn't bother to write down their orders. She wouldn't forget. As Ida headed for the kitchen, Ellie said, "I've kept my Friday afternoon clear, Livie, if you need help preparing the decorations for Saturday. I can meet you after my crazy quilting group finishes. We are embroidering spider webs," she added. "Such fun."

Allan Meyers pulled a cell phone from his trouser pocket and frowned at the caller ID. "This is a new client," he said. "I'd better —"

"Allan." Ellie's narrowed her eyes ever so slightly. Olivia and Jason exchanged a quick

99

glance. They knew that look.

"Sorry, force of habit," Allan said, a shade too heartily. "I'll let it go to voice mail."

"Why don't I keep the phone for you," Ellie said, producing one of the many macramé bags she had created. "That would make it so much easier for you to concentrate." She held out a small, slender hand with shiny rose nails.

Allan grinned. "You're a marvel, Ellie. And right, as always." Handing over his phone, he said, "The next time I have an irate customer, I might just turn him over to you."

"Don't be silly, dear. It would make me cranky."

"Much as we're enjoying your repartee," Olivia said, "could we hammer out the final details for the engagement party that's happening in a mere three days? Because you know how I hate meetings. I want this one to be over before we start breakfast, or I will demonstrate cranky."

"I need to get to the garage soon," Jason said. "Struts hired Wade back, and she wants me to keep an eye on him. She's afraid he's started drinking on the job again. He might botch a brake job or something."

Ida appeared with a tray of breakfast plates and a fresh pot of coffee. Clattering eggs and bacon in front of Olivia, she said, "Bertha tried to call, but you've got your phone turned off. That new girl of yours called in sick, so Bertha's going to the store to help Maddie. But here comes Mr. Willard." Ida pointed a plate of cheese omelet toward the window as a tall, painfully thin older man approached in long, loping steps. Aloysius Willard Smythe, known to one and all as Mr. Willard, smiled at the group inside, a gesture that tightened the skin across his prominent cheekbones. As Olivia's attorney, Mr. Willard had more than once helped her with sticky problems, including her friend Clarisse Chamberlain's murder.

As Mr. Willard seated himself, Ida delivered his pancakes, syrup, sausage, eggs, blueberry muffin, and coffee. "If you order any more food," Ida said, "I'll have to drag over another table."

"We can finish our business in short order," Olivia said, scanning her notes. "Mom has agreed to help with the decorating details."

"I've already spoken with several friends, as well as my poetry-writing group," Ellie said. "So far, eight women have agreed to help. I'm sure we'll have more volunteers than we'll need."

"I don't know how you do it, Mom," Olivia said. "I mean, short of holding a knitting needle to their throats."

"Completely unnecessary, dear."

Olivia turned to her brother, who looked bored and hungry. "Jason, would you mind being a general 'gofer' on Saturday? Events never go off without a hitch. We always run out of something or need to find a broom in a hurry."

"Okay," Jason said. "Can we eat now?"

"We need a couple volunteers to offer toasts to the bride and groom," Olivia said, her eyes flitting between Allan and Mr. Willard.

"Sure, I'd love to," Allan boomed, startling several diners at nearby tables.

"I would be delighted." Mr. Willard said. "I am quite fond of Maddie and Lucas."

Olivia drained her second cup of coffee and held out her cup as Ida returned with the pot. Wearily squinting at her own handwriting, Olivia said, "I think we've covered the most important tasks both before and during the engagement party on Saturday. Bon Vivant will provide staff to help with the serving. That will cost a bundle, but it's better than trying to do it all by ourselves. I'll take care of the expense. Most of the refreshments will be provided by Bon Vi-

"I can't answer that question with precision," Mr. Willard said. "Bertha was recounting what she heard from a friend of hers who is also a bank employee. However, it was her impression that very little was disturbed inside the bank. Or, I should say, that is the rumor Bertha heard. Perhaps the sheriff will reveal more soon?" He directed his last question to Olivia.

"You all realize, don't you, that Del doesn't automatically contact me when he is called to a crime scene? He'd be more inclined to suggest I get lost."

"Oh, Livie, I'm sure he does so out of kindness and concern for your safety," Ellie said.

"Or not." Olivia took the biggest gulp of coffee she could manage.

"Well then, we'll simply have to wait for further word on the poor head teller's condition," Ellie said. "He is in good hands; we must hope for the best. Would you pass the cream, Allan, dear?"

Chewing replaced conversation as they enjoyed their breakfasts. Olivia gazed out the window as she ate. The town square bustled with dog walkers, reminding her that she'd been neglecting Spunky during the frantic preparations for Maddie and Lucas's engagement party. As she was getting ready to leave her apartment earlier that morning, the little guy had propped his head on his front paws and whimpered. His sad brown eyes had flitted between his mistress and his leash, which hung near the door. Olivia couldn't take much more of that. Maybe she and Spunky could sneak in a run through the park before the demands of baking claimed her attention again.

Among the shop clerks and early customers cutting through the spring grass, one slender, bright pink figure caught Olivia's attention. The woman's gait was brisk yet wobbly, as if she might be wearing high heels. Her floppy hat, also pink, flapped in the breeze. When it threatened to leave her head, she clamped down on the crown with one hand. Olivia couldn't see the woman's face, but she knew who it had to be: Lenora Tucker Bouchenbein. Stage name: Lenora Dove. In Chatterley Heights, she was known as Herbie Tucker's aunt Len.

"Uh-oh," Allan said as he caught sight of Lenora heading straight for Pete's Diner. "That woman terrifies me." He shifted his chair away from the window.

"Allan, dear, I think 'terrified' is an exaggeration." Ellie patted her husband's muscular upper arm. "I think you could handle her in a street fight."

"That's not what I'm worried about. Last week she followed me into the hardware store and talked my ear off. Confused the heck out of me. Suddenly I realized I'd agreed to give her free business advice. I'm not sure, but I think I might have offered to 'loan' her money to buy a used computer so she can write the story of her life."

"How kind of you, dear," Ellie said. "The poor thing was left destitute, and she has led such an interesting life."

Olivia's sympathies were with her step-father. "I know Gwen and Herbie feed Lenora, but she acts as if her survival depends on the free cookies we put out every day."

"Lenora doesn't wish to be a burden," Ellie said.

Lenora had recently moved back to town after the death of her husband, Bernie Bouchenbein, a Hollywood producer who had believed in spending money as soon as it reached his hands, if not before. He'd left Lenora with very little. Consequently, she'd shown up on Gwen and Herbie Tucker's doorstep, offering her glorious presence, as well as help with their new baby. According to Gwen, her visit had quickly become permanent, but the helping-with-the-baby part had yet to materialize. Aunt Lenora had, however, relieved Gwen and Herbie of

107

every bottle of wine in their cellar. She required a steady new supply, which put a dent in the young couple's budget.

Still and all, Olivia enjoyed Lenora. Which was a good thing, because Lenora was at that moment breezing into Pete's Diner, a woman with a mission. She headed straight for the group at Olivia's table, smiling as warmly as she could after several too many facelifts.

"Darlings, I'm so glad I finally tracked you all down." Lenora dragged over a chair from another table and wedged it between Allan and Mr. Willard. "You don't mind if I join your little gathering, do you?" Lenora appropriated Mr. Willard's unused knife and speared one of his sausage links. "The food here is a bit heavy for my delicate figure, but the sausages are lovely." As Lenora devoured the sausage, she eyed the other offerings around the table. Jason snugged his plate closer to keep it out of her reach.

"We would love to have you join us, Lenora," Ellie said. "We were just discussing the upcoming party at Bon Vivant to celebrate Maddie and Lucas's engagement. Olivia is planning it." Ellie reached over to an unoccupied table for a clean, empty coffee cup and a spoon and fork. "May we offer you some breakfast? Allan and I are treating this morning."

Allan shot his wife a look that begged for mercy. Ellie smiled as she patted his arm and said, "Allan is so sentimental about weddings, aren't you, dear?"

"Oh no, I couldn't," Lenora said. "I eat so little, these huge breakfasts simply overwhelm me. I'll just sample here and there." She liberated Mr. Willard's one remaining sausage. Ever the gentleman, Mr. Willard did not object, but his eyes followed the sausage as it left his plate. "I'm just helping you finish quickly," Lenora told him with a coquettish smile. "You see, we must leave very soon if we want to get to the airport in time." It was well known that Lenora, hoping to steal Mr. Willard away from Bertha Binkman, was forever plotting ways to spend time with him.

As Mr. Willard's eyebrows puckered in confusion — and possibly dread — his eyes appeared to sink into his skull. "Airport?"

Lenora scooped up a forkful of pancake. "Oh, silly me," she said. "Did I forget to tell you? It's so thrilling. Two of my dearest Hollywood friends are flying in this morning for a lovely visit. I don't have a car, and I simply must meet them myself. They are staying at my place, of course. I wouldn't have it any other way."

Olivia wondered how Gwen and Herbie felt about the visit, since Lenora's "place" was, in fact, their home. She was trying to think of a sneaky way to mention that fact when she caught her mother watching her. Ellie raised her eyebrows a mere fraction, enough to warn her daughter that she could read minds. *Drat the woman! How does she do it?*

Ida appeared next to Mr. Willard and refilled his coffee cup. "Once a moocher, always a moocher," she muttered.

Ellie aimed her eyebrow weaponry at Ida, who shrugged her shoulders and retreated. Around the table, forks busied themselves with remaining morsels, while Lenora opened a gold compact and patted her hair.

To her own surprise, Olivia took pity on Lenora. "Tell us about these friends of yours," she said. "Are they actors?"

Lenora snapped shut her compact and paused for dramatic effect. Olivia tried not to wince as Lenora's smile pulled to the right. "My dear friend, Trevor Lane, is a well-known actor. I'm sure you're all familiar with his work. He is best known for his portrayal of the brilliant psychiatrist Dr. Patch Treadwell." When the character's name failed to produce sighs of recognition, Lenora added, "On *Midnights in Manhattan*."

happened to Bertha?"

"What? Oh no, Bertha is fine. I just spoke with her, in fact." Mr. Willard shook his head as if to clear it. "Bertha relayed the most astonishing news about that incident at the bank early this morning. I suppose you heard that a young teller was injured by an assailant?"

Everyone nodded, with the exception of Jason, who was wiping up scrambled egg scraps with a slice of toast. Olivia did not point out that the teller was in his forties. Everyone was young to Mr. Willard.

Mr. Willard wrapped his long, bony fingers around his coffee cup as if he felt chilled. "Bertha told me the poor unfortunate man could not describe his assailant. He remembered only that he unlocked the bank's outer door and someone jumped him from behind. His nose and mouth were covered with a wet cloth. His assistant arrived at the bank shortly thereafter and found the victim propped up against the building, unconscious. He promptly called the police department. The poor young fellow was rushed to the emergency room, where his wounds are being treated."

Allan rested his elbows on the table and asked, "Any idea how much the assailant stole from the bank?"

vant, except for the cookies and the cake. The Gingerbread House, meaning Maddie and I, are handling those. Maddie insisted on helping, and thank goodness for that. I've been working with Mom on two new recipes for the event. I'll be using one of the new recipes to construct a cookie cake. Wish me luck."

A cell phone played a snippet of what sounded to Olivia like Mozart, though music wasn't her strong suit. Mr. Willard checked his caller ID. "I need to take this call," he said. "It's a client. Do start without me." He walked outside, where he stood in view of the waiting group. Mr. Willard's call ended quickly, but before he could rejoin the group, he answered a second call. As he listened, Mr. Willard slowly shook his skull-like head. Only Jason began eating, immune to the frank curiosity exhibited by his companions.

By the time Mr. Willard returned, his normally benign expression had evaporated. He looked worried. He collapsed into his chair and frowned at his eggs and sausage as if they disturbed him. "Oh dear," he said. "This is quite unfortunate."

The group waited for Mr. Willard to elaborate. When he didn't, Ellie touched his hand with her fingertips. "Has something

103

"I can't answer that question with precision," Mr. Willard said. "Bertha was recounting what she heard from a friend of hers who is also a bank employee. However, it was her impression that very little was disturbed inside the bank. Or, I should say, that is the rumor Bertha heard. Perhaps the sheriff will reveal more soon?" He directed his last question to Olivia.

"You all realize, don't you, that Del doesn't automatically contact me when he is called to a crime scene? He'd be more inclined to suggest I get lost."

"Oh, Livie, I'm sure he does so out of kindness and concern for your safety," Ellie said.

"Or not." Olivia took the biggest gulp of coffee she could manage.

"Well then, we'll simply have to wait for further word on the poor head teller's condition," Ellie said. "He is in good hands; we must hope for the best. Would you pass the cream, Allan, dear?"

Chewing replaced conversation as they enjoyed their breakfasts. Olivia gazed out the window as she ate. The town square bustled with dog walkers, reminding her that she'd been neglecting Spunky during the frantic preparations for Maddie and Lucas's engagement party. As she was getting ready to leave her apartment earlier that morning, the little guy had propped his head on his front paws and whimpered. His sad brown eyes had flitted between his mistress and his leash, which hung near the door. Olivia couldn't take much more of that. Maybe she and Spunky could sneak in a run through the park before the demands of baking claimed her attention again.

Among the shop clerks and early customers cutting through the spring grass, one slender, bright pink figure caught Olivia's attention. The woman's gait was brisk yet wobbly, as if she might be wearing high heels. Her floppy hat, also pink, flapped in the breeze. When it threatened to leave her head, she clamped down on the crown with one hand. Olivia couldn't see the woman's face, but she knew who it had to be: Lenora Tucker Bouchenbein. Stage name: Lenora Dove. In Chatterley Heights, she was known as Herbie Tucker's aunt Len.

"Uh-oh," Allan said as he caught sight of Lenora heading straight for Pete's Diner. "That woman terrifies me." He shifted his chair away from the window.

"Allan, dear, I think 'terrified' is an exaggeration." Ellie patted her husband's muscular upper arm. "I think you could handle her in a street fight."

"That's not what I'm worried about. Last week she followed me into the hardware store and talked my ear off. Confused the heck out of me. Suddenly I realized I'd agreed to give her free business advice. I'm not sure, but I think I might have offered to 'loan' her money to buy a used computer so she can write the story of her life."

"How kind of you, dear," Ellie said. "The poor thing was left destitute, and she has led such an interesting life."

Olivia's sympathies were with her step-father. "I know Gwen and Herbie feed Lenora, but she acts as if her survival depends on the free cookies we put out every day."

"Lenora doesn't wish to be a burden," Ellie said.

Lenora had recently moved back to town after the death of her husband, Bernie Bouchenbein, a Hollywood producer who had believed in spending money as soon as it reached his hands, if not before. He'd left Lenora with very little. Consequently, she'd shown up on Gwen and Herbie Tucker's doorstep, offering her glorious presence, as well as help with their new baby. According to Gwen, her visit had quickly become permanent, but the helping-with-the-baby part had yet to materialize. Aunt Lenora had, however, relieved Gwen and Herbie of every bottle of wine in their cellar. She required a steady new supply, which put a dent in the young couple's budget.

Still and all, Olivia enjoyed Lenora. Which was a good thing, because Lenora was at that moment breezing into Pete's Diner, a woman with a mission. She headed straight for the group at Olivia's table, smiling as warmly as she could after several too many facelifts.

"Darlings, I'm so glad I finally tracked you all down." Lenora dragged over a chair from another table and wedged it between Allan and Mr. Willard. "You don't mind if I join your little gathering, do you?" Lenora appropriated Mr. Willard's unused knife and speared one of his sausage links. "The food here is a bit heavy for my delicate figure, but the sausages are lovely." As Lenora devoured the sausage, she eyed the other offerings around the table. Jason snugged his plate closer to keep it out of her reach.

"We would love to have you join us, Lenora," Ellie said. "We were just discussing the upcoming party at Bon Vivant to celebrate Maddie and Lucas's engagement. Olivia is planning it." Ellie reached over to an unoccupied table for a clean, empty coffee cup and a spoon and fork. "May we offer you some breakfast? Allan and I are treating this morning."

Allan shot his wife a look that begged for mercy. Ellie smiled as she patted his arm and said, "Allan is so sentimental about weddings, aren't you, dear?"

"Oh no, I couldn't," Lenora said. "I eat so little, these huge breakfasts simply overwhelm me. I'll just sample here and there." She liberated Mr. Willard's one remaining sausage. Ever the gentleman, Mr. Willard did not object, but his eyes followed the sausage as it left his plate. "I'm just helping you finish quickly," Lenora told him with a coquettish smile. "You see, we must leave very soon if we want to get to the airport in time." It was well known that Lenora, hoping to steal Mr. Willard away from Bertha Binkman, was forever plotting ways to spend time with him.

As Mr. Willard's eyebrows puckered in confusion — and possibly dread — his eyes appeared to sink into his skull. "Airport?"

Lenora scooped up a forkful of pancake. "Oh, silly me," she said. "Did I forget to tell you? It's so thrilling. Two of my dearest Hollywood friends are flying in this morning for a lovely visit. I don't have a car, and I simply must meet them myself. They are staying at my place, of course. I wouldn't have it any other way."

Olivia wondered how Gwen and Herbie felt about the visit, since Lenora's "place" was, in fact, their home. She was trying to think of a sneaky way to mention that fact when she caught her mother watching her. Ellie raised her eyebrows a mere fraction, enough to warn her daughter that she could read minds. *Drat the woman! How does she do it?*

Ida appeared next to Mr. Willard and refilled his coffee cup. "Once a moocher, always a moocher," she muttered.

Ellie aimed her eyebrow weaponry at Ida, who shrugged her shoulders and retreated. Around the table, forks busied themselves with remaining morsels, while Lenora opened a gold compact and patted her hair.

To her own surprise, Olivia took pity on Lenora. "Tell us about these friends of yours," she said. "Are they actors?"

Lenora snapped shut her compact and paused for dramatic effect. Olivia tried not to wince as Lenora's smile pulled to the right. "My dear friend, Trevor Lane, is a well-known actor. I'm sure you're all familiar with his work. He is best known for his portrayal of the brilliant psychiatrist Dr. Patch Treadwell." When the character's name failed to produce sighs of recognition, Lenora added, "On *Midnights in Manhattan*."

"Afraid I don't have time for the soaps," Allan said.

"Gotta get to work," Jason said, scraping back his chair.

Ellie pushed the muffin basket closer to Lenora. "How delightful your friend was able to take a break from his demanding schedule to come visit you."

"Well, Trevor is on a bit of a hiatus," Lenora said. "He so longs to return to his first love, the theater. We began our careers together in the theater, you know. Bernie — that's my dear late husband, Bernie Bouchenbein — invested in a lovely play in which Trevor and I performed together. Bernie usually stuck to movies, but plays always seem more respectable. I've never understood why. However, I was an ingenue at the time, and Bernie wanted me to have a good start."

Olivia wasn't an expert on the soaps, but she knew that "on hiatus" usually meant the actor's character was dead or in a coma. And wanting to "return to the theater" sounded a lot like wanting "to spend more time with my family" after one has been fired. And now that she thought of it, a "good start" in theater suggested that Bernie Bouchenbein didn't want his pretty young wife to begin her acting career as a

111

disposable starlet. Olivia found herself liking Lenora's deceased husband.

"Naturally, Trevor is bringing along his assistant, Dougie Adair." Lenora took a delicate sip of coffee. "Dougie has been tremendously helpful to Trevor's career. Dougie isn't an actor, of course, but he is such a clever young man, and he knows so much about the business." With a sigh, Lenora said, "It will be such a lovely reunion."

"A reunion?" Ellie asked. "So you haven't seen Trevor and Dougie for some time?"

"Alas, no," Lenora said. "Although by reunion, I meant having all of us back home together."

"Back home?" Olivia asked. "Here in Chatterley Heights?"

"Oh, didn't I say? Trevor and Dougie grew up here. Well, not in Chatterley Heights, but close by, in Twiterton. They went to high school together. Naturally, both of them played on the football team."

Jason's face lit up. "No kidding. I spent a year on the Chatterley Heights football team, and we played the Twiterton Twits. That's not what they called themselves, of course. Anyway, they usually beat us."

"They still do." Allan scraped back his chair and stood up. "I need to get to work. Ellie, I know you'll be helping Livie prepare for Maddie's shindig, but you won't forget we have dinner plans?"

Ellie said nothing as she reached a slender, graceful hand toward Allan's wrist. Allan sat down. Turning to Lenora, Ellie said, "I know that poor Mr. Willard is snowed under with work at the moment, and it's so important that you pick up your friends at the airport. Would you mind if Allan and I drove you instead? I would love to meet them."

"Mom, don't you have —"

Ellie turned on her brightest smile. "Don't fuss, Livie. I'm sure I'll be back in plenty of time for my meditation class. Unless you would care to drive Lenora and me to airport?"

Allan gazed toward Olivia with desperate hope in his eyes. It lasted only a moment, though. With a firm shake of his head, he said, "Now, Ellie, Livie is a businesswoman. She has a store to run. It takes time and dedication to keep a business going. We can't send her off on errands during her workday. And don't forget, Livie is preparing Maddie's get-together almost single-handedly."

"I agree completely," Ellie said, looping her arm around her husband's elbow. "Besides, your online businesses are humming along nicely, and you worked until nearly midnight last night. You need a break."

Lenora's ability to show emotion had been lost to surgery, but her wary eyes were asking, *What just happened here?* Olivia had the same question. Her mother could get anyone to do anything, but normally she used her powers for a clear and just purpose. Ellie might simply be trying to rescue Mr. Willard from Lenora's clutches and keep Bertha from losing her love. However, Mr. Willard, befuddled as he might seem at times, was shrewd, insightful, and completely devoted to Bertha. Ellie knew this better than anyone.

It struck Olivia that her mother might have the same questions that had crossed her own mind. Were these younger men truly taking a few days out of their busy professional lives simply to spend quality time with Lenora Tucker? Nothing against Lenora, but it seemed unlikely. Were they out-of-work moochers? Did they assume Lenora had inherited a fortune from her producer husband? Did Ellie suspect the two men might try to take advantage of Lenora, not to mention her nephew and his wife? Well, if the Tucker family needed protection, Olivia could think of no one more capable of providing it than her mother.

CHAPTER SIX

The Gingerbread House had been open for over an hour by the time Olivia returned from her breakfast meeting. Several customers were browsing while two women waited for assistance at the cash register. Bertha, alone on the sales floor, was busy helping a harried mother decide between two cookie cutter themes: baseball or zombies. Olivia went directly to the sales counter and got to work. Spunky would have to stay in her apartment for a while. She'd make it up to him. Meanwhile, thank goodness for puppy pads.

From the sweet, buttery smell of freshly baked cookies drifting through the leaky old kitchen door, Olivia knew that Maddie was hard at work. It wasn't like Maddie to ignore the sales floor, especially when the store was short staffed. Even on ordinary days, though, she could so easily slip into her own world filled with music, dancing, and decorated cookies. And this was no ordinary Wednesday. In three days, the town of Chatterley Heights would celebrate Maddie and Lucas's engagement, and one week later, they would marry in a tiny, private ceremony. Olivia and Del had agreed to be their witnesses, and Maddie's aunt Sadie would be the only other guest. Maddie, who reveled in crowds and loved to dance, was nervous. She joyfully anticipated a huge turnout for her engagement party, but for her nuptials she wanted quiet.

When the customers had dwindled to two women looking through cookbooks, Olivia beckoned Bertha over to the cash register, and asked, "Did Jennifer ever call to say why she didn't show up this morning?"

"I found a message from her on the machine." Bertha's round face puckered with concern. "I know she hasn't been working here for long, but I can't help but think something is terribly wrong. . . . I mean, for Jennifer to simply leave a message with no details. She's such a conscientious young woman, so good with the customers."

The last two browsing customers headed toward the front door, so Olivia asked, "Are you comfortable working the sales floor on your own for a few minutes while I check

116

with Maddie in the kitchen? She might have heard from Jennifer by now. If not, I'll ask her to call around and see if she can find temporary help on such short notice."

"Oh, I'll be just fine. Don't fret now," Bertha said with a maternal pat on Olivia's arm. "If a busload of customers suddenly bursts through that door, I'll poke my head in the kitchen and ask for help."

Olivia opened the kitchen door to hear Maddie singing "Can't Take My Eyes off of You" along with her earbuds. In time to the music, she squirted tiny electric purple flowers on a cookie shaped like a wedding dress. Olivia waited for Maddie to finish before waving to get her attention.

"Hey." Maddie pulled out her earbuds. "How was your meeting? And more important, how did your baking session with your mom go yesterday?"

"Fine, and none of your business," Olivia said. "Any word from Jennifer? Is she ill? If she isn't coming in at all today, we'll need some backup."

"About backup, remember that soul-numbing institution called school? The one that doesn't release its prisoners until June?" Maddie selected a pastry bag and squeezed a minuscule dab of forest green icing to create a leaf. "School is where most of our temps are for the next month or so. The rest of them graduated, got desperate for full-time work, and moved to DC or Baltimore. I found one who could come in next week, but right now she's filling in for a waitress at the café. And to answer your first question second . . . nope, no word from Jennifer. All she said in her message was she had to deal with a family emergency."

"Hard to argue with a reason like that," Olivia said.

"Except . . ." Maddie capped her pastry bag and sank into a chair. "Maybe I misunderstood, but I thought she said during her interview that she didn't have any family in this area."

Olivia opened the kitchen door wide enough to peek into the store. Bertha was discussing sanding sugar with a middle-aged woman, while two more customers chatted near the mixers. "Under control for the moment." Olivia pulled up a chair across the worktable from Maddie. "Any idea where Jennifer is staying?"

"She's renting a room from Gwen's aunt Agnes," Maddie said.

"That makes me think she doesn't have family in or near Chatterley Heights," Olivia said. "Maybe that's what she meant. If her 'family emergency' is in another town or state, we have no clue how far away she is or when she might return. Did you try calling her cell? Or Aunt Agnes?"

"I did," Maddie said. "Her cell goes directly to voice mail, and Aunt Agnes didn't even know she was gone. She checked Jennifer's room, and her belongings are still there. She has paid up through May. I'm out of ideas. I promise I'll never again hire someone without your prior written and notarized approval. Jennifer seemed so perfect. And I'm normally such an extraordinary judge of character."

The kitchen door opened, and Bertha's plump, friendly face appeared. "You'll never guess who just showed up. Jennifer." From anyone else, those words might have been sarcastic, but Bertha sounded her usual cheerful self.

"Did she offer any details about her family emergency?" Olivia asked.

Bertha slipped through the door and closed it behind her. "Not a word, but then, maybe it was too personal. She hunkered right down and got to work helping a couple of women looking for cookbooks. You know, I do worry that she is trying to hide how upset she is. If there was a death in her family . . ." Bertha's eyes glistened, and Olivia wondered if she might be remembering the cruel murder of her beloved employer, Clarisse Chamberlain. With an emphatic shake of her head, Bertha said, "It isn't healthy to push your feelings down too far, it just isn't. Maybe I should talk to —"

"Why don't I talk to Jennifer and see how she's doing," Olivia said. "I haven't had a chance to get to know her." She knew Bertha wouldn't push too hard for information. Olivia, however, wanted very much to learn why Jennifer was suddenly disappearing from work.

Olivia returned to the sales floor as Jennifer unlocked the cabinet containing The Gingerbread House's stock of valuable vintage and antique cookie cutters. A well-dressed woman, her face lit with excitement, watched Jennifer select one of the store's most valuable and expensive cutters, a duck shape with a flat back. Jennifer held the cutter in the palm of her hand and discussed its attributes. Olivia moved closer to listen. Jennifer and her customer seemed absorbed in their exchange and unaware of Olivia's presence.

"We think this dates back to the early twentieth century, possibly even the late nineteenth century," Jennifer said. "It was handmade by a tinsmith and has been lovingly used by several generations of bakers. As you can see, it has an air hole cut into the back to allow air to escape. It's large enough to put your finger through if you need to push the cookie dough out of the cutter."

Jennifer placed the cutter in the customer's hand. The woman ran her finger over the metal, and said, "It's in such good shape. Although clearly it has seen use. There's the sweetest little dent right there on the duck's bill. I can just imagine a child playing with it like a toy while his mother baked cookies for him." She stared into space as if envisioning the scene. "Or maybe she was his grandmother. Grandmothers are generally more tolerant. His mother would probably have told him to stop playing with the cookie cutter before he damaged it."

Olivia smiled at the customer's comment. Vintage cookie cutters had that effect on people. Her smile faded when the store's front door opened and in walked Chatterley Heights's least favorite postal carrier, Sam Parnell. Though it was still spring, Sam had already switched to his United States Postal Service summer uniform, complete with hat. Olivia tried to quell her more judgmental reactions, especially when it came to looks, but she had to admit the outfit wasn't flattering to Sam. It included shorts, which revealed Sam's spindly legs. If he were a kinder person, Olivia thought, she probably wouldn't notice.

Jennifer and her customer were too engrossed in vintage cookie cutters to notice Sam's entrance. He held a white box with a red stripe and blue print. Sam always personally delivered Priority Mail, hoping to get a sneak peek at the contents, and he headed straight toward Olivia. She wished she'd been quick enough to slip back into the kitchen.

"Is that package for us?" Olivia asked.

"So that's the new girl." Sam cocked his head in Jennifer's direction. "First time I've seen her. I deliver mail all over Chatterley Heights, and I'd remember a pretty girl like that. Looks kind of standoffish, though. That type usually is."

Olivia caught herself before she launched into an automatic defense of Jennifer's personality. Sam elicited gossip with well-honed skill, then delivered it to Chatterley Heights citizens as if it were First-Class Mail. It was part of his daily routine. If he didn't have any new gossip to dispense, he would invent some. Olivia found it best to show as little interest as possible.

"I hope this is the shipment of cutters I've

been waiting for." Olivia slipped the package from Sam's hand while he studied his newest quarry. Sam stared at his empty hand, then at Olivia. She tried not to squirm as his watery blue eyes narrowed to slits. She reminded herself that Sam could be irritating, but he was usually harmless . . . unless he felt humiliated.

"Sorry to hear about you and Del." Sam's sneery smile exposed his crooked front teeth. "But I guess it's easy to understand, now that I see how young and pretty your new clerk is."

Old news, Olivia thought with relief. "Now, Sam, everyone knows that was one of Binnie's little attempts to invent news."

"Huh. That's not the way I heard it." Sam's expression reminded Olivia of a vulture. "Of course, it all depends on how much you trust your own friends. Someone sure is feeding Binnie some juicy insider information about you and the sheriff." When Olivia didn't respond, Sam added, "Maybe you and Stacey Harald had a fight? She's been mighty touchy lately, what with that husband of hers going off the wagon. And then she got laid off from her job."

Olivia so dearly wanted to grab Sam by his scrawny neck and stuff a very sharp cookie cutter down his throat; on the other hand, that might damage a perfectly good cookie cutter. "You're not making sense, Sam, and I have work to do." Turning her back on him, Olivia said, "Thanks for bringing the package so quickly." She tried not to look back as she closed the kitchen door, but she couldn't keep herself from glancing at Sam's profile as he watched Jennifer discuss vintage cookie cutters with her enthusiastic customer. Sam was smiling, and it wasn't in a friendly way.

Olivia sorted through her new shipment of cookie cutters, adding each to the store's inventory list, but her mind was on Stacey Harald, a good friend since childhood. Stacey hadn't mentioned anything about losing her job, which she sorely needed. Her ex-husband Wade's now-and-then child-support payments weren't nearly enough to round out Stacey's income from her position as office manager at the Chatterley Heights Elementary School. The couple's two teenage children lived with Stacey. If Wade was drinking again and had lost his job at the Struts & Bolts garage, Stacey and the kids would be in serious trouble.

"Livie? Are you with us, or have you left for your own little happy place?"

Olivia, startled by Maddie's voice, turned

too quickly and whacked her hand against the arm of her wooden chair. "Ouch!"

"Oh dear," Bertha said. "I know how to stop that from bruising very much. My great aunt taught me. She knew such wonderful home remedies." Bertha dug to the back of the freezer for a tray of ice. She emptied the cubes into a dishtowel, which she folded into a makeshift ice pack. "Hold this on your hand as long as you can stand it," she said as she handed the lumpy concoction to Olivia.

"Will that really work?" Maddie asked.

"It will, if you use it right away," Bertha said.

"If I remember to use it at all." Olivia fumbled with the loose pack, which wanted to come apart.

"Or you could stop walking into solid objects," Maddie suggested.

"Yeah, that'll happen." Olivia examined the array of cookies covering the table. "You've made great progress on the extra cookies for Saturday. They look great."

"Of course they do," Maddie said. "Bertha helped with the decorating while you were handling the Jennifer situation. How did that go, by the way?" The oven timer dinged. Maddie opened the oven and switched a batch of baked wedding dresses for unbaked ones.

"Unfortunately, the Jennifer situation became the Snoopy standoff, so I never managed to speak with her. She's still up-selling vintage cutters to a fascinated customer, or she was when I escaped from Sam. By the way, he insinuated it was Stacey Harald who started the rumor that Del dumped me for Jennifer."

Maddie snorted in derision. "Stacey? Not a chance. And for Jennifer? Oh, please, that's the silliest part of the rumor. I mean, Jennifer is certainly pretty in a serious, intense sort of way, but she seems so . . ."

"Serious?" Olivia lifted the ice off her hand to give it a rest.

"Exactly," Maddie said. "And intense. Del is sheriff; he has enough intensely serious stuff in his life."

"So I'm light and fluffy?"

"Don't be silly, Livie. *I'm* light and fluffy. You are . . . well, I guess you verge on serious, at times anyway. However, you are never intense, or hardly ever. The point is, you're a lot more fun than Jennifer, unless there's a side to her I haven't seen. For instance, I can't imagine Jennifer hiding with me in a root cellar while a deranged killer runs amok right above our heads."

"I must admit, that was fun, in a terrifying sort of way." Olivia dumped her melting ice cubes into the sink and wrung out the sopping towel. She examined her hand and was impressed. There were only light signs of bruising.

"Oh, you two," Bertha said. "I should head back to the sales floor to help Jennifer, unless you need me here."

"I'll join you later," Olivia said. "Leave Jennifer to me. I intend to find out about this mysterious family crisis of hers."

When the kitchen door closed behind Bertha, Olivia selected a nearly empty pastry bag and used the last bits of lilac royal icing to accent a pale pink wedding gown cookie. "Maddie, have you heard a rumor that Stacey Harald got laid off from her administration job at the elementary school?"

Maddie's deep green eyes widened. "Not a word. Is it true? School funding must be really low. Stacey is the principal's right-hand woman."

"The rumor came from Sam Parnell, so the odds are it isn't true." Olivia mixed a couple drops of teal gel food coloring into a small batch of royal icing. Teal was her favorite color, and she was getting tired of purple in all its various hues. "On the other hand, I did see Stacey and Wade arguing in the park this morning. She doesn't normally waste energy like that."

"You don't think they're back together, do you?" Fluffy tendrils of red hair escaped from Maddie's purple bandana and softened the outline of her face. Although she was in her early thirties, at that moment she looked barely old enough to date, let alone marry. "Because if those two reunited," Maddie said, "that would be tragic. I'd have to intervene."

"I'd pay to see that." Olivia checked the kitchen clock. "It's going on noon, and Spunky hasn't been out today. I didn't even bring him down to the store this morning. Could you cover the lunch hour with Bertha and Jennifer? I need to take Spunky on a run. Maybe I can call Stacey at the same time. I'm worried."

When Olivia opened the door of her apartment, Spunky leaped into her arms. The force of his little body nearly knocked her backward. She used a foot to close the door behind her before he realized he could escape down the stairs.

"I'm glad to see you, too, Spunks." Olivia held him under one arm and rubbed his silky ears as she headed down the hallway toward the kitchen. When they reached the bathroom, Olivia poked her head inside. "I see you used your puppy pad," she said. "Good boy. That deserves a treat." Spunky wriggled out of her grasp, ran into the kitchen, and skidded on the tile. He came to a stop in front of the magical cabinet door that made dog treats appear and disappear. Standing on his hind legs, Spunky clawed at the plastic container as Olivia drew out two of the recently purchased bone-shaped doggie treats that always reminded her of cutout cookies. She broke the bones in two and slid them across the kitchen floor. While Spunky chased the pieces and devoured them one by one, Olivia gathered his leash and a couple plastic bags.

When he saw the leash, Spunky trotted over to his mistress. He squirmed with excitement as she slipped his fluffy head and front legs through the harness. "Hey, don't get your fur in a bunch," Olivia said as she tried to secure the leash. "There, done. No thanks to you, you squirmy little . . ." Spunky gazed up at her with warm brown eyes full of innocence and adoration. "You are such a little con artist, and I fall for it every time." She ruffled the long, silky hair nearly hiding his eyes.

"Okay, let's go." As Olivia said those hopeful words, the kitchen phone rang. She hesitated, tempted to let it go. Most people called her cell first. Unless . . . Olivia picked up her cell phone, which she'd set on the counter to charge. Only it wasn't plugged in. And the battery was dead. Again. Meanwhile, she had listened through her voice mail spiel on the kitchen phone.

The message began with a deep and familiar sigh. "All right, Livie, I get the point," Maddie said. "I didn't know you hated 'Chapel of Love' so much. Would you please turn your cell back on? We've got a situation —"

Olivia grabbed the telephone receiver. "What situation?"

"Wait, you were monitoring *my* call?"

"Come on, Maddie, I wasn't really monitoring —"

"*And* you turned off your cell to avoid me? All because you hate the Dixie Cups? You do realize 'Chapel of Love' hit the top of the charts in 1964. Or are you mad at me for some reason?"

"Maddie, I'm not mad at you. I like 'Chapel of Love,' I own all the Dixie Cups CDs, my *mother* loved the Dixie Cups. *What situation?*"

"Oh right, the situation," Maddie said.

"Well, it's Jennifer. She disappeared again. Herbie's aunt Len . . . I mean Lenora Dove, just stuck her head in the kitchen and asked where everybody was. I ran out to the sales floor, and Jennifer wasn't there. Not anywhere. I checked the cookbook nook and the entryway and even the backyard. No Jennifer. And no note. You might want to get down here right away."

"Where was Bertha?"

"She's helping me in the kitchen. Jennifer insisted she could handle the floor alone."

"Could Bertha fill in on the floor for fifteen minutes? I promised Spunky a run in the park. He hasn't been out today." At the sound of his name, Spunky whined and tried to jump up Olivia's leg.

"Um, well . . . it's kind of even more complicated. Lenora brought a couple friends along, and they're famous or something, or one of them is famous. I never got hooked on soaps, so . . ."

Olivia groaned. At Pete's Diner that morning, her own mother had arranged for Allan to drive Lenora to the airport to pick up a couple of Hollywood friends. Lenora must have brought them to the store to show them off.

"Anyway," Maddie said, "a customer recognized Lenora's friend, the famous one.

She ran out into the park and started telling everyone that he — whose name I can't remember, but I'll admit he's hunky. Although nothing compared to Lucas . . . What was I saying? Oh yeah, the customer was Polly Franz, and you know she can get out about a million words a minute. So The Gingerbread House is filling up really fast. I'm thinking of calling Del for crowd control."

Polly Franz ran the Chatterley Heights food shelf and was well known for her ability to talk nonstop without pausing for breath. "Don't bother Del about this," Olivia said. "I'll be right down. I'm sure the excitement will wane eventually, and maybe we'll get a few sales out of it." After she hung up, Olivia removed Spunky's leash. "I'm so sorry, Spunks. Our run will have to wait for a while. I'd take you downstairs with me, but apparently the entire town of Chatterley Heights is currently occupying the store. I know crowds make you nervous, plus there's that little escape trick you like to pull. You'll have to stay up here for now. I promise to come back once everything returns to normal, or what passes for normal in this town."

Spunky whimpered, whined, and begged. As Olivia returned his leash to its hook, the poor pup sank to the floor as if he'd given up on life.

"Nice try." Olivia bent over and rubbed his ears. "You must be exhausted after all that work. Take a nap."

Olivia plugged in her dead cell phone and headed toward the living room. Before leaving her apartment, she glanced out her front window, which looked down on the town square. She saw a thin but steady stream of Chatterley Heights citizens funneling in the general direction of The Gingerbread House.

With a sudden sense of urgency, Olivia locked the front door behind her and hurried down the stairs. When she unlocked the door at the bottom of the staircase, she found three people in the foyer. She locked the staircase door and followed them into the store.

Bertha was the first to spot her. "Oh, Livie, I'm so relieved you're back. Maddie is usually good at handling swarms of people, but she's upset about something. I'm not sure what."

"Maybe she's upset about Jennifer disappearing again?" Olivia scanned the crowd, which was no worse than the biggest event they'd ever hosted. She noticed there were even a few men. The Gingerbread House

133

rarely attracted men, though special store events sometimes brought in more. They might show up for the cookies and coffee, then slip out. Olivia didn't see either enticement on hand. Nor did she see her friend and business partner.

"Speaking of Maddie, where is she?" Olivia asked.

"I think she's in the kitchen." Bertha was about the same height as Olivia, five foot seven, so both were able to see over many of the visitors' heads. Maddie was not in sight, but Lenora Tucker and her two Hollywood friends stood together in the warm sunshine that radiated through the large window facing the park. Olivia was quite sure their location was not accidental. They couldn't have chosen a better spot to see and be seen. Tiny Lenora Tucker (stage name: Lenora Dove) stood between two men, her arms interlinked with theirs. The men, one tall and the other a couple inches shorter, faced away from Lenora as if they wanted to escape but couldn't break the iron grip of a ninety-pound woman who was well beyond fifty, though she would never admit her age.

"How have sales been since these folks appeared?" Olivia asked.

Bertha crossed her arms over her stomach,

which had slowly shrunk since she and Mr. Willard had found each other. "Dreadful," she said. "Worse than the Tuesday last winter when we had that awful blizzard."

"Nobody came to the store that day," Olivia said. "As I remember, we sold one cookie cutter, and you were the customer who bought it. You wouldn't even take your employee discount."

"I felt terrible when you sent me home early and insisted on paying me for a full day. And you call yourself a hardheaded businesswoman." Bertha's stern tone came from many years spent raising two boisterous and rather spoiled boys who were not her own.

As several more gawkers crowded into the store, Olivia decided it was time to take action. "Let's have a little talk with these Hollywood folks . . . assuming we can crawl close enough to make ourselves heard."

"Let me go first," Bertha said. "I'm bigger."

With a firm smile and relentless pressure, Bertha cleared a path toward the three celebrities — if they counted Lenora, which Olivia supposed they ought to do — who were holding court by the window. Nearby, Olivia saw the flash of a camera. Sure enough, Binnie Sloan and her niece, Ned, were slithering through the throng, gathering twistable quotes and embarrassing photos for *The Weekly Chatter* and the evil blog it had spawned.

Finally, Olivia got a good look at the taller of the two men standing with Lenora. If Olivia thought she was too mature to do a double take at the sight of an attractive man, she was wrong. She assumed he must be Trevor Lane, star of *Midnights in Manhattan.* Broad shouldered and lean, he was the type of man who looked great in . . . well, just about anything. He wore a tan cashmere sweater, sleeves pushed up to emphasize elegant hands and nicely shaped wrists. His forearms were firm without the bulge of excessive muscle, as if he exercised just enough and no more.

Bertha pushed to the front of the crowd, and Olivia scurried to catch up with her. Finally, Olivia was able to get a clear look at Trevor's face. He had classic features, almost too perfect, with a strong jaw and cheekbones. His dark brown hair looked thick and natural. The overhead lighting revealed emerald green eyes, although Olivia suspected they owed their intensity, and perhaps their color, to contact lenses. She guessed Trevor's age to be early thirties, given the length of his career. So far, the years had been kind to him, adding definition to his features. Trevor Lane was, Olivia admitted, the most gorgeous man she had ever encountered. Either he was very lucky, or he'd found a supremely skilled plastic surgeon.

Olivia's mother materialized at her side. "Hello, dear," Ellie said. "I saw you working your way through the adoring crowd. Although you did stop and stare for such a long time, I wondered if you had suddenly frozen, like Snow White."

If Olivia possessed a skin tone inclined to blush, she would have. "Snow White ate a poisoned apple, Mom. She didn't freeze."

"You were always so precise about details." Ellie looked especially petite and graceful in a silky, pale pink skirt that wrapped around her slender hips and tied with a thin ribbon. A matching top with loose sleeves tied at her waist. Underneath she wore a black leotard and tights.

Olivia glanced at her mother's feet. "You aren't wearing your tap shoes."

"How observant, dear. My enthusiasm for tap dance has not waned, if that's worrying you. As it happens, I'd just finished my ballet lesson when word reached me about the population movement toward The Gingerbread House."

137

Word always seemed to reach Ellie, usually without any effort on her part. Olivia had given up trying to figure out how she did it.

"Would you like to meet Trevor and Dougie?" Ellie asked. "I see Trevor is putting his pen away, so I assume he is signaling the end of his appearance. He and his friend intend to stay in town for a week or so. There will be plenty of time to satisfy everyone's craving for a Trevor Lane autograph. I'm sure he would be willing to sign for you right now, though."

"I couldn't care less about autographs," Olivia said.

"Of course not, dear. Only it would mean a great deal to Lenora. She is so thrilled that Trevor and Dougie have come to visit her. She misses the excitement of her former life. And, of course, she misses her husband. Lenora and Bernie Bouchenbein were truly a love match, no matter what anyone says."

The audience dispersed quickly as Lenora guided the two men toward the store kitchen. Olivia hadn't seen Maddie in the adoring crowd. Bertha was no longer in front of her and hadn't gone back behind the cash register, which wasn't like her . . . though no customers were lined up to pay for purchases, so it didn't matter. "Mom, have you seen Maddie or Bertha?"

"Bertha headed toward the cookbook nook with a customer, and I believe Maddie stayed in the kitchen to work on cookies. I'm afraid she was rather miffed at Lenora for demanding refreshments. I do enjoy Lenora," Ellie said, "but she can be exasperating at times."

"We should probably make sure no fights break out in the kitchen," Olivia said. "Bertha will send an SOS if any actual customers show up."

"Lucas is in the kitchen." Ellie paused at the sales counter to adjust her wraparound skirt. "His presence will keep Maddie calm. The faucet was dripping or something like that, so he dropped by to fix it." She hooked her arm around Olivia's elbow. "Come on, I'll introduce you."

"I hate to admit this, but I barely noticed Trevor's companion," Olivia said.

"I'm sure Dougie is used to that, dear."

As they entered the kitchen, Olivia could feel the tension in the air. One look at Maddie's face told her the source. Lenora was busy appropriating decorated cookies, meant for the engagement party, and arranging them on a plate. She glanced up briefly and said, "Do brew us a fresh pot of coffee, Maddie. There's a dear."

Maddie's pale, freckled cheeks reddened. She crossed her arms and glared at Lenora's back, but she said nothing. Nor did she pour the existing coffee, a nearly full pot, into the kitchen sink, where her fiancé, Lucas Ashford, wrench in hand, was listening to the rhythmic drip from the faucet. Olivia suspected her best friend since age ten of angling for a fight.

Usually it was Ellie who smoothed the waters, but this time rescue came from Trevor's friend, the man Olivia had barely noticed, who lifted the coffee pot, sniffed it, and said to Maddie, "This smells wonderful. Just let me know where you keep the cups, and I'll pour." When he smiled, Maddie relented. She opened a cabinet and the two of them took out seven cups.

Very impressive, Olivia thought as she assembled cream and sugar. What was his name again?

As if she'd read her daughter's mind, Ellie said, "Thank you, Dougie . . . if I may call you Dougie?"

"Please do. And you are Ellie, correct?" With a light laugh, Dougie added, "Actually, I'm surprised you remembered my name. Most people don't. Trevor is the main attraction; I'm just along to fetch and

140

carry." His tone and demeanor betrayed no trace of resentment. Olivia couldn't help but notice the impressive muscles in Dougie's upper arms as he reached for the last cup. She wondered if he might be more bodyguard than friend.

The subject of the interchange, Trevor Lane, had done little more than smile now and then since Olivia and her mother had arrived in the kitchen. At close range, the rather attractive crinkling around his eyes looked more pronounced. Olivia ratcheted up her estimate of Trevor's age by a few years, though he was every bit as attractive as he'd appeared from a distance.

"There," Lenora said as she lifted a heaping plate of decorated cookies. "I have only a tiny appetite, but I know you two boys must be famished. It was quite a long flight from Los Angeles. I doubt you've had a bite of food since you left. I'm afraid this isn't the most substantial offering, but at least it will keep you going until we can get a proper meal for you." Lenora placed the cookies on the counter between Trevor and Dougie. As her hand disengaged from the plate, two cookies left with it. Maddie rolled her eyes, and Olivia had to clamp her teeth together to keep from snickering.

Trevor drank his coffee black and ignored

the cookies. In fact, with the exception of Lenora, no one showed interest in the cookie plate. As she sipped her coffee, Lenora filched a third cookie, a lovely wedding gown shape that Maddie had decorated to match the colors of the dress Aunt Sadie had designed and created for her.

"Oh, do eat some cookies, Trevor," Lenora said. "I know you avoid sugar, but really, you are too thin. And Dougie, you need to keep up those lovely muscles."

As Lenora nibbled along the hem of the lavender-and-yellow wedding-dress cookie, Maddie's eyes metamorphosed to crystalline orbs, much like the emeralds in her engagement ring. Meanwhile, Lucas tested the faucet and watched for drips, unaware of his true love's burgeoning rage. Olivia searched desperately for a topic that might break the tension.

Once again, Trevor's friend intervened. "Everyone knows Trevor Lane," he said, "but I should introduce myself. I'm Dougie Adair, general sidekick." Dougie had a warm smile, which he bestowed on Maddie. "Your cookies are stunning," he said. "I've never seen anything like them in New York City or in Los Angeles, and I've lived in both cities. I understand you are getting married on Saturday? And you are creating these cookies yourself for the occasion?"

Maddie unclenched her teeth enough to say, "It's an engagement party. Everyone is invited." Lenora sidled up to the cookie plate and reached out her hand.

"That's a lot of cookies," Dougie said, "in very little time, and you'll need every one. However, I'm always available to devour leftovers, if by some miracle you have a few left after the party."

Lenora withdrew her hand and pretended to examine her nails.

Olivia was impressed. Dougie had masterfully halted the raid on the cookie supply, and he'd accomplished it without directly offending Lenora.

Maddie softened to her usual friendly self. "How long are you two staying in town? If you're still here on Saturday, you'll be honorary Chatterley Heights residents and hereby invited to our engagement party. Right, honey?" Maddie winked at her beloved.

Lucas was hovering near the sink as if he didn't trust his repair work. When all eyes turned to him, he flushed. "Um, sure."

"This is my fiancé, Lucas Ashford," Maddie said. "He can't cook, but he can fix anything."

"Lucas Ashford," Trevor said. "I know that

name, don't I?" He glanced over at Dougie for confirmation.

"Sure, we remember Lucas," Dougie said. He reached his hand out toward Lucas, who hesitated before shaking it. "You played football in high school."

"Of course," Trevor said. "I remember now. What was the name of the Chatterley Heights team again? The Chatterley Cheaters?"

"It was the Chatterley Cheetahs, Trevor." The reproof in Dougie's voice was subtle but clear. "As I remember, Lucas, you also played basketball. You were really good. Trevor and I weren't so versatile. We just stuck with football."

"And now you're a plumber," Trevor said.

"Lucas is a businessman." Maddie radiated righteous indignation. "He *owns* the Heights Hardware."

Trevor bestowed a dazzling smile upon Maddie. "You mustn't take me too seriously. We had a long and tiring flight, and much as I love my fans, they can be exhausting. Dougie is forever warning me to keep my mouth shut when I'm tired, and he's right." With a slight bow, Trevor added, "Many, many congratulations on your upcoming nuptials. I wish you far better luck at marriage than I ever had." Trevor tilted his head toward Dougie. "Or should I have left out that last part?"

Dougie laughed. "Yes, but nice try."

Olivia felt relieved that the mood had lightened, but the interchange had piqued her curiosity about Dougie. The conversation was winding down. Lucas packed up his tools, and Maddie said she'd walk him back to the hardware store. Trevor tried to convince Lenora to take them to the Tucker home, where they would be staying. Lenora insisted that if Trevor ate a cookie, he wouldn't feel so tired, while Ellie suggested that fatigue responded better to rest than to sugar. Olivia cornered Dougie by the coffeepot. "I'm curious about something," she said. "If my question is rude, just tell me."

"Now *I'm* curious," Dougie said with a good-natured grin. "Ask away."

Olivia didn't want to ask outright about their relationship, so she chose a less direct approach. "Trevor implied that you help him navigate interactions with the public. Are you his . . . manager?"

"In a manner of speaking," Dougie said with a rueful laugh. "And in answer to your cleverly concealed question, we are no more than friends. Between us we have three former wives. Trevor lost his two by cheating on them, starting with the maids of

145

honor at both weddings, and I'm still in love with mine."

Olivia glanced over at Trevor, who was discussing with Lenora the energy-draining qualities of sugar. "I've only just met Trevor, but he does seem hard to manage."

"He is, believe me. Trevor can be charming, funny, rude, you name it. He's actually quite a good actor. He really belongs on Broadway, but he's stuck in daytime drama. That's where the steady money is."

"So you're his agent?"

"No, Trevor's got an agent, for all the good it does him. I'm his writer."

"He has his own writer?"

"He does. You'd be surprised how much writing Trevor is expected to do on his own, and it isn't his thing. He's great at extemporaneous speaking, but having to put pen to paper or fingers to keyboard . . . well, the very thought enervates him. And you saw what he's like when he needs a nap. So he does the speaking, and I do the writing. I answer his fan mail and email. I deal with his stalkers. I write his press releases, charming and witty answers to interview questions, blog posts, tweets, you name it."

As the sugar forum came to a close, Trevor called across the kitchen to Dougie, "You might have to carry me to Lenora's place.

I'm dead on my feet."

"And sometimes I'm his muscle," Dougie said quietly as he nodded toward Trevor. "I do what needs to be done."

CHAPTER SEVEN

Olivia and Bertha spent over an hour putting The Gingerbread House back together after the hordes of fanatic Trevor Lane fans departed. By the time Olivia untangled the last cookie cutter mobile, it was time to close the store. During the reconstruction, only two people walked through the front door. Both of them left as soon as Bertha informed them that Trevor Lane was long gone. No one asked about Dougie Adair. Olivia wondered if Dougie resented his invisible status . . . or if he preferred it that way.

The one person Olivia hadn't heard from was Jennifer Elsworth. Bertha and Olivia had taken turns calling Jennifer's cell from the kitchen phone, but their calls all went directly to voice mail. "You go on home, Bertha," Olivia said. "I'll reconcile the receipts, since there aren't very many."

"I feel so bad for you, Livie." Bertha

removed her embroidered apron, which depicted two little gingerbread girls joyfully swinging on a vine over a lake. When she'd bought the apron, Bertha had said, "You wouldn't think it to look at me now, but I was a daredevil as a little girl."

Maddie's aunt Sadie had proposed the idea for a series of aprons based on The Gingerbread House logo, which featured tumbling gingerbread men, women, and children. Using exotic colors and a touch of humor, Aunt Sadie continued to create endless variations on the original theme. Her most recent batch depicted gingerbread boys and girls having fun in serious adult jobs. The aprons all sold quickly.

"I do hope nothing has happened to Jennifer," Bertha said as she headed toward the front door. "You hear such terrible stories about folks dying in car crashes while they are rushing off to be with sick family members. It's just not fair. But we'll hope for the best. Now, Livie, if you need me to fill in tomorrow, don't hesitate to call. Dear Willard and I are planning to meet for lunch, but otherwise . . ."

"I can't believe Jennifer won't try to contact us before tomorrow. I'll let you know, and many thanks for your flexibility. If we keep having sales days like this one, we won't need any staff at all." Olivia locked the front door behind Bertha and gravitated toward the kitchen, from which luscious aromas drifted. As she opened the kitchen door, the phone rang.

At the kitchen table, Maddie swayed to her earbuds, oblivious to the ringing. Wielding a pastry bag, she squiggled purple icing down the sides of a wedding cake cutout cookie. She glanced up, startled, as Olivia lunged for the phone.

"Livie?" It was Del's voice. "Is that you breathing heavily?"

"Sorry to disappoint you, Del, but I tripped over a chair trying to reach the phone. I thought it might be Jennifer."

"Jennifer?"

"Our new clerk. You met her briefly," Olivia said. "She's the attractive younger woman you dumped me for, remember?"

Del responded with a reassuring chuckle.

"Frankly, if we don't hear from her soon, she'll be our former clerk," Olivia said. "You haven't heard anything about an accident involving a young woman, have you?"

"Nope, haven't heard about any accidents today, but I'll keep my ears open. Maybe her car broke down. Or she ran over her phone."

"You're making excuses for Jennifer because you thought she was cute," Olivia said. "Or that's what Sam Parnell said. So if that's why you're calling . . ."

Del heaved an exaggerated sigh. "Poor old Snoopy. He keeps forgetting I carry a loaded gun. Anyway, that's not why I called. I thought you might want to eat this evening."

"The thought had occurred to me," Olivia said. "I did miss lunch. Only I have to bake and decorate some very special cookies before Saturday, and I seem to be down a staff member. It's been quite a day."

"So I heard," Del said. "Hollywood and the paparazzi converge in the quaint little Gingerbread House. It has the makings of a murder mystery."

"Don't even think it." Olivia glanced up at the kitchen clock. "I don't know about dinner. There's just so much work —" Maddie put down her pastry bag and began waving at Olivia with both hands. "Hang on a moment, Del. Maddie seems to be having a seizure." Olivia held the telephone receiver against her shoulder.

"Okay, here's an idea," Maddie said. "Abbreviated version. You are stressed, which makes me and many others crazy. So go have a quick meal with Del, maybe for an hour or so. I'm nearly finished with this last

151

batch of extra cookies for Saturday. Then I'll work on the recipes for the special cookies. Tell me the flavors you want to use, and let me take a crack at the early experimentation. Don't give me that look, Livie. It's my engagement party, so I get a say. I don't care if your creations are a surprise. I'd much rather join in the fun of making them. Well?"

Olivia hesitated for a moment before shrugging her shoulders. "I don't know. I love baking with Mom, like when I was a kid. On the other hand, I am feeling pressured and cranky, which stresses Mom . . . and she is missing her yoga classes to help me."

With a sage nod, Maddie said, "Now see, that's a setup for disaster."

Olivia heard a squawking noise close to her ear. "Oops. Sorry, Del. Heavy negotiations going on here. Yes, dinner now, Pete's Diner. See you in five." Olivia hung up, and said, "Okay, you win. I could use some help creating cookie recipes with lavender-lemon and rosewater-lemon." Olivia grinned at Maddie. "Me, businesswoman; you, cookie genius."

"There," Maddie said. "Don't you feel better? Now scram and let me concentrate." She reinserted her earbuds and squirted a tiny pink flower on a wedding-cake cookie.

As Olivia entered Pete's Diner, she felt calmer than she had in days. She spotted Del at a table by the front window. In place of his uniform, he wore dark brown slacks and a crisp tan shirt. His uniform hat usually left a dent in his light brown hair, but now it hung straight over his eyes as he scanned the menu. He must have showered before meeting her. When Del looked up and saw her, his face lit with pleasure. Olivia was finding it harder and harder to remember that he could be downright irritating at times. "Hi there," she said. "Catch any bad guys lately?"

"Well, I did stop a fellow driving a Lexus erratically through the north end of town. He kept drifting into the oncoming lane."

"Drugs?" Olivia asked. "Or was he drunk?"

"Texting." Del handed a ketchup-stained menu to Olivia.

"Young people these days," Olivia said, shaking her head.

"He was thirty-six. Oh, and the car was a rental. Good-looking guy, a bit arrogant, said something about needing to reassure his fans that he'd be back, whatever that means."

"You're teasing me, right?" Olivia's menu dropped onto the table. "You did not stop Trevor Lane for texting."

"I did." Del grinned at her. "I don't understand what women see in him. He struck me as kind of a self-obsessed jerk."

"Don't look at me, he isn't my type. Though he is handsome and famous, and he probably knows people who know people. Lots of women go for that." Olivia paused before adding, "Not me, of course."

Ida appeared at their table and plunked down two plastic tumblers of merlot. Her unruly gray hair was pinned back in a tight bun and free of her usual hairnet, so she wasn't on cook duty. "Real cops drink beer," Ida said. "I can give you a deal on the meatloaf and mashed potatoes, two for one. A certain cook, not me, made too much of the stuff. All I gotta do is slap it on a couple plates. How about three for the price of one? You could take some home for breakfast tomorrow morning."

"Sounds good to me." Olivia loved Pete's meatloaf, especially for breakfast.

"Done." Del handed the menus to Ida, who heaved a weary sigh and shuffled off to deliver the order.

"So I hear you had an exciting afternoon," Del said.

Olivia sipped her merlot. Despite the presentation, the wine was excellent. "Exciting isn't the word I'd choose. Exhausting, frustrating, expensive . . . yet interesting. Del, when did you stop Trevor Lane?"

"About half an hour ago."

"And was he alone in the car?"

"Yes. Why?

Ida plunked down three plates filled to capacity with hunks of meatloaf and piles of mashed potatoes. Olivia estimated each plate held about four portions.

"Pete said to get rid of the stuff before it gets old," Ida said. "All for the price of one. He fired the cook, so don't go expecting anything like this again."

When Ida was out of earshot, Olivia said, "Trevor has a sort of bodyguard/handler/writer/companion named Dougie Adair traveling with him. Lots of muscles. I got the impression it was part of his job to keep Trevor out of trouble. I don't suppose you got a look at who he was texting?"

"Well, Livie, there's this little thing called a subpoena. I didn't really have any reason to ask for one. I explained to Mr. Lane that in Maryland it's illegal to text and drive, but I let him off with a warning, since he was from out of state. He was suitably contrite, and I let him go. I watched him drive off in an impressively straight line at an appropriate speed." Del took a generous bite of meatloaf and washed it down with merlot.

"How disappointingly lenient of you," Olivia said. "I'd love to know who Trevor was texting."

"Why?" Del used his spoon to capture a large hunk of mashed potatoes, poured sauce on top, and shoveled the mixture into his mouth.

"Show-off." With exaggerated delicacy, Olivia ate a small bite of her meatloaf. "Did you know you've got tomato sauce dribbling down your chin?"

Del grunted and swiped his chin with his napkin. "Thanks. About your interest in Trevor Lane's texting behavior, is it just prurient curiosity, or are you suspicious of him for some reason?"

"I'm not sure I'd call it suspicion, but . . . Del, does it strike you as odd that Trevor Lane — well-known star of stage, screen, and daytime drama — suddenly decided to visit little Chatterley Heights, Maryland, bringing along his entourage of one? Yes, I know they both grew up in Twiterton, so why not stay somewhere there? Why stay out at Chatterley Paws with an aging, unsuccessful actress and two people they don't know, not to mention a baby, plus animals everywhere? They haven't seen Lenora in years. From what I've observed, they barely tolerate her. Let's face it, Lenora is one of us, we love her, but she's a bit, well . . ."

"Bizarre?" Del pushed his plate aside and drained his tumbler of wine.

"Irritating," Olivia said. "Maybe I'm building a case out of imagined connections. Or a cake out of cookies, which is what I'm supposed to be doing right now." Olivia glanced up at Pete's bird-call clock. "The Cooper's hawk is about to strike seven."

As Olivia finished her merlot, Ida appeared at their table and nodded at the empty tumbler. "You want another one of those?" When Olivia declined, Ida said, "We got cherry pie for dessert. Want any?"

"Too full, but thanks."

"Pete said it's on the house for you two. I'll make 'em to go, along with this stuff." Ida picked up the leftover meatloaf and left.

"Have I mentioned how much I love dating a cop?" Olivia asked. "I get free food."

"I thought it was the free coffee you loved, but you're welcome."

"Tell me honestly, Del, has past experience made me too suspicious? About Trevor and Dougie, I mean."

Del shrugged. "Livie, I'm trained to be suspicious, only we like to think of it as keeping our eyes open. On the other hand, it wouldn't hurt to look into Trevor's and Dougie's backgrounds a bit, especially since their arrival comes close on the heels of a break-in at Lady Chatterley's and the attack on a bank manager."

"Good idea. Unless there's something I should know about, I'll understand if you don't share what you find." *Maddie can probably dig up the same information, anyway.*

Del's cell phone rang. He checked the caller ID and answered at once. "Maddie? You okay?" As he listened, Del's expression relaxed. "Yeah, she can be forgetful, but she's got her good qualities. Hang on." As he handed his cell to Olivia, Del said, "Apparently you are once again not responding to your cell, or it's dead, or you are still mad about having to go to chapel or something."

Olivia groaned and took the phone. "Maddie, I am not now, nor have I recently been, mad at you. I left my cell to recharge at my apartment. What's up?"

"Jennifer is back."

"And what does Jennifer have to say for herself?" Olivia glanced at Del, who looked puzzled and interested.

"You're going to be mad at me," Maddie said.

"Maddie, please, what's going on?"

"Jennifer is really, truly upset. I know this sounds like the kind of excuse a kid would give a teacher — you know, like the dog ate my homework, or I didn't finish my paper because my grandmother died, sniffle, sniffle."

"Jennifer's grandmother died? Maddie, don't make me work so hard."

"Okay, Jennifer told me her aunt suddenly got sick and called her from someplace in DC, where she lives . . . lived. Anyway, that's why Jennifer ran off so fast this morning. She couldn't convince her aunt to call her doctor. Then Jennifer got to worrying and tried to call her aunt back but got no answer, so she just took off in a panic."

"Jennifer didn't think to call a neighbor or even the police?" Olivia asked. Del's eyebrows shot up, but he didn't interrupt.

"Panic is like that, I guess," Maddie said. "Jennifer said she found her aunt weak and feeling awful, so she took her to the emergency room. They were concerned enough to admit her to the hospital for observation. Jennifer drove right back here and came to work. She said everyone was busy then, so she figured she'd explain when things got

159

quieter. Then she got a call from the hospital that her aunt was going downhill fast, so she took off again."

"So did her aunt rally?" Olivia asked.

"Well, no. She died. Jennifer was really broken up about it. She said this aunt was her last living relative and practically raised her. I guess I felt a lot of sympathy because of Aunt Sadie. I'd have been an orphan at ten if Aunt Sadie hadn't taken me in when my mom and dad died."

"Maddie, you know I understand. Why did you think I'd be mad at you?"

"Well, I told Jennifer she could keep her job."

"I'm fine with that," Olivia said. "We have no evidence Jennifer has been lying to us. Not yet, anyway. I'll be back soon, but first that poor pooch of mine needs attention. All he's gotten today are a couple quick visits to the backyard and extra guilt-induced treats. I'll take him on a quick run, and then we can start baking up a storm."

"Great!" Maddie sounded more like her hyper-enthusiastic self again. "Although I've already gotten a head start on the baking. You know me, can't keep my hands away from cookie dough."

"I do have a favor to ask, if you need a break soon." Olivia sneaked a glance at Del, who was checking his voice mail and text messages. "Would you use your magic computer fingers to do a little research for me? I'd really like to know more about our new employee. And maybe our other new-comers." Del looked up from his cell phone, gave Olivia a quick smile, and went back to reading his messages.

"You really do suspect Jennifer is lying, don't you?" Maddie's curiosity had reasserted itself.

"I think things aren't adding up, that's all. It's probably not a big deal. I mean, it's not as if there's been a murder."

CHAPTER EIGHT

Olivia heard Spunky whine as she slid the key into the lock of her apartment door. She prepared herself to intercept a five-pound missile. Spunky burst through the opening and right into Olivia's arms.

"Gotcha!" Holding tight to the squirming Yorkie, Olivia pushed into her apartment and closed the door with her backside. "I'm getting good at this, aren't I, Spunks?"

Spunky wriggled as Olivia made sure the front door was latched. When she released him, he raced toward the kitchen. Olivia arrived to find him stationed next to his empty food bowl. He tilted his little head and whimpered. The long silky hair on his head fell to one side, revealing sad, starving eyes.

"Oh, you're good," Olivia said. "I know this is how you survived on the streets of Baltimore, but remember, I'm on to you. I gave you a big bowl of food this morning plus extra treats."

Spunky whimpered again with increased pathos. He sank to the floor as if he were too weak to sit upright any longer. Against her will, Olivia felt herself melt. After all, the little guy had missed his daily run, and he'd stayed alone in the apartment all day instead of enjoying his usual time in the store, lapping up attention.

Olivia caved in and opened Spunky's bag of dry food. "I realize this is a precedent-setting mistake," she said, "for which I will pay and pay." She poured a small pile of kibbles into Spunky's bowl, the sight of which gave him the strength to leap to his paws. "I will live to regret this, won't I?" Olivia murmured. Spunky ignored her.

While Spunky licked his bowl clean, Olivia changed into her jeans and running shoes. When she returned to the kitchen and lifted his leash from its hook on the kitchen wall, Spunky held still barely long enough for her to attach the leash to his collar. Olivia sprinted behind as Spunky pulled her downstairs with an urgency she understood and took seriously. They made it outdoors just in time.

"I'm so glad you aren't a puppy anymore," Olivia said.

Dusk had given way to darkness, deepened by the cloud-filled sky. Around the town

163

square, only a few shops, the Chatterley Café and Pete's Diner, remained open. The old-fashioned street lamps lining the sidewalks revealed a handful of folks heading home from work or out to dinner. The park looked dark and empty, the way Spunky liked it. No screaming children or rowdy teenagers who might step on him or pull his tail. Spunky yanked on his leash to inform Olivia that he thought a run in the park sounded like a good idea. Olivia wasn't so sure. The only light deep within the park came from one streetlamp that lent a golden glow to the old band shell. Only the rounded exterior showed in outline against the dark sky, reminding Olivia of a seashell-shaped cookie cutter.

Spunky had set his heart on a run in the park. He made his desire clear by pulling so hard on the leash that his front paws lifted off the ground. Olivia had bought the determined five-pound creature a harness leash to keep him from strangling himself; unfortunately, it also enabled him to yap at full volume.

"Oh, all right," Olivia said. "We'll brave the park. Only I'm counting on you to protect me." She trotted behind Spunky into the darkness. Her eyes adjusted quickly, and she found she could make out the benches scattered around the park, as well as the statue of Frederick P. Chatterley and his horse, toward which Spunky ran with terrier determination. He had a fondness for the horse's legs, which seemed to remind him of fire hydrants.

Before they'd reached the founder's statue, Spunky halted so suddenly that Olivia nearly tripped over him. His sensitive Yorkie ears perked as he stared toward the dark interior of the band shell. Her heart pounding as if she were still running, Olivia scooped him up and carried him to the deeper shadows, out of sight. She put him on the grass and tugged on his leash, but he wouldn't budge. She told herself it was nothing. Spunky wasn't yapping or growling, just listening. Olivia suspected he heard a courting couple inside the band shell. Or a squirrel, scrounging for crumbs.

She tugged again at the leash. "Come on, Spunks, remember how fond you are of Frederick P. and his trusty steed? Also, Maddie and I have work to do, so if we could move it along . . ." Spunky gave Olivia a momentary glance but quickly refocused on the band shell. Then she heard it, too: a voice, male, angry, and harsh. The voice sounded familiar, but she couldn't place it. She edged closer. A faint murmur answered, followed by another outraged response. Olivia caught the word "lied." She thought back to the one-sided conversation she'd overheard in the garden behind Bon Vivant. But no, this voice sounded lower, a bit slurred, and definitely male.

Spunky growled. Olivia knew from experience that a volley of yaps would quickly follow. She grabbed her fierce protector, who had no idea how tiny he was, and headed past the band shell at a casual pace. Spunky refused to be thwarted. He growled and barked and tried to squirm his way out of Olivia's tight hold.

"Don't you dare," Olivia hissed as she found herself clutching Spunky's hind legs. He had managed to wriggle up to peek over her shoulder. Hanging on to one of his legs, Olivia reached up and grabbed a handful of the hair on his back, which hadn't been trimmed in some time. She might never trim it again. Spunky whimpered, but Olivia didn't loosen her grip. She turned toward the band shell, forcing Spunky to look in the opposite direction, toward the statue. As she did so, she saw the figure of a man standing next to the band shell, staring in her direction. She couldn't see his face. From his silhouette, Olivia guessed he was on the small side, thin but broad shouldered. He didn't gesture or call to her. He simply stared as if he might be trying to identify her. It wouldn't be hard. Everyone in town knew Spunky.

In an instant, the figure turned and walked away, weaving slightly as he melted into the darkness. There was something about the way he moved, bowlegged and belligerent . . . Olivia flashed to her breakfast meeting at Pete's Diner. Olivia had watched her friend Stacey Harald argue with her ex-husband Wade. Normally a gentle person who loved his children, Wade became combative when he drank, and he'd probably been drinking already that morning. When he'd stalked away from Stacey, his gait had been wobbly and angry. Wade was slight yet muscular, and he was bowlegged. Olivia promised herself a talk with Stacey as soon as possible.

"Olivia? Is that you?"

Olivia's heart skittered up her throat. Spunky spewed a torrent of outraged yaps and renewed his struggle to free himself. Olivia held him so tightly he yelped.

"Sorry, I didn't mean to startle you." A tall man stepped out of the band shell and into the light.

"Mr. Lane, I didn't expect . . ." Olivia loosened her stranglehold on Spunky but held firmly to his leash.

"Even total strangers call me Trevor." As he tilted his head, a lock of hair fell across his forehead.

Olivia envisioned female fans longing to brush the hair away from his eyes. This was not her own reaction, which Spunky expressed perfectly by snarling at Trevor. "Everyone calls me Livie," she said.

Two more men emerged from the band shell. The first, Olivia recognized as Dougie Adair. "Livie, we truly are sorry if our sudden appearance scared you," Dougie said. "My fault, really. I heard frantic barking and thought someone might be in danger. I guess it comes from having lived in big cities most of my adult life. We were just enjoying your lovely band shell. If I called Chatterley Heights home, I'd come here every evening to think and write."

Olivia began to understand how Dougie managed to keep Trevor out of trouble, if that was, in fact, his role. She had to wonder why Trevor had escaped from Dougie's protection earlier in the day. What had been so important that he had to risk a ticket, not to mention an accident?

The third man looked very familiar to Olivia, but she couldn't place him. He was a couple inches shorter than Dougie. From his wiry build, she guessed he might be a runner, yet his pasty complexion placed him indoors for long periods. With a slight nod to Olivia, the man said, "I'm Howard Upton."

"Come off it, Howie," Trevor said. "You simply aren't a Howard, not even in a suit."

In the muted lamp light, Olivia could see Howie's cheeks redden. "Howie is fine with me," he mumbled.

Where have I seen him before? "Do you live in Chatterley Heights?" Olivia asked Howard.

"Howie still lives with his mother in Twiterton," Trevor said, emphasizing the word "mother." "We three went to Twiterton High together, graduated the same year. Although Dougie and I were friends all through high school, played football and basketball, dated a lot, so we rarely crossed paths with Howie. Poor little Howie was the class genius."

"You make it sound like a fate worse than death," Dougie said with a light laugh. "Howie really was a child genius. He skipped two grades and graduated from high school at sixteen, right, Howie?"

Howie's tight expression relaxed. "I was younger than the other boys, and maybe a bit chubbier as I prepared for a growth

169

spurt, so naturally I was at a disadvantage in sports. And high school girls aren't interested in dating boys who are much younger. After high school my age became less of a hindrance, and I made up for my earlier dating deficit. I went into finance; that gave me a distinct advantage with women."

Olivia heard a tinge of defensive arrogance in Howie's voice, but she imagined being a child genius wasn't easy. And then she remembered where she'd seen him before: behind the teller window in the Chatterley Heights National Bank. He must be in his thirties. By "going into finance," did Howie mean working as a bank teller? Management trainees were often required to work as tellers before graduating to managers, but even so, she would expect a "child genius" to have progressed further by now.

"Come inside and chat with us awhile, won't you?" Trevor asked with his fetching smile.

Spunky growled at the invitation, and Olivia thought about all the cookies she had to create before Saturday. On the other hand, her curiosity had shifted into overdrive, and besides, Maddie wanted to help with the baking and decorating marathon. Come to think of it, Maddie would be deeply disappointed if Olivia failed to learn as much as possible about these mysterious strangers.

"Maddie is expecting me in the store soon," Olivia said, "but I'd love to chat a bit." She followed Trevor up the broad steps leading into the band shell. Dougie and Howie followed behind. A stone bench circled the inside perimeter. Olivia chose a spot near the front entrance, lit by the streetlamp, and nestled Spunky on her lap. The location gave her a quick way out. Not that she was nervous. Just cautious. Spunky allowed Dougie to sit on Olivia's right without incident. However, when Trevor tried to sit on Olivia's left, her canine guardian growled at him. With quick grace, Trevor moved next to Dougie. Olivia caught the satisfied expression that flickered across Dougie's face. Howie followed Trevor but put some distance between himself and the two other men.

For Olivia, the band shell had always offered a sense of peace. It was well over one hundred years old, but the town had kept it fairly well maintained. The rounded structure, with its curved entrance and open floor plan, hosted band concerts, dances, and a variety of other town events. For musical performances, the town provided folding chairs and music stands. During a flush period in Chatterley Heights's history, the town leaders had sprung for lighting, which they now used sparingly. As a young girl, Olivia had spent many summer hours in the cool interior of the band shell, happily reading historical novels and imagining music and dancing from eras long before her birth.

Now the band shell felt abandoned, despite their presence. As always after a long winter, the floor could do with a good scrubbing, and the decorative paintings on the walls needed touching up. From what she could see of the stone bench they were sitting on, she was glad she'd changed into jeans.

Spunky fussed in Olivia's firm grip, though he wasn't growling or yapping. He was impatient to be home, and so was she. No time to beat around the bush. "Wasn't that Wade Harald I just saw leaving the band shell? Do you know him, too? What brought all of you together this evening?" Olivia's bright tone was, she hoped, a decent imitation of Maddie's at her most innocently blunt. She noticed the quick glance between Trevor and Dougie. Howie crossed his arms over his narrow chest.

"Pure accident." Dougie's tone was

smooth, unconcerned. "We don't really know Wade well, but Trevor and I were exploring this lovely park, and we ran into Howie. We haven't seen each other since . . . How long has it been, Howie?" Dougie and Trevor turned their heads toward Howie and away from Olivia. Howie squirmed as if he felt uncomfortable. "High school."

"Graduation day, to be precise. Howie was valedictorian, naturally." A faint undertone in Trevor's voice made Olivia wonder if these three former classmates shared a more complex history than they were willing to discuss with a stranger. Trevor's cell phone rang to a syrupy tune that Olivia had heard but couldn't identify. Trevor checked the caller ID and sighed. "It's dear old Lenora."

When Trevor failed to answer by the second ring, Dougie said, "Lenora is our hostess." The quiet authority in his voice was unmistakable.

"Oh, I suppose. . . ." Trevor flipped open his cell. "Lenora, dearest. So sorry to have abandoned you. Pressing business, you know how it is." Trevor stared out into the dark park as he listened to her response. "What an intriguing idea, my dear. I was hoping for a rest, but I wouldn't dream of disappointing my fans. And you know how I love animals. Have you spoken with Mad-

173

die about it?" After a pause as Lenora responded, Trevor asked, "Well, have you at least run the idea past your nephew? No? Don't you think the restaurant might have a few objections?" Trevor glanced toward Dougie and rolled his eyes. "All right, Lenora, why don't you talk it over with everyone involved, then let me know." Apparently, Lenora agreed. "Kiss kiss to you, too," Trevor said and snapped his phone shut.

"What now?" Dougie asked.

Trevor groaned. "Lenora had one of her brainstorms. She has decided there should be entertainment at Maddie's party, and she and I should be the featured stars. Her nephew, whose name I've forgotten, used to write little plays in high school, so Lenora wants him to create some skits or something. And she thinks cookies should be involved in the performance, since that's the party theme."

"Really," Olivia said. "And here I thought the party was to celebrate Maddie and Lucas's engagement." Her cell burst once again into "Chapel of Love," inducing snickers from the three men. The noise roused Spunky, who had been snoring gently in Olivia's lap. He dropped off again as soon as Olivia opened her cell and silenced the Dixie Cups. Olivia heard Maddie's voice before the phone reached her ear.

"Livie, were you planning to make an appearance anytime soon?" Maddie did not sound like her irrepressibly cheerful self.

"Sorry, Maddie, I didn't mean to stick you with all the baking. I've been in the band shell chatting with Trevor, Dougie, and Howie from the bank, but I'm heading right back to the store."

"No, don't move," Maddie said. "I'll be there in two minutes. I need to get out of this kitchen before Lenora calls with more about her brilliant idea for my engagement party. Tell the guys I'm bringing cookies so they won't leave."

"Understood," Olivia said, but Maddie had already hung up. "I'm afraid I'm under orders to hold you three captive for a while," Olivia said to the men. "Maddie is rushing over with cookies."

Howie checked his watch. "I need to get going soon. I start work early in the morning."

"Well, I wouldn't pass up Maddie's cookies even if I were offered the role of Rhett Butler in a remake of *Gone with the Wind*," Trevor said. "Besides, I missed dinner."

"I'll bet you did." Howie snorted too loudly. "I heard about your antics this

175

afternoon. Sheriff Jenkins caught you speeding and texting. I wonder who you were so desperate to have a conversation with . . . another married woman? I guess Dougie needs to keep you on a tighter leash."

With a soft chuckle, Trevor said, "Ah, the simple pleasures of small-town life, I remember them well. The rumor mill churns incessantly." To Olivia, Trevor's comment sounded like a line from a play.

Olivia's bench seat offered the fullest view of the park, so she was first to notice a figure jogging toward the band shell. The moonlight revealed a fluffy head of bouncing hair that could belong to no one in town but Maddie Briggs. Spunky lifted his head and watched her approach with eager, perked ears.

"Where did you say you worked, Howie?" Trevor's voice was too smooth. "The local bank, isn't it? Funny how things turn out. Howie Upton, math genius, destined for great success in the financial world . . . and here you are, thirty-four years old, a teller in a small-town bank."

Maddie must have reached hearing range, because she halted and stood quietly in the grass. Olivia had to remind herself to breathe. She'd wondered about Howie's lowly position, too, but Trevor's tone implied he possessed information that Howie wanted to keep secret. Of course, Trevor's insinuations might be wild guesses based on a plausible-yet-fabricated theory about Howie's failure to achieve what his schoolmates expected of him. Either way, Olivia decided to keep her distance from Trevor Lane. Although she found herself very curious about the past relationship among these three men.

"I come bearing cookies," Maddie announced heartily as she climbed the bandshell steps. Exchanging a swift glance with Olivia, she handed the plate to Dougie, who expressed delight as he selected a teal heart-shaped cookie. Dougie passed the treats on to Trevor. "There's plenty for seconds," Maddie said. "I've been a busy baker."

"How delightful," Trevor said in his silkiest voice. He made a show of trying to choose between a peppermint-striped wedding cake and a rose-covered chapel.

"Take both," Maddie said.

"I believe I will, one for dinner and one for dessert. Thank you, Maddie." With the plate on his lap, Trevor picked up each cookie with long, graceful fingers and placed them side-by-side on the palm of his left hand. "And by the way, don't worry about Lenora's plan for you to provide even more cookies for her little amateur playlet. We adore Lenora, of course, but she does occasionally mistake herself for the center of the universe."

"When everyone knows *you* are the center of the universe," Howie said under his breath.

"Are you excited about your celebration and upcoming nuptials, Maddie?" Dougie asked.

"Sure," Maddie said. "I always love a party. I get to wear a fantastic dress, be surrounded by friends and total strangers . . . what's not to get excited about? I hope you're all planning to be at Bon Vivant Saturday afternoon. There will be wine, cookies, and little sandwiches with the crusts cut off."

Olivia noticed that Trevor hadn't passed the cookie plate on to Howie. She also observed Howie's stiff posture and wooden expression. Maddie must have noticed, too, because she snatched the cookie plate from Trevor's lap. After claiming a deep pink wedding gown for herself, Maddie offered the plate to Howie. His shoulders relaxed as he reached for a cookie shaped like a gift box wrapped in pink-striped icing.

"Be careful of your weight, Howie," Trevor said. "You worked so hard to lose it."

Trevor's warning, delivered so casually, silenced everyone. Olivia froze, her own cookie halfway to her lips. Maddie recovered first, and said lightly, "You're too skinny, Howie. And I'm not just saying that because I myself have quite generous proportions." Howie glanced up at Maddie with an expression that reminded Olivia of Spunky when she gave him an extra treat.

"You both look great," Dougie said. He chomped on his cookie and nodded in approval. Before taking a second bite, Dougie lifted up his cookie heart, now minus one lobe, to offer a toast. "To Maddie and Lucas," he said, "and a long and happy life together."

All but Trevor echoed the toast. Olivia noticed his tight jaw and narrowed eyelids. Trevor Lane was very angry, which startled Olivia. *Why? Just because Maddie and Dougie tried to soften his nasty comment to Howie?*

With a jerky movement, Trevor raised one of his cookies, as Dougie had done, and said, "I wish you the very best of luck, Maddie, as you enter that challenging condition known as married life. And may you be spared the fate suffered by Anna Adair, my good friend Dougie's former wife."

CHAPTER NINE

"Wow, talk about drama," Maddie said as she scooped up an assortment of gel food colors and arranged the bottles on the kitchen counter. "Trevor's mysterious line about Anna Adair is such a great ending for a scene in a play. I was impressed. Trevor would be totally convincing as Rhett Butler. I might have to start watching the soaps."

"Trevor Lane doesn't like to be crossed, that's for sure." Olivia noticed the sugar supply was running low and started a shopping list. "Dougie told me he was still in love with his former wife. I would love to know what terrible fate befell her. I wonder if Lenora knows."

"I'm not sure we could trust Lenora's version of anything, but I bet I can find the information online." Maddie fired up Olivia's laptop, which doubled as the store computer. "Although Trevor might have been ad-libbing to punish Dougie for contradicting him when he told Howie to watch his weight. Honestly, I feel like we've been in the middle of a joie de vivre or something."

After puzzling for a moment, Olivia said, "Well, this evening was intriguing in a tense sort of way, but 'enjoyment of life' isn't the description I'd have chosen."

Maddie lifted her fingers from the computer keyboard. "Déjà vu?"

"Not unless you'd heard Trevor's show-stopping toast before this evening."

"Ménage à trois?"

"Please stop."

Olivia sat at her little kitchen desk, where she'd left a notebook in which she'd been scribbling ideas for cookie recipes. The lavender cookie recipe was close, thanks to her mom's input, but she was ready to scratch the lemon verbena idea altogether. Olivia felt as if the time pressure had frozen her brain. Maddie created recipe variations all the time, but she never wrote them down. Too boring, she always said. Olivia enjoyed recording her ideas. She liked to watch an idea develop into a project, even if the goal was as mundane as reorganizing a shelf. Her current project, creating two new recipes for Maddie's engagement party, was far more intriguing than reorganizing a shelf, but also a whole lot tougher. Olivia thought back to her business-school training, specifically her class on entrepreneurship. *I'm supposed to think of this as a challenge, right? So why do I feel tempted to clean the bathroom instead?*

"Livie, do you know you're mumbling to yourself?"

Olivia tossed her pen on the nearly blank page. "Let's face it, I'm no good at making up recipes."

"Don't be silly." Maddie's hands paused over the computer keys. "Here's your problem: you're going at this like it's a school assignment that requires icky things like logical thinking. Making up cookie recipes is really more like playing in a sandbox. Sometimes numbers are involved, but once you get the hang of it, you can estimate. I'll show you what I mean in a minute. Give me a little more time to sate my curiosity about Trevor, Dougie, and Howie, okay? I mean, it's sort of your fault I'm doing this search."

"Your rampant curiosity is *my* fault?"

"Well, not when I'm wondering, for example, what beets taste like in sugar cookies, but you are the one who got me hooked on mysteries. Books aren't enough for me anymore. Now I need regular doses of mystery delivered right to my door. So go organize the fridge or something while I get my sleuthing fix." Maddie's fingers hopped around the keyboard. "And stop all that muttering about addictive personalities."

Suddenly, cleaning out the freezer did sound like a good idea. Olivia began by extracting an unlabeled container made of clear plastic. She pried off the lid and found two cookies: a purple tree and a pink bell. The Gingerbread House had hosted a holiday event in early December, nearly five months earlier. Way too long to keep fully decorated cookies. She dumped the cookies and tossed the empty container into the sink. Next she found a small, rusting tin so filled with ice crystals she'd need carbon dating to identify the age of the contents.

"Eureka!" Maddie said.

Olivia tossed the tin and its contents into the wastebasket and abandoned her task. "I remember now why I never clean the freezer," she said. "It reminds me of digging through layers of sedimentary rock. What did you find?"

"First, about Dougie Adair. I've been piecing together bits of his past from several sites. The most recent stuff is from Hollywood gossip blogs. The bloggers write mostly about Trevor Lane, of course, but

Dougie's name pops up from time to time. There was no mention of a wife, which made me really curious. I tried searching his full name, Douglas Ray Adair, and I found some older records. It looks like he moved to New York City in 1995 to try his luck at playwriting."

"Dougie mentioned living in New York City. How was his luck?" Olivia lifted a clean mixing bowl from the dishwasher and used a kitchen towel to wipe off any moisture that hadn't evaporated during the energy-save dry cycle.

"Really bad," Maddie said. "In the late nineties, a couple of Dougie's plays got produced way, way off Broadway. I found some scathing reviews."

"How far off Broadway?"

"One of them was in New Jersey." Maddie peered at the screen. "Listen to this: 'Mr. Adair may have intended to tell a tale of unrelenting darkness and despair, and I must admit that he succeeded, in as much as the audience longed for the lights to go on and despaired of ever seeing the final curtain.' "

"Ouch."

"No kidding," Maddie said. "I suspect the reviewer stole those words from someone else, but still . . . I'm sticking to decorated cookies. Everybody likes decorated . . . Whoa."

"What did you find?" Olivia dropped her towel in the dishwasher and scooted a chair next to Maddie.

"This looks like a 1999 obituary list of people in the arts." Maddie pointed at a short entry in a series of death notices. "It says here that *'Anna Adair, twenty-three, died unexpectedly at her home in New York. Cause of death unknown. Anna was a poet, married to writer Douglas R. Adair, who was out of town at the time of her death.'* Evidently, Dougie found her when he returned home. Golly. What Trevor said about Dougie's wife sort of implied that she might have killed herself, didn't it?"

"I wonder if . . ." Olivia shook her head to clear it. "My friend, your engagement bash is in two days, and we have a lot of work to do before then. Our curiosity can wait."

"Point taken." Maddie put the computer to sleep by lowering the lid. "This is unsettling and wildly fascinating, but we have fabulous cookies to invent and produce in practically no time. Fire up the trusty Artisan, and let's get to work!"

By midnight, Olivia felt more hopeful that her promised wedding gift to Maddie and

Lucas might materialize in time, even though Maddie had contributed a good portion of the creativity. In the Gingerbread House kitchen, the luscious aromas of lemon and lavender competed for dominance. Olivia's legs felt wobbly, and even Maddie's pace had slowed down to that of an average human, but they had accomplished a miracle. They'd created at least one promising original cookie recipe.

"Your idea for speeding up the experimentation process was pure genius," Olivia said. "I was afraid it would take weeks to come up with an edible recipe. I would never have thought of mixing quarter batches until we got the texture and flavor right."

"Aw shucks. I couldn't have done it without your superior math skills." Maddie sampled a barely cooled cookie. "I do believe we've done it," she announced. "Here, taste this and tell me what you think."

Olivia bit into a heavenly melding of lemon and lavender flavors. "The texture came out just right this time, and the lavender flavor is pretty good. Maybe we could lighten it a bit. And I'm fine with ditching the lemon verbena idea and sticking with good old lemon cookies. I'll save the lemon verbena for green beans or something."

"Yeah, like you ever cook vegetables," Maddie said.

"Hey, I have a can opener, and I know how to use it." Olivia sat at her desk with pen and paper. "Do you have an estimate of how many guests might attend your engagement party?"

"Livie, that would be math. How many people live in Chatterley Heights and the surrounding countryside?"

"Too many. Hand me the laptop, would you?" Olivia woke up her computer, looked up the population of Chatterley Heights, and added in what information she could find about the areas nearby. "Several thousand," she concluded, "not including nearby towns like Clarksville, where I know you have some friends. I do recall suggesting that you use the invitation-only approach."

"I get it, Livie; you told me so. Only it wouldn't have worked because Binnie took it upon herself to advertise the event in both *The Weekly Chatter* and her infernal blog. All I can hope is that most people would rather die than do anything Binnie Sloan tells them to do."

"I doubt Binnie's following goes much beyond Chatterley Heights, anyway," Olivia said. "I guess we'll just have to bake as many cookies as humanly possible, and when they're gone, they're gone."

"We'll limit the wine, too," Maddie said. "Lucas and I are footing the bill for drinks. Poor Lucas is still paying off the loan he took out to pay for his parents' care before they died. This recession has really slowed down business, even for Heights Hardware, the best hardware store in the entire country. Luckily, my income has been more or less steady, thanks to The Gingerbread House."

While the last batch of experimental lavender-lemon cookies cooled on racks, Olivia began filling the dishwasher. "Tomorrow evening we'll need to start baking the cookies for Saturday," she said. "I'll check and make sure we have enough supplies."

Maddie bounced up from her chair with altogether too much energy. "Livie, it's already tomorrow, and there aren't many tomorrows left before the party. I'm wound up anyway, so I intend to keep baking. You get some sleep. You are two months older than me, after all; you could get a heart attack or something."

"I'll remind you about that comment two months from now, when you've reached my advanced age," Olivia said. "I was planning to stay up a while, too. I brought home several boxes from Clarisse's cookie cutter collection. We're only using a few of them, so I thought it would be fun to put together a new display for the store. I mentioned the idea to Bertha, and she loved it. She still misses Clarisse. So do I."

"Aren't you worried they might be stolen?" Maddie asked. "Del hasn't caught whoever broke into Lady Chatterley's and/or attacked the head teller at the bank."

"I'll lock the cutters in a case and put it in the safe at night," Olivia said. "Del keeps telling me to install an alarm system, but it's so expensive. Knowing me, I'd probably trip the alarm on a daily basis."

"I see your point. Hang on a sec, let me check something." Maddie turned toward the computer screen. "I hate reading Binnie's blog, but if there's any new information about the break-ins, she'll hear it first."

"Or she'll make it up." Olivia cleared her desk and began to lay out the cookie cutters she'd selected from Clarisse's collection.

"Nothing from Binnie," Maddie reported, "except that your ongoing feud with the love of your life, Sheriff Del Jenkins, is heating up again. Apparently, you are in desperate denial and won't let go. Oh my . . ."

"What? No wait, do I really want to know?"

"Binnie has redefined nasty. She dug up

information about Del's divorce," Maddie said. "According to Binnie's blatant innuendo, Del was such a difficult husband he drove his wife back into the arms of her ex-husband. Del will kill Binnie."

"No, he won't, but I will." Olivia slapped a dishtowel on the counter. It felt good. "Del told me his wife left him to return to her ex-husband. It hurt him deeply. Binnie finally says something partly true, and it's more vicious than any lie she's ever printed."

Maddie stared at the screen in silence for a moment. "You know," she said, "that's not the sort of insider information I usually find easily on the Internet. Not impossible, of course, but . . ." Her hands bounced around the keyboard for a few minutes. "Nothing so far. Del's ex-wife was named Lisa, right? Okay, here's a notice about his wife's remarriage, but it doesn't mention Del, or that she is remarrying her ex-husband. I'm sure I could find more, but only because I know what I'd be looking for. Binnie must really hate Del to go to such lengths to trash him." Maddie clicked away for several more minutes. "Okay, I can find references to Del as the arresting officer in various places other than Chatterley Heights, probably in previous jobs. A couple quotes about more recent cases. Lisa doesn't appear to be a tell-all sort of person. Del never posts anything online himself."

"Of course not," Olivia said. "He isn't the celebrity cop type. He's very private."

"I hate to break it to you, Livie, but that wouldn't stop someone who really wants to find out about him. Private investigators manage to dig up all sorts of information the rest of us wouldn't know how to find. Even an average citizen can use sites that find personal information for a fee. I don't, of course. My curiosity wanes when I have to shell out money."

"I need sustenance," Olivia said as she selected an undecorated lavender-lemon cookie. "Herbs are good for the brain, right?"

"I'm sure I've read that somewhere," Maddie said. "While you're at it, hand me one of those babies. I could use a few more IQ points."

Olivia relaxed on a kitchen chair and propped her feet up on the seat of another one. "Binnie Sloan can be a bulldog when it comes to hunting down information, especially when she's miffed at someone. She doesn't like you and me. She's still angry with Del for all the times he has interfered with her so-called investigative reporting. If she could find damaging or humiliating information about any of our pasts, she'd gladly use it, but I can't see her hating us enough to pay anyone to find the information for her. Can you?"

"Not a chance," Maddie said. "*The Weekly Chatter* isn't exactly the *Baltimore Sun*. Binnie operates on a frayed shoestring. Plus she's been paying for her niece's journalism training. Ned's been burning through lots of online classes, plus she's taken a couple courses at American University."

Olivia nibbled her cookie and felt herself relax. Her mother always told her that lavender potpourri would calm her, if only she'd give it a chance. She concluded that cookies worked much better. "And don't forget," Olivia said, "Binnie has her pride. She'd have to be desperate to pay someone else to dig up dirt for her."

"So do you think Binnie might be really desperate to embarrass Del?"

"Can't imagine why." Olivia finished her cookie and brushed the crumbs off her lap. "No, I have a feeling Binnie came by the information about Del's divorce without much effort. I suspect someone else fed it to her."

"I don't get it," Maddie said. "Who would do that? Maybe somebody Del arrested?"

Olivia stood and stretched her arms above

her head. "I don't know. But I can't help thinking maybe there's —"

Fierce barking penetrated into the kitchen from the store's sales area. Maddie's chair toppled to the floor as she leaped to her feet. Olivia scrambled toward the door with one worry in her mind: Spunky's safety. She'd left him to snooze in the dark store while she and Maddie baked the night away. She hadn't wanted him to wake up alone in the apartment. He might fear he'd been abandoned.

With Maddie close behind, Olivia threw open the kitchen door and flipped on the lights. "Spunky? What's wrong, boy?"

Spunky yapped as he skittered back and forth in front of the large window that faced onto the Chatterley Heights town square. Olivia didn't try to stop him. Instead, she doused the sales floor lights and stood at the window. Maddie joined her.

The outside porch lights revealed nothing out of the ordinary. Olivia saw no movement in the store's dimly lit front yard. Clouds hid the moon, while streetlamps dropped glowing circles along the sidewalk surrounding the park. Nothing suspicious there, as far as Olivia could tell. The park itself was dark, except for the single lamp by the band shell.

When Spunky quieted down, Olivia scooped him into her arms. "What did you see, my fierce protector?" The tired little guy snuggled against her shoulder, ready to call it a night.

"Maybe he woke up suddenly and panicked?" Maddie suggested.

"Maybe." Olivia stroked her pup's silky back to soothe him.

"Or it might be time to install that alarm system Del keeps urging us to go into hock for." Maddie yawned. "I'm reconsidering the all-night baking idea. I think I'll go home, grab a few hours of sleep, and get here early tomorrow morning."

"Maybe you should sleep in my guest room," Olivia said.

"Come on, Livie, this isn't Baltimore. Besides, your mom has been teaching me some basic self-defense moves. Have you any idea how strong that teensy woman is? Maybe I should ask her to walk me home at night. Anyway, Aunt Sadie and Lucas will worry if I'm not there in the morning, and I don't want to call and wake them. Tell you what, I'll give you a ring when I'm safely home, so you won't fuss all night."

"Call the phone in the store kitchen," Olivia said. "I'll finish cleaning up and prep for opening tomorrow."

They returned to the kitchen, where Maddie grabbed a full garbage bag she'd left next to the alley door. "I'll call the instant I get in the door. You need your beauty sleep."

"I'd feel better if you left that trash until morning," Olivia said. "And go out the front door. It's far better lit."

"Will you stop fussing? Anyway, this stuff will start to stink if we leave it here. What would Bertha think of us?" Maddie opened the alley door wide and made a show of scanning the alley for movement. "Nope, no crazed murderers as far as the eye can see. Take a look for yourself."

Maybe she had lived in Baltimore too long, but Olivia's first couple years back home hadn't convinced her that little Chatterley Heights was immune to big-city problems. "I'll do more than 'take a look' at that alley," she said. "I intend to watch you until you're around the corner of the house."

"Have it your way." Maddie chuckled as she headed into the alley.

Olivia found her best friend's attitude a bit, well, insulting, but they were both tired, so she let it pass. Everything would return to normal once the engagement party was a delightful memory. Olivia was looking forward to that moment. She watched from the doorway as Maddie dropped the garbage bag into the trash can and replaced the lid. She turned and waved to Olivia before skipping down the alley to the corner of The Gingerbread House, where she would cut through the lawn to reach the well-lit sidewalk. Olivia was tempted to sneak a peek through the store window to watch Maddie pass the building, but she figured Spunky would be making a racket if anything wasn't right. Olivia closed, locked, and latched the alley door.

While she waited for Maddie's call, Olivia dampened a cloth and began to clean the countertop in preparation for the next round of baking. If she set up the ingredients, they could hit the ground running and maybe finish a batch or two before they had to open in the morning. Knowing Maddie, she'd sleep a few hours and wake up with the energy of three cookie bakers. Olivia intended to get up early, but she wouldn't even try to match Maddie's —

The kitchen phone rang and interrupted Olivia's rambling thoughts. She glanced up at the clock over the sink. Maddie had left only a few minutes earlier. Olivia lunged for the phone without checking the caller ID.

"Livie? Could you come to the door, please?" Maddie's voice sounded more subdued than usual, but Olivia was so relieved to hear it she felt almost giddy.

"Sure, did you forget something?" Olivia carried the phone with her and opened the alley door as she spoke. No one was there. "Maddie? Where are you?"

"I meant the front door. Right now. Please?"

Olivia slammed the alley door, dropped the phone receiver on the kitchen counter, and sprinted into the store. She was halfway across the sales floor before it occurred to her she ought to have brought her cell, just in case. However, Maddie had her phone, and Spunky didn't seem upset. In fact, the little guy was wagging his tail as he looked out the front window onto the porch. Olivia didn't stop to confirm what Spunky saw, but she assumed it was Maddie. So maybe nothing was all that wrong.

The store's front door, which led into the foyer, was locked and bolted, as was the door leading outside. It would take Olivia a couple minutes to open both. Spunky jumped down from his chair and trotted over to her.

"No, Spunks, you stay in here," Olivia said. "If we need your ferocious help, I'll come back and get you."

Apparently, Spunky heard his mistress say

they were going outside, because he wagged his tail with gusto. As she opened the store door, Olivia put her foot out to stop him. He leaped over it and pranced across the foyer to the front door. Olivia gave up. She picked Spunky up and held him tightly against her side while she fumbled with the deadbolt.

When Olivia flung open the front door, no one was there. Momentarily confused, she stepped out onto the porch and listened. She heard nothing. Spunky squirmed and strained his head around to the right, where the narrow front porch wrapped around the corner of the house. Maybe Maddie was there, out of sight? Why wasn't she calling out?

Olivia felt Spunky stiffen as he sniffed the air. "What is it, Spunks?" Olivia whispered. He responded with a low growl. At the same time, he wagged his fluffy tail. "Maddie?"

"Livie, over here." It was Maddie's voice.

Olivia entered the curve in the porch as it rounded the southeast corner of the house. Her heart whacked at her ribs as if it were desperate to escape. When she saw Maddie, her first reaction was relief. Maddie leaned against the porch railing and stared out at the darkened park. She certainly looked unhurt. Yet she seemed oddly still, as if she'd been stunned.

Spunky growled again, but not directly at Maddie. He was focused on something behind her, just out of range. Olivia eased through the corner of the wraparound porch. She saw the wicker chair she enjoyed relaxing in after closing the store on a summer evening. She loved the full view it gave her of the town square.

It took Olivia several seconds to process the fact that someone else was seated in her spot. The chair's wicker back curved around enough to hide the head and torso, but the hands and legs belonged to a man. A tall, well-dressed man. With a sinking feeling, Olivia recognized the khaki slacks and sleek burgundy loafers Trevor Lane had been wearing in the band shell earlier in the evening.

"Is he . . . ?"

"Yes." Maddie spoke in a whisper. "I couldn't find a pulse. Trevor is very dead."

"I see. Hush, Spunky." With her free hand, Olivia rubbed the Yorkie's ears to calm him. "Did you call Del?"

"Yes, right after I called you. I got him out of bed, but I really wanted Del here instead of someone else."

"I can understand that," Olivia said. "Would you take Spunky for a bit? Hold on tight, he's in a mood." She handed her restive pet over to Maddie, who clutched him to her chest.

Without turning around, Maddie said, "Please tell me you aren't going to examine the body."

"I was just wondering . . ." Olivia steeled herself before facing Trevor's lifeless form. She didn't see any evidence of blood. His shoulders slumped forward, his hands crossed right over left as if someone had arranged them. Trevor's head hung down, so Olivia could see only his dark brown hair. Olivia knew better than to touch the body, but she forced herself to squat down to get a look at his face. "What's that on his left cheek?"

"All I did was take his pulse," Maddie said with an hint of panic. "I didn't look at his left cheek or anything else. Why on earth would you?"

"Well, he died on my porch," Olivia said. "Even if he was killed somewhere else, he was brought to my porch. I need to know why. Del will be here soon, and he'll have called the crime-scene folks. I won't have another chance." She straightened, and said, "I'll be right back."

"Hey, you're supposed to keep me from getting hysterical."

"That's what Spunky is for." Olivia had left the front door unlocked, so she quickly reentered the foyer, where she kept a small antique desk with business cards. She had stashed a flashlight in the drawer in case she came home to find the electricity out, which happened during violent thunderstorms. She hoped no one had requisitioned the little flashlight for their own use. When she opened the drawer, the flashlight rolled forward. Now, if only the batteries hadn't died . . . She'd bought good-quality flashlights from Heights Hardware and tried to change the batteries regularly, but somehow she always forgot this one. She tried the switch. The light flickered weakly, but it would be enough.

Del and the crime-scene personnel would object to an amateur messing with evidence. Olivia understood the importance of an untouched crime scene. On the other hand, if the mark on Trevor's cheek was what she feared, she and Maddie might be sucked into the investigation through no fault of their own.

Olivia heard a faint siren in the distance. She almost wished Del would arrive and chase her off, so she wouldn't have to do what she was about to do. Spunky whimpered for Olivia's attention as she forced herself to kneel in front of the wicker chair. She pointed her flashlight up toward Trevor's handsome, dead face. Her hand shook as a shiver went through her. The light died.

As Olivia lowered the flashlight, it flicked on again. She must have jolted the batteries when her hand shook. Keeping her movements steady, Olivia raised the flashlight and aimed it toward the left side of Trevor's face. The mark on his cheek looked like a hammer drawn with a dark substance, perhaps charcoal. Whoever killed Trevor hadn't been satisfied with leaving this strange symbol. The murderer had added a final touch: a decorated cookie stuffed into Trevor's mouth. Olivia wondered if he'd died first or been left alive long enough to experience this final humiliation. "Oh dear," Olivia whispered.

"What? What?" Maddie spun around, and Spunky yelped.

"Maybe you should take a look at this." Olivia offered her flashlight to Maddie.

"Do I have to? Couldn't you just tell me?" Maddie took a step toward the wicker chair. She hesitated, as if caught between horror and curiosity.

"Of course, I could describe it to you, only I could use your expert opinion. Please,

Maddie?"

"Expert?" Maddie was starting to sound like herself again.

"You'll understand when you see Trevor's cheek. But hurry, I can hear a siren. We don't have much time. Then I'm afraid we'll have to compose ourselves and play innocent, at least for a while. I guarantee Del will ask us questions about this."

"Geez, now I really have to look at him. I don't want to be caught off guard." Maddie exchanged a jittery Yorkie for the flashlight and dropped quickly to her knees in front of Trevor's body. When the flashlight conked out, Maddie shook it. "These things are crap," she said. "Lucas stopped carrying them in the hardware."

"Now you tell me," Olivia said.

Maddie got the flashlight going again and wasted no time. "Whoa," she said as she examined Trevor's face. "Okay, I see what you mean. This'll take some explaining. I wonder if it was one of ours."

"I suppose . . . I mean, that cookie sure looks like one of ours, but anyone could have taken it at any time during the last couple days."

Maddie switched off the flashlight and stood up. "I'm not talking about the cookie."

"Wait, you mean you know something

about the hammer drawing on Trevor's cheek?" Olivia found herself talking to air. Maddie had already slipped into the foyer to return the flashlight to its storage place.

As the siren announced the imminent arrival of the police, Maddie reappeared. "Livie, it isn't a drawing of a hammer," she said. "It's the imprint of a cookie cutter shaped like a judge's gavel, and it is *burned* onto his cheek."

CHAPTER TEN

It was nearly three a.m. when Olivia, Maddie, and Del settled in the Gingerbread House kitchen. The crime-scene investigators had finally left for the lab, and Trevor Lane's body was bound for the morgue. Olivia and Maddie had permission to open the store at its usual time. They hadn't yet decided whether that would be such a good idea. Once word spread around Chatterley Heights that Trevor Lane had been found dead on The Gingerbread House porch — and it would spread, they had no doubt of that — hordes of citizens would crowd into the store wanting only to satisfy their avid curiosity. Olivia was tempted, oh so tempted, to keep the store closed. They could bake all day, which might give them a fighting chance of finishing the cookies for Maddie and Lucas's engagement party in two days.

Olivia poured three cups of freshly made

coffee and delivered them to the table. After seeing the damage to Trevor Lane's face, she couldn't bring herself to prepare a plate of decorated cookies. No one asked for any. "Del, please tell us. Was Trevor poisoned with one of our cookies?"

Del's eyebrows shot up, revealing tired, red eyes. "No, Livie, it would seem Trevor was killed by a hammer blow to the back of the head." Del opened his notebook. "Okay, let's go over this step-by-step. Maddie, you found the body, so we'll start with you. If you left the store by the alley door, how did you notice him in the dark? The way he'd been placed in that chair, I doubt you'd have seen him as you walked around the side of the house."

Maddie wrapped her hands around her warm cup as if she felt chilled. "Livie leaves the porch light on at night, which I used to think was a good idea." She shivered and sipped her coffee. "Even so, you're right, I wouldn't have noticed the . . . Trevor if I hadn't looked back at the store from the front lawn. I'm not really sure why I did look back." Maddie looked puzzled and tired, and her mop of red hair had lost its fizzle. Tangled curls hung loosely around her face as if the energy had drained out of them.

"Think," Del said. "Did something catch your attention, like a movement or a sound?"

Maddie's face puckered as she relived those dreadful moments. Olivia felt so sorry for her friend, she almost wished she had found the body instead. Almost.

"I think I heard a rustling sound," Maddie said, "and I just turned automatically. Yes, I remember now. I thought maybe Spunky had come to the window to see me off. He's such a friendly little guy." Maddie's eyes teared up. "I'm so glad he wasn't outside."

"Okay," Del said, "so you turned around toward the window because you thought Spunky might be looking out at you?"

"Yes. Except the curtains were closed, and I could see that they weren't rippling, which they would have been doing if Spunky had wormed around in front of them. That dog is incapable of being still unless he's napping, and even then . . ." Maddie held her coffee cup suspended in midair as if she'd forgotten to take a sip.

"Did you hear any sounds after that?" Del asked. "Or maybe you saw a movement out of the corner of your eye?"

Maddie lowered her cup and shook her head. "Nothing after that, I'm sure of it.

Right away, I noticed the chair on the porch wasn't empty. I saw . . . legs. I thought . . . I don't know what I thought, except at first I didn't feel scared. This is Chatterley Heights, after all. Besides, Livie is the one who finds bodies, not me." Maddie slapped her hand over her mouth. "Sorry, Livie, that just popped out."

Olivia patted Maddie's other hand. "Not a problem. I'll assume you're hysterical."

"Thanks. I think." Maddie's cheeks had regained a hint of color. "I might never eat a decorated cookie again."

"Nonsense," Olivia said. "I have it on the best authority that decorated cookies counteract the effects of shock. Also, I'm pretty sure they cure the common cold." Olivia selected three iced cookies shaped like wedding cakes. She put each cookie on a plate, handed one to Del, the second to Maddie, and saved the last for herself.

Maddie stared at her plate. "Livie, remember when we were all in the band shell? We passed around that plate of cookies? Trevor took two cookies and held them on his hand, like this." Maddie placed her wedding cake cookie on the palm of her left hand.

"I remember," Olivia said. "He ate one and made that awful toast with the other one."

"Do you remember their shapes?"

Olivia shook her head. "I think one had peppermint stripes. Usually I can remember cookie shapes. It must be shock."

"A peppermint-striped wedding cake and a rose-covered chapel," Maddie said.

"What is it, Maddie?" Del asked. "Are you thinking the cookie in Trevor's mouth might have come from the plate you took to the band shell?"

Maddie shook her head. "Just the opposite," she said. "Livie, you probably can't remember the icing colors because all the cookies I brought were dark pink. I got enthusiastic and made too much rose pink icing, so I used the extra to decorate a bunch of cookies that hadn't turned out absolutely flawless. Not that I'm a perfectionist."

"And the cookie in Trevor's mouth was blue," Olivia said. "At least what we could see of it."

Del scribbled something in his notebook. "Can you remember the last time you offered blue cookies in the store?"

Maddie grimaced. "Unfortunately, yes. It was yesterday afternoon, when Lenora descended with Trevor and Dougie in tow."

"And most of the citizens of Chatterley Heights showed up to see them," Olivia said.

"So just about anyone could have taken that cookie," Del said, rubbing his chin. "Or gotten it somewhere else."

"Tell me the flavorings in that cookie," Maddie said, "and I can probably tell you if it was one of ours. If you can determine what shape it was, that'll help, too. I used blue icing on lots of cookies, but only on two shapes."

"Which were?" Del asked, his pen poised over his notebook.

"One was a gift box with a blue ribbon, and the other was a little girl in a pale blue dress with a darker blue sash. She was supposed to represent a flower girl."

"Got it," Del said. He closed his notebook. "I'll check with the crime lab about the shape. Now what about the gavel imprint on Trevor's cheek? How sure are you that it was made with a cookie cutter?"

"I'm virtually positive." Maddie shivered. "It was burned on his skin, wasn't it? Olivia thought it might be a charcoal drawing."

"No, the image was definitely burned on," Del said. "Have you sold a gavel-shaped cookie cutter recently, or ever?"

Olivia shook her head. "Clarisse's collection includes a whole set of legal-themed cutters, but I haven't had a reason to use them. In fact, I've never taken them out of storage. So far there hasn't been much demand for events with a legal theme." She suppressed a nervous giggle as she envisioned a cookie party to welcome an ex-con home from prison.

Del flipped his notebook shut. "That's enough for now. I may have more questions once I hear what the medical examiner has to say."

"You know where to find us," Olivia said. "We'll be the ones with confectioners' sugar in our hair."

With a faint smile, Del said, "I'll allow you to keep baking, and I promise not to eat the inventory." He gave Olivia's cheek a light stroke with his fingertips before reaching for his uniform hat. "You two get some sleep. I recommend you keep the store closed tomorrow. Lie low, try not to answer the phone. I don't want everyone in town pumping you for information."

Maddie and Olivia exchanged quick glances. They both knew that nothing could protect them from the intense curiosity of Chatterley Heights residents.

It was four a.m. when Olivia rinsed out Mr. Coffee's carafe and Maddie tried to find space in the already-stuffed dishwasher for the cups and plates they'd used while Del questioned them about their grim discovery. The color had returned to Maddie's cheeks, but she had been uncharacteristically quiet since Del left. Olivia hoped it was only exhaustion.

"I'm beat," Olivia said. "What if we grab a few hours of sleep before we tackle the baking again?" Before Maddie could respond, the phone rang. "Leave it," Olivia said. "We can listen for a message."

Maddie glanced at the caller ID, and said, "Oh jeez, it's Lucas. I was supposed to call him about three hours ago. He must be worried sick." She grabbed the receiver. "Lucas! I'm so sorry I forgot to call, but . . ." Maddie's eye widened as she listened to him for a few minutes. "Well, all I can say is, I'm impressed. Even I would be hard pressed to learn all that information in" — she glanced up at the clock — "in less than an hour. Especially in the middle of the night." Maddie listened a moment, shaking her head. "I'm fine, honey, really. A little shook up, that's all. You get some sleep. I'm staying here. And no, we are not postponing our engagement party. Livie and I plan to catch a nap and then start baking again. Neither sleet nor snow nor . . . whatever the rest is. I'll call you at a decent hour. Love you."

"Did Lucas already find out about Trevor's murder?" Olivia asked as Maddie hung up.

"Yep."

"But how?"

"Well, it started with Polly, who was working really late at the food shelf because she was trying to find a safe place for a homeless family with a bunch of children to spend the night. After they left, Polly went upstairs to her little office to do some paperwork. She heard sirens, so she looked out her office window, which gives her a view of Pete's Diner. She saw a light on in the diner and figured Ida was doing some personal cooking. Pete lets her do that because she doesn't have a kitchen in her rented room, though she's allowed to heat things up in the landlady's kitchen. Anyway, Polly called Ida, who got her binoculars and went outside. She saw all the lights on in The Gingerbread House, then the crime-scene van arrived." Maddie paused for breath.

"So, how did Lucas find out?" Olivia asked, fascinated in spite of herself. "I have a hard time believing that Ida would think to call him."

"Patience, Livie. The gossip vine is a tangled web. And now is not the time for a

213

lecture on messed metaphors."

"Mixed metaphors."

"Whatever. Anyway, Polly has a new boyfriend, did you know that? I just found out a few days ago. He's working as a night janitor at the Chatterley Café. They stay open really late, you know, and the cooks arrive at five a.m., so they need cleanup during the night. Polly called her boyfriend's cell. He was just about to leave the café, so he locked up and walked down Park Street until he could see The Gingerbread House. He watched the body get carried off the porch. He knew it wasn't one of us because he saw us on the porch with Del. Although he did wonder if one of us had killed someone, like maybe an intruder."

Olivia was starting to feel dizzy. "So I ask again, how did Lucas find out?"

"Easy," Maddie said with a grin. "Polly called him. Well, actually, she wondered if maybe *I'd* killed *Lucas.* He said Polly sounded a bit disappointed when he answered his own phone."

"Hold on, Maddie. Lucas hasn't used that many words as long as I've known him. How did he remember all that detail?"

Maddie laughed. "Here's what Lucas said: Polly called him and said she'd talked to Ida, who called her boyfriend, who said

214

something about a body. Period. I filled in the detail. And I'll bet you a dozen cookies it's all accurate. Wow! I feel energized! I need to bake. You go take a nap, Livie."

"Good idea." Olivia had been tired before Maddie's recitation. Now she was ready to drop. "We'll keep the store closed, at least until afternoon. I'll put a sign on the front door before I go upstairs. We'll need to notify Bertha and Jennifer, too."

"I'll do that," Maddie said. "Bertha gets up at five thirty to take a long walk, so I'll call her then. Jennifer turns off her phone at night because she has trouble sleeping. That means I can leave her a message without disturbing her."

"How do you *know* these things?"

"Well, Livie, it's very simple. I didn't waste ten years living in Baltimore and avoiding my neighbors."

"I'll ignore that," Olivia said. "See you in a couple hours."

"Oh, Livie, make it three hours at least. I'm fired up enough to do the work of a team of bakers."

Olivia pretended she hadn't heard. Maddie was already humming along to her earbuds as Olivia closed the kitchen door.

Spunky's head popped up when Olivia flipped on the light for the sales floor. "Hey,

Spunks, time for bed." She searched the shelf under the cash register and found a blank sheet of paper, a pen, and a small Scotch tape dispenser. Spunky jumped down from his favorite chair and trotted over to her. "You've been a patient little boy," Olivia said as she scrawled a quick message on the sheet of paper. Aiming for indefinite and uninformative, she wrote, *Closed for Inventory.* The sign would fool no one.

Spunky trotted beside Olivia into the foyer. He waited at the door leading up to Olivia's apartment while she unlocked the front door. Her heart began to pound as soon as she cracked the door open. "It's all over," she whispered. Her heart wasn't convinced. She took a deep breath, then another before wedging her arm through the opening to tape the note on the outside. *Okay, that felt a little silly, but I don't care.*

Olivia led Spunky upstairs, comforting herself with the knowledge that, by daylight, everyone within a fifty-mile radius would have heard about the body on The Gingerbread House porch. Maybe then she wouldn't feel so alone.

CHAPTER ELEVEN

At twelve minutes past eight, Olivia opened the kitchen door of The Gingerbread House to a blast of sensory overload. The aroma alone nearly knocked her off her feet. The dominant fragrance was lavender, but Olivia thought she smelled lemon, rose, and a hint of tuna fish.

Maddie's hair, a mass of fluffy red springs dotted with flour and confectioners' sugar, resembled a powdered wig. She sang along with the Dixie Cups as she danced around the worktable with a pastry bag full of electric purple royal icing. Olivia noticed several flower girl cookies with electric purple hair. Either Maddie had overdosed on coffee, or she'd cracked from stress. Possibly both.

Maddie waved with her pastry bag and sang, "So did you sleep well?" as if it were "Goin' to the chapel," a line from "Chapel of Love." When Olivia didn't so much as smile, Maddie stopped dancing and pulled out her earbuds. "Are you okay?" she asked.

"I'm just wondering the same thing about you," Olivia said. "How did you do all this baking? Why do I smell lavender, lemon, and *rose*? Did you have tuna salad for breakfast, and is there any left?"

Maddie sniffed the air and wrinkled her nose. "Sorry about the tuna. It's all I could find for breakfast, and I'm afraid I devoured all of it." Maddie capped her pastry bag to keep the icing fresh. "About the other, more pleasing aromas . . . Livie, I realize I've taken over creating the special cookies for my wedding gift, but you know how it is. I get carried away. Ideas pop into my mind, and I can't resist trying them out. I thought about Trevor and that rose-covered chapel cookie he held on the palm of his hand. That memory upset me at first, but then I thought, 'Hey, instead of plain lemon, why not use lemon and rose together for the cookie cake?' I tried that combination, but it tasted awful, so I dumped the lemon altogether and went with rosewater and vanilla bakery emulsion. I know it's been done before, but I've been varying the flavoring measurements to try for a somewhat rosier effect. I thought we could sprinkle rose-colored sparkling sugar on the cookies and use rose-flavored icing to hold them together in a pyramid."

To be honest, Olivia felt considerable relief that the project was progressing so much faster than she'd feared it would.

Maddie's eyes lit up like green sparklers. "And my best idea of all, my pièce de . . . de . . . don't tell me. My pièce de persistence!" Noting the pained expression on Olivia's face, Maddie said, "Blew it again, huh?"

"It's pièce de résistance, but I like your version, I really do. And I'm sure the Académie française would agree, after a glass of wine or two. So elaborate on your idea for me."

"Okay, this isn't entirely new, either," Maddie said, "but what is? We'll 'sprinkle' organic rose petals on the cookie cake and hold them in place with little dabs of icing. What could say 'wedding' more lusciously than red and pink rose petals? Plus, it will sort of match my hair."

Olivia had to admit it all sounded beautiful and delicious . . . and labor intensive. "It's a great idea," she said. "How would we get the rose petals in time for Saturday? I don't think Bon Vivant uses them, do they?"

"No, but don't worry. Problem already solved." Maddie uncapped her pastry bag.

As she added decorative loops to a wedding cake cookie with the last of her electric purple icing, she said, "I know a little online company based on a farm outside Clarksville. I emailed them. Someone was already up and on their computer, checking orders. They promised to have dried organic rose petals in our hands by tomorrow morning. We'll have the cookie cake ready by then."

"Sometimes I wonder if I'm really needed here," Olivia said.

"Don't be silly," Maddie said as she mixed pale daffodil yellow gel coloring into a small bowl of icing. "You're the one with the money. Also, you can add and subtract."

Olivia dumped old coffee grounds and rinsed out the Mr. Coffee carafe. "I smell a lot of lavender in here," she said. "You didn't increase the lavender in the other experimental recipe, did you? I may not have mentioned this before, but lavender is not my favorite flavor." Seeing Maddie's worried expression, Olivia added, "Though I love the color and, of course, the stunning gown Aunt Sadie made for you, in which you look gorgeous."

"Nice save," Maddie said with a grin. "To put your mind at rest, I got a bit too rambunctious with the dancing, and I spilled half a bottle of lavender oil. Think of it as cleaning solution."

"Believe me, I do."

"Here, try one of these." Maddie handed Olivia a bright yellow and purple daisy.

Olivia sniffed the cookie. The lemon fragrance was stronger than the lavender. Good sign. She took a small bite. "Nice," she said. "Very yummy. It's even better than our experimental lavender recipe. What did you change?"

"I used lemon bakery emulsion instead of extract. It didn't change the texture of the dough, but the lemon flavor is stronger and sort of mellows out the lavender better. I agree with you, a little lavender goes a long way."

"So did you get any sleep at all?" Olivia asked.

"Nope. I hit a slight energy dip, so I sneaked into Lucas's house for a shower and a change of clothes. Only please don't tell Aunt Sadie that I keep some clothes at his house. She never married, you know."

"Maddie, I hate to shatter your innocent image of Aunt Sadie, but I'm quite certain she wouldn't die of shock. According to my mom, Aunt Sadie was quite the popular young woman. Mom said she broke off at least two engagements." Olivia had to laugh when she saw Maddie's stunned expression.

"How come she didn't tell me?"

"You were her little girl," Olivia said. "Mom never shared a word with me about her scandalous past. I was nearly eighteen when I found an album with pictures of mom and dad dressed in hippie clothes. That was the first I'd heard about them living together in a commune. Of course, now she won't shut up about it. There are some things we don't need to know about our parents, at least not too soon or in too much detail."

"I see what you mean," Maddie said.

Olivia poured cream into two fresh cups of coffee. "Did you mute the phone? I thought it would be ringing nonstop."

"It was." Maddie filled a clean pastry bag with daffodil yellow icing and gave a flower girl a head of perfectly reasonable blond hair. "I figured no one should be calling the store phone in the middle of the night, so it wouldn't matter. My cell was going crazy, too, so I turned it off."

"I guess we should turn the wretched things back on," Olivia said. She began with the kitchen phone, which began to ring immediately. Olivia checked the caller ID. "It's Bertha." She picked up the receiver, and said, "Sorry, Bertha, have you been trying to reach us for long?"

"Oh my, no, Livie. I knew you'd be trying to get some sleep. Goodness, what a night you two had! Are you both okay? Do you need me to cover the store today? I know how to handle gossips. They won't get through me."

"That's sweet of you, Bertha, but we decided to stay closed for a while, maybe all day. Frankly, we need the time to bake. What are people saying?"

"Well, Mr. Willard and I had an early breakfast at Pete's Diner, and you wouldn't believe . . . Ida figured you and Maddie must have killed an intruder trying to rob the store. Then Polly came in and said she'd heard it was that handsome actor who died, the one who came to The Gingerbread House. Only don't you tell me anything, Livie. It's best I don't know. I'd get too flustered trying to remember what to keep to myself."

"That's wise, Bertha. If anyone asks, just say Maddie and I are unharmed, neither of us is under any suspicion, nothing was stolen from the store, and the police will release more information when they are good and ready."

"I can do that, Livie. Honestly, some people are so . . . Oh dear."

"What's wrong, Bertha?" Olivia exchanged a worried glance with Maddie, who held her pastry bag suspended above a daffodil-shaped cookie.

"Well, Mr. Willard bought me a sweet little laptop for my birthday so we could email each other, and I just got a message from Polly. She wrote to a whole list of folks. She says that a friend of hers heard that Sheriff Del has arrested Wade Harald for murder! Oh, that can't be right. Poor Wade does have a bit of a drinking problem, but I can't believe —"

Olivia's breath caught in her throat. "Bertha, what does the email say? Is Stacey okay?"

"Stacey Harald? Oh yes, I should think so. Polly says Wade killed Trevor Lane. But, dear me, whatever for?"

Olivia had been trying for forty minutes to reach either Stacey Harald or Del. She'd left several messages to no avail. The police department's answering machine directed her to 911 for an emergency. Olivia gave up, at least for the moment.

Maddie interrupted her cookie-icing project and settled at Livie's desk with the laptop. Her fingers danced across the keyboard while Olivia checked her cell in case she had missed a message.

"Livie, come look at this," Maddie said.

Olivia peered over Maddie's shoulder at the laptop screen. "Tell me you aren't checking Binnie's excuse for a blog. What use is that?"

"Binnie doesn't mention anything about a cookie cutter in her post about Trevor Lane's murder," Maddie said. "All she says is the body was found on the porch of The Gingerbread House. Oh, and the police probably suspect us but haven't yet collected enough evidence to charge one or both of us. Binnie is certainly predictable," Maddie said. "She takes a kernel of information and builds an outrageous story around it. If I can figure out where she started . . ." Squinting at the screen, Maddie scrolled through an array of photos taken by Ned, Binnie's niece and the photographer for *The Weekly Chatter.* Ned rarely opened her mouth, but her photographs spoke for her. The last photograph in the series practically shouted. It was a photo of Olivia holding a wriggling Spunky and staring open mouthed into the darkness. "Binnie must have used these photos to fabricate her story," Maddie said. She returned to the first one.

Olivia pulled over a kitchen chair, so she could see the screen more clearly. "That's a night shot," she said. "It's the inside of the band shell. How on earth did Ned do that without being seen?"

"Knowing Ned, she made herself invisible," Maddie said. "She must have taken this before you arrived at the band shell last evening. Those three men standing inside look like Trevor Lane, Dougie Adair, and Howie Upton."

"See over there, near the left edge of the band-shell entrance?" Olivia touched the screen. "That looks to me like the toe of a work boot. And up above, that's a hand. See the finger pointing toward the three men? When Spunky and I were in the park, walking toward the band shell, we heard a man's angry voice. The man came stalking out and stared at me as if he were trying to figure out who I was. Of course, Spunky was yapping in his own unique way, so that would have been a clue. I recognized him; it was Wade Harald. I meant to call Stacey, but . . ."

"You never mentioned this to me," Maddie said. "Well? What was the argument about?"

"I don't know. Like I said, all I could hear was a man's angry voice. Except, wait . . . I did hear one word. The voice was distorted by rage. I think he said the word 'lied,' but I'm not absolutely positive."

Maddie scrolled to the next photo, which showed a man leaving the band shell. His face was hidden as he looked down at the steps. Olivia recognized the spare, bow-legged figure she'd seen. "That's Wade. I recognized him a few seconds later when he turned to stare at me."

"The last two photos show a man walking away," Maddie said as she scrolled quickly through them. "So we have our answer, more or less. Wade had some sort of argument with Trevor, Dougie, and Howie, and now Trevor is dead. That doesn't prove Wade killed Trevor. Maybe Wade drove drunk and Del arrested him. Maybe Binnie, being Binnie, heard about the arrest and connected the dots to conclude that Del arrested Wade for murder."

"I agree Binnie is prone to wild leaps of logic," Olivia said, "but for once she might be right." She flipped open her cell phone and tried Stacey's home phone, then her cell, and finally her number at work. "Still no answer, only the usual recorded messages. I have a really bad feeling about this."

"But Livie, why would Wade Harald, of all people, dump Trevor on *our* porch with a cookie stuffed in his mouth and a gavel shape burned on his cheek? Wade is normally a sweet guy, except . . ."

"Except when he's been drinking," Olivia said. "Maddie, Wade sounded so angry that night. Trevor must have wronged him in some way. They went to different high schools, but maybe they crossed paths as teenagers." Olivia ran her fingers through her tangled hair. She couldn't remember when she'd last washed it. Thank goodness the store was closed.

"Do you really believe Wade would kill Trevor over some incident from high school? Who does that?"

Olivia thought back to the slights she had experienced in high school. She remembered the worst of them, perpetrated by a pretty, popular cheerleader named Sara. Sara was competitive, with a jealous streak. She had to be the best at everything. Olivia had outscored her on an important math test. Sara had taken revenge by hinting to Olivia that the quarterback, also popular, had a crush on her. Then Sara told the quarterback that Olivia was telling everyone they were a couple, which enraged the quarterback's girlfriend. Olivia could still feel her deep embarrassment, as well as her fury. She'd certainly felt like murdering Sara. However, Olivia's life got better after high school. She forgot those feelings, and she hadn't thought about Sara until now.

Wade Harald hadn't been as lucky. His life had been unraveling for years, and he'd turned to alcohol for comfort.

"All I know," Olivia said, "is how angry Wade sounded on Wednesday evening. If he'd had a weapon, I think he might well have used it."

"But where would Wade come up with a gavel cookie cutter and a decorated cookie?" Maddie asked. "I can't imagine him taking the time and effort to . . . to do what was done to Trevor."

"Maybe he had help."

"Not from Stacey," Maddie said. "I refuse to believe that."

"Wade is suggestible when he's been drinking, and he is easily enraged. If someone pushed the right buttons and gave Wade a little encouragement, I'm afraid I could see him as the killer," Olivia said. "For Stacey's sake, I hope it didn't happen that way."

"But, Livie, could you really see Wade arranging Trevor's body on our porch? And again I ask, what about the gavel brand? The cookie in his mouth? That took planning ahead. Wade is not a planner ahead."

"I know." Fear seeped through her brain like sludge, slowing her ability to reason. "He is a hothead, though."

"So you're thinking there are two murderers?"

"I'm thinking we have three other suspects: Dougie, Howie, and Jennifer. All three strike me as coolheaded. And I'm thoroughly convinced they are all hiding something."

CHAPTER TWELVE

The worktable in The Gingerbread House held a mountain of undecorated cookies by mid-afternoon. Olivia and Maddie had baked their way through twenty pounds of flour, all but a few cups of their sugar supply, and every available drop of lavender essence, rosewater, and lemon and vanilla bakery emulsion. They'd also run out of clean baking equipment, and the dishwasher was full.

"Do I look as bedraggled as I feel?" Olivia asked.

Maddie looked her up and down. "Worse. I remember your hair used to be auburn. Now it's white. Sad, really." Maddie dug through the clutter on the kitchen counter to find a pen and a pad of notepaper. "I'll make a list and ask Jennifer to do some shopping. Today is Thursday, so she might have to order an overnight delivery of flavorings." She plunked down on a chair. "But first, I need to catch my breath. I know as soon as I rejoin the world, hordes of people will pummel me with questions about Trevor's murder."

"Tell them to ask the police. Say you've been too busy to even think about it. Pretend to faint." Olivia filled the dishwasher soap dispenser and punched the on button.

"Oh yeah, that'll work. Remember where you are, Livie." Maddie stretched her arms above her head. "Sorry, I'm a bit cranky. Maybe I need a teensy nap. There's a little space under the kitchen table I could curl up in."

"Not a chance." Olivia dug her apartment key out of her jeans pocket. "Use my guest room. Sleep as long as you need to, and I'll keep cleaning the kitchen. Maybe I'll turn the phones on and catch up on messages."

"Not without me, you won't," Maddie said, perking up. "What if we've missed another development? What if Del has identified Trevor's killer? What if it isn't Wade Harald, after all? Del would call to tell you, wouldn't he?"

"Probably not. He'd be too busy." Olivia sank into a chair and put up her feet on the edge of Maddie's seat. "Okay, let's revive the phones and rejoin the world together." Olivia and Maddie retrieved their cells and switched them on. Neither phone rang instantly. "The excitement must be waning," Olivia said. "On the other hand, I have fourteen new voice mail messages and twelve text messages."

"I win," Maddie said. "I have seventeen new voice mail messages and twenty-three text messages. One is from Jennifer Elsworth. She begs our forgiveness again and offers to take care of the store while we prepare for the party. Shall we forgive and forget as I initially told her we would?"

Olivia ran her fingers through her tangled hair and a dusting of flour fell onto her jeans. "I have serious questions about Jennifer's reliability, among other things, but we'll need her help. Tell her yes. We can't work Bertha to death." Olivia scrolled through her own messages and missed calls. "That makes three calls from my mother." She listened to the messages in order of time. Ellie's first two messages were cheerful and supportive, so Olivia deleted them. When she listened to the third call, she knew at once that her mother was worried about more than just the dead body on her daughter's porch.

"Okay, Jennifer is duly forgiven and assigned to work tomorrow morning," Maddie said as she sent a text message.

"Maddie, do you have any messages from Stacey Harald?"

"Not a one, why?"

"Stacey left one short message early this afternoon, asking if she could talk to me, but that's all. About half an hour ago, Mom called. She wants me to come over this evening if I can. She and Allan had a surprise visit from Stacey, along with both her kids. Stacey asked if they could stay. Mom said she seemed really shaken up."

"Wow, things must be bad out there," Maddie said. "Stacey is usually so unshakeable, even about her family."

"We certainly have been in our own little cookie world," Olivia said. "Unbeknownst to us, the press — as in the notorious paparazzi — has descended upon Chatterley Heights. That's what the rest of my voice mails and texts are about."

"Mine, too." Maddie jumped to her feet and stretched toward the ceiling. "With the most important party of my life coming up the day after tomorrow . . ."

"I know, Maddie. I'm so sorry all this is happening right now. This is supposed to be your time."

"Oh, I'm not fussing about that," Maddie said. "We're missing all the action. We can't bake or decorate right now, anyway. Not until we have clean dishes, cooled cookies, and more ingredients. I'm inclined to give Jennifer a test run right away and see how she does with the shopping. Give me a few minutes to send our lists to her via email." Maddie cocked her eyebrow as she gave Olivia a once-over. "You could use a shower and a change of clothes. Meanwhile, I'll dust myself off while I wait to hear from Jennifer. Then, my sleuthing friend, let us make tracks for your childhood home and sink ourselves knee deep into this mess. Remember, Stacey Harald and I go way back, too. Stacey and her kids need us! Or was that over-the-top?"

"A bit," Olivia said. But Maddie wasn't listening. She'd already begun to pound out an email to Jennifer.

Olivia, Maddie, Spunky, and a box of cookies arrived at the Greyson home by early evening. Both Olivia and Maddie had decided to shower and change, assuming that hugs would be forthcoming. When Olivia rang the doorbell, the living room curtain twitched. "I think Mom is having flashbacks again," she said. The front door opened a sliver, enough for Ellie's slender arm to shoot out, clutch her daughter's sleeve, and yank her into the house.

Ellie poked her head outside and hissed, "Make it snappy, Maddie. They are out there, I can feel it." Maddie barely made it inside before Ellie slammed the door.

"Wow," Olivia said, "you sixties types are paranoid." She noted that her mother had dressed for the occasion in a rainbow-colored, tie-dyed blouse and long, matching skirt that Olivia remembered seeing when, as a child, she had hidden in the back of her mother's closet. Olivia felt a prick of envy about how well the outfit still fit.

Ellie reverted to her yoga-centered self and said, "Nonsense, Livie, dear. It isn't paranoia when the danger is real." Ellie pried the box of cookies from Maddie's stunned grasp. "Good, you brought sustenance. We will need it. Now, hugs all around, and then let's get to work."

Ellie led the way to her husband's home office at the rear of the house. The room had once been Olivia's ornithologist father's office, where he had spent days and evenings bringing bird behavior to life on the page. His charming, lively books became minor bestsellers and provided a comfortable, though not lavish, lifestyle for the Greyson family. At least they had not been left destitute when he died in his late forties.

When Ellie ushered the group into Allan's

office, Olivia felt as if she'd walked into a spy novel. With the blinds closed and only the computer screen for light, the room's inhabitants were hard to recognize at first. As her eyes adjusted, Olivia recognized Stacey Harald, seated in Allan's guest chair, with her teenage son and daughter next to her, cross-legged on the rug.

"Livie and Maddie," Stacey said in her rich alto voice. "It's about time." She joined her old friends, looping an arm around each of them. "The Three Mooseketeers, together again."

Olivia grinned at the confused look on her stepfather's face. "We three go back to elementary school, Allan."

"Yes, well, I hope the other students didn't call you mooseketeers," Allan said. "Or if they did, I hope you punched a few of their noses."

With her gentle laugh, Ellie said, "Now Allan, violence wasn't necessary. In high school, all three girls sprouted up at the same time. They took a while to — shall we say, 'even out?' — so their legs were unusually long and slender."

"Oh," Allan said. "So it wasn't an insult?" He looked so perplexed that everyone laughed.

"It's okay, dear," Ellie said. "We are laugh-

237

ing for you, not at you. You see, sometimes it is wiser to turn an insult into a joke."

"Ah," Allan said. "Well, then, let's get to work. I've taken the liberty of jotting down a few ideas to help guide us through this troubling situation." He handed around some typed pages from his computer.

"Allan, dear, this isn't a business plan," Ellie said.

"Wait, Mom. Plans are good," Olivia said as she scanned Allan's list. "There are some good ideas here. Although I suspect Del might object to the part about emailing us a daily report about the investigation."

"Well, I was assuming that Del, being the sheriff, would be the one to find the real murderer," Allan said. "That is, after all, his job."

"Dear, sweet Allan," Ellie said. She opened the cake pan filled with the last of the frozen cookies Maddie had prepared to serve at The Gingerbread House. They were simple round cookies, all decorated quickly with leftover icing. "Have a cookie, dear."

Allan accepted his demotion with good humor, took a cookie, and passed the pan to Stacey.

"So," Ellie said. "I am game for anything. Livie, Maddie — you have experience with these situations. What would you like me to do? Infiltrate the police department?"

Stacey's thirteen-year-old daughter, Rachel, snickered. She stopped at once when her mother glanced at her with dangerously slitted eyes.

"Mom, you and Allan are doing a great job of protecting Stacey and her kids from the paparazzi. Keep it up."

"Ellie, Allan," Stacey said, "we don't want to put you in a tough situation. We'll have to emerge at some point."

"Only when you are good and ready," Ellie said. "Meanwhile, you can count on us to scare off those vultures. I would feel better, though, if I could do something more active."

"There's one thing you could do, Mom. You could bake some cookies for us to offer at the store. We'll have to open again tomorrow, and we've run through all our extra cookies, ingredients, and time. Any type of cookie will do. Drop cookies would be fine. We'll need only about half a batch, so Rachel and Tyler could eat the rest, assuming they help you with the baking."

Rachel looked mildly interested, but Tyler said, "I'd rather just eat the extras."

"I'm sure you would, Tyler," his mother said, "but that won't happen. If Rachel is the only helper, she gets the extra cookies."

Rachel stuck out her tongue at her brother. Tyler made a face at his sister, and said, "Okay, fine, whatever." Stacey smirked, and Ellie winked at Stacey. For a moment, Olivia felt left out of the Mothers Club. Well, at least she and Maddie could try to prevent Wade Harald from being wrongly convicted of Trevor Lane's murder . . . unless, that is, their friend Stacey's husband, the father of her children, was a killer.

"Stacey, could I have a word with you before Maddie and I take off?"

Stacey's eyes widened, though her kids didn't seem alarmed by the question. "Sure," Stacey said. "Tyler, Rachel, you two start winnowing down that pile of homework. You can help Ellie bake after you've finished."

Tyler groaned. "But, Mom —"

"Right now."

The teenagers shuffled off toward the bedrooms that used to belong to Olivia and Jason. Ellie had handed the box of cookies to Stacey as she followed her kids into the hallway. "There's coffee in the carafe," Ellie called after Stacey as she headed toward the kitchen.

Maddie stifled a yawn. Olivia pulled her aside, and said quietly, "Maybe you should go home and get some rest. You have a big day coming up very soon."

"Not a chance."

"Please?"

"You want to question Stacey alone, don't you?" Maddie sounded miffed.

"I'm afraid two of us might feel intimidating."

"Well . . . Jennifer did promise to deliver our baking supplies tonight, so we could bake first thing in the morning. I might be able to start another batch of cookie dough."

After Maddie left, Olivia went to the kitchen, hoping to find Stacey. When she flipped on the kitchen light, Olivia found her friend hunched over the table, cradling her face in her hands. Olivia poured two cups of coffee and sat down across from her.

Stacey slumped back in her chair. "I know what you're going to ask me. You want to know if I think Wade might actually have killed Trevor Lane. The answer is, I don't know for sure. How could I? Wade is a gentle guy at heart. He gets argumentative when he drinks, and I hate that, but he has never, ever raised a hand toward me or the kids. Sometimes I've been afraid he would, but he hasn't." Stacey sipped her coffee and shook her head. "Usually, he starts to cry. I guess that's pathetic, but it sure isn't violent."

"Thanks, Stacey, that's helpful," Olivia said, although she knew it wouldn't save Wade from a murder charge.

Stacey ran her fingers through her tousled blond waves. Her fingernails looked bitten to the quick, and brown roots showed along her hairline. Olivia felt a wave of concern for her tough childhood friend. In high school, Stacey had been an anchor for Olivia as she coped with the death of her father. That she was tall, willowy, and gorgeous had never spoiled Stacey's down-to-earth nature. She'd come from poverty, which she'd been determined to escape. And she had. Stacey was smart and focused. She had worked her way through junior college, landed a job as a secretary at Chatterley Heights Elementary, and had quickly risen to office manager.

Olivia didn't waste time treading softly. "Stacey, is there a reason why Wade started drinking again?"

Stacey opened the box of cookies and selected a bunny rabbit with pink stripes and a purple mustache. Sounding, for a moment, more like herself, she said, "My, you're a fine-looking fellow," and bit off an ear.

Understanding her friend's need to gather her thoughts, Olivia excused herself to search for two small plates in her mother's frequently reorganized cupboards. In a drawer, she found two cloth napkins.

By the time Olivia returned to the table, Stacey had finished consuming both bunny ears and the fluffy tail. "We're on the verge of bankruptcy," Stacey said. "We could lose the house. Wade feels responsible, and he should."

"I thought you got the house in the divorce settlement," Olivia said.

"I did, and I refinanced to get the payments down to what I could handle from my own salary. I didn't really trust Wade to stay sober and employed. He was paying child support, though, and we needed that. Still, the kids and I were doing okay, even after this recession hit. We cut back, the kids pitched in. . . . They both got little jobs like babysitting and lawn mowing. Then Wade did something stupid. For the right reasons, of course, but still . . . He hated that Rachel had to quit ballet, and Tyler would miss out on sports, so he started paying for all that himself. I guess it made him feel good, so he bought them clothes and new bikes and so on. He kept telling me his boss was giving him raises. Only she wasn't. He was maxing out his one credit card. You can guess the rest." Stacey bit off her bunny's head.

"Wade sank underwater, his debt compounded, and he started drinking again?" Olivia's own stomach tightened as she imagined how that would feel. She still owed a hefty chunk on the mortgage for her Queen Anne, as well as on a business loan. At least she had savings, thanks to a surprise inheritance from her friend, Clarisse Chamberlain.

Olivia picked out a daisy-shaped cookie and nibbled on its teal petal. Decorated cookies always had a calming effect on her. She reached across the table to squeeze her friend's arm. "Stacey, if I'm to help, I need to understand the history between Wade and Trevor Lane. Wade went to Chatterley Heights High, so how did he and Trevor know each other?"

"There's more to Wade than meets the eye," Stacey said. "I divorced him for good reason, but he wasn't always a drunk. I don't know if you remember, but in high school Wade was an amazing athlete. He was short and skinny, but that didn't matter one bit. You should have seen Wade run across that field. Boy, was he fast. Nobody could catch him once he got going. He'd catch that ball so quick, take off running, and he'd make a touchdown before the other players could focus their eyes." Stacey smiled at the memory.

Olivia felt saddened by the love and admiration in Stacey's voice, all for the man who had let her down. Wade had squandered that devotion. Yet he'd done so with the intention of providing for his family. Olivia reached for another cookie and steeled herself to drag out yet more painful information.

"Well," Stacey said, "that's about enough wallowing for one day. Wade may be a screwup, but he's the father of my children, so I'm inclined to help save his scrawny neck. I don't trust the police, not even Sheriff Del. So it's you and Maddie and me. Now, what do you need to know?"

"The Three Mooseketeers," Olivia said with a smile. "I need to understand why the police think Wade killed Trevor. Can you think of a motive?"

"Oh yes, I most certainly can," Stacey said, shaking her head. "Good old Trevor Lane. There was a man asking to be murdered, even in high school." Stacey leaned her elbows on the table, ready to work. "Like I was saying, Wade was a wonder on the football field, despite his size. His teammates loved to watch the opposing players underestimate him. After a while, of course, other teams caught on. This was high school football, so the same teams played each other every year. Wade made quite an impression his first year, and the next year the coach made him quarterback."

"When was this?" Olivia asked. "As you probably remember, I wasn't much of a sports fan. I can barely make it across the room without tripping over my own feet . . . as my mother keeps pointing out to me."

"Many of us have noticed that endearing trait," Stacey said. "Wade became a quarterback in the fall of our freshman year. He was a junior."

"So Trevor Lane and Dougie Adair were about the same age as Wade?"

"Yep," Stacey said. "All three were juniors. Trevor and Dougie played on the Twiterton football team. Trevor was their quarterback. A very popular quarterback, I might add. At least, that's what Wade told me at the time. When the two teams played each other the year before, Wade was playing defense, and he did some fancy move, the name of which I've forgotten. Trevor got distracted by it and fumbled the ball. Boy, did he make a stink about that trick, even threatened to kill Wade, but the ref let it go. Wade was

246

really looking forward to a repeat humiliation."

"Uh-oh," Olivia said. "Trevor Lane was not one to take humiliation lightly."

"No kidding." Stacey's eyes strayed to the cookie box, but she resisted. "Trevor certainly took his revenge on Wade. It altered the course of Wade's life and foretold his future. I should have seen it coming. . . . If I had, I might not have married the poor guy."

"Do you wish you hadn't married him?" Olivia asked.

"Not for a minute. Rachel and Tyler are great kids. I can't imagine life without them. Wade and I had some good years, and I'm grateful for those, too. However, things are what they are, and I have to protect my kids. Wade knows I won't let them spend time with him if he's been drinking. Up until lately, he's been careful."

Olivia poured the last of the coffee into their cups. "What did Trevor Lane do to Wade all those years ago?"

Stacey poured a dollop of cream into her cup. "Trevor used his acting skills, such as they were. He and that sidekick of his, Dougie, invited Wade to meet them before the game for a 'friendly' drive in Trevor's old Cadillac. I think it was a hand-me-down

247

from Trevor's father, who'd kept it in really good shape. Wade couldn't resist the chance to ride in a car like that. Even back then, he was in love with cars."

"I'm surprised Wade was willing to go off with those two right before a game," Olivia said. "Especially after Trevor's threat the year before."

"That's my Wade," Stacey said. "Trusting to a fault. That's actually one of his more endearing qualities. When Trevor said he wanted to let bygones be bygones, Wade never questioned. Just like he wasn't suspicious when Trevor offered him a large bottle of cola that was already open."

"Oh no."

"Yep." Stacey gave in to temptation and commandeered another cookie, a pale blue dove with a silver dragée eye. "Too pretty to eat," she said. "Almost." Nestling the cookie on her plate, Stacey said, "Poor, sweet Wade . . . he didn't get suspicious even when Trevor and Dougie drank nothing. The cola was, of course, spiked with pills."

"And with a game coming up in . . ."

"In a couple hours," Stacey said. "They were supposed to be on a dinner break. Coaches around here weren't too rigid about knowing where their players were until they were due to start warming up. It was assumed they were home with their families. After that night, the rules changed."

"So I gather Wade was not at his best during the game?" Olivia couldn't help feeling sad for the young, naive Wade Harald. Adolescence could be a minefield.

"If by 'not at his best' you mean doped up, as well as hyped-up on caffeine, then you got it right. Wade was kicked out of the game, off the team, and questioned by the police. He told them what happened, but Trevor and Dougie denied any involvement. They tested clean for drugs, so the police believed them. It didn't help Wade's credibility that he lost his temper very publicly and vowed to 'get' Trevor and Dougie no matter how long it took."

"Which would be why Del arrested him for Trevor's murder?"

Stacey nodded. "He made himself the perfect suspect. Only I don't believe for a minute that my Wade has it in him to murder someone, let alone the imagination to create such a weird scene on your porch. From the rumors I've been hearing, the killer branded Trevor. In my wildest, most bizarre dreams, I can't imagine Wade having the forethought to bring a branding iron along to a murder. Unless that didn't really happen?"

Olivia grimaced. "I really shouldn't . . ."

With a shrug, Stacey said, "Understood. Anyway, I've said my piece, and now I'm hungry. Excuse me while I eat the blue dove of happiness." She removed the silver dragée eye and bit an impressive chunk from the dove cookie's upper body.

Although Stacey sounded like her old no-nonsense self, Olivia noticed the shadows under her cornflower blue eyes. "Speaking of rumors," Olivia said, "there's one going around that you were laid off from your job at the elementary school."

Stacey shook her head. "Not yet. There's talk of layoffs at the school, but I haven't heard anything definite. I'll admit the possibility is wedged somewhere at the back of my mind. However, knowing our administration, layoffs would be a last resort. We're down to the bone as it is." Stacey swept a few crumbs off the table and onto her empty plate. A worry wrinkle had formed between her eyebrows, adding years to her lovely face.

"Just one more question for now, Stacey, and it may have nothing to do with Trevor's death. It's about our new employee at The Gingerbread House, Jennifer Elsworth."

"I caught a glimpse of her in your shop,"

Stacey said. "Didn't look familiar."

"It seems Jennifer grew up in Twiterton, left for parts unknown, and now she's back in the area." Olivia measured her words carefully. Stacey might feel desperate to find another suspect. "Jennifer is working out well at the store. She is quiet but good with customers. In fact, she sold the red mixer, so —"

"The red mixer? No kidding. 'Good with customers' is an understatement."

"Agreed," Olivia said with a light laugh. "It's just that Maddie hired her without consulting me, and Jennifer didn't have any references. You see, I like to know the background of the people we hire."

Stacey's teasing grin brightened her eyes. "Oh, I see, all right. Maddie hired Jennifer without telling you, she's terrific, so you're looking for something wrong with her. Besides, I heard that silly rumor Binnie's been spreading about Del and Jennifer. It isn't true, right?"

A firm denial popped into Olivia's mind, but she squelched it. Maybe it was best to leave some doubt about why Olivia wanted information about Jennifer rather than peg her as a possible killer. Not that Stacey was the type to spread unsubstantiated rumors, but these were not ordinary circumstances.

"I meant to call you about Jennifer," Olivia said, "but I haven't had time. Jason met her once, years ago. He said she went to Twiterton High School. Since you've worked so many years in school administration, I thought you might know an easy way to find out a bit about her background. Not her school records, of course, just a little about her family, that sort of thing."

Stacey chuckled. "The easiest way I know of is to ask your mother. I'm guessing you've tried that, and she drew a blank?"

"Hard to believe, I know. I was aghast. Mom isn't perfect. She said Twiterton residents were wealthier and didn't mix much with the likes of Chatterley Heights folks. Maddie looked for Twiterton yearbooks online and only found the last three years."

"I'm not surprised," Stacey said. "Chatterley Heights High has managed to put two past yearbooks online, and that was with volunteer help. There's no money to spare. With kids from well-to-do families attending private schools, even schools in wealthier areas are struggling to stay open. The office manager at Twiterton High happens to be a friend of mine. I'll call her and see what I can dig up for you."

"That's great, thanks."

"It's the least I can do." Stacey yawned and stretched.

Olivia gathered their plates and carried them to the kitchen sink. Before closing the box of cookies, she asked, "Sure you don't want another? Cookies have been known to induce a sweet and restful sleep."

"Or a tummy ache," Stacey said. "Don't fret; if I wake up in desperate need of a cookie, I know where to find them."

As Stacey headed toward the guest room, Olivia knocked on Allan's closed office door. Ellie opened the door a crack. "Oh good, it's you," she said as she poked her head into the hallway. She glanced up and down the corridor. "Is Stacey in her room?"

Olivia nodded. "Although given the number of cookies she ate, she will probably reappear to brush her teeth. I should take off for home soon. Sorry we took so long. You can ignore my request for cookies, Mom. I think Maddie has been baking."

"Not a chance," Ellie said. "Rachel and Tyler finished their homework in record time, so they have an hour to bake before bed. We were just waiting for you and Stacey to finish in the kitchen. I won't ask how your conversation went."

"Thanks," Olivia said. "I assume Spunky is still napping next to the computer?"

Ellie pulled Olivia into the office and closed the door behind her. "There's something you need to see first." She pointed toward the computer screen, which Allan was reading.

Olivia took one look at the text and said, "Oh no, not Binnie's blog again. Can't we just ignore her?" Spunky's eyes popped open in response to his mistress's irritated tone. Once he determined Olivia wasn't angry with him, he resumed napping.

"It is wise to keep informed, dear," Ellie said. "Though it isn't always pleasant. Once all this is over, I'll need to double up on my yoga classes."

"It's darned nasty," Allan said. "You'd better read this for yourself, Livie."

With a sense of foreboding, Olivia settled in front of the screen and read the first few lines of Binnie Sloan's blog about Wade Harald's arrest on suspicion of murder. Although, predictably, Binnie had left out the suspicion part and jumped directly to a murder charge. "We know all this, don't we?"

"Keep reading, dear," Ellie said. "Think of it as an exercise in creating emotional distance."

Olivia began again at the beginning of the blog post.

The streets of Chatterley Heights are safe once again as of this afternoon, when Sheriff Del Jenkins finally found time in his busy social life to arrest Wade Harald for the murder of visiting soap star Trevor Lane. The hunky Mr. Lane was found dead in the early morning hours, posed in a rocking chair on the porch of The Gingerbread House. That little cookie store, and the would-be sleuths who run it, do seem to attract a surprising number of violent deaths. This time, at least so far, there's no direct evidence linking the murder to Olivia Greyson and Maddie Briggs. Or is there? Maddie is soon to be married to the strong, silent owner of Heights Hardware, who might want to reconsider whether marriage to the flighty redhead is good for his health.

"Okay, those were snarky cracks about Del, Maddie, and Lucas, but otherwise this piece is fairly low key . . . for Binnie."

"Keep reading, Livie," Ellie said.

Olivia scrolled to the next page, a photo of Olivia and Maddie chatting with Trevor and Dougie in the band shell. Howie Upton was a shadowy figure partly hidden by Dougie, who had turned his back on Howie. "This must have been one of the photos

Ned Sloan took Wednesday evening. Only yesterday . . ."

"And only hours before Trevor's murder," Allan said.

"I think Livie knows that, dear." There was a hint of sternness in Ellie's voice.

"It's okay, Mom. Allan is right; this doesn't look so good. You can see Maddie and me laughing. It's almost as if we know these men better than we let on."

"Which is quite ridiculous," Ellie said.

"Whoa. Down, girl." Allan wrapped his arm around his wife's slender shoulders. "No one takes Binnie's innuendoes seriously."

The next page contained the remainder of Binnie's blog.

Our busy sheriff seems convinced he has his man. Maybe he does. Lately, Wade is drunk more than sober, and rumor has it that Struts Marinsky, the tough-as-nails owner of Struts & Bolts Garage, fired Wade for coming to work all liquored up. If you've had your brakes worked on recently, you might want to take your car back and demand a redo.

Meanwhile, Wade's ex-wife and kids have taken a powder. Have they disappeared to escape the press, or are they in protective custody? We'll ask them when we locate their hiding place, which shouldn't be long now.

But what about Olivia Greyson? What's her part in this drama? Olivia enticed Mr. Lane to visit her store so she could impress her customers, who showed up in droves. Sounds like a teenage crush to us. Olivia has been divorced for several years now. Her relationship with the sheriff has hit a bump in the road — the young, pretty Jennifer Elsworth. Must be quite a shock for poor Olivia. First she gets dumped by her husband, a successful surgeon, and then she can't even hold on to a small-town sheriff. Did she make a play for the darling of daytime television, only to be rejected yet again?

So we have to ask ourselves: do we have one murder suspect or two? You be the judge.

"Wow," Olivia said. "You've got to admit — Binnie is cunning. She even managed to get in a dig at Del. It should be entertaining to read the responses to her post."

"You seem to be taking this quite calmly," Allan said in a hopeful tone.

"If I took Binnie too seriously, I'd have had a stroke by now." Olivia closed down the offensive blog. "Or I'd be in jail for murder."

CHAPTER THIRTEEN

By the time Olivia and Spunky arrived
home, it was nearly eleven p.m. Allan had
insisted on driving them. When he saw the
unlit porch, he walked them to the door and
waited to hear the click of the lock. As Allan had explained to Olivia, he believed
Wade Harald was innocent of Trevor Lane's
murder, mostly because it seemed to involve
more planning than Wade could muster. So
it logically followed that the true murderer
was still out there, possibly roaming the
streets of Chatterley Heights.

As always, her stepfather's logic was unas-
sailable, so Olivia hadn't argued with him.
Besides, a ride would get her, plus one
pooped pup, back home more quickly. As
she unlocked the door to The Gingerbread
House, she composed a mental list containing only one item: finish the cookies for
Maddie and Lucas's party, even if it took
till dawn.

A sliver of light under the kitchen door told her that Maddie was still working. *Good.* Between the two of them, maybe they could finish the cookies in record time. Olivia had promised Stacey she would do what she could to clear Wade of murder, and she intended to try.

"One of my dumber promises," Olivia said to her sleepy Yorkie as she nestled him on the soft, embroidered seat of his favorite chair. With a whimpering sigh, Spunky collapsed in a tired heap. "When all this excitement is over, you need a trim." Olivia stroked the silky hair cascading over his eyes. "Get some rest, little one. I may be needing your fierce protection."

The kitchen door opened, and Maddie poked her head around the edge. She looked entirely too alert. "Hey, you're back. How's Stacey holding up? Has Del arrested Binnie yet?"

"For what? Evil blogging?"

"One can dream. I saw what Binnie wrote about us. She sure knows how to have a good time at our expense . . . or at your expense, to be more accurate." Maddie held the kitchen door open, releasing a strong whiff of lemon blended with a subtler flowery fragrance.

"Sorry I was gone so long," Olivia said.

"Have you been working all this time?"

"I don't think of baking as work, Livie. Cookies are my canvas, and icing is my paint. Plus, decorated cookies taste good, so there's really no downside."

"Wow, you've been . . ." Olivia gazed in awe at the scene in the kitchen. Decorated cookies covered the worktable, the counter, the chair seats, even her little desk. When she'd run out of cooling racks, Maddie had spread the cookies on whatever she could find: cake pans, lids, even kitchen towels. The kitchen looked like a huge abstract painting covered with swaths of yellow, purple, and red, in every conceivable shade. The sweet, flowery scent of a garden in full bloom swirled around the kitchen. Olivia felt deliciously light-headed . . . and hungry.

"I've been what?" Maddie prodded. "On fire with creative genius? Gloriously imaginative? The van Gogh of the cookie world?"

"I was going to say you've been busy." Olivia felt the need to sit down, but all the chairs were occupied with cookies.

"Well, that's true, though disappointingly prosaic," Maddie said. "Jennifer met the challenge and found all the ingredients we needed. I was inspired to get the baking out of the way, so we could move on to other fascinating pursuits."

"Such as your engagement party?"

"Well, that, too. I was thinking of the hunt for Trevor Lane's killer. Not so much for Wade's sake, but for Stacey's peace of mind, not to mention her child support checks. Before you fill me in," she said, "did you read all of Binnie's latest blog or just the highlights?"

"All of it, as did Allan and my mom. I'm not worried. Binnie had to go so far out of her way to implicate me in Trevor's murder, I doubt anyone will take it seriously."

Maddie lifted a cake pan of cookies off a chair so Olivia could sit down. "Don't count on that," she said. "Chatterley Heights is well supplied with gullible, gossipy citizens." Maddie opened a storage cupboard and shoved the pan on top of a folded pile of aprons.

"Are those new embroidered aprons from Aunt Sadie?" Olivia asked.

"No, just a few from her last batch. I forgot where I'd stored them. I'll put them out on the sales floor tomorrow."

"Hand them to me, will you?"

"Livie, I'll agree that Aunt Sadie's aprons are stunning, and they sell quickly for amazing prices, but right now we have other —"

"Just let me see them, okay? I want to check something."

Maddie lifted up the pan of cookies and pulled the aprons off the shelf. "You'll have to put them back when you're finished. Or we could put them out right now. They are already tagged."

While Olivia looked through the small pile of embroidered aprons, Maddie opened the lid of her computer to awaken it. She pulled out the chair from under the desk and found yet another pan of cookies. Unable to find a spot for it, she sat down and balanced the pan on her lap. "The computer is open for business," she announced. When Olivia didn't respond, Maddie twisted in her seat and said, "Earth to Livie, we don't have all night. Well, actually, we do, but eventually we'll have to open the store, and I'd like to clean up the kitchen and maybe have a shower before . . . Livie? Are you okay?"

"Hmm? Oh, sorry, I was lost in speculation, probably pointless. Did the other aprons from this batch sell already?"

"No, why?"

Olivia opened up the top apron and spread it on her lap. The embroidered scene depicted a cocky gingerbread girl with puffy red braids. She was dressed as a lumberjack, held an axe, and stood next to a partially cut tree.

"Oh, I love that one," Maddie said. "Aunt

Sadie named it the Lumberjill and said I was her model. Put that aside; I want to buy it."

"The scenes on the aprons all related to professions, right? I remember one was in a courtroom. There was a gingerbread judge in robes, and he was —"

With a squeal, Maddie said, "I remember that one, too. I don't know why it hasn't sold yet. It was a hilarious courtroom scene. There was a jury of gingerbread men and women all dancing around, and the judge was holding a gavel in the air, trying to call the court to order. Hey, you don't suppose Trevor's killer got the gavel idea from that apron, do you? That means we're looking for a woman."

"Slow down a bit." Olivia folded the Lumberjill apron and handed it to Maddie. "The store was packed when Trevor, Dougie, and Lenora made their appearance. Granted the audience was mostly women, but I noticed some men, too. Anyone could have seen that apron. Now, if we could track down the gavel cookie cutter, that might lead us somewhere. I know we've never carried one in the store."

Maddie sighed. "Jennifer's into cookie cutters, and she would certainly have seen the apron. I sure hope the murderer isn't

Jennifer. She's a fabulous clerk. I mean, let's face it: neither of us could sell that red mixer. And she found all the ingredients we asked for in record time."

"Jennifer is very talented," Olivia said, "which is no guarantee of innocence. Let's leave our new employee for later. Right now, we don't have any reason to connect her with the murder except that her behavior has been a bit odd at times."

Maddie reawakened her computer, which had drifted off while they talked about aprons. "Okay, whither should my fingers goeth?"

"Let's try Howie Upton," Olivia said. "He seems to have held quite a grudge against Trevor since high school. He hasn't been very successful for a child genius, which might explain why he can't let go of the past."

"Okay, this could take a while," Maddie said. "I'm going to check professional and social network sites. Howie strikes me as someone who might use the Internet to provide himself with a social life. He can be anyone he wants online, but if he uses his own name, I'll find him."

While Maddie tapped away, Olivia began to pack up the finished cookies. Many were dry enough to layer in cake pans, which she stacked one on top of another. She had cleared half the table before she began to tire. The remaining cookies were either still cooling, or the icing hadn't hardened yet. Olivia pulled up a kitchen chair, rested her feet on another, and relaxed. Within moments, her head drooped forward as she drifted toward a lavender, rose, and lemon nap.

"Yes!" Maddie announced at full volume. "I am Queen of the Internet!"

Olivia jerked awake and her feet slipped off their perch. Her chair began to wobble backward. She grabbed for the table edge but missed. Hearing sounds behind her, Maddie spun around and caught the chair before it reached the point of no return. "Whew," Maddie said. "Talk about a close call." She righted the chair while Olivia clutched the table edge to help pull herself upright.

"Maybe you should take a nap upstairs," Maddie suggested. "In your own bed. At least, I assume you don't fall out of bed often."

"Not more than once a week," Olivia said. "Have you found anything interesting about Howie Upton?"

"Interesting, yes." Maddie righted the kitchen chair Olivia had pushed over with her feet. "He seems to have trouble with women."

"Not surprising. What kind of trouble?"

"They don't like him." Maddie settled in front of her computer again and awakened the screen. "In fact, one woman complained quite vocally about his 'clodishness.' Is that even a word?"

"Maddie, you didn't hack into his email, did you?"

"Don't fuss, Livie. Hardly anyone is as easy to hack as you are, especially a child mathematics prodigy who works in a bank. By the way, you have an email from Del. It's time sensitive, so you might want to read it soon. Anyway, I found plenty of posts from Howie on a variety of blogs, plus a number of my own local Facebook friends allowed Howie to become their friends, a decision many of them are reconsidering."

"Wait, back up." Olivia leaned against the counter so she could face Maddie. "You hacked into my email and read a message from Del? That's going too far, even between best friends since age ten. This has got to stop."

"I've tried, Livie, I really have, but it's such fun to crack a password that's in French. It lightens the terrible psychological burden I carry from that D in high school French. Besides, would you have checked your email before morning?"

"Probably not, but —"

"Then I rest my case," Maddie said. "I might add that it's sort of inconsistent to get mad at me for hacking you when you're always encouraging me to hack other people."

"That's hacking for the greater good," Olivia said. "It's important."

"So is your love life. Read Del's email."

"Fine," Olivia said. "You clean the kitchen." She took Maddie's place at the computer, and read:

Livie, I hope you're getting some sleep, but knowing you two, you're baking, so maybe you'll get this in time. Any chance we could meet at the Chatterley Café early for breakfast? I have to meet the medical examiner at nine a.m., so I should leave town by eight. Could you make 6:30? I miss you. Del

Olivia checked the clock over the sink. "It's about two a.m.," she said. "That should leave plenty of time for more hacking . . . I mean investigation. To be followed by a nap, and a shower."

"If you're worried about the timing,"

Maddie said, "I can clean up. I'll open in the morning, too. Bertha and Jennifer both agreed to be here by eight thirty to help handle the curious crowd we can expect by opening time."

"Del has to leave the restaurant by eight, so I'll be back in time for opening." Much as Olivia wanted to see Del, at the moment she was more interested in what he might be willing to tell her about Trevor Lane's murder and the evidence against Wade Harald. Olivia wrote a quick acceptance for breakfast and hit send. "Okay, breakfast with Del is a go."

"Excellent." Maddie punched the on button for the dishwasher. "Shall we begin with my summary of the Howie Upton hack — ? Sorry, 'investigation' has too many participles."

"Syllables. Could we move on to Howie?"

Maddie threw a wet towel at Olivia. "Isn't this fun? Okay, on to Howie Upton. I found a blog all women should know about, devoted to warnings about men. It's for women only. You have to sign in to access it, so first you have to answer some questions and give an email address that can be traced back to a person. Obviously, a male hacker could get in without breaking a sweat, but the real purpose of the blog isn't obvious unless you're in. Apparently, the women are keeping the secret pretty well. My guess is they've got several members who are electronic geniuses, so . . ."

Olivia cleared her throat.

"Right, interesting but not relevant," Maddie said. "The bloggers all use aliases, but they don't hesitate to name names. Howie Upton came up several times, and never in a good way."

"Any indication that he's violent?" Olivia asked.

"Not physically, no. One woman called Howie 'self-obsessed' and 'arrogant,' but we knew that. He doesn't like to be rejected, but who does? The most interesting entries came from a woman who said she dated him for about four months before breaking off with him.

"During the time they were together, she said, Howie seemed to change. At first, he acted attentive and confident. He complimented her, brought her gifts, and so on. Then he started taking her for granted. Worst of all, she said Howie seemed obsessed with hatred for other men. He kept pointing out how stupid they were, or that they didn't deserve the attention they got from women. The blogger finally broke off the relationship when Howie began criticiz-

270

ing her own older brother, who she loved dearly."

"Sounds like our Howie," Olivia said. "Although, when it comes to nasty comments, Trevor was the clear winner. Howie and Dougie were his victims."

Olivia's mind was spinning with ideas, though the rest of her had begun to wilt. "That makes me wonder if Trevor was the original source of Howie's anger issues with other men. Maybe he fell back into the victim role around Trevor."

"Which is, of course, pure speculation," Maddie said. "Not that I myself don't indulge in the purest of speculation from time to time. For instance, maybe Howie's father was hypercritical, and men like Trevor remind him of daddy. Or was that over-the-top Freudian?"

"Don't ask me. All I can do is add and subtract." Olivia brushed her tangled hair back from her forehead and wondered if she'd have time to wash it before breakfast. "I'm convinced Howie hated Trevor, that's what counts. Although it isn't enough to accuse him of murder. What we need are some solid motives. Did you find anything that might explain why Howie hasn't achieved the career heights he seemed destined for?"

"So glad you asked that, Livie. I don't yet

have the absolute, most final answer to that question. However, I did happen on a few mentions of the name Howie Upton in connection with an investment-banking firm in DC. Howie was at one time an up-and-coming investment banker. Then he fell off the radar. I am highly motivated to find out why."

"Good." Focused on her next step in the investigation, Olivia picked up Maddie's wet towel and began to fold it. "I'll email Allan. Maybe he has some DC financial-type buddies he could tap for information. Allan loves building businesses on his own, but he makes friends easily. He might be able to find out if Howie was simply laid off from his investment-banking job — as in 'last hired, first fired' — or if he was let go for something worse."

"I'm rooting for something worse." Maddie stood up and stretched her arms toward the ceiling. "Meanwhile, it's past three a.m. I'm ready to close up shop, and you, my friend, could use some sleep. You need to be on your toes by six thirty a.m., so you can wheedle classified information out of Del."

"Sounds like an excellent plan. I'll shoot an email to Allan before I head upstairs. Maybe I can wake up in time to wash my hair, too."

"I didn't want to say anything, but . . ." Maddie jumped aside just in time to avoid being winged by a wet towel.

Olivia thought fondly of her bed as she closed the kitchen door behind her. She could navigate her way across the sales floor, thanks to the streetlamp positioned outside the front window, but why take the chance of tripping over a table leg? As she reached toward the light switch, her hand froze. She didn't see Spunky's furry form curled up in his chair.

"Spunky?" Olivia whispered. He couldn't have gone far. "Where are you, Spunks? Time to wake up so we can go to bed."

A faint clicking sound brought Olivia's attention to the front window. Spunky's nails needed cutting. He must be hidden behind his chair, looking out the window. "Okay, what's so interesting that you can't even —" A low growl interrupted her. She hurried to the window and found Spunky standing on his little hind legs, with his front paws pressed against the glass. "What is it, boy? What do you see?"

Spunky growled again. His head moved slowly as if he were following a moving target. Olivia stared in the same direction but saw nothing. She suspected Spunky's keen eyesight could see movement invisible to her, possibly even in the park. Olivia suddenly felt exposed. If someone was outside, she might be visible. *Get a grip, Livie. Spunky growls at squirrels.*

"Come, my mighty warrior, time for bed. Tomorrow morning, Maddie will take you for a walk, and you can give that squirrel a piece of your mind."

Spunky responded with a frustrated whiney growl and transferred his front paws from the window glass to Olivia's shins.

"Ouch," Olivia said as she lifted her pup and cuddled him in her arms. "Tomorrow we clip those nails, and no complaining this time." Spunky snuggled against Olivia's arm. "My hero," she whispered. If anyone had been in the park, he or she was gone now. Yet Olivia hesitated, uneasy. Maybe she should call Del? No, Del was trying to snag a few hours of sleep before their six thirty a.m. breakfast date. Olivia could roust him out of bed, of course, but . . . over a squirrel?

Spunky had drifted to sleep. The feel of his soft little body in her arms was so comforting, Olivia couldn't stifle a yawn. If Spunky had seen anything truly threatening in the park, she told herself, the next county would've heard his yapping. Surely it was safe to go to bed. She silenced that last niggling worry by making a mental note to mention the incident, if it could be called an incident, during breakfast with Del.

CHAPTER FOURTEEN

The Chatterley Café opened for breakfast at six a.m. on weekdays, usually to a waiting crowd of hungry customers. When Olivia arrived at six thirty, the line stretched from the front door to the street. With a smile and an apologetic explanation, she managed to slip past a determined cluster of folks guarding the entrance like sentinels. Once inside, Olivia searched the crammed restaurant for Del. All tables and booths appeared to be occupied, but she wasn't worried. Del always managed to secure a booth for them.

A waitress with long blond curls and a loaded tray cocked her head toward the back of the restaurant. "Sheriff Jenkins is waiting for you, third booth from the end." The young waitress was gone before Olivia could thank her.

Olivia saw the corner of a newspaper on the table as she approached, so she knew Del was facing the rear, as he always preferred. As she'd learned, he liked his privacy.

Olivia poked her head around the booth's high back said, "Hi, stranger. You look lonely. Mind if I join you?"

"Sure," Del said without missing a beat. "I'm waiting for someone, but she's never on time."

"Her loss, my gain," Olivia said. She had tried to startle Del many times before, but she had yet to succeed. Sometimes she wondered if he'd been born without a startle reflex. "Have I mentioned how glad I am to be dating a cop?" Olivia slid into the seat across from Del, appreciating the feeling of seclusion. "Cops get all the best tables."

"And I thought it was my winning smile," Del said. He leaned across the table to give her a quick kiss. She wished it had been just a bit longer.

"That, too," she said.

Del pushed aside his newspaper and reached for Olivia's hand. "How are you and Maddie holding up?"

"Oh, you know how it is. The baking is fun but time-consuming, and the party details are endless, but we'll make it."

"Livie, what I meant was . . . how are you doing after finding a murder victim on your front porch?"

"Oh." Against her will, Olivia flashed back to the scene on The Gingerbread House porch. *Was that really less than two days ago?* "I guess there's an advantage to being crazy busy," she said. "We've been too distracted to stay upset."

"Good," Del said. "Then I won't have to worry about you and Maddie getting sucked into another murder investigation."

Olivia sensed a warning in Del's comment and was relieved when rescue appeared in the shapely form of the young blond waitress. She poured coffee into Del's cup. "On the house, of course," she said with a fetching grin. Olivia got the coffee minus the smile. The waitress produced a pen and order pad from her apron pocket. "Our special today is a nice, light omelet with roasted shallots and chèvre cheese. Comes with whole-wheat toast. What would you like, ma'am?"

Being called "ma'am" by a young thing made Olivia feel like throwing a plate. She was only in her early thirties, after all. Maybe she should take up kung fu with her mother. Or run a marathon. "I'll take the special."

Del glanced at her with raised eyebrows. "What? No blueberry pancakes and cheesy eggs?"

"At my age, I need to begin thinking about whole grains," Olivia said.

"At your —" Del took a deep breath. "Nope," he said quietly, "not going there."

The waitress ignored Olivia's comment. "You want your usual, Sheriff? Scrambled eggs with roasted potatoes?"

"I have no idea what chèvre cheese is, so yes."

The waitress laughed in a light, flirtatious way, or so it sounded to Olivia. Del didn't seem to notice. As the waitress sashayed off, Olivia took a sweet, creamy gulp of Italian roast and told herself that she wasn't ready for a permanent relationship, anyway.

"Our murder made the *Baltimore Sun*," Del said, sliding the paper toward Olivia.

"Lucky us." Olivia skimmed the article. "At least the story doesn't dwell too much on previous murder cases in Chatterley Heights."

"That's in a separate article." Del flipped several pages and pointed to the top of page six. "The account does concede that Trevor Lane was a well-known figure, so the killer might have followed him here."

"What do you think?"

"I wait to hear what the evidence says." Del drained his coffee and pushed his empty cup aside. Blondie the waitress, as

Olivia had begun to think of her, appeared at once to fill his cup. Del said, "Thanks," without looking up.

"Trevor graduated from Twiterton High," Olivia said, "so it's conceivable his reappearance here stirred up something from the past. From my brief interaction with him, I'd say he had a nasty side."

"Sounds like you've been giving this some thought."

"Well, he was left on my porch," Olivia said with what she hoped was nonchalance.

"Livie, whoever *killed* Trevor has a nasty streak, too." Del leaned toward her and lowered his voice. "Be careful. Better yet, don't get involved. At least not any more than you already are. It's only a matter of time before someone figures out that Stacey and her kids have disappeared to Ellie and Allan's house."

"How did you — ?" Olivia watched Del's slow smile and knew she'd been tricked. "You didn't know for sure, did you?"

"Nope. It seemed logical, but there were other possibilities. The high school called me when Rachel and Tyler didn't show up. I checked with the elementary school and was told Stacey had left town for a family emergency. I didn't want to search for them, obviously, because I might accidentally point the press, or worse, in their direction. But I'm relieved to know nothing has happened to them, so thanks for that."

The arrival of breakfast gave Olivia a chance to think. Del dug into his scrambled eggs. Her omelet smelled delicious, though the cheese looked awfully . . . white. She tried a bite. Not bad, in a fluffy sort of way. Roasted shallots could make almost anything palatable.

Although Olivia trusted Del's investigative skills and took his warning seriously, she had no intention of abandoning Stacey's family to the fates. On the other hand, it was foolish to keep anything from him, at least not without a very good reason. "Del, this might be nothing, but . . ." She had Del's immediate attention. "This morning after Maddie and I finished baking — it was shortly after three a.m., I think — I went into the store to get Spunky so we could go to bed." Olivia hesitated, wondering if she'd overreacted to Spunky's behavior.

"And? Just tell me," Del said. "I trust your instincts."

Olivia relaxed. "Thanks," she said. "That helps. Anyway, Spunky is usually a good little sleeper, but I found him wide-awake and staring out the front window of the store. I couldn't see anything. Spunky can see better in the dark than I can. I wondered if something or someone might be out there, maybe in the park. Spunky was so intent, he barely noticed me. Then he growled a couple times. I told myself that he growls at squirrels. . . ."

"One question," Del said. "Would the movement of a squirrel out in the park normally be enough to awaken Spunky from a sound sleep?"

"He does have acute hearing," Olivia said. "Remember when he heard Buddy howling in the park in the middle of a stormy night?" Cody Furlow, Del's deputy, had also adopted a rescue dog, a huge black lab with a penchant for running away. Buddy and Spunky had bonded over their shared compulsion to escape confinement.

"That dog can howl like a banshee," Del said. "As I remember, you said you could hear Buddy's howling, too, right?"

"Not at first, but yes. Once I got close to the window, it was hard to miss. And you're right, when I'm inside The Gingerbread House, I would never hear a squirrel in the park. I doubt I'd hear one even with the windows open. Come to think of it, when Spunky notices a squirrel, it's only when he is watching out the window. I think he is seeing it move, rather than hearing it.

However, even if someone was in the park last night, making enough noise to awaken Spunky, it might not be relevant to Trevor's murder."

Del didn't comment. He rubbed his chin and frowned at nothing in particular. Olivia had seen this behavior before. Either Del was thinking through a problem, or he needed a shave. All she could do was wait. With some reluctance, Olivia picked up her whole-wheat toast. She didn't mind wheat toast, but this piece looked really . . . hearty. She took a small bite. It was sweeter than she'd expected. However, when Del took a deep breath, Olivia abandoned her toast without regret.

Del leaned across the table and captured Olivia's hand. She had to shift closer to the table to hear his voice. "From now on, Livie, if you see or hear anything even the least bit suspicious, call me at once. Or 911, if you can't get hold of me. What I'm about to tell you must not get out. Okay? Don't even tell Maddie." Del paused, waiting for her to respond.

Olivia nodded. "I promise. I know you'll have good reasons." It was tough to keep anything from Maddie, but it probably wouldn't be for long. In Chatterley Heights, secrets had a way of leaking out.

"All right, then." Del's shoulders relaxed, but he kept his voice low. "Sometime during the night, someone placed a hammer on the bench inside the band shell. He or she did this after taking a swing at the outside of the band shell, leaving a neat and very noticeable hole in the wood near the foundation. There's paint on the hammerhead that matches the band shell paint."

"Is it the murder weapon?"

"Can't be sure," Del said. "It's still going through forensics." He checked his watch. "I need to leave in about twenty minutes to meet with the medical examiner. I should know more after that."

"Del, I just thought of something you said about the break-in at Lady Chatterley's. Wasn't a hammer used to try to force the safe open? Could the murder weapon be that same hammer?"

"Until we have evidence to the contrary, we're assuming it's a coincidence that hammers were used for both crimes."

"Okay, but if the hammer you found this morning turns out to be the murder weapon, wouldn't that clear Wade Harald? Obviously, Wade couldn't have whacked the band shell this morning because he was in custody. Right?"

Del ran his fingers through his hair, a sign

of frustration. "Livie, I wish it were that simple. Wade might have tossed it away after the murder. Maybe someone else found it, wanted to turn it in, but didn't want to get involved. Or the hammer we found might not be the murder weapon. And you might want to consider that someone left that hammer at the band shell to create reasonable doubt about Wade's guilt." Del rolled his shoulders in circles as if they felt stiff.

"You mean someone like Stacey Harald?" Olivia asked. "You think she sneaked out of Mom and Allan's house in the wee hours to plant that hammer?"

Del paused before answering. "Livie, I know you're worried, but I promise you, we are covering every angle. It's just that . . . well, there's no point in speculating until we learn if the hammer we found is the murder weapon. Then we'd have to check alibis. However, thanks to you and Spunky, we are closer to knowing when that hammer was delivered to the band shell. You can understand why I don't want anyone to get wind of —"

"I gave my word, Del, okay?"

"Okay."

"Okay, then." Olivia grumpily pushed aside her plate with the leftover whole-wheat toast.

Del chuckled and snatched her hand again. "And thank you," he said.

"For what? Doing my duty as a citizen?"

"That, too." Del pulled her across the table for a goodbye kiss, longer this time. "And for covering breakfast for me." He slid out of the booth and into his uniform jacket. "I'm sorry, Livie. I know I invited you, but I've been so busy, I haven't had time to get to the bank."

"And you don't use a credit or debit card," Olivia said, "for reasons I've never understood."

"Too easy to overspend. My salary isn't great, and I'm afraid I don't have your head for math," Del said with a sheepish smile.

"Jerk," Olivia said, a bit louder than necessary.

Del chuckled. "I love you, too." He grabbed his uniform hat and disappeared into the breakfast throng.

From a block away, Olivia knew something was wrong at The Gingerbread House. The store wasn't due to open for at least forty-five minutes, yet she recognized a number of Chatterley Heights citizens standing on the porch. Additional clusters of people milled around on the grass and the sidewalk. Lenora Dove was holding court amid a group of camera-toting strangers. Olivia hesitated. She didn't see Maddie's unmistakable mop of red hair. She must be inside the store.

Olivia quickly changed her route, scooting across the grass between the Chatterley Café and a small toy store next door. To keep out of sight, she walked two blocks north, then turned east and continued until she reached the alley that ran behind The Gingerbread House. Olivia scanned the alley and saw no signs of activity. She sprinted to the store's back door. Luckily, Lucas had installed a new lock as well as a peephole for those times when Snoopy Sam Parnell made one of his surprise visits to deliver an "urgent package."

Olivia reached The Gingerbread House without interference. She slid her key into the lock and pushed. The door shifted, opened a crack, and stuck. Maddie must have used the old latch. Olivia knocked, hoping no one was lurking nearby in the alley. She thought she heard a gasp from inside the kitchen.

"Maddie? Are you in there? It's me, let me in."

Through the open crack, Olivia heard a soft, frightened voice ask, "Livie?" It sounded breathless, like Bertha when her

287

asthma was acting up. "Livie, are you sure it's you?"

"Absolutely certain." Olivia heard voices nearby, perhaps from the side yard. "Bertha, hurry, let me in. Someone is coming."

"Oh dear." Hands fumbled with the latch and the door opened.

Olivia slipped into the kitchen and slammed the door behind her. She turned to see Bertha looking far from her usual cheerful self. Her red cheeks alarmed Olivia, who remembered how precarious Bertha's health had been before she'd lost sixty pounds. "Sit down and take deep, slow breaths," Olivia ordered as she pulled out a kitchen chair. She gave Bertha's shoulder a gentle push until she sank onto the seat.

"My goodness, you wouldn't believe —" Bertha gasped for air.

"First, breathe," Olivia said. "Then you can talk." By now, she could hear voices outside in the alley. She glanced back at the door and realized she'd closed the old latch but had neglected to flip the new lock. The latch should hold, but she wasn't about to take the chance. The lock made a faint clicking sound as she secured it. From the chattering outside, Olivia assumed someone had heard. Well, they'd have to hack down the door to get inside the kitchen.

Olivia felt as if she'd wandered into a vampire movie. She pulled over a chair for herself and said, "Okay, Bertha, you may now speak. What the heck is going on here?"

"Oh, Livie, it's the strangest thing," Bertha said. "Maddie and Jennifer and I were restocking shelves, getting ready to open, you know? I looked out the window. For no particular reason, you understand, just to admire the morning. We weren't due to open for over an hour, and with three of us there at one time, well, there wasn't any reason to go rushing about —"

Olivia began to regret giving Bertha permission to speak.

"— and anyway, there she was!" Bertha shuddered. "She was on the porch with her face up against the window, staring right at me with that awful grin that makes her look like the Bride of Frankenstein. I nearly fainted."

"Whoa, wait a moment, are you talking about Lenora Tucker?"

"I certainly am," Bertha said. "Or whatever her name is today. I thought I'd have a heart attack right then and there. I guess I sort of screamed, and Maddie came running. Then I looked back at the window, and there were more of them!"

"More . . . people?"

"If you can call them that," Bertha said. "Leeches, that's what I'd call them. Horrible clingy things trying to suck our blood. They had cameras, and they started flashing away right through The Gingerbread House window. Binnie was there, too, with that skinny little niece of hers holding up a camera bigger than she was. Maddie quick closed the curtains for the little window, but there's no thick covering for the big front window. Jennifer and I tried to find a sheet or something. We finally gave up. We've been pretending to ignore them. The kitchen door to the alley was locked, but I bolted it, too, because you never know what creatures like that will do." Bertha's breathing began to slow down. Sharing her horror had weakened its power.

Olivia was relieved to see Bertha's color return to normal. "Why are they being so persistent? What can they possibly want from us? And why don't they just call and ask like normal people?"

"They did," Bertha said. "We found a million phone messages when we got to the store this morning, so we turned off the message machine and let the dang thing ring its silly head off. Those monsters finally gave up and came on over to the store, thinking they'd just walk right in. They want to hound Stacey and her kids, that's what they want. Like the poor things don't have enough trouble and strife. Lenora Tucker got it in her head that you'd spirited them off somewhere. She convinced those ruffians you must be hiding them in the store or maybe your apartment. I'm surprised they haven't scaled the walls and broken in."

Olivia almost suggested boiling oil but censored herself in time. "Did you call the police department?"

"All we got was a recording," Bertha said with disgust. "We decided it wasn't worth bothering 911, as long as the locks held. Maddie said we should wait for you."

Olivia sat next to Bertha and pondered what to do. The first idea that popped into her head involved a cookie and a long nap with Spunky snuggled behind her knees. It was a tempting course of inaction. With great reluctance, she let the notion drift away. "Well," Olivia said, "I guess we have about half an hour to think of some way to get rid of them. I suppose it ought to be legal."

With an appreciative laugh, Bertha said, "Don't see why they deserve to be treated with kid gloves. I didn't say anything to Maddie because it isn't my place, but I learned a thing or two taking care of Clarisse's two sons all those years. You know I loved Clarisse like a sister, but she spoiled those boys. They got everything they wanted. They'd beg and whine, and Clarisse would just give in. She knew she wasn't doing them any favors, letting them get so selfish and demanding. One day we had a long talk about it. Clarisse decided to let me take over. From then on, those boys had to get past me if they wanted something."

"That was smart," Olivia said, not sure where Bertha's story was leading. "I'm guessing you said no a lot more than Clarisse did?"

"You bet I did, and it was all for their own good, because I really did love those boys." Bertha went quiet for several moments, lost in her memories. A tentative knock on the alley door brought her back.

Olivia looked through the peephole in the door. No one was there. She assumed it was a reporter staying out of sight in hopes she'd open the door to check the alley. "It's nothing," she said, to reassure Bertha.

"Anyway," Bertha said, "that's my long way of saying we've been hiding in this store like skittish cats. Well, it's time to bare our claws. We can't let those vultures control us." Bertha slapped her plump knees. "They don't have the right to keep us from doing our jobs." With an emphatic nod of her head, Bertha added, "I can tell you, I'm in a mood to give those creatures what for if they even try."

Olivia was tired of hiding. She liked the idea of going on the offensive, but she wished she had a clue what "what for" meant. "Vultures play by their own rules," she pointed out. "They will poke and prod and snap their cameras, hoping one of us breaks, lets something slip. You and I and Maddie will probably hold up under the pressure, but I don't know Jennifer well enough to predict how she might react."

"You let me handle Jennifer," Bertha said. "I'll give her a good talking-to and keep an eye on her."

According to the kitchen clock, The Gingerbread House was due to open in twenty minutes. They couldn't afford to stay closed for another day. Besides, the thought that Binnie and her ilk could keep them trapped inside infuriated Olivia. "We'll open on time," she said. "Bring the others in here right now. We'll have a meeting to set the rules. I'm counting on you to monitor Jennifer, but I realize the situation is unpredictable."

"Yes, ma'am," Bertha said. She sounded

like a drill sergeant itching to whip the soldiers into shape. Olivia imagined the consternation Clarisse's spoiled sons must have felt when they'd heard that tone and known the gig was up.

"I'll leave a message for Del and Cody," Olivia said. "And I do believe I'll give my mother a quick heads-up."

Promptly at nine a.m., Olivia unlocked the door of The Gingerbread House. Olivia and Maddie were prepared to handle the main sales floor, while Bertha and Jennifer were assigned to defend the cookbook nook. Olivia had brought an eager Spunky downstairs to yap and nip at heels. She intended to hold on to him for the entire ordeal. Once the press had crowded into the store, she would lock the door to keep out customers, if there were any. After that, they'd wing it.

"Places, everyone," Olivia announced. She took a deep breath and opened the front door of The Gingerbread House. To her relief, the first person to slip inside was her mother, Ellie Greyson-Meyers, dressed in heels and a tailored suit. "Mom? What . . . ?" Spunky jumped out of Olivia's arms, but it didn't matter. No rabid throng of sensation mongers surged through the door behind Olivia's mother.

A sleek black ribbon held Ellie's neatly brushed hair back from her face, transforming her former-hippy hairstyle into a professional look. "Good morning, Livie, dear," she said. "I've been having a lovely chat with your eager visitors, but I'm afraid quite a number of them decided they couldn't stay any longer." Ellie hooked elbows with her daughter and spun her around to face the front window. Olivia nearly lost her balance. Wielding remarkable strength for one so tiny, Ellie kept the two of them upright. "Now you can understand why I wouldn't let you take tap dancing as a child, don't you, dear?"

"Unfair," Olivia said. "You caught me off guard." She did a double take when she looked out on the empty front porch. "I could have sworn I saw the press swarming outside. How did you get rid of them?"

"You may not be aware of this, Livie, but I am a trained negotiator. While you were living in Baltimore, poor little Chatterley Heights went through rather a bad patch. Several new families had moved into town, you see. They were perfectly nice people, but I'm afraid they, as well as their offspring, were rather openly critical of small-town life."

"I imagine that didn't go over well?"

"You imagine correctly," Ellie said. "Sadly, several school fights erupted, neighbors squabbled. . . . So sad. Several of us brought in a lovely young man to train us in the fine art of mediation."

"I also imagine you were top of the class."

"I was the only one who finished the class, dear."

"Okay, but how did you convince the press to leave us alone? Although, not all of them, I'm afraid," Olivia said as Binnie and her niece Ned barged through the front door. Lenora Dove lingered in the open doorway, gazing out at the departing press vans.

"Oh, Bertha is more than equal to Binnie and Ned," Ellie said. "As for the others, I simply applied the art of negotiation, and they decided on their own that it would be best to withdraw."

"Yes, Mom, but what negotiation technique did you use?"

As Ellie tilted her head, her beribboned hair swayed to one side. "Oh, I simply explained that the poor souls had been suckered. I softened the blow by feeding them the chocolate chip cookies Stacey's kids and I baked last evening. I tried to handle the situation quietly, of course. I didn't want to embarrass Lenora too publicly, although, between you and me, she is not blameless. You see, Lenora told Binnie that you were almost certainly hiding Stacey and her children in your store or apartment. As you know, Binnie craves respect from the bigger papers. She called them with her 'scoop,' only she did so without checking her facts. So unprofessional."

"Sometimes you are the best mom ever."

"Only sometimes, dear?"

"Now how do we get rid of Binnie and Ned?"

Ellie gave Olivia's arm a quick squeeze, and said, "I'll just go help Bertha with that task, shall I?"

"This I've got to see. Maddie can hold the fort." Olivia glanced around the nearly empty store to find Maddie dancing as she restocked a shelf. Olivia heard what sounded like a soft growl and noticed the empty chair near the front window. "I hear Spunky. Did you see where he went?"

"I believe he trotted into the cookbook nook after Binnie," Ellie said.

"Oops. Spunky isn't fond of Binnie, and vice versa."

Ellie speed-walked toward the cookbook nook, with Olivia straggling behind, as the growling exploded into a volley of yaps. Olivia arrived in time to see a tableau that would remain forever etched in her mind. Nedra, Binnie Sloan's ethereally thin niece, crouched on top of an antique mahogany buffet, wielding a camera almost as big as she was. She snapped shot after shot of Spunky as he yapped wildly and hopped on his back legs, attempting to scale the buffet to reach Ned.

Binnie's more substantial form, clothed in her usual cargo pants and flannel shirt, sat cross-legged on a large side table, amidst a scattered cookie cutter display. The table wobbled when Binnie so much as turned a page in her notebook. She scribbled rapidly, her expression verging on maniacal.

Jennifer Elsworth cowered well off to the side, staring at the scene with her mouth hanging open. Her sleek brown hair fell across her face like a protective curtain. Trusty Bertha had planted her sturdy body between Binnie and Ned. Strong arms crossed over her ample bosom, Bertha glared at the two invaders like an avenging Valkyrie judging the right moment to strike.

Olivia couldn't help herself; she doubled over in laughter. She knew her antique buffet would never recover from Spunky's claws. The display table was about to collapse under Binnie's weight, and several new cookie cutters were already bent beyond repair. Binnie would undoubtedly intensify her efforts to smear Olivia and The Gingerbread House in her *Weekend Chatter* blog. But Olivia couldn't stop laughing. Her mother grinned, and even Jennifer looked a shade less horrified. When Olivia heard laughing behind her, she turned her head to see Maddie and a customer holding their stomachs as they gasped for breath.

Ellie quickly regained her gentle demeanor. She scooped Spunky into her arms and carried him a safe distance away from his captives. The fierce Yorkie wriggled for a few moments, then relaxed as Ellie stroked the hair on his neck and whispered in his ear. He snuggled closer to her. His head dropped against her shoulder, and he closed his eyes.

Binnie Sloan's plump cheeks reddened, a rare display of embarrassment. She slapped shut her notebook and slid off the end table, taking its contents with her. With a quick nod at Ned, she strode toward the entrance to the cookbook nook, crunching several cookie cutters along the way. Ned jumped down from her perch and followed her aunt.

At the entrance to the main sales floor, Binnie spun around and pointed her index finger at Olivia. "You are hiding the family of a murderer, and, trust me, I will find them. They know more about the killing of Trevor Lane than the police realize, and I think you're in on it. I'm going to blow this case wide open."

Binnie turned and strode toward the front door with Ned scurrying behind her. As she passed him, Spunky awakened from his hypnotic state and yapped at her. She paused in the entryway long enough to yell, "That dog of yours is a public menace."

Following Binnie and Ned's dramatic exit, no one spoke. Even Spunky had nothing to add. Eventually, Maddie said, "Jennifer, would you work on straightening up the cookbook nook? The rest of us will handle the sales floor."

"Of course," Jennifer said. "I could use a chance to calm down."

As the others straggled back to the main sales floor, Maddie asked, "Binnie wouldn't dare go after Spunky. Would she?"

"She might," Ellie said, "but Spunky will prevail. Won't you, sweetheart?" Spunky lifted his head and gazed adoringly at Ellie.

Olivia felt the merest prick of envy. "Mom, have you been studying with that dog whisperer again? I thought you'd mastered all there was to know."

"I've moved on to terrier whispering," Ellie said. "It's an advanced class. Quite chal-

300

lenging." Ellie settled Spunky on his favorite chair, where he melted against the soft fabric and went into a deep sleep. "He's exhausted, poor dear."

"Those two have a lot of nerve," Bertha said, "barging in here and upsetting poor little Spunky. He was minding his own business, and that skinny girl put her camera right in his face and started flashing those terrifying lights at him. He's just a tiny tyke. How did she expect him to behave?"

Ellie sighed. "Exactly as he did behave, I expect. I suspect it was Binnie's idea to create a distraction, so she could slip away. She wanted a chance to search for Stacey and her children."

"Well, Binnie Sloan should be ashamed of herself," Bertha said. "Spunky gave her just what she deserved."

Ellie stared out the front window of The Gingerbread House so long that Olivia began to feel concerned. "You look worried, Mom. Do you think Spunky might be in danger?"

Ellie started. "What? Oh, I don't think so. I'm just having one of my bad feelings. Perhaps I'd better get going."

"Is your bad feeling about Stacey and the kids?" Olivia asked.

"Yes, dear, it is. Binnie is no fool. She'll

301

figure out that if Stacey hasn't left Chatterley Heights, our house is her second most logical hiding place. Binnie knows that I am at The Gingerbread House. She might think this is a good time to peek inside my home for Stacey and her kids. She might even try to force her way inside." Without saying good-bye, Ellie zipped out the front door, already dialing her cell phone.

CHAPTER FIFTEEN

Business in The Gingerbread House was surprisingly light all Friday morning, a welcome relief from the crowd of reporters gathered on the porch before the store opened. Olivia wondered if her customers had grown bored with cookie cutters and only showed up when they expected excitement. Maddie had scrounged enough cookies to fill a tray, but the free treats had hardly been touched. Could an entire town lose interest in such delectable delights? Leaving Bertha and Jennifer to handle the nearly empty sales floor, Olivia sought out Maddie in the kitchen, where she was decorating the rosewater cookies for her cookie cake.

"Nonsense, Livie," Maddie said when Olivia posed the question to her. "It is physically and spiritually impossible for anyone to become tired of decorated cookies. I suspect the population of Chatterley

Heights is saving its collective appetite for the party tomorrow." Maddie plunked tiny pale pink dots on the forest green icing foliage of a rosebush cookie. She'd decided to surround the perimeter of the cookie cake with a rose-garden motif. As she aimed her pastry bag at another cookie, the kitchen phone rang. "Would you get that, Livie? I've been letting it go so as not to waste a minute of precious decorating time. I figured folks were checking to be sure there'll be plenty of cookies for everyone and his second cousin twice removed. I've never understood what that meant."

Olivia answered the phone and was surprised to hear Stacey Harald's voice. "Livie? Don't say my name out loud, okay? Can you talk?" Stacey sounded rushed.

"Yes, I'm in the store kitchen with Maddie. Are you okay?"

Maddie paused in her decorating to lock eyes with Olivia, who nodded when Maddie whispered, "Stacey?"

"We're en route to somewhere or other," Stacey said. "Your stepdad is driving. He sneaked us out into the alley behind your house, where we got into an unmarked van. There are curtains on the back windows, so we won't be seen. I'm relieved we don't have to crouch on the floor. I don't know how he got hold of this van so fast."

"Allan knows people," Olivia said. "Sounds like serious subterfuge. Has something happened?"

"Your mom had one of her bad feelings. She told us to git, and we're gittin' right now. Listen, Livie, I can't talk long, and I have a lot to pass on. So don't ask questions until I'm finished, okay?"

"Understood," Olivia said.

"Allan got me this disposable cell phone. When the minutes are gone, we dump the phone. I'm not even sure where he is taking us, but it doesn't matter. He just wants to get us away from the ravenous press, especially Binnie Sloan, may she rot in . . . never mind, waste of time.

"Here's the scoop: Wade is being arraigned for murder, possibly as we speak." Stacey's next words were muffled, but Olivia told herself her friend was probably trying to calm her kids' reactions to their dad's arrest. "Okay, I'm back. That hammer the police found in the band shell? It had Trevor Lane's blood on it. Most of it was washed off, but I guess there was still blood in some cracks, enough to test. It was Wade's hammer, the one he always used at Struts & Bolts Garage. Wade claims it disappeared right before the murder, and

Struts backed him up. The police found Wade's prints on the handle, smudged but identifiable. That's all I know. Tell Maddie I'm sorry. It looks like we won't be able to make her engagement party."

"When you are back home with all of this behind you, we three will celebrate," Olivia said. "Meanwhile, Maddie and I will do whatever we can to help. It's possible somebody killed Trevor with Wade's hammer and somehow managed to preserve Wade's fingerprints."

"I'd like to believe that," Stacey said with a long sigh. "But when Wade is drinking, he can be really dumb. I could see him losing it, killing Trevor, and forgetting to wipe off his own prints. Anyway, thanks for your support and . . . you know. Oh, and before my phone croaks, I have a bit of information to pass along. I called my friend Susie at Twiterton High and asked about Jennifer Elsworth. No such name appeared in the school records, and no one who fits her description graduated from Twiterton High when Jennifer would have, or even the following year. However, here's a wrinkle you might find interesting." Stacey's voice disappeared again.

Olivia took advantage of the break to whisper the information about Jennifer to

Maddie.

"I'd better be quick," Stacey said. "Allan says we're almost there, wherever 'there' is. Susie told me there was a Jennie who dropped out of Twiterton High after her junior year. She'd just turned eighteen, so the school didn't follow up very well. Jennie had a rough life. She hadn't made it to school on picture day since middle school, so there's no photo in their high school records. Susie asked around the office and found someone who remembers Jennie vaguely. She was a pretty girl, blond, bright, but very quiet. Missed a lot of school even before she dropped out. Her mom was an addict. Jennie sort of became the grown-up who took care of the house and her mom. Her dad was out of the picture, walked out when Jennie was about eleven.

"Here's the real interesting part, Livie: Jennie had an older half sister who was what they used to call "slow." Susie didn't know much about the older girl because she didn't attend school. There was a rumor Susie didn't have time to follow up on. The older half sister died when Jennifer was young, maybe about nine — apparently, that part is fact. The rumor part is she was murdered."

"Really? Did Susie mention any suspects?"

Olivia saw Maddie's eyes widen at the mention of suspects.

"Nope, that's all I've got."

"Thanks, Stacey. Unless Jennifer connects up with Trevor's murder, I'll probably leave her past alone. After all, she did sell the red mixer for us."

"Seriously, that thing has been hogging your shelf since you first opened the store. Must be quite a relief to have it off your hands."

"Words cannot express . . . Anyway, hang in there, my friend. You're in good hands. Maddie and I will do what we can from this end. Keep those rabid press hounds at bay."

"I can handle them," Stacey said. "If they go after my kids, I'll make them wish they hadn't."

Olivia realized she'd been checking her watch, on average, every five minutes. More customers might help distract her from her worries about Stacey and her family, but so far only the curious had stopped by. Olivia had sent Bertha to join Maddie in the kitchen to help with the decorating. Bertha was delighted with her new assignment. If she were a smart businesswoman, Olivia told herself, she would send Jennifer home. But something stopped her. Despite the paucity of customers, Jennifer kept busy, industriously dusting all the shelves, the cookbooks, even the individual cookie cutters hanging in mobiles around the room. To a casual observer, Jennifer might appear calm, but Olivia thought her single-minded focus had a frantic quality.

On impulse, Olivia poked her head into the kitchen. Maddie had just removed a sheet of rosewater cookies from the oven. For a moment, the sweet floral fragrance helped soothe Olivia's jitters. *Who needs meditation when there are cookies fresh from the oven?*

"Bertha," Olivia said, "would you mind filling in on the sales floor for a bit? I just want to confer with Maddie."

"Of course." Bertha capped her pastry bag of royal icing and left.

Maddie set the cookie sheet on a cooling rack. "What's up? Did you think of someone to investigate, I hope? Because much as I love baking and decorating, this is getting a bit old. I could use a little distraction. Plus, I was thinking we ought to clear up this murder thing before my engagement party. It could seriously get in the way of Lucas and me being the center of attention tomorrow. Or is that selfish and callous?"

"No comment," Olivia said, laughing for

the first time since breakfast. "How about a breather from the baking? I need some computer magic."

"Sure. In fact, I declare the baking finished. More or less. I made a couple extra batches, just in case. We do have to complete the decorating and assemble the cookie cake . . . assuming our organic rose petals ever arrive. The company did call, by the way, to tell us there'd been a delay, but we should be getting the package this afternoon." Maddie washed flour off her hands, and asked, "What would you like my dancing keyboard fingers to ferret out for you?"

"First, I don't want anyone to know what you're doing, so keep the screen out of sight," Olivia said. "I'm frustrated. We have bits and pieces, but they don't add up to much. Nothing leads anywhere. This is just a hunch, but see if you can track down anything about —" Olivia paused to peek out at the sales area. Jennifer was helping a customer, and Bertha had taken over the dusting. "Let's move out of earshot." She led Maddie to the storage cabinet at the far end of the kitchen.

"Ooh, clandestine research," Maddie said. "How exciting."

"As I said, I might be way off base, only the dates are suggestive." Olivia spoke softly,

aware that Jennifer was in the store. "Remember what Stacey said about 'Jennie'?
The girl she thought might be Jennifer? She
said there was an older sister who might
have been murdered when 'Jennie' was
about nine. I think that was about the time
Trevor and Dougie were juniors or seniors
in high school."

"And Howie, too, though he was a couple
years younger," Maddie said. "So you're
looking for a possible connection between
those guys and this Jennie's older sister?
Yeah, that's a long shot. Yet somehow
intriguing." Maddie rubbed her hands
together in gleeful anticipation. "You tell
Bertha to keep Jennifer busy on the sales
floor, so she won't pop into the kitchen."

When Olivia returned, Maddie had turned
the laptop screen so it couldn't be seen by
someone entering the kitchen. After furi-
ously tapping for about thirty seconds, she
stopped and said, "Oops."

"Oops what?"

"I know it's masochistic, Livie, but I
requested an alert when Binnie Sloan
publishes one of her wretched blog posts.
I'm skimming her latest and . . . Oh my."

"Oh my *what*?"

"Short version," Maddie said. "Binnie
leads with a picture of Spunky snarling at

her, but the rest is way different from what I expected after this morning. She claims Spunky is merely reflecting the rage of his owner because she . . . that is, you . . . have been dumped."

"I have?"

"Yep, says so right here. Del finally dumped you, once and for all eternity, in favor of Jennifer. Okay, here's the scoop: Binnie found out about the hammer the police found in the band shell. She claims Stacey put it there to protect 'that useless drunk' Wade. Binnie's words, not mine."

"Somehow I guessed that," Olivia said.

"Del let Stacey leave town because, according to Binnie, he is too distracted with Jennifer to do his job as sheriff. Ooh, and here's the best part: Binnie speculates that Jennifer might be the real murderer. Jennifer and Trevor came to Chatterley Heights at about the same time. Jennifer came from Twiterton, as did Trevor originally. And Jennifer got a job with the sheriff's girlfriend, maybe to keep an eye on the sheriff *while she carried out her plan for cold, calculating revenge.'* I think Binnie has finally snapped."

"Finally?"

"Wow. Livie, listen to this: *'We suspect that Jennifer lured Trevor Lane to Chatterley*

Heights for her own secret reasons . . . a childhood crush, perhaps? Did the great Trevor Lane once brush her off like a gnat? Did he do so again after returning to his ancestral home? And has he paid for it with his life?' "

"Ancestral home?" Olivia leaned against the kitchen counter so she could keep an eye on the door. Something about Binnie Sloan's bizarre assertions sparked Olivia's curiosity. If she could only figure out —

"Livie? This is planet Earth hailing your ship. Please tell me you don't believe anything Binnie says."

"Hm? Oh no, of course not. Binnie is speculating wildly, as always, but . . . well, why isn't she making up a nasty fictional story about *us*?"

"I'm okay with that, really I am." Maddie sounded confused, verging on impatient. "Are you saying you feel slighted because Binnie is picking on Jennifer more than you? Because I'm thinking gratitude makes a lot more sense."

Olivia began to pace around the kitchen table, hoping her thoughts would fall into logical order. "Okay, we — that is, you and I, Mom, Spunky, even Bertha — humiliated Binnie, and she vowed vengeance. After that, she wrote a blog post that rehashed

313

her earlier innuendos about Del and Jennifer. Old news, no one cares. Then she singled out Jennifer and accused her of 'cold and calculating' murder. That strikes me as very strange. It doesn't make sense." Olivia pulled a chair next to Maddie, angled so she would notice if the kitchen door began to open. "I think Binnie is privy to information we haven't discovered yet," she said. "Either she has been scouring the Internet, or she's getting information from someone else. You and I need to do some serious dot-connecting."

"Cool." Maddie flexed her fingers. "My computer skills are at your command."

"See if you can find any evidence that Trevor, Dougie, Howie, and Jennifer are all linked to one another in some way, perhaps in their teenaged past. Besides the fact that they're all from Twiterton, that is."

"Jennifer is a lot younger than the guys," Maddie said. "She wouldn't have gone to school with them."

"True, but what about her older half sister? Stacey mentioned she didn't attend school because she was 'slow,' but it's an angle worth investigating. I really want to know how she died. I'd also like to know more about the tensions among the three men, especially post–high school. While you're at it, hack into my email and see if Allan sent an email about Howie."

"I'd love to," Maddie said. "Have you changed your password?"

"Haven't had time."

"Well, it isn't hacking if I know the password. It won't be as much fun."

"I think I'll have a chat with Jennifer. I'll have Bertha watch the sales floor, so you'll be alone in here."

Jennifer was ringing up a sale when Olivia joined her at the register. As the customer left with her package, Olivia said, "We seem to be short on customers today."

Jennifer smiled, but her deep green eyes were unreadable.

"Why don't you and I straighten the cookbook nook for a while?" Olivia said, leading the way into the nook. "Bertha can keep an eye on the sales floor, in case a customer wanders in by mistake. Honestly, I don't know what's happened to Chatterley Heights. You'd think we'd be swarmed with curious citizens, what with a murder and the press descending on us this morning."

"I wondered about that, too. Maybe they're saving their appetites for the party tomorrow." Jennifer rescued a bouquet-shaped cookie cutter from under the bookcase, where it had bounced during Binnie's destructive exit from the cookbook nook. As Jennifer ran her finger over a new dent in the top edge, her pale eyebrows drew together in an angry frown.

"Or maybe they're too busy emailing each other and reading blogs to sate their curiosity about this morning's drama in The Gingerbread House. You know what outlandish stories find their way online."

With a slight shake of her head, Jennifer said, "I'm afraid I'm out of step with my peers. I don't have a computer, so I don't use the Internet much. My cell phone has Internet access, but I rarely use it, and I have no interest at all in blogs. Cookie cutters are much more fun."

"I agree," Olivia said. "You are very knowledgeable about cookie cutters. Did your mother teach you?"

For the first time since Jennifer's arrival at The Gingerbread House, Olivia saw a genuine smile light her face. "Oh yes," Jennifer said, "my mother loved cookie cutters. We had lots of them, all passed down from my grandmother and great-grandmother. My mother told us about the cutters while we baked."

Jennifer had said "us," yet had made no mention of any possible siblings. Much as she wanted to ask directly, Olivia was afraid Jennifer would shut down. Instead, Olivia asked, "Does your mother still have all those cutters?"

"No, she . . ." Jennifer's smile faded. "My mother passed away. I'm keeping the collection of cutters packed away for now."

Hoping to lighten the mood, Olivia asked, "You lived in Twiterton as a child, didn't you? Was it as gossipy as most small towns?"

Jennifer hesitated for only a moment. "Yes, I suppose so," she said. "I do remember my mother complained that everyone was into everyone else's business. She was a very private person."

Olivia took a bound notebook and pen from a locked drawer in an antique bureau. "Since it's so quiet, let's do a little inventory, shall we? I like to keep track of stock in the cookbook nook, since customers are often alone in here. Not that I don't trust my customers."

"It's smart to be careful," Jennifer said with an edge in her voice. "People can't always be trusted."

Olivia handed the notebook and pen to Jennifer. "I'll rearrange the cookbooks in alphabetical order, and you can mark them off on the inventory list." They had worked through the A's and B's before Olivia said, casually, "I don't know many folks from Twiterton. I can only think of one who lives here in Chatterley Heights. He works at the bank. His name is Howie . . . Howie Upton, I think. Do you know him?"

Jennifer dropped her pen and bent down to pick it up. "The name doesn't sound familiar," she said, focusing on the inventory list. "I haven't had a chance to open an account yet. Anyway, I was a kid when we left Twiterton."

"Why did you decide to move to Chatterley Heights instead of back home?"

"Twiterton isn't the town I remember. Now it's more of a bedroom community," she said, responding with ease and confidence. "I wanted more of a small-town feel."

"Well, you've come to the right place," Olivia said. "I guess that's why I'm a bit of a small-town gossip myself. I am so curious about Trevor Lane and Dougie Adair. I know they were both from Twiterton."

With a light laugh, Jennifer said, "I can understand your curiosity, given what's happened. I honestly can't tell you anything about them. They were a lot older than I was. All I ever heard was that Trevor and Dougie played football."

Since Jennifer sounded more relaxed, Olivia decided to dig a little deeper. "If my experience is any clue, high school football heroes leave a mark for years. I remember seeing our school corridors lined with trophies and photos of quarterbacks. And, of course, there were photos of prom kings and queens, who were usually football players and cheerleaders."

"Oh yeah," Jennifer said. "I heard Trevor Lane was a big football hero, even after he left town. Especially after people found out he'd become an actor."

"I'm amazed that he and Dougie Adair maintained their friendship over all these years."

Jennifer was marking off cookbook names as if she'd done inventory her whole life. "I'm not positive that Trevor and Dougie are such great friends," she said.

"Really?"

Jennifer's pen froze in midair. "I don't know for sure, you understand, only it seemed to me that Trevor hogged the spotlight, and I don't think Dougie Adair was very happy about that. I mean, when they were here in the store. That's what I heard, anyway."

Was Jennifer in the store when Trevor, Dougie, and Lenora were holding court? I thought she hadn't shown up for work. "You could be right," Olivia said carefully. "Trevor

319

did seem to outshine his companions." Olivia sneaked a peek at Jennifer's profile as she made quick work of the cookbook inventory. The shy softness of her mouth had tightened. She looked nervous . . . or angry.

"We've got to stop meeting like this," Olivia said. Maddie barely smiled, she was so engrossed in her computer search. "Bertha is back on the sales floor keeping Jennifer busy. I had an interesting and revealing conversation with Jennifer."

"Uh-huh," Maddie said without taking her eyes from the screen.

"While we were talking, a herd of performing rhinoceroses entered the store. They want us to do a circus-themed cookie party under a big top."

"Aha!" Maddie leaped up from her chair and did a little celebration dance.

"Why do I suspect your joy has nothing to do with the rhinoceroses?" Olivia glanced at the screen but had no idea what she was looking at.

"You're seeing rhinoceroses?"

"Never mind," Olivia said. "What have you found?"

Maddie plopped onto her chair and pointed to the computer screen. "Somebody scanned this newspaper article and posted it online. It's an old article, wrinkled and yellowed, so it's blurry in spots. However, since my eyes are two months younger than yours, I can read it to you. Pull up a chair. We don't want curious ears to hear this."

Olivia peeked out to the sales floor and was pleased to see three customers. Bertha was showing one woman their extensive array of sanding sugars, while Jennifer explained a variety of decorating tools to the other two. "All quiet on the sales front," Olivia said as she moved a kitchen chair next to Maddie at the computer.

"Mostly I found bits and pieces of information, which I'll go over in a minute," Maddie said. "But this is the mother lode. This piece appears to be cut from the *Twiterton Times* weekly newspaper, a 1993 edition. The rest of the date isn't legible. However, we can gather from the content that it probably was published in late May. The article is about the death of Melissa Nortenson, and it mentions she had a younger sister. I don't see the sister's name, though."

"So in 1993 . . ." Olivia did a quick calculation. "If Jennifer told the truth during her interview, she is now twenty-eight years old, which means she was about nine in 1993. Supposedly, that's when Jennie's half sister died."

"Yep," Maddie said. "So I'll bet you another red mixer that your brother was right: Jennie Nortenson and Jennifer Elsworth are indeed one and the same. She attended Twiterton High at least through junior year, so she couldn't have left town before about 2000 or 2001."

"Interesting." Olivia mentioned Jennifer's comment that, during their recent visit to The Gingerbread House, Trevor had "hogged the spotlight," and Dougie was unhappy about it. "I wonder if someone told Jennifer about it, or if she really was in the crowd somewhere," Olivia said. "She's been insisting that she didn't know Trevor or Dougie at all, but clearly she knew *about* them."

"I sure didn't see her during the event, but it was awfully crowded," Maddie said. "She wouldn't have been in high school when they were, but she might have heard about them. Why would Jennifer want to hide the fact she went to Twiterton High?"

Olivia stretched to loosen a tight shoulder muscle. "Perhaps to keep her identity a secret." She squinted at the fuzzy print on the computer screen. "I wonder who posted this piece. It looks choppy, as if someone cut it apart and reassembled it, maybe to delete specific information. If your eyes are so great, tell me what it says."

"Sure, but first, about how this piece got itself posted . . ." Maddie clicked away and scrolled through some unintelligible information. "It's sort of like an anonymous website. Whoever did this knew what he or she was doing. This involved skilled programming. The identifying information is encrypted. I can't figure out where it was sent from."

"Jennifer just told me she doesn't use the Internet," Olivia said.

"Then either she's lying, or someone else did this. I'm good, but not good enough to translate all this stuff. We'd need a younger computer genius with a more extensive skill set than even I possess. However, I can tell you what the article says, minus a few unintelligible words."

"I'll settle for that," Olivia said. "But use your low-energy voice, just in case."

"I'll be positively pooped," Maddie said. "In fact, to save energy, I'll simply summarize this article for you. Anyway, it's too sad to read word for word. Melissa Nortenson, age sixteen, was found dead at the base of a cliff not far from Twiterton. Cause of death was a broken neck. Foul play not ruled out but no viable suspects were identified. Some unnamed persons were questioned but apparently had alibis. Bruising on the arms and wrists suggests a possible struggle. Victim described as a pretty redhead with limited mental capacity. Due to the latter, she did not attend the local high school but was homeschooled."

"Homeschooled," Olivia said. "By her addict mother and nine-year-old sister?"

"Don't be hasty, Livie, we don't actually know that the mother was an addict at the time of Melissa's death."

"Good point." Olivia thought about how she would feel if she had a daughter whose life was cut short in such an ugly way. "I suppose the addiction might have followed the death of her daughter. Or she returned to a habit she had kicked earlier, maybe for the sake of her children."

Maddie stared at the screen for a few moments. "We keep hearing about Melissa's 'slowness' or 'mental incapacity.' What if her mother was hooked on drugs when she had Melissa, then kicked the habit when she realized how her child had been affected? That might explain why Jennifer seems quite intelligent."

"Makes sense," Olivia said. "Grief led the mother back to drugs, and her younger, healthier daughter became her caregiver. Poor woman."

"Poor Jennifer." Maddie closed the computer screen.

"Stacey's friend said Jennifer had a half sister," Olivia said. "So the father who left after his wife turned back to drugs might have been —"

"Jennifer's father!" Maddie clapped her hand over her mouth. "Oops. Sorry, too much energy." Settling back in her chair, Maddie skimmed the text again. "An unnamed younger sister is mentioned, but that's all."

"Which makes me wonder if Jennifer might have posted this piece herself."

Maddie shrugged. "Because she isn't identified by name? I've never seen Jennifer go near a computer, so I can't judge her skill level. She could be a genius hacker for all I know and lying about her abilities. On the other hand, maybe she had help with this post."

"The real question," Olivia said, "is *why*? What did she, or possibly someone else, hope to accomplish by posting this anonymous piece about Melissa's death?"

"Perhaps she hopes someone out there knows her sister was murdered and by whom." Maddie slumped back in her chair and stared at the screen. "Here's the odd part. There's no way to post comments. Maybe this was meant as a warning to one person. 'I know what you did. . . .' You know, to flush out a suspect."

"How would it reach the suspects?"

Maddie laughed. "Easy, the same way folks download malware. You hack into address books and send an email with a link in it to all the people on the list. The email looks like it's coming from a friend, so some recipients won't think twice about clicking on the link. *Et voyeur,* you've downloaded something nasty to your computer." Maddie frowned. "I didn't get that French phrase right, did I?"

"I don't keep you around for your expertise in French," Olivia said.

"Thanks ever so much."

Olivia's mind was spinning with too many possibilities. "If Jennifer had anything to do with this post, maybe Binnie is on to something. I can't believe I said that."

"There's no way Jennifer could have carried Trevor to our porch."

"I know," Olivia said.

"Do you think she had help? Dougie could have carried him. Or Howie, or Wade? Or maybe all of them?"

"I'm not sure I —"

"Ooh, maybe it was like that short story we read in English class. Remember, Livie? There was this lottery, and everyone in the village had to take a number . . . I forget the rest. Anyway, maybe Jennifer, Dougie, and Howie are all in on it together, and they picked straws to see who would kill Trevor. Maybe they picked Wade as the fall guy because he's such an obvious suspect with an obvious motive."

"Down, girl," Olivia said. "No more sugar for you."

Maddie hopped out of her seat as if her energy had reached the point of explosion. "I think better on dancing feet." She executed a quick spin toward the worktable. "If I may take a leap of logic," she said, "what if Jennifer suspected Trevor had something to do with Melissa's death? What if that post was also sent to Trevor personally as a warning that she was on to him? What if Trevor tracked Jennifer down and trekked all the way to Chatterley Heights, um . . . to buy her off or something? I'm running out of what-ifs."

"Thank goodness."

"Fine, let's hear your theory," Maddie said as she began to pack up the remaining cooled and decorated cookies for the party.

"I don't have a clear theory yet." Olivia

stood up and stretched. "However, I do think you've done a good job of identifying the suspects in Trevor's murder. I'd still add Wade Harald to the list. And yes, we need to consider the possibility that two or more of them cooperated in the murder."

"As long as my brilliance is recognized," Maddie said. "Oh, and I almost forgot." With no apparent effort, she accessed Olivia's account. "As requested . . ."

Olivia took Maddie's place and read Allan's email:

Livie, here's the scoop on Howie Upton. He wasn't simply laid off. He was fired from his investment job for suspected insider trading. Howie hid his tracks well. My buddy said the firm was in a bind. They suspected Howie had set up a coworker to look like the guilty party, but they couldn't prove it. So they ended up just firing both of them, but neither was prosecuted. That's why Howie was able to get a teller job at the bank. The other guy wasn't so lucky. He shot himself. Hope this helps.

Love, Allan

By the way, our mutual friends are in good hands.

"I assume you read this?" Olivia asked.

"I did. Sobering."

Olivia deleted Allan's message and closed the computer lid.

"So, what's next?" Maddie asked. "More computer searches?"

"Did you look for any other references to Melissa Nortenson's death?" Olivia asked.

"I meant to dig deeper for that," Maddie said as she opened the laptop. "Thanks for reminding me." Her fingers bounced around the keyboard at a dizzying pace. "Ah, this looks like a good one. It's from the *Baltimore Sun,* a few weeks after Melissa's death."

Olivia drew her chair closer. "Good choice. This discusses the investigation. Looks like the police hit a brick wall until . . ." She pointed to a paragraph near the end. "Can you read this?"

"Oh. My. God. Trevor Lane was a suspect. I knew it! This could be the connection we've been looking for," Maddie said. "A classmate claimed to have seen him with Melissa earlier in the evening. The classmate isn't named."

"Not surprising," Olivia said. "I see that Trevor was questioned and released due to lack of physical evidence, plus a friend, also unnamed, came forward to give him an alibi."

"Do you think the friend was Dougie?" Maddie's mood had sobered. "I sort of liked Dougie. Would he lie for Trevor?"

"Probably. If he did, that lie might have secured a lifetime job for him." Despite the warmth in the kitchen, Olivia shivered.

"Golly."

Olivia glanced up at the kitchen clock. "We close in two hours. How ready are we for the party tomorrow afternoon?"

"We have baked and decorated with superhuman speed, so we're nearly finished. The cookie cake is ready for assembly, which will be a snap. All we'll need is a small batch of royal icing to glue the cookies together in a pyramid. Oh, and we need those rose petals, though I'm beginning to lose hope. If they don't arrive in the next —"

As if on cue, they heard a tentative knock on the kitchen door, and Bertha poked her head inside. "Snoop — I mean, Sam Parnell is here with a package for you, Maddie. I tried to get it away from him, but he insisted it's his duty as a representative of the United States Postal Service to deliver important packages in person. What should I do with him?"

"Knock him on the head, tie his hands, gag him, and lock him in the inventory closet," Maddie said with unseemly glee.

"Only don't damage the package."

Bertha's lips parted, but no words emerged.

"Tempting," Olivia said, "but impractical. There isn't much room in the closet, and Sam might mess with the inventory. You'd better bring him into the kitchen. Thanks, Bertha."

Bertha nodded and withdrew. Olivia heard a distinct giggle before the door shut.

Olivia shot a stern glance at her friend. "Have you gotten those snarky impulses out of your system, Maddie? Because we don't need Sam on the warpath more than he already is."

Maddie smiled in a way that wasn't entirely reassuring. "Just girlish high spirits," she said. "Or maybe wedding nerves. Take your pick. And don't look at me like that, Livie. I'll be good."

Before Olivia could respond, Sam barged into the kitchen as if a stove had caught fire and he was rushing in to save the womenfolk. "My shift's over," Sam said in a nasal whine that made everything sound like a complaint. "I volunteered to drop off this Express Mail delivery on my way home. I figured it was important for your little shindig tomorrow." He held a white box with a blue stripe tightly against his chest. When

Olivia reached toward the package, Sam took a step back and sniffed the air. Focusing on a cooking rack covered with decorated cookies, he said, "Smells good in here. I got a shift tomorrow afternoon, so I won't be able to make it to your little get-together. I sure hate to miss those cookies."

Olivia exchanged a quick glance with Maddie. "We can fix that, Sam. Why not have a cookie now? We've made plenty of extras. Have a seat, and I'll pour you a cup of coffee." Olivia emptied the last of the coffee into a clean cup and placed it on the kitchen table.

"Don't mind if I do." Sam scraped a chair over to the table and sat down. The smug grin on his face made Olivia uneasy. When Sam was in a good mood, it usually meant he was about to deliver unsettling gossip.

Maddie plunked two cookies on a plate and clattered it on the table near Sam. He picked up a fuchsia-striped wedding cake, and said, "I suppose you're all in a tizzy about that party. Women get so worked up over these things."

Maddie and Olivia were standing on either side of Sam's chair. They locked eyes over his head. Maddie's expression said, *May I tear him limb from limb now?* Sam squirmed in his seat as if he sensed the silent communication between the two friends. He scooped up the second cookie, scraped back his chair, and stood up. "Well, gotta get going," he said. Leaving a nearly full coffee cup, Sam took a step toward the kitchen door, hesitated, and turned around to face the women. "I'm surprised to find you two acting so calm, like nothing is wrong," he said. "I mean, considering the trouble your friend is in."

Olivia's body tensed, but she tried not to show it. "I have a number of friends," she said.

"Only one of them's on the run, though, right?" Sam's thin lips formed what Olivia supposed was a grin. His crooked front teeth peeked through. "Looks like she's as guilty as that no-good drunken husband of hers."

Stacey? Guilty? Olivia clenched her teeth to keep herself from screaming at Sam. She heard Maddie's light gasp. From Sam's expression, he'd heard it, too.

"Yeah," Sam said, "from what I hear, the police found that cookie cutter. You know, the one the killer used to brand that actor fellow? Everybody knows all about that. No use trying to keep secrets around here. Stacey Harald should know that better than anybody."

Olivia knew Sam wanted to hear her beg for details, and she so wanted to deprive him of that pleasure. But she needed to know. "I hadn't heard," she said.

With a disdainful snicker, Sam said, "Women. They get into a habit and don't bother to think. Looks like Wade's faithful ex-wife ran that cookie cutter through the dishwasher to get rid of the fingerprints and blood and all. Guess she figured that would fix everything. Silly woman. Her dishwasher didn't quite do the job. Must be an old dishwasher." With the exquisite timing of a born gossip, Sam nodded to them and slipped through the door to the sales floor. As he closed the door behind him, Olivia could hear his whiny chortle.

CHAPTER SIXTEEN

After Del's cell phone sent Olivia to voice mail for the third time, she gave up. "Doesn't anyone answer their phones anymore? I thought cell phones were supposed to keep us all connected twenty-four/seven." Olivia hit a key on the kitchen laptop just to see it wake up. "I can't get ahold of my mom or Allan, the police department sends me to 911. . . . How am I supposed to find out if Sam was fibbing about Stacey? I can't believe our Stacey would try to destroy evidence."

"Down, girl," Maddie said. "Stacey wouldn't be dumb enough to put evidence through the dishwasher and leave it there for the police to find." Maddie opened a kitchen drawer and took out her own cell. Punching in a speed-dial code, she said, "I'm trying Lucas's cell. Drat, it went right to voice mail. Really, he should bear in mind that his bride-to-be might be desperate to reach him."

"Where is everybody?" Olivia plopped down on the chair at the kitchen desk. "I feel like I'm in one of those movies where everyone on earth vaporizes, and we're the only ones left."

"Whoa," Maddie said. "That sounds like something I'd say."

"Okay, let's pull ourselves together," Olivia said. "A plan. We need a plan if we're going to save Stacey from being railroaded for murder." Olivia pawed through the desk drawer until she found a small notebook and a pen. The pen was dry, which irritated her beyond all reason.

"I agree, we need a plan," Maddie said as she handed Olivia a working pen, "if only to keep you from imploding."

"Sorry. It's Sam. I'm mad at myself for letting him annoy me."

"You aren't alone," Maddie said. "Remember, Sam practices his craft all day, like we practice creative cookie baking. That's how you get good at something. Say, I don't suppose we could make Snoopy Sam look good for Trevor's murder?"

"What an uplifting thought, but no. We'd only waste precious time." Olivia flipped through her notebook until she found a clean page.

"You could work a lot faster at the computer," Maddie said.

"I know, but sometimes I focus better with a pen in my hand. Plus there's the satisfaction of ripping out a page and balling it up."

"I get that." While Maddie cleaned the kitchen, Olivia wrote. When she'd finished, she tore out the page, and said, "Okay, Maddie, read through this and tell me if I've left anything off."

Maddie hitched herself up onto the kitchen counter and began to read the notes Olivia handed her.

"These aren't in any particular order, and I listed motives next to the names." While Maddie read through it, Olivia continued scribbling in her notebook.

- Trevor Lane: Why did he come to Chatterley Heights? Did he kill Jennifer's sister, Melissa? (He was questioned and released.)
- Dougie Adair works for Trevor, but doesn't seem to like him much. He could have been Trevor's alibi for Melissa's murder. Why did he come to Chatterley Heights with Trevor?
- Wade Harald: Trevor and Dougie got him kicked off his high school football team, which seems to have ruined his

life. His hammer killed Trevor. But he isn't someone who plans ahead. He argued with Trevor, Dougie, and Howie in the band shell — what about?

- Howie Upton clearly hated Trevor, who picked on him in high school and beyond. Howie is a financial genius who lost everything due to accusations of insider trading. Did he know Melissa? Does he know Jennifer? Might he be helping Jennifer search for her sister's killer?
- Jennifer Elsworth/Nortenson/ Whatever: She lied about when she left Twiterton and seems to have known Trevor better than she is willing to admit. Did her move to Chatterley Heights have something to do with her sister's death? Has she been searching online for her sister's killer?
- Stacey in cahoots with Wade: Ignoring for the moment that a gavel cookie cutter turned up in her dishwasher, Stacey has no motive for killing Trevor. However, her loyalty to her family might be a motive for trying to help Wade by planting the murder weapon in the band shell while he was in custody. (Improbable if Stacey remained in hiding.)

Maddie pondered a moment. "Trevor wasn't what I'd call a likable guy. I suppose someone we don't know might have hated him enough to follow him to Chatterley Heights. Maybe this stranger stayed out of sight and waited for an opportunity to kill him?"

"That assumes Wade Harald was set up," Olivia said, "which is possible. But a stranger would have to know that Wade had reason to hate Trevor, that Wade worked at Struts & Bolts, and which hammer was his . . . among other coincidences too complicated to mention."

"Well, if you're going to use logic . . ." Maddie hopped off the kitchen counter and began to pace. "From this list, it seems to me Wade has the only real motive for the murder. Trevor ruined Wade's chance to be a football hero, and his life has been going downhill lately."

"Exactly," Olivia said. "We know very little about Trevor's past with Dougie and Howie. Dougie has been loyal, but maybe he carries hidden resentments."

"And Howie seems like a guy who collects resentments," Maddie said.

Olivia tore another page she'd been writing on from her notebook and handed it to Maddie. "We need to do some targeted

research. We don't have much time, so ef-
ficiency is the word of the day." She tapped
the top of her pen against her cheek.

"Livie, you are so in your element. You
come up with the ideas, and then I do my
thing on the computer." Maddie pushed the
start button on the dishwasher.

"I'm thinking we'll need to do some quick
fieldwork."

"Goody, a trip to Chatterley Paws," Maddie said. "You read this to me." She handed
back Olivia's notes. "I need caffeine and
sugar to nurture my brain cells."

While Maddie started a pot of coffee and
sneaked a few cookies from the extras for
the engagement party, Olivia read through
her list out loud:

- What kept Dougie and Trevor linked
  together all these years?
- What is the real story behind Dougie's
  wife's suicide?
- Did Howie Upton have any reason to
  hate Trevor, aside from the fact that
  Trevor teased and taunted him?
- Why were Howie, Trevor, and Dougie
  in the band shell the night of Trevor's
  murder?
- Did Trevor know that Howie was accused of insider trading?

- Are the murders of Melissa Nortenson and Trevor Lane related?
- Why did Jennifer disappear from the store when Trevor and Dougie showed up?
- Who has been breaking into Chatterley Heights businesses, and why? Do the break-ins connect in any way with the murder?

"Okay, what do you think of this list? Anything we should add?" Olivia handed her notebook and pen to Maddie.

"Looks like a lot of work to me," Maddie said as she skimmed through the list. "Interesting work, though. Give me some time, I'll see what I can come up with." Maddie began to scribble rapidly. "This is why I use a computer," she said. "Pens run out of ink without any warning." She tossed the pen aside and switched to the computer.

Olivia felt impatient and very anxious for news about Stacey. She longed to corner suspects and shake information out of them. But she knew it wouldn't work. They needed cool heads and, of course, a plan of action. Olivia drained her coffee and finished off a cookie, which only increased her agitation. Settling at her desk, Olivia tried to remember what her mom had taught her about calming and centering her mind. Wasn't she supposed to breathe deeply or something? She tried it. Her heart rate slowed a bit, and her chattering mind grew quieter, quieter. . . .

"Livie, how can you nap at a time like this?"

Olivia's head jerked upright. "I was meditating."

"Well, don't do it again. Meditation makes you cranky."

"I couldn't agree more," Olivia said. "Get back to work." Her eyes closed of their own accord.

"Livie, wake up. You can catch up on sleep later."

"What time is it?"

"You were snoozing for about twenty minutes," Maddie said. "Did you know that you snore?"

"Do not."

Maddie grinned. "Okay, I lied, but I had you going there. I hope you're refreshed, because it's planning time." She thrust the laptop computer toward Olivia. "These are my additions to the list. I think you'll agree I can pull my weight in this sleuthing caper."

- What's with the gavel cookie cutter brand on Trevor's cheek, and the

342

cookie in his mouth? Symbolic of justice and humiliation? Are they false clues? Just plain mean? Really, why bother? And where did the cookie cutter come from?

- Did Wade sneak the gavel cookie cutter into the dishwasher when Stacey wasn't looking? (Assuming Snoopy's rumor was true, which it probably isn't.) Stacey is sharp. If she knew the incriminating cookie cutter was in the dishwasher, she'd have taken it out before she left the house unattended. Wade, however, would be dumb enough to forget about it.
- How did Trevor's body get onto The Gingerbread House porch? Wouldn't that take two people? Or one really strong man? And why our porch? (Again, Wade is an idiot, so he might not think about the risks.)
- Is someone feeding rumors to Binnie Sloan's blog?
- How did Melissa Nortenson really die?

"These are terrific questions," Olivia said, scanning Maddie's additions. "Now comes the really hard part: How do we find the answers to these questions in a very short time? Your engagement party is tomorrow afternoon."

"As it happens, I know the answer to the last question," Maddie said. "I found another online mention of Melissa's death. It's a site that caters to aficionados of old, unsolved mysteries, so I can't vouch for its accuracy. Bearing that in mind, the blogger says that Melissa was mildly brain damaged, as we've heard. She was also very pretty and rather free with her favors, though only if she liked the boy. Melissa died in 1993 from a broken neck. She was found at the base of a cliff by her nine-year-old sister, Jennie, who had slipped out of the house early that morning to find her older sister before their parents discovered her absence."

"That poor child." Olivia felt her limbs go limp as she imagined the young girl finding the lifeless body of her beloved older sister. "It sounds as if Melissa made a habit of meeting boys in secret."

"Apparently," Maddie said. "Here's the really interesting part. . . . There was only one response to the original post. The response said that two high school boys were questioned in connection with the murder. Their names were withheld because neither was charged. There wasn't enough evidence, although both had been seen several times in Melissa's company."

"Interesting," Olivia said. "So . . . Trevor and Dougie? Of course, we can't assume this information is accurate."

"Nope. It's worth noting that I didn't find this information anywhere else. The newspapers reported Melissa's death as a possible homicide. Suspects were questioned and released."

"Any idea when the original post first appeared?"

"Good question," Maddie said with a grin. "Naturally, I have an answer. It was in 2008, on the fifteenth anniversary of Melissa Nortenson's death. Livie, what if Jennifer posted this along with that first article?"

"It's possible. . . ." Olivia sank back in her chair to think. "Thanks for tracking this down. You are officially a genius. This feels important, only I'm not yet sure what it means. Let's leave it to compost for now and go back to our notes."

Maddie scanned the questions, frowning. "We did leave Stacey completely off the suspect list. Is that wise?"

"Maybe not, but I'm assuming Del and Cody are investigating Stacey and Wade exhaustively. Our job is to create reasonable doubt." Olivia pointed to the reference regarding Snoopy Sam's rumor. "I'll bet I can get the answer to this one," she said.

"Give me a minute." Olivia flipped open her cell and speed-dialed Sheriff Del Jenkins. She was sent to voice mail yet again. "Hi, Del, it's me. I know you're busy, but I wanted you to know that Sam Parnell is going around town claiming that Stacey Harald tried to clean the gavel cookie cutter by running it through her dishwasher. Sam hinted the police found blood or something else on the cutter. Maybe in the seams? Del, please let me know if Sam is telling the truth, or if he is doing his usual hatchet job on an innocent friend of mine. This is really important to me. Call anytime; Maddie and I are just prepping cookies at breakneck speed for the extravaganza tomorrow. Any chance you can still come to the party with me? Thanks, Del. I miss you."

"Ooh, nicely played," Maddie said.

"I really do miss him."

"Well, of course you do. I meant the whole outraged-for-Stacey tone, plus the part about how we're baking and decorating cookies, rather than interfering in a police investigation. Think Del will fall for it?"

"Oh, he'll be suspicious," Olivia said with a light laugh. "But he won't leave me hanging. He knows how we feel about Stacey."

The kitchen door creaked, and Olivia instinctively sat on her notebook. "Who is it?" Olivia sounded more demanding than she'd intended.

"Livie? It's just me."

"Mom?"

The door wedged open, allowing Ellie Greyson-Meyers's slight form to slip into the kitchen. "I'm so sorry if I alarmed you two, but I knew how intensely focused you would be right now. I didn't want to startle you into squirting . . ." Ellie's gaze had taken in the table, cleared of all but a few drying cookies. "Are you . . . taking a break?"

"Mom, am I ever glad to see you." Olivia pulled out a kitchen chair, and said, "Sit."

Ellie sat as instructed. "I realize you are distracted, Livie, but have you perhaps confused me with Spunky?" Ellie had shed her power suit and liberated her hair, which hung loosely down her back. In her ankle-length calico skirt and long-sleeve knit top, she projected comfort and serenity.

"Don't be silly, Mom. Spunky isn't allowed in the kitchen. Although now that you mention it, you're both teeny tiny with hair that always needs trimming, and you both —"

"My, my, such a light, carefree attitude," Ellie said. "Does this mean you have solved the murder of Trevor Lane and saved your dear friend Stacey Harald from a life on the run?"

Olivia capitulated with an exaggerated sigh. "No, Mom, and we are running out of time before Maddie and Lucas's engagement party."

Maddie added, "It's not really about the party, Ellie. We won't feel much like celebrating with all of this still up in the air. So you've heard Snoopy Sam's latest rumor?"

"I have heard Sam's rumor," Ellie said, "and dismissed it."

Olivia's cell phone sang out the opening lines of "Chapel of Love" yet again. Olivia groaned.

"Sorry," Maddie said. "I promise I'll change that to something dirgelike."

As the tune began a second time, Olivia grabbed her cell and checked the caller ID. "It's Del," she whispered. "Hi, Del. Thanks for getting back to me so fast. I don't mean to be a pest, but —"

"Not possible, Livie. Anyway, I understand. You're worried about your friend and —" The blast of a car horn drowned out Del's words.

"Hey, are you driving? What have I told you about calling me when you're driving?" Olivia heard a distinctive snicker and glared at Maddie.

"That it makes you anxious, and I wouldn't want to make you anxious, would I?" Del said. "However, I reasoned that your anxiety about Stacey might be a wee bit stronger than your concerns about me driving while talking on my official police cell phone. It would be different if I were texting. Which I would never do except in a dire police emergency."

"Is there any other kind? But you're right: I'm worried about Stacey. Just try not to have an accident until I hear everything you learn. And next time, take a squad car so the other drivers slow down and pay attention."

"Yes, ma'am," Del said. "It's good to know you care. Now about that cookie cutter in her dishwasher. The rumor is partly true. We did find a gavel-shaped cookie cutter mixed in with a load of clean dishes in her dishwasher."

"Oh no! What about —"

"Don't panic yet, Livie. I said the rumor was only partly true, and Sam stretched it even more if he claimed there was blood in the seams."

"There wasn't any blood in the seams?" Olivia saw Maddie's face light up. "What else did he get wrong?"

"We aren't convinced it's the same cookie

cutter used to brand Trevor. I mean, it's definitely the exact same shape, and it looks well used. It had been cleaned but not by a dishwasher, at least not recently. We did find traces of dirt in the seams. We expected to see evidence that the edges had been exposed to heat and . . ."

Olivia guessed he was hesitant to say "flesh." "I get the point. Thanks, Del. So you think someone planted a second gavel cutter in Stacey's dishwasher? Wouldn't it have been more convincing to plant the real cookie cutter used to brand Trevor?"

"Probably," Del said. "Maybe he or she isn't knowledgeable about forensics."

Or has no respect for police competence . . .

"By the way, Livie, this will all be general knowledge soon, even though we tried to keep it under wraps. And before you assume we police are hard-hearted and manipulative, we did quietly let Stacey know the cookie cutter evidence looked bogus. She promised to keep quiet. Since you didn't know, and neither did Sam, Stacey must have kept her word."

"Of course she did," Olivia said.

"One more thing before I sign off," Del said. "We never released any information to the public about the cookie cutter in the dishwasher."

"But who would . . . ? Oh." The truth hit Olivia a second before Del confirmed it.

"Yep. We suspect that whoever sent that rumor into the world might be the person who murdered Trevor Lane. That part is just between you and me, Livie. Be careful."

"Any idea who passed the rumor on to Sam Parnell?"

"He claims he was sitting in the park reading the paper when he overheard someone on a cell phone. He couldn't describe the voice or remember the exact words used. He didn't look around to see who might have been speaking. All in all, Sam is a lousy witness, so it's anyone's guess what really happened."

"Or how much Sam embellished or made up," Olivia said.

"Or if someone fed him the informa—" The blast of a car horn drowned out the remainder of Del's comment. "Sorry, Livie, some idiot cut in front of me without a signal. Anyway, keep your ears open and do not take any chances."

"Will you make it to Bon Vivant tomorrow afternoon?"

"I plan to," Del said. "I'll probably be late, though. Don't worry about Stacey right now. Just focus on Maddie and Lucas's party. Okay?"

"Understood."

"Why don't I feel reassured?"

"Bye, Del."

CHAPTER SEVENTEEN

"Mom, are you sure you'll be okay minding the store?" Olivia asked as she and Maddie prepared to go AWOL during the workday.

"Of course, Livie. The store will be open for only a couple more hours. Bertha is here to manage things, and Jennifer will be there, too. I will probably have time to work on some decorations for the party tomorrow. Bertha said she and Jennifer will be alone in the store tomorrow morning, as well." Ellie said. "Shall I come in and help them?"

"Could you, Mom? You aren't skipping too many yoga classes, are you? You know what that does to you."

"I attended an extra class yesterday. I'm certain the customers will be safe in my presence."

Olivia gave her mother a grateful hug. "You're a lifesaver, Mom. Thanks."

"You may reward me with cookies," Ellie said with an impish grin.

"Done. Call if you need me, and definitely call if you hear anything about Stacey or . . ."

"Of course. You will be careful, won't you, Livie?"

"Don't fuss, Mom. We're going to chat with a few people, that's all."

"Well, I'm glad you're taking Spunky with you for protection."

When he heard his name, Spunky yapped and wriggled to free himself from Olivia's encircling arm. "I'll let you down as soon as we're outside, Spunks." Olivia was glad her mother felt comforted by the little Yorkie's protective persona, but Olivia was counting more on his charm. She had no intention of exposing her pooch to danger.

Ellie opened the kitchen's back door. Maddie poked her head out to check the alley behind the store. "All clear," she said. "No sign of Binnie . . . or of Ned's camera."

"Come on, team: time to roll." Olivia stepped into the alley. As soon as she lowered Spunky to the pavement, he tried to run. Olivia was familiar with his instinctive need to take off, so she kept a firm hand on his leash. She waited to hear her mother lock the door behind them before allowing Spunky to pull her down the alley.

"I already forgot," Maddie said, rushing

354

to keep up. "What's first on the agenda?"

"First, we avoid attention while we head for the car," Olivia said. "Then we drive to Chatterley Paws for an impromptu visit with Lenora Dove and her dear bereaved friend, Dougie Adair. While you were talking to Bertha about watching the store, I quickly called Gwen Tucker. She said Lenora and Dougie are watching an old movie on DVD, and she promised not to mention we were coming. Gwen warned me that Dougie is making noises about flying back to Los Angeles. I want to get to him first."

"Won't it look suspicious if he leaves town during a murder investigation?" Maddie asked. "Trevor was supposed to be his best friend."

Olivia put her finger to her lips as they reached the side street where she always parked her car. "Gwen said Del told him to stick around," she whispered, "but Dougie claims he has to make arrangements for Trevor's Hollywood memorial. I'm not sure what that means exactly, but I don't think it makes Dougie look guilty of murder. He might be a man who is mourning his best friend's death, feels trapped in a small town, and wants to go home. Anyway, unless there's evidence against him, it'll be tough to make him stay here for long."

Olivia led the way to her PT Cruiser and unlocked the doors. For once, she barely noticed the spicy scent as she opened the door. Maddie slid into the passenger's side, and Spunky willingly settled on her lap.

Olivia drove through an alley to avoid the street around the busy park. Within minutes, they were beyond the Chatterley Heights town limits, heading west toward Chatterley Paws. Gwen and Herbie Tucker had recently relocated their veterinary clinic and animal shelter to an old farm.

"Okay, let's get to the specifics," Maddie said. "Shall I search Dougie's room while you keep him distracted? I can say I'm taking Spunky on a play date with some of the shelter dogs."

"Good heavens, no. I want you to charm Lenora and Dougie."

"That goes without saying, but what else?"

"Maddie, I really don't have this plotted out step-by-step. We need to keep in mind our list of questions. I do desperately want to know more about the death of Dougie's wife. Also, about his friendship with Trevor . . . They were friends in high school, played football together, and they continued their relationship until Trevor's death. And yet Trevor treated Dougie like something between a slave and a bodyguard."

"Almost like a handler," Maddie said. "You know, like someone who takes care of everything for you, makes everything turn out right no matter how badly you've messed up."

"Or someone who makes things go away," Olivia said. "Inconvenient things."

"Are you thinking Dougie knows too much about Trevor's secrets? But wouldn't that give Trevor a reason to murder Dougie, not the other way around?"

Olivia slowed down as the new fence around the Tucker property came into view. "I suspect it went both ways, that they knew each other's secrets," she said. "Dougie might know a good deal about Howie, too."

"Ooh, the possibilities." Maddie ruffled Spunky's ears. "What about Lenora?"

"We'll need to take whatever she says with a shakerful of salt," Olivia said as she pulled up to the Tucker barn. "On the other hand, at some point it might be helpful if you took Lenora off for a glass of wine. You know how much she likes her wine."

"Oh yes," Maddie said, "and I know how talkative she becomes when she imbibes. I shall allow dear Lenora to chatter to her heart's content, with perhaps a wee bit of direction from me."

As Olivia turned off the ignition, Gwen

Tucker emerged from the barn and waved to them. Waving back, Olivia said quietly, "Showtime."

Gwen and Herbie Tucker cared for a growing family of orphaned, injured, or abandoned animals of all types, in addition to their own little son and, now, Herbie's widowed Aunt Len. Gwen led Olivia and Maddie through a cluttered living room to their family room, equally cluttered, where Lenora Dove sat curled up on a comfortable sofa. Her long hair, dyed auburn, was wound like a turban around her head, and a pale pink satin sheath hugged her waif-thin body. Lenora looked like a stand-in for an elderly Audrey Hepburn.

"Oh, Dougie, look who's come calling! It's Livie and Maddie." Lenora held out a self-manicured hand in greeting. With her other hand, she retrieved a large wineglass from a table next to the sofa. Her eyes strayed to a television showing a black-and-white movie, which Olivia recognized as one of the Thin Man stories, starring William Powell and Myrna Loy. The dimmed overhead lights created a movie theater ambiance.

Dougie Adair sat in a deep plush armchair, ignoring the movie. Instead, he read a newspaper by the light of a lamp on a side table. The banner identified the paper as the current *Los Angeles Times*. Olivia wondered how Dougie had managed to find a daily copy in little Chatterley Heights. Even the Chatterley Café offered only the *Baltimore Sun*. Perhaps Dougie had driven to one of the bigger nearby towns to buy the paper.

Dougie seemed momentarily irritated when they walked into the room. He quickly composed himself, smiled, and put aside his newspaper. "Lenora, darling," he said, "perhaps we could interrupt Nick and Nora for a bit? We have guests."

"Oh, and you've brought sweet little Spunky, too." Lenora picked up the television remote but made no effort to mute the sound. "Gwen, be a dear and bring our guests some wine. Perhaps you'd be kind enough to open another bottle, so we won't run short?"

With a quick wink at Olivia, Gwen excused herself.

Maddie scrunched onto the sofa next to Lenora. "I *love* Nick and Nora Charles," Maddie gushed. "Is this the one where Nick shoots the ornaments on the Christmas tree? I never get tired of that scene."

Lenora smiled indulgently. "No, my dear, this is *Another Thin Man,* the one where little

359

Nicky tags along." With a long sigh, Lenora said, "I'm devastated by dear Trevor's death, and little Nicky always seems to lift my spirits."

"I *love* little Nicky." Maddie kicked off her shoes and settled against the back of the sofa, her legs snuggled up against her chest. "Oh, and there's Asta. I *love* Asta." Sensing a threat to his status as number-one terrier, Spunky jumped onto Maddie's lap and yapped at the television. "But not as much as I love you, Spunks. I promise."

Olivia worried that Maddie might be overacting, though one look at Lenora's contented expression reassured her.

"My dear, the truly adorable one was William Powell," Lenora said with a sigh. "I so hoped to meet him after I moved to California. Although I was already married to my darling Bernie, I was still young and quite the romantic. I'd seen so many William Powell movies, only I hadn't quite grasped the age difference between us. I was still an ingenue, you see, and dear William Powell . . . well, when he died in 1984, he was ninety-one. It was not meant to be. But he will always be handsome and dashing to me." Lenora sighed as she watched her lost love down yet another martini.

Olivia did some rough calculations and

concluded that Lenora must have been an ingenue for a long, long time.

Maddie gave Olivia a quick wink that said, *We'll do just fine, Lenora and I. Run along and question Dougie.*

Olivia glanced at Dougie, who'd given up trying to read the paper. He stared at the floor, clearly bored. "I hear you'll be leaving us soon," Olivia said to him.

"If the sheriff will let me. There's nothing for me here. I need to make arrangements back in California."

"Understandable," Olivia said. "How about a walk outdoors? I've seen this movie several times."

With evident relief, Dougie put aside his newspaper. "I'll see you later, Lenora, dear."

Lenora stared at the television screen, attentive only to William Powell's presence. A parade of emotions molded her features as best they could, given the limiting effects of plastic surgery.

Dougie followed Olivia from the room. Closing the door behind them, he said, "It's sad, really. Lenora, I mean. She lives in a past of her own imagining."

As they stepped outside, the sun floated from behind a cloud and warmed Olivia's face. A gentle breeze ruffled her hair. She had to remind herself she was pressed for time. "I didn't get to know Trevor well," she said, "but to me it seemed his world was much like Lenora's. They both grew up in small towns. Lenora isn't adapting well to being back, and from what I observed, I doubt Trevor would have adjusted any better. Do you?"

Dougie gave her a startled look, and Olivia noticed gold flecks in his light brown eyes. Del's eyes were much the same, yet somehow warmer. "That's an intriguing question," Dougie said. "Trevor lived and breathed Hollywood. Sometimes it seemed as if Hollywood was the only reality in his life. People didn't count. Don't get me wrong; Trevor had scores of relationships, but he didn't have friends."

Dougie opened the barn door and waited for Olivia to pass through. She felt a moment of discomfort, as if she were entering a danger zone. She tossed it off and entered the cool, dark interior of the old barn. The smell of hay and the cacophony of animal sounds comforted her, made her feel safe. In addition to the barks and meows of dogs and cats, Olivia heard the lowing of cattle, a sheep baaing, and several animal sounds she couldn't identify. Everyone within a fifty-mile radius knew that Herbie and Gwen welcomed any and all homeless animals, so creatures appeared on their doorstep with overwhelming regularity. Gwen often insisted they'd reached capacity, but somehow the next abandoned animal always found a home with them.

A half-grown black kitten poked its head around a hay bale to check out the new arrivals. Without hesitation, it ran up to Olivia and rubbed against her ankle. When she picked it up, the kitten purred and cuddled against her. Olivia wondered how Spunky would feel about a feline companion.

"You wouldn't see this sort of place in Hollywood." Dougie stopped at a stall and produced an apple from his jacket pocket. A chestnut mare clopped over to him for a nibble. "Old habits . . . ," Dougie said. "I grew up in Twiterton and worked summers on several farms. I always kept my jacket pockets filled with treats." When the mare had finished her snack, Dougie turned to Olivia, and said, "I suspect you and Maddie didn't stop by to be neighborly. What's on your mind?"

Olivia lowered the kitten to the barn floor and watched it streak off after something she was glad she couldn't see. "I'm curious," she said. "You mentioned Trevor didn't have friends. Didn't you count yourself as his friend?"

Stroking the horse's forelock, Dougie said, "Trevor and I went to high school together, and we played football together. But that was high school. Trevor was the handsome star, even then. I was the tagalong and, if necessary, the muscle. I was also the better student. Trevor got by on C's. I'd make him study harder when the coach got after him to raise his grades. Not that I didn't benefit from the association. Trevor usually passed his girlfriends on to me when he grew bored with them. In return, I made him look good on the football field." Dougie's matter-of-fact tone made the arrangement sound unremarkable, merely a business deal. "Trevor was quarterback, but I was the better strategist. I set up plays for him, so he could be the hero." Dougie leaned against the stall. The powerful muscles of his upper body strained against his cotton shirt as he crossed his arms over his chest.

Olivia's own muscles tightened against a vague sense of danger. She told herself there'd been no personal threat in Dougie's comments. When he relaxed his stance and gave the mare a final pat, Olivia began to feel silly . . . until he focused those intense, nearly translucent eyes on her face. She shivered in spite of herself.

"Now, Livie, I have a question for you,"

Dougie said. "How much do you think you know already about Trevor? And about me?"

"I —" Olivia's mastery of language took a sudden hike.

Dougie chuckled. "Okay, I suppose that wasn't fair. However, you might want to bear in mind that you and Maddie aren't the only ones on the planet who have computers. I'm a writer. My laptop travels with me wherever I go. I have access to the Internet, and I use it often. It seems you two have gained quite a reputation as sleuths, at least locally."

"I see," Olivia said. "Then I won't beat around the bush."

"I have no intention of sharing any personal information with you, if that's what you're hoping." Dougie momentarily closed his eyes and took a quick breath. More calmly, he added, "Sorry, Livie. Even though I wasn't deeply fond of Trevor, this has all been a shock for me. I've been thoroughly grilled by the police. All I want to do now is go home. I didn't kill Trevor. Period." When Olivia didn't respond, Dougie said, "By the way, I heard that Wade Harald was arrested for Trevor's murder. I vaguely remember him from our high school football days, when he played for the Chatterly Heights team. He's the ex-husband of a good friend of yours and Maddie's, isn't he? So that gives you two a powerful motive to finger another suspect."

Despite his light, conversational tone and the absence of any overt threat, Dougie's blunt observation couldn't have been clearer. He was warning Olivia to back off. She felt a chill and suddenly longed for sunshine . . . and maybe a nearby witness or two. However, this might be her only chance to question Dougie before he left town. "I suspect your memory of Wade is clearer than you're willing to admit, since you and Trevor drugged him to get back at him for besting Trevor on the football field."

Dougie didn't flinch. "Not according to the police. I'm sure you're aware of that fact."

"You're wrong about one thing," Olivia said. "If Maddie and I found evidence that Wade Harald was guilty of murder, we wouldn't hesitate to turn him in to the authorities. We're concerned only about our friend, Stacey Harald. It looks like someone is trying to implicate her in Trevor's murder, and we won't allow that to happen."

"If that's a threat," Dougie said, "it is misdirected. I had nothing to do with Trevor's death, and I don't much care who did kill him. I came back here to the farm right after our impromptu meeting at the band shell. And before you bring up those photos that appeared in that amusing little blog, yes, Wade did wander into the band shell the night Trevor died. Wade was drunk, of course. He threatened Trevor and stalked off."

Olivia sensed that Dougie was on the verge of cutting off their conversation, so she decided against pushing the issue. "That night in the band shell," she said, "Trevor and Howie didn't appear to be old friends. Why were the three of you there together?"

With a throaty snicker, Dougie said, "Those two never pretended to be civil. Howie simply showed up at the band shell while Trevor and I were relaxing. Trevor was bored, so he was already in a foul mood. Howie's presence didn't help any. I couldn't understand why Howie stuck around. He knew Trevor's abuse would only escalate."

"Did the three of you leave the band shell together?"

"I've told all this to the police."

"I know," Olivia said, "but Trevor's body was left on my porch. I take that personally."

Dougie shrugged. "Howie left soon after you and Maddie did. Trevor decided to stay in town for a while, so I took off in the rental car. That's the last time I saw him alive."

"How was Trevor planning to get back to the farm without a car?"

"I didn't much care. I assumed he had found another place to sleep." Dougie scooped up a stone from the barn floor and heaved it with such force that it lodged in a bale of hay.

"So are you suggesting Trevor had a friend in town? Perhaps a woman friend?"

"How delicate of you," Dougie said with a mirthless chuckle. "I wouldn't know. Trevor wooed and deserted women 'friends' with remarkable speed." Dougie's casual tone contrasted with his tight jaw. "In answer to your earlier question," he said, "no, I did not consider myself to be Trevor's friend. He paid me well to do exactly what I'd done in high school: to make him look good. I managed to keep his reputation more or less intact, no matter how big a mess he got himself into, and I tolerated whatever abuse he felt like hurling at me. I didn't like it. However, I was highly compensated for my calm forbearance."

"What will you do now?" Olivia asked.

"Celebrate."

"Trevor's death?"

"Trevor's exit from my life. But I did *not*

kill him."

"Look, I'm not here to accuse you. It's just that . . ." Olivia decided to change her tactics. Dougie might be more willing to share information that could implicate someone else in Trevor's murder. "I'm really not trying to set you up as a suspect," Olivia said, "but you are my best source of information about Trevor's past. It seems he alienated a number of people during his life. Since he was murdered here and not in Hollywood, I can't help thinking his killer might be someone from his youth in Twiterton, or even someone here in Chatterley Heights. You're the only one I can think of who might be able to fill me in about people from that period of his life."

"Like who?"

"You tell me."

Dougie appeared to sink into his thoughts. As he headed toward the barn door, Olivia followed, wondering if he were sifting through memories or calculating how to transform someone else into the prime suspect for Trevor's murder. Dougie remained silent as he closed the barn door behind them and led the way to a barnyard pasture where a small herd of sheep grazed on grass. To protect the sheep while maintaining the traditional look of their farm,

Gwen and Herbie had added wire mesh to the bottom half of an old, but still functional, rail fence. Dougie leaned against a fence post and gazed at the pasture. A sheep munched its way closer until Dougie could reach out and lightly stroke its fleece.

"By the time I started high school," Dougie said, "I was one of the few farm kids left in Twiterton. Trevor's family moved to town from Baltimore, where his father worked as an attorney. They were well-to-do, and I was . . . well, we did fine, but developers were rapidly eating up family farms. Most of the kids I knew in high school were from DC or Baltimore or even farther away."

Olivia felt a prick of irritation. Was Dougie reminiscing so she would give up and leave him alone? Hoping to get a reaction, she said, "It sounds like Trevor might have fit in at school better than you did."

Dougie hesitated, as if he were giving her suggestion serious thought. "Funny thing is, he didn't fit in well at all, not really. Trevor was Trevor, always and forever. He wasn't chronically nasty on purpose; he just didn't know how to be anything else. I'm not saying Trevor wasn't one of the popular kids. Girls went crazy over him, other boys wanted to hang out with him. . . . He could turn on the charm when he wanted, but it didn't take long to realize that if Trevor bothered to be charming it was because he wanted something. If you were unlucky enough to become what he called a friend, he dropped the facade. Everyone saw through him, anyway. Trevor wasn't a complex character. He knew how to embarrass another student in public, but he didn't have the follow-through to, say, blackmail someone."

"Doesn't sound like Trevor was much fun to be around," Olivia said. "Why did you put up with him all those years?"

"It was a living," Dougie said as he shrugged one muscular shoulder. "I'm afraid I can't think of anyone from Trevor's distant past who would go to the bother of killing him. Including me."

"What about Howie Upton?" Olivia said.

"Howie?" Dougie sounded genuinely surprised. Maybe even hopeful? "Have the police been questioning him, too?"

"I really don't know," Olivia said. "That night in the band shell, Trevor was quite hard on Howie, and Howie didn't take it well. I wondered if there was bad blood between them. Perhaps, in the past, Trevor did or said something that Howie couldn't simply laugh off?"

Dougie watched a determined English sheepdog herd an errant sheep back toward the others. "I'm envious of Gwen and Herbie. I could write in a place like this. On the other hand, the animals would eventually starve," he said. "About Howie. Back in high school, I probably wasn't as sensitive as I should have been, and good old Trevor was but a younger version of the man he became. Howie and Trevor were dueling egos. Howie was probably the smartest kid ever to grace the halls of Twiterton High, and he knew it. He was a genius when it came to anything involving numbers. We were in the same calculus class. Howie would correct the teacher, and he'd be right every time."

"Was Howie arrogant about his superior talents?" Olivia asked.

"There should be a stronger word than 'arrogant.' Even the teachers disliked him, although they predicted a great future for him. Now, if Howie had looked and sounded like Trevor, high school would have gone much better for him, but he was pudgy and whiny. The girls sneered at him. Boys beat him up. It was sad . . . or it would have been if Howie had possessed even one appealing personal quality."

"In the band shell," Olivia said, "you were

kind to Howie when Trevor insulted him."

"Not out of sympathy for Howie, believe me. I was just doing my job. When Trevor went out of bounds, I was to pull him back and remind him that he had an image to sustain. That evening it didn't work. Howie was one of Trevor's preferred whipping boys."

"Really? Why?"

"Howie was so easy to pick on. Trevor couldn't resist. I have to admit, I wasn't fond of Howie, either, so I wasn't really exerting myself much in his defense."

As Dougie watched the sheep graze, Olivia studied his profile for hints to his mood. He gave little away. Olivia found herself more curious than ever about this articulate man with the face and body of a fighter.

Dougie reached into the pocket of his flannel shirt and drew out two bone-shaped dog treats, like Spunky's, only bigger. When Dougie whistled, the sheepdog abandoned his post and galumphed across the pasture toward him. "Good boy," Dougie said. "You've been working hard. You need sustenance." He tossed the treat over the dog's head. Apparently used to the game, the sheepdog had already determined the treat's trajectory and found it with no difficulty.

An unexpected thought flashed through

Olivia's mind: *Are these displays of kindness for my benefit?* As if he'd sensed her doubt, Dougie said, "I frequently prefer animals to people. Animals hunt because they are hungry." He raised his arm to throw another treat to the sheepdog.

"I suppose there are many types of hunger," Olivia said.

Dougie's arm dropped to his side, the second dog treat still in his hand. "You really should stay out of this, Livie."

"My friend is implicated in a murder she didn't commit. I'll do whatever I have to do."

"Trevor had many enemies, some of them as ruthless as he was." Dougie focused those translucent, impenetrable eyes on Olivia's face. "I'm going to tell you something about Trevor and hope it will serve as a warning to you. It involves me, as well. I'm certain the police know already, so it won't be a secret for long." Dougie turned to gaze at the pasture. The sheepdog trotted over to him, hoping for another snack. Dougie threw the dog-bone treat in the air. The dog caught it in his mouth, wagged a thank-you, and ran toward a wandering sheep.

"Given your reputation," Dougie said, "I'm guessing you already know part of my story. I was once married, for a short time, to a sweet and talented young poet. I loved her deeply, but she wasn't very stable. She suffered severe bouts of depression. Pills didn't help, and sometimes my presence seemed to worsen the condition, especially when I was consumed by my own writing. So I began to take trips away from home, during which I lived in cheap motels and wrote plays. I thought I was helping. In fact, she became resentful, as if I were abandoning her. She began to have affairs. Her last affair was with Trevor. He was doing mostly commercials at the time. While I was gone, Trevor would fly to New York to stay with my wife. Then he tired of her. He broke off with her by never communicating with her again."

"And then she killed herself," Olivia said.

"I thought you might have learned about that," Dougie said. "Yes, she killed herself. I found her when I returned from one of my writing holidays."

Or writing escapes? Olivia could imagine how Dougie's helpful absence might have felt more like desertion to his wife.

Dougie leaned against the fence and stared down at the grass. "Trevor was self-obsessed and cruel. His brutal treatment of Anna is only one example. He assumed others existed to fill his needs. I could name fifty people who are angry enough to have murdered Trevor and mutilated his body. Some of them might attend Maddie's engagement party tomorrow."

Including you. The bright sunlight couldn't stop the chill that went through Olivia as she considered how many of Maddie and Lucas's guests might have known and despised Trevor Lane. Would one of them turn out to be his killer?

CHAPTER EIGHTEEN

The Gingerbread House kitchen qualified for disaster status, but Olivia and Maddie had finished, in record time, a rose-petal cookie cake and many dozens of garden-themed lavender-lemon decorated cookies. Only their fragrances lingered in the kitchen. Lucas and several Heights Hardware employees had carted the goodies to the Bon Vivant garden to join the dozens of wedding-theme cookies they'd delivered earlier.

"Maddie, stop fidgeting." A tiny pearl button slipped from Olivia's grasp as she tried to push it through a loop. She leaned her hip against the kitchen counter to steady herself. "There must be a million of these little buttons. No wonder Aunt Sadie's eyes bothered her while she was making your dress."

"You must admit, it's the most gorgeous wedding dress ever created. And I get to wear it twice! First, to my engagement party, where it will be seen and admired by scads of people, and then to my quiet, little wedding. I hope no one spills wine on it today." Maddie hugged herself with happiness.

"Now you're making it even harder to button."

"Oops, sorry," Maddie said. "I need to calm and center myself, as your mother would say. You know what would calm and center me? We should discuss our investigative strategy for this afternoon."

"Our strategy is to relax, have fun, and keep the cookies flowing." Olivia slipped another button through its loop. "Just half a million to go," she said.

"Livie, everybody will be at the engagement party; it's the perfect time to unmask the murderer. Tomorrow, everyone will scatter."

"You're right: your dress is stunning, one of a kind, priceless. Aunt Sadie risked her fragile eyesight to design and create it for you, her beloved niece and adoptive daughter. She slaved over it day and —"

"I get it, Livie, I get it. If I chase down and subdue a killer, I might get my dress dirty."

Olivia buttoned the last button and spun

Maddie around to face her. *"Dirty?* Your lovely dress might be torn to shreds."

Maddie let out a sigh worthy of a spoiled teenager. "Okay, fine. You're right. But has Del figured out who killed Trevor, or is he going to railroad poor, dumb Wade? What'll happen to Stacey and the kids?"

"Del gave me a quick call this morning to assure me he is covering all the bases."

"But Livie, what bases is he covering, and are they the right ones?" A spiral of red hair plopped onto Maddie's nose. "I knew this hairdo was a mistake. Hang on, I'll get the mirror." She picked up her long skirt, sprinted to the tiny kitchen bathroom, and returned with the small mirror Olivia had hung from a nail. "Hold this up for me." Maddie grimaced at her reflection. "This might take a while," she said as she ripped pins from her hair. Curls cascaded nearly to her shoulders and across her face.

"Anybody home under there?" Olivia asked as she pushed the curls away from Maddie's face.

"Oh sure, go ahead and mock." Maddie sounded distinctly irritable. "This is what always happens when I try to look glamorous." She pawed through the kitchen junk drawer until she found a piece of twine. "This will have to do, since I can't find any of those thick rubber bands in vivid colors."

"I bought a whole bag of them only a week ago," Olivia said. "Hang on, something is making this drawer stick." She reached her hand toward the back of the drawer, where she felt a soft package. "I'll bet this is the bag of bands," Olivia grasped ahold of the package and pulled. She felt the bag stretch, but it remained stuck, as did the drawer.

"Here, let me. A little muscle ought to do it." Maddie yanked the drawer pull with the strength and impatience of a frazzled bride-to-be with disastrous hair. The drawer broke free and exploded from its cavity. The contents flew in all directions. "There," Maddie said. "I feel much better now."

Olivia began to gather up the detritus. "It was time to clean the junk drawer, anyway." She scooped up a small paper bag. "What's this?"

"My guess is, it's junk," Maddie said. "It doesn't look familiar, though. Open it."

Olivia reached inside the bag and withdrew a paper towel wrapped around a light object. She opened the towel.

"What is it?" Maddie asked. "Livie? What's wrong?"

Olivia held out her hand. A cookie cutter nestled in the crinkly paper towel.

"Geez." Maddie reached for the cutter. "That sure looks like a gavel."

"Don't touch it." Olivia jerked her hand back, out of reach.

"But how did it get here? At least one of us has been in this kitchen almost nonstop since before Trevor . . ."

"The operative word is 'almost.' I can think of numerous times when the kitchen was empty. In fact, when Jennifer dropped off all the baking supplies we needed, she used your key to the store."

"Are you sure it's *the* gavel cutter?" Maddie asked. "How do we know it isn't another plant, like the one in Stacey's dishwasher?"

"We don't know for sure. We'll have to wait until it goes through forensics." Olivia used the kitchen phone to call Del. When the call went to voice mail, she said, "Hi, Del. Maddie and I are about to leave for the party, but I've got something important to tell you. We just found another gavel cookie cutter, this time in the Gingerbread House kitchen. Call me."

"Should we drop it off at the police department?" Maddie asked.

"Let's give Del some time to —" Olivia's cell rang. She flipped it open and said, "What a coincidence. Hi, Del. I was just . . . Okay, we'll wait for you. He'll be here in a few minutes," she said as she hung up.

Olivia rewrapped the gavel cutter in its paper towel. She placed it on the counter, out of Maddie's line of sight, and pulled a chair next to her friend. "I'm sorry, Maddie," Olivia said.

Maddie started, as if her thoughts had carried her far away. "What?"

"I said, I'm sorry this had to happen today, of all days."

"Don't be silly, Livie. I'm envisioning the wonderful stories I could tell my children about how their mother caught a killer at Mommy and Daddy's engagement party."

Olivia couldn't think of anything to say, though apparently her expression spoke for her.

"You think I couldn't do it, don't you . . . totally subdue a killer, I mean. Making decorated cutout cookies day in and day out isn't for weaklings, you know. Plus I've been helping Lucas out in the hardware store when I have Sundays free. You should see me wield an electric saw."

"Were you planning to bring an electric saw to your engagement party?" A vivid image flashed through Olivia's mind. She saw Maddie in her slinky satin dress, her hair spiraling out like curls of flame . . . and an electric saw in her hands, aimed like a semiautomatic rifle at a terrified criminal.

"You're missing the point, Livie. I want to be an inspiration to my children and grand-children . . . should I ever have any, that is. And I don't plan to just yet. Why is it always the guy who saves the day?"

Olivia was excused from answering by a firm knock on the alley door. She checked the peephole to be sure Sam Parnell wasn't hand-delivering yet another package. "It's Del." Maddie retrieved the paper towel package, while Olivia opened the door.

"You're still in your uniform," Olivia said as Del entered the kitchen.

Del took the paper towel from Maddie and slid it into a plastic bag. "This'll have to go right to forensics. Show me where you found it." Maddie pointed to the kitchen floor. "The drawer was stuck, so . . ."

"I get it," Del said. "Leave everything as is, in case forensics wants to dust for finger-prints. Sorry, Livie, but I'll have to meet you later, at the party. This goes straight to the lab." He gave her a peck on the cheek and reached for the door. "I keep forget-ting," he said, twisting his head around. "Maddie, you said you could identify whether the cookie we found in . . . whether the cookie was one you'd made."

"I could, almost certainly. Give me the

specifics."

"The lab said it was a sugar cookie shaped like a girl in a dress," Del said. "A light blue dress. Ring a bell?"

"I decorated several girl shapes and iced them in different colors. Light blue was one of the colors. If the cookie had lemon flavoring, then it was definitely one I put out in the store in the morning, the same day Trevor, Dougie, and Lenora held court here."

Del's face puckered as if he was thinking hard. "Thanks. I'll double-check about the lemon flavor." He opened the alley door and left without another word.

"The last of the great romantics," Maddie said.

Olivia grinned. "Oh, Del has his romantic moments. When he's working, he's working. I can understand that."

"But we have fun when we work," Maddie said.

"Trust me, Del is having fun. It just looks different." Olivia glanced up at the kitchen clock. "We need to get going. Mom will already be at Bon Vivant, along with a cadre of her friends, waiting for instructions."

"I wish we could take Spunky along," Maddie said.

"Way too many people. He'd take off, and

we'd never see him again."

"Speaking of all those people," Maddie said. "What information do you want me to probe for while I'm being giggly and charming?"

"I really, really want you to relax and enjoy your engagement party." Olivia slipped her cell into the pocket of her new gray linen slacks. "Where's my sweater?"

"Right where you tossed it, on a chair." Maddie lifted the thin gray sweater, bought to match Olivia's slacks, and handed it to her. "Nice silk blouse, by the way. You look good in peach. I forgive you for not wearing a dress to my engagement party."

"I didn't want to outshine the bride."

"Uh-huh." Maddie threw a pale yellow silk shawl over her shoulders. "Do you honestly think any outfit could compete with this?" She twirled around to show off the delicate purple blossoms Aunt Sadie had embroidered on her shawl.

"No contest."

"Wise woman. In this outfit, I figure I could wheedle information out of anyone, so you might as well give me an assignment, Livie."

Olivia slipped her sweater over her head. "Maddie, I honestly have no idea where to go from here. My mind is filled with details

385

that don't lead anywhere. I doubt Dougie or Howie will even show up for your party. Dougie will probably fly out tomorrow morning, if he hasn't already left. This case is too much for me. We'll have to count on Del."

"Poop head," Maddie said. "Well, never mind. I'll figure it out by myself."

That's what worries me.

The recently watered garden behind the Bon Vivant restaurant sparkled in the bright sunlight, but Olivia barely noticed. Maddie and Lucas's engagement party would officially begin in five minutes. Bon Vivant staff and Ellie's troupe of volunteers scurried to and from the kitchen, toting appetizers and drinks to the serving tables on the terrace behind the restaurant. Guests had begun to arrive.

Olivia finished arranging a plate piled with lavender-lemon flower-shaped cookies. She stepped back from the table to inspect her work, but her mind refused to pay attention. She wished she could take her own advice and forget about Trevor Lane, at least for the duration of the party. But her dear friend Stacey Harald, through no fault of her own, was in hiding with her kids, because she'd been set up to look complicit in Trevor's murder. Time was running out. Soon the suspects would scatter, and Stacey would have to come home to face the stares and the gossip and . . . Binnie Sloan.

Olivia's mother, Ellie, floated across the patio toward her, wearing a flowing dress of teal silk, tied at her slender waist with a pale yellow silk scarf. Her husband, Allan, tagged along behind. He looked sharp in a three-piece pinstripe suit he'd once worn as a corporate executive.

"Livie, dear," Ellie said, "you are looking lovely, yet glum. The refreshments are under control. Perhaps you would feel better if you began to mingle."

"Helping Stacey would make me feel better, Mom. Or baking and decorating cookies. But mingling? That would make me cranky."

"I know this is a tough situation for you," Allan said. "Anything we can do to help?"

"Maybe . . . Allan, your knowledge of the Internet is pretty sophisticated, right?"

"Oh, well, I —"

"Allan's knowledge of the Internet is superb," Ellie said. "What do you need him to do? Hack into the police files?"

Allan glanced nervously at a young couple approaching them. "Ellie, I don't think —"

"But dearest, it's for the greater good,"

Ellie said. "You are so clever."

"You wouldn't have to do anything illegal," Olivia said. A group of party guests, filling their plates with goodies, had moved close enough to hear their conversation. Olivia led her mother and stepfather farther away from the serving tables. "Allan," she said, once they were out of earshot, "is it possible to post something anonymously?"

"Depends on who's reading the post," Allan said with a grin.

"If you were reading it?"

Allan's grin widened. "Unlikely. Back when I worked for . . ." He glanced at Ellie. "Back when I worked for bloodsucking corporations, I was the one they called upon to trace hackers to their lairs. I got pretty good at it."

"Oh excellent Stepfather, thank you for marrying my mother. Here's what I need: have a chat with Howie Upton, assuming he shows up here."

"Howie is already here, Livie." Ellie pointed her head toward the chow line. Howie Upton was dressed in a three-piece suit that hung loose on his thin body. He was piling his plate with a little bit of everything.

"Just have a chat with him," Olivia said. "Bring up the subject of posting online. I want to know if he has the expertise to post something in such a way that your average hacker, like Maddie, couldn't trace the source of the post."

Allan grinned. "Intriguing. And here I thought I'd be bored at this shindig."

"Please be casual about it," Olivia begged. "Howie is smart. I don't want him to get suspicious about why you are talking to him."

"Livie, Howie and I are the only guests wearing three-piece suits. It's entirely natural that we would cluster together."

"Why do I think the rest of us have just been insulted?"

Allan winked at her, bent over to give his petite wife a peck on the cheek, and strode toward Howie.

"It was kind of you to send Allan on assignment, Livie," Ellie said. "He does love to feel his expertise is useful."

"I wasn't being kind. Believe me, I don't know what I'd do without him."

"Me neither, dear." Ellie tapped her daughter's arm with teal-polished fingertips. "You seem so distracted, Livie. Surely you can count on Del to resolve this troubling murder. In time, that is."

"That's my worry, Mom. Del is a great cop, I know that. He's careful and thorough, which takes time. Only we don't have much of it left. We need to resolve this mess soon for Stacey's and her kids' sakes, and also for ours." Olivia told her mother about the gavel cookie cutter she and Maddie had found at The Gingerbread House, stuffed in a kitchen drawer. "We could get added to the suspect list, too, along with who knows who else. And here I am, too busy and flustered to think straight. My mind is so crammed with bits of information, and I can't make any sense of them."

As Olivia reached up to run her hand through her hair, Ellie's quick, strong arm grabbed her wrist and forced her to stop. "You will figure it all out, Livie. There's no need to ruin your hairdo."

Olivia laughed in spite of herself. "I forgot to brush my hair before we left. Maybe I should leave it tangled more often. Besides, tangled is what my mind feels like."

"Oh, Livie, you are too close to the details. As your father used to say, data collection is essential, but at some point you must stop and look for the connections. Maybe you need to step back to perceive what is truly important." Ellie tucked an errant wave under the pale yellow ribbon that held her hair away from her face. "Now, I believe I will select a cookie and mingle a bit. I see that Herbie Tucker has kindly brought his aunt Lenora to the party. I'm sure Lenora is devastated by Trevor Lane's death. I'll go chat with her . . . if you are okay?"

"I'm fine, Mom. You go mingle. Let me know if you learn anything interesting." Olivia followed her mother to the cookie display, where she chose a yellow tulip with lavender sprinkles.

Ellie picked up two identical daisy shapes, grape purple with bright yellow outlined petals. "I might as well bring an extra for Lenora," she explained. "If I only have one cookie, those sad, hungry eyes will con me into giving it to her."

"She reminds me of Spunky," Olivia said.

"I suppose that's why we love her."

"Speak for yourself." Olivia bit off a chunk of her yellow tulip. "Wow, this is good. I wish I could take credit, but Maddie is the real genius behind her own wedding cookies." Ellie didn't respond. "Mom?" Olivia followed her mother's gaze to one of the restaurant's small gardens. She saw a man in tan slacks and matching sweater, possibly cashmere, over a white shirt. His back was to Olivia, but she recognized the broad shoulders that stretched the sweater across his back.

"I'm rather surprised to see Dougie Adair

here," Ellie said.

"I'm stunned," Olivia said. "I thought for sure he'd be on a plane headed for Los Angeles. Is it possible that Lenora talked him into coming?" She searched the terrace and found Lenora, with her nephew Herbie beside her, talking to Maddie and Lucas.

"This is quite fascinating," Ellie said. "I'll go chat with Lenora now."

"Report back, okay? Mom?" But Ellie's powerful little legs had already carried her out of range. Olivia considered tagging along behind, but she saw her stepfather barreling toward her like a confident bull.

"Mission accomplished," Allan said, a shade too heartily.

"Let's move out of earshot." Olivia took two more cookies and led Allan to an isolated table close to the restaurant, where they could keep an eye on the crowd. After they sat down, she handed him one of the cookies.

"Is this my reward?" Allan took a bite. "Yum. Almost as good as money."

"Glad you think so. What did you find out from Howie?"

"Fascinating young man," Allan said. "Sociopathic, of course, but in the right environment, that would be a plus."

"I think I'd be happier not knowing about

that," Olivia said. "It sort of makes my skin crawl."

Allan threw back his head and guffawed. "You and your mother," he said, "two peas in a pod. That's a compliment, by the way." He bit off a large chunk of cookie and made appreciative sounds as he chewed.

"So what do you think? Could Howie create an anonymous post?"

"With his eyes closed," Allan said. "Mind you, a real expert could probably track the path, but that boy has impressive computer skills. Back in the day, I'd have been tempted to hire him, if he weren't so . . ." Allan frowned as he searched for the right word.

"If he weren't so sociopathic?"

"Hm? No, that's not the problem, though I'd sure keep an eye on him. He's too arrogant, too certain of his own genius. Not to say he isn't a genius, he surely is, but . . . Well, there's such a thing as too much confidence, if you know what I mean."

"I know what you mean."

An hour later, the engagement party was in full swing, and Olivia felt as confused as ever. She'd been so focused on helping the festivities run smoothly, she'd barely spoken to anyone but the restaurant staff. The time had come for her to mingle. She hung her apron on a hook in the restaurant kitchen and returned to the patio. She ought to check in with Bertha and Jennifer before abandoning her post.

Olivia waved to Bertha, who was restocking the cookie supply. Bertha motioned Olivia to join her. Seeing the concerned look on Bertha's face, Olivia hurried to her. "Is something wrong?"

"I hope not," Bertha said. "It's just that I haven't seen Jennifer in some time. She agreed to keep the cookie platters filled, but I found them all practically empty."

"Thanks for stepping in," Olivia said. "I'll see if I can find her." Olivia remembered she'd seen Jennifer wearing brown slacks and a beige sweater. She was average height but pretty enough to stand out, even in a well-dressed crowd. Olivia walked through the kitchen and restaurant, looked over the crush of guests on the patio, and examined the open gardens in back. There was no sign of Jennifer. Was this another of her disappearing acts? Olivia was about to give up when she spotted movement through a break in the trees behind the gardens. She remembered her early morning visit to that very spot — was it only last Tuesday?

Olivia decided not to investigate. An

amorous couple had probably escaped to the woods to "get to know each other better," and she cringed at the thought of interrupting them. Olivia was about to give up on finding Jennifer when a figure emerged from the woods. The slight figure wore a long sweater coat, large sunglasses, and a brown scarf covering her hair. She looked similar in size and build to Jennifer Elsworth. When the woman paused to slip something into her pocket, Olivia immediately thought of a cell phone.

Olivia spun around and quickly scanned the guests for cell-phone users. She saw one man gesticulating and pacing while he talked on his cell. No one appeared to have just hung up. Howie Upton was chatting with a young woman in a short, tight skirt, who wobbled on her stilettos. Olivia couldn't find Dougie Adair in the crowd. Maybe he had left already.

Olivia lectured herself about jumping to conclusions. The young woman might be a loner by nature, someone who needs to escape from people on a regular basis. But Olivia's gut told her she was right, that the figure approaching the restaurant was Jennifer, and she seemed to be trying to hide her identity.

With exquisite timing, a familiar voice

spoke from behind Olivia. "I should get engaged more often," Maddie said. "Isn't this fun?"

"Maddie, am I glad to see you. Come on, we have to talk." Olivia led her around the patio and toward Bon Vivant's packed front parking lot. Luckily, the PT Cruiser was easy to spot.

"Are we running away?" Maddie asked.

"Conferring." Olivia unlocked the car, and they slid into the front seat. "In private." For the next few minutes, Olivia sped through a summary of what she'd learned from her stepfather and what she'd observed on her own. "Mom suggested we step back from the details to determine what's really important. I know you've been too busy to —"

"In fact," Maddie said, "I had a chance to chat with Dougie. Although it was more chatter than chat. I wanted to disarm him . . . you know, make him think he's getting information from me when I'm actually watching his reactions. That sort of thing."

"Does that actually work?"

"It does for me," Maddie said. "You'd never be able to pull it off. You're too mature."

"Thank you . . . I think."

"So here's the scoop: I mentioned Jennifer, and I let it slip that I wondered why he and Trevor had really come to Chatterley Heights."

Feeling squeamish, Olivia said, "I hope you didn't give him a reason to skip town."

"Livie, you have no faith in me. But I'll let that go because it underscores how good I am at babbling. I told him that, though we all love Lenora, I couldn't understand why he and Trevor would want to keep in touch with her, let alone visit. Anyway, then I told him something Ellie told me — she wanted me to pass this information along to you, by the way, so this is a 'two birds with one stone' thing. I told Dougie that Lenora had chattered all over town that he and Trevor were coming to visit her. Dougie didn't look surprised by that, but I guess it's important."

"I don't get why this is significant," Olivia said.

"Okay," Maddie said, "I'll back up. Ellie told me to tell you that Lenora visited every business on Town Square to spread the news that Trevor Lane and his buddy, Dougie Adair, were coming to Chatterley Heights expressly to visit her." Maddie paused a moment, looking confused. "Ellie said you'd understand. She didn't want to elaborate because there were so many people around."

"Didn't she say anything else at all?" Olivia asked.

Maddie frowned in concentration. "I think she said something about looking for the threads. Does that mean anything to you?"

Olivia relaxed against the back seat of her PT Cruiser. "I think she's referring to what I relayed to you earlier . . . you know, about stepping away from the details. The threads . . ." Olivia massaged her forehead. "This case is so complex, and we haven't time to figure out which details are important." She closed her eyes and released her mind to follow its own path.

When Olivia had been silent for more than three minutes, Maddie asked, "Livie? Are you having a catatonic seizure or something?"

Olivia's eyes popped open. "I think I understand what Mom meant," she said. "Several unexplained events have taken place in or near Chatterley Heights, all in the last week." Olivia began counting on her fingers. "First, Jennifer showed up at the store and wanted a job. Second, there were break-ins at Lady Chatterley's and the bank. Third, I overheard a mysterious, angry phone call in the woods here at Bon Vivant.

Fourth, Trevor Lane and Dougie Adair showed up in Chatterley Heights. And fifth, Trevor Lane was murdered. Have I missed anything?"

"What about those rumors in Binnie Sloan's hateful blog?" Maddie asked.

"The rumors . . . I think you're right, Maddie. Those rumors have escalated to the point where it's hard to imagine Binnie creating them. They started the same time as the break-ins."

"And right after Jennifer began working for us," Maddie said. "So where does this get us?"

"I'm not sure," Olivia said, "but let's assume these events are all related, which would mean they are all related to Trevor Lane's murder."

"Yes!" Maddie bounced on the car seat. "So I repeat, where does that get us?"

Olivia felt herself wilt. "Not a clue. However, I know what Mom would tell us."

"To have a cookie?"

"To keep the threads in mind and see where they join together," Olivia said. "Or words to that effect."

"Your mom is very wise," Maddie said. "Although she doesn't always make sense."

By late afternoon, the crowds began to thin.

Toasts had been offered and wine had been drunk, at times to excess. The rose-petal cookie cake rested on a wheeled cart draped with a linen tablecloth. Olivia had assumed guests would break off pieces throughout the party, but every organic rose petal remained intact. The Bon Vivant staff had given it a place of honor at the edge of the patio, with the gardens and hills for a backdrop. The guests had admired the lovely creation but thought it too gorgeous to consume.

As the late afternoon sun drifted behind a ridge of fluffy white clouds, cameras appeared among the remaining guests. Maddie and Lucas had decided against hiring professional photographers, due to the expense. They'd counted on friends and family to fill the void. Olivia's stepfather, among many others, welcomed the challenge with enthusiasm. Olivia relaxed at a patio table, her sore feet resting on a chair, to watch the photo session.

When Maddie and Lucas posed beside the rose-petal cookie cake, the clicking of cameras commenced. After a time, Maddie wheeled the cake aside and led Lucas into the early rose garden for another round of photos. Maddie's wild hair had cooperated for once. The curls jumbled together as if a stylist had spent hours arranging them just so. Lucas looked relaxed and happy with his arm around his soon-to-be-bride. Within minutes, the sun reemerged, and the cameras disappeared. A group of muscular, and perhaps less then sober, male employees from Heights Hardware called to Lucas to join them. Maddie waved him away. Lucas kissed her and followed his coworkers. A few women stayed to chat with Maddie amid the roses.

Olivia began to feel impatient. She glanced toward the restaurant, where she saw Jennifer conferring with Bertha and a Bon Vivant staff member. Olivia made a mental note to corner Jennifer when she was alone and ask point blank if she'd slipped away to the woods earlier.

Olivia's cell phone vibrated in her pocket. Her caller ID told her Del had sent a text. Olivia thought about leaving it, making him wait. He had now missed nearly the entire party without explanation. Yeah, Del was sheriff, investigating an unsolved murder, but jeez . . . He could at least tell her if he was hot on someone's trail. In case he was doing just that, Olivia opened the text. It read, "Got a lead. Hope to be there soon." Olivia snapped her cell shut with unnecessary force.

No dramatic breakthrough in the case had come to Olivia, and she was close to giving up. She'd find some other way to help Stacey and her kids. Or maybe Del was on the verge of arresting the killer, and all would be well.

Olivia looked around for her mother and saw her chatting with Lenora and Herbie Tucker. To Olivia's surprise, neither Dougie nor Howie had left yet. Howie checked his watch. With a tight expression, he glanced toward a patio table where Jennifer was clearing empty plates. Olivia had the impression he knew her and was perhaps waiting to take her home. Yet he hadn't spoken to Jennifer during the party, at least not to Olivia's knowledge. In fact, she had never seen Howie speak to Jennifer.

Dougie Adair joined Lenora, Herbie, and Ellie, though he didn't participate in their conversation. His attention shifted from the gardens to Howie and then, suddenly, toward Olivia. When she held his gaze, Dougie broke away from his group and strolled toward her table.

"I'll be flying out tomorrow morning," Dougie said as he dropped into a chair next to Olivia. "The sheriff knows how to find me." When Olivia didn't respond, Dougie gazed out at the rose garden. "Maddie looks

402

lovely and happy," he said. "Lucas is a lucky man."

Dougie, Trevor, Howie, Jennifer . . . all connected to one place, Twiterton, and to one person, Melissa Nortenson. "Who do you think killed Melissa Nortenson?" Olivia hadn't meant to ask the question so bluntly, but she was glad she'd done so. Her peripheral vision told her Dougie's body had tightened. Moments passed in silence. Olivia fully expected him to bolt, but he didn't.

"Not me," Dougie said finally.

"Trevor?"

"I don't know, but I don't think so."

"But you gave him an alibi, didn't you?"

Dougie shrugged. "We were buddies, of a sort, remember?"

"And he repaid you by having an affair with your wife and driving her to suicide," Olivia said.

Dougie jerked in his chair as if he'd been poked with a sharp knife. "Trevor also destroyed Wade Harald's football career and possibly his life, and he relentlessly tortured Howie Upton."

"Why did you and Trevor come to Chatterley Heights?" Olivia asked. "And don't say it was to visit Lenora."

"No comment."

"Do you know who our clerk, Jennifer Elsworth, really is?"

Dougie laughed. "Well, that was obvious, at least to us. She grew up and dyed her hair, but those eyes are unmistakable. Her sister Melissa had the same green eyes."

"How well did you know Melissa?" Olivia asked.

"Not as well as Trevor did. I'm not proud of our treatment of Melissa. Her mind might have been slow, but when it came to boys, we'd never known a faster girl. It was just too tempting." Dougie shifted in his chair. "I should point out that Jennie was the one who went in search of her after she disappeared. That had become her job, searching for her sister when she'd run off." Olivia felt a sudden surge of sadness. She wasn't convinced of Dougie's innocence, but she was tired of asking such awful questions. She spotted Maddie in the garden and waved. Maddie waved back and pushed the wheeled cart, which held the cookie cake, out of the rose garden and onto the patio nearer to Olivia's table. Maddie ran back to the garden to pick a rose. Olivia began to feel more relaxed.

The sound of raised voices drew Olivia's attention. She was surprised to see Jennifer and Howie walking down a path between two gardens, engaged in a heated discussion. Jennifer pulled away from Howie and headed toward Bon Vivant's kitchen, leaving him alone on the path. As he watched her leave, Olivia came into his field of vision. She turned away, but not soon enough.

Transcend the details, Olivia thought. All the suspects are connected to a past crime: the death of Melissa Nortenson. They all converged on Chatterley Heights at about the same time, give or take a few days. One of them, Trevor, was subsequently murdered. Olivia jerked upright with a sudden realization. Trevor's accused killer, Wade Harald, had gone to Chatterley Heights high school. It was likely he'd never even met Melissa Nortenson.

Olivia's cell phone vibrated, and she flipped it open. A text message from Del read, "I'll be there in a couple minutes. Hang tight." Olivia snapped her phone shut. *Hang tight? What's that supposed to mean?*

When Jennifer appeared in the doorway to the kitchen, Olivia thought it might be a good time to confront her about why she'd left her post at the refreshment tables. Jennifer glanced in her direction and saw Dougie. Olivia waved to her, but Jennifer spun around and went back inside the building as if she didn't want Dougie to see her. It struck Olivia that Jennifer had never been around when Dougie and Trevor showed up. Had Jennifer lured them to Chatterley Heights in order to . . . what? To kill whichever one she assumed had murdered her sister?

"Dougie?"

Dougie started. He eyed Olivia warily.

"I am just going to keep asking you until you tell me the truth. Why did you and Trevor really come to Chatterley Heights? Was it because someone was blackmailing you?"

Dougie's jaw dropped, but he didn't move.

"Please, Dougie, just tell me. I don't think you killed Trevor."

Dougie stared into Olivia's eyes, cleared his throat. "Yes," he said, "someone was trying to blackmail both of us over something that happened a long time ago."

Olivia nodded. "The murder of Melissa Nortenson. And you were innocent." She made it a statement of fact.

"Yes. Trevor said he was innocent, too. He needed an alibi, and so did I, so we alibied each other. I was never sure of his innocence until . . ."

"Until when? Please, Dougie. I don't think we have much time."

Dougie's eyes searched the patio.

"Are you looking for Jennifer Nortenson?"

Dougie nodded. "She was the only one we could think of who would try to blackmail us . . . the only one who might care enough to follow through after all these years. Trevor refused to pay. He insisted on confronting her. That's when I felt more sure that he might be innocent."

"Are you sure Trevor wasn't intending to silence Jennifer permanently?"

"I was his muscle," Dougie said. "Permanent silencing would have been my job. But Trevor never so much as hinted that he wanted me to frighten Jennifer or 'handle' the situation in any other way. We both met with her, together and separately, and she's still alive and kicking." Dougie stared out at the gardens. "Back when the police questioned me about Melissa's murder, they showed me a photo of her body. I think they were trying to shock me into saying something self-incriminating. They seemed certain she'd been pushed over that cliff, but they didn't tell me why they thought that. Trevor was never rough with women. Not physically, anyway. If Melissa had refused his advances, which I sincerely doubt, he would have walked away. To Trevor it was all a game. Women weren't really individuals to him; they didn't truly matter."

"I don't understand why Jennifer tried to blackmail the two of you in the first place. Was she just hoping to make some money?"

Dougie shook his head. "She was absolutely convinced that one of us had killed her sister. She was trying to figure out which of us was guilty. She was open about that. Then when we both showed up, she thought maybe we'd done it together. She acted confused."

Was Jennifer acting? If Jennifer wasn't the killer, then it had to be . . . Howie. Brilliant, ruthless, unattractive. Howie was a genius, but he'd always been unsuccessful with the opposite sex, both in high school and beyond. He'd lost his high-level job because he broke the law, but he was skilled enough to cover his tracks.

Though small, Howie worked out, kept fit. He was probably strong enough to transport Trevor's body. But why would Howie arrange the body on The Gingerbread House porch? Olivia thought she knew the answer. Jennifer moved to Chatterley Heights, using a different last name. Maybe Howie already knew about her blackmail scheme, or maybe he learned about it later. But he did find out that Trevor and Dougie were coming to Chatterley Heights because, as her mother had told Maddie, *Lenora had visited every business on Town Square to spread the news.* Howie surely knew they weren't coming to visit Lenora. That's when he realized he'd need to make one of them look guilty of Melissa Nortenson's murder. Trevor was the most believable suspect, and Howie hated him, so he chose to implicate Trevor. For extra measure, Howie branded Trevor's cheek with a gavel cookie cutter to point to Jennifer as a possible suspect. It had been an extra bonus when Wade showed up at the band shell and lost his temper with Trevor. *That's why I felt so overwhelmed with clues. There were too many suspects.*

Poor, pretty, "slow" Melissa must have seemed like a sure conquest to Howie. But she wasn't. Olivia could well imagine Howie's rage, and the resulting violence, when Melissa resisted his advances. Olivia had no idea how Howie had made contact with Melissa's younger sister. Maybe they'd simply run into each other. It made sense that Howie might keep an eye on Jennifer, especially once he realized she couldn't let go of her sister's unsolved murder. Maybe Jennifer reached out to Howie for help with the anonymous post about her sister's death. Or perhaps he found the post online and deciphered the programming, which led him to Jennifer.

Olivia sank back in her chair. The break-ins . . . What about those? They happened before Dougie and Trevor arrived in town. They might be unconnected with Trevor's murder, but if they were connected . . . Olivia glanced toward Howie, still standing on the path between the two gardens. He was watching her. No, not her, something behind her. Olivia twisted around in her chair. She saw Del striding in her direction. His eyes, however, were focused on Howie.

The rolling cart bearing the rose-petal cookie cake was not far from where Howie stood. Olivia saw him glance sideways at the cart. Maddie was watching him, too. Her eyes narrowed with suspicion as Howie sidled up to the cart and reached toward the handle. What Maddie could not see was the small silver object Howie drew from the pocket of his suit coat. Olivia couldn't tell a pistol from a revolver, but she knew a gun when she saw one.

Olivia and Dougie sat between Del and Howie, right in harm's way.

Olivia looked back and saw Del push a server to the ground. Del drew his weapon but kept it at his side. As he neared Howie, Del aimed his gun. Howie grasped the handle of the cart with Maddie's wedding

410

cookie cake.

"Dougie," Olivia whispered.

"Oh jeez," Dougie said as he saw Howie's gun. He grabbed Olivia by the shoulder and pulled her under the table with him. Olivia watched in horror as Maddie, who stood behind Howie, took off at a run. But she wasn't running away. She ran straight at Howie. As Howie pulled the cart back to give it a good shove forward, Maddie leaped onto his back. Her satin gown glowed in the late afternoon sunlight as she flung her knees around his waist.

With the fearless passion of a bride defending her wedding cake, Maddie wrapped her arms around Howie's neck, and yelled, "Touch that cookie cake and you're a dead man!"

Howie lost his balance. He toppled backward, choking, and fell on top of Maddie. The gun flew from his hand and slid out of his reach. Del kicked the gun farther away. He yanked Howie to his feet and cuffed his hands behind his back. Lucas arrived at a gallop, pulled Maddie to her feet, and threw his arms around her.

"Wow," Dougie said. "That's quite a woman."

"That she is," Olivia said. "That she is."

CHAPTER NINETEEN

When a volley of Yorkie yaps jolted Olivia
from deep sleep, her chest began to thump.
It took a few moments for her groggy brain
to realize the thumping came from her own
heart. She had no idea what had caused
such a reaction. Her dreams, when she
remembered them, usually contained im-
ages like cookies dancing in nonpareils or
sprinkles. A nightmare, for Olivia, might
involve a volcano spewing royal icing in all
the colors of the rainbow.

Olivia lifted her head off the pillow and
saw Spunky, ears perked, staring at her
bedside table. "What's up, Spunks?" His
ears twitched, but he didn't offer an explanation. Olivia struggled upright and examined the table, which held a lamp and her
cell phone. "Did my phone vibrate? At this
hour?" She checked for recent messages and
found a missed call from the store's kitchen
phone. No message. The date read May 6,

which was . . . *Today? From the kitchen phone?* "Maddie cannot be baking at five thirty a.m. only a day and a half after she subdued a murderer at her own engagement party. Can nothing slow that woman down?"

Olivia slid out of bed and into the laceless, worn-out tennis shoes she used as slippers. "Come on, Spunks. Maddie needs a stern lecture and possibly a sleeping pill."

When Olivia arrived downstairs and unlocked the door of The Gingerbread House, she found the sales floor lit as if they were opening in five minutes. Spunky sneaked past her and trotted toward the cookbook nook. Maddie's voice said, "Hey, Spunks, did you unlock that door all by yourself? What a clever boy."

Spunky answered with his happy yap.

"Little fibber," Olivia called out. "Don't think you can fool anyone but Maddie. I'm the one with the opposable thumbs, and don't you forget it." Spunky emerged from the cookbook nook and made straight for the front window, where he settled on his favorite chair.

Maddie poked her head into the room, looking all too alert. "I'm sorry, Livie. My call woke you up, didn't it? I forgot what time it was. However, now that you're up, I can start the music."

"The music?"

"Don't worry, Livie, not the Dixie Cups. You'll love this." Maddie disappeared back into the cookbook nook.

A moment later, Olivia heard a familiar strain, followed by a man's voice singing, "I'm getting married in the morning. . . ."

"Maddie? What is Stanley Holloway doing in our cookbook nook?"

Maddie joined her, a puzzled expression on her freckled face. "Because I'm getting married, Livie."

"I hate to break it to you, but your secret is out. The engagement bash was a big giveaway."

"Let me explain, Livie. Lucas and I are getting married in the morning. *This* morning. At ten a.m. The ceremony will be here, so I'm decorating the store."

"You're . . . I . . ."

"You need coffee," Maddie said. "And a cookie." With a critical up-and-down look, she added, "And a long shower."

"But why the change in plans?"

"Because, Livie, I'm not scared anymore. There's nothing like a brush with death to make lifetime commitment look less terrifying. Also, no one at the party touched our gorgeous cookie cake, and it won't last for a week." With a broad grin, Maddie said,

414

"Besides, now I have a story to tell my kids and grandkids. Grandma once captured a killer!"

"She did indeed." Olivia gave her best friend since age ten a one-armed hug. "Do you need help with the arrangements?"

"All done," Maddie said. "Del is still your date, by the way. Too late to swap him out for a new one. So run along and get ready. Be down here by nine forty-five, ready to party once again. This time we'll lock the doors to keep itinerant murderers on the streets, where they belong." Maddie disappeared into the cookbook nook.

Spunky hopped off his chair and joined Olivia as she left the store. During their journey back upstairs to her apartment, Olivia hummed the tune to "Get Me to the Church on Time." She had no idea what the lyrics were.

By noon, Maddie and Lucas had been giddily married for over an hour, and the rose-petal cookie cake had dwindled by nearly half. To be fair, Olivia's brother, Jason, was responsible for a substantial portion of the dwindling. Olivia was delighted to see Aunt Sadie sitting next to Maddie. She hadn't felt up to attending the big engagement party. Though now confined to a wheelchair,

Aunt Sadie looked delighted to be part of their more intimate group.

The wedding guest list had been expanded from the original three, not counting the wedding couple, to include Olivia's family, Bertha, and Mr. Willard. It was Mr. Willard who had procured a justice of the peace to perform the hastily scheduled ceremony.

Despite the early hour, Olivia's stepfather produced several bottles of chilled champagne. He popped the cork and began to pour. After several toasts, the guests nibbled on rose-petal cookie cake and chatted together in one group.

"So, Del, how about clearing up a few details for us," Olivia asked with her most fetching smile. She stroked the back of Spunky's neck as he snoozed on her lap.

"Like what?" Del lightly brushed the tip of her nose with his index finger.

"Like, is there any news about all those extra gavel cookie cutters that keep appearing around town . . . including in our kitchen?"

"Oh my," said Mr. Willard and Bertha at the same time. They giggled and leaned closer to each other.

"The gavel cookie cutters all appear to be clear of incriminating evidence," Del said. "So you and Maddie will remain free for the time being."

"So good to know," Olivia said. "Were those cutters attempts to create as many suspects as possible?"

"Howie hasn't been terribly talkative," Del said. "But that's what we assume. We are relatively certain the gavel brand on Trevor's cheek was intended to represent 'justice,' thereby implicating Jennifer in his murder. About the cookie in Trevor's mouth, the girl in a light blue dress . . . We dug into Melissa Nortenson's death and discovered she had been wearing a light blue dress when her body was found. Given that it was her younger sister who found her, we assume the cookie is yet another attempt to implicate Jennifer in Trevor's murder."

"That's plain evil," Bertha said. "Poor child."

"Well, Jennifer has had her revenge on Howie for using her to hide his responsibility for her sister's death. She filled in a number of the blanks. Jennifer admitted that she'd been convinced that Trevor and/or Dougie caused Melissa's death, either willfully or by accident. She couldn't let go until she knew the truth. She devised a plan, but she needed help from someone with strong Internet skills. So she brought Howie into the picture."

"Slow down," Olivia said. "How did Jennifer know about Howie's skills?"

Del chuckled. "Because Howie's ego is approximately the size of the universe. Jennifer found him online, where he was constantly trolling for female companionship. He bragged incessantly about his online prowess. Jennifer contacted him and pretended to be impressed. She initiated an online romance before offering to move to Chatterley Heights to be near him."

"Back up a bit," Maddie said. "Getting Trevor and Dougie to come to Chatterley Heights must have taken some time and effort. How did that happen?"

While Allan topped off champagne glasses, Del said, "Jennifer was single-minded in her pursuit of the truth about her sister's death. It took many months. Once she'd convinced Howie that she was in love with him, she told him she couldn't fully commit herself to a relationship until she let go of losing her beloved sister. She believed Melissa had been pushed off the cliff, and she wanted to know who was responsible. When she broached the idea of using the Internet to lure her two suspects, Trevor and Dougie, to Chatterley Heights, Howie jumped in feet first. Jennifer had hooked him by his ego . . . and his need to protect himself. He saw the situation as a chance to nab a grateful girlfriend while, at the same time, sending someone else to prison for his own actions. A win-win, so to speak."

"Or a lose-lose, depending on your perspective," Olivia said. "Did Jennifer suspect Howie might have been involved in Melissa's death?"

"No, she did not." With a slow shake of his head, Del added, "I wish people would leave the investigating to the professionals."

"Well, I can sure understand Jennifer's frustration," Maddie said. "The police have had years to investigate her sister's death, and it looks like they just let it go." Lucas slipped his arm around her shoulders.

Del opened his mouth to respond, but he remained silent when Olivia cocked a warning eyebrow at him. "Anyway," Del said, "Howie was convinced he was smart enough to implicate Trevor or Dougie in Melissa's death. When they showed up ready to fight for their reputations, Howie panicked. At the moment, I can only guess what happened, but I suspect that Trevor confronted Howie, maybe even accused Howie of pushing Melissa off the cliff because she resisted his questionable charms."

"That sounds like Trevor," Olivia said.

"He was arrogant to the point of foolishness."

"Fatal foolishness," Ellie murmured. "Howie and Trevor were prone to self-delusion. Del, am I correct to think that Howie tried to implicate Jennifer because she had begun to suspect him of killing Trevor?"

"Oh yes, Ellie, you would be correct. Jennifer admitted as much. Of course, Jennifer knew she was innocent, so by setting her up to take the fall, Howie only convinced her that he was guilty."

"Oh, what a tangled web, and so forth," Ellie said. "So very sad."

The group heard a tentative knock on the door of The Gingerbread House. Olivia handed Spunky over to Maddie and opened the door. Jennifer Ellsworth took a few shy steps inside. "Um, I just came to say goodbye," she said, "and thank you."

"Come in and have some champagne," Maddie said. "And maybe half a cookie cake."

Jennifer smiled, and her features softened. "No, really, thanks. I need to get going. I wanted to tell you that I'm leaving town. I . . . I've really enjoyed working here, but I think it's best that I get on with my life, now that . . . well, now that my sister's killer is behind bars. That has been my only goal for so many years, and now it's accomplished. I just wanted to thank you for all you've done and to explain why I disappeared from the store sometimes. You see, I thought Howie was on my side, that he was helping me, so I had to meet with him on short notice. And I look a bit like my sister, so I didn't want Trevor or Dougie to see me and get suspicious that I was the one pretending to blackmail them. I got more and more angry with Howie because he was doing stupid and dangerous things, like breaking into Chatterley Heights businesses and hurting people. I should have seen through him earlier, but . . . Anyway, I'm truly sorry for all the trouble I caused." She slipped out the door so fast that no one had a chance to respond.

The group fell silent for some time before Allan said, "Well, seems I was right about that lad, Howie Upton. I'm certainly glad I'm no longer in the corporate world."

Ellie regarded her husband with puzzlement. "So am I, dear, but what brought that up?"

With his hearty laugh, Allan said, "I'd pegged Howie as a sociopathic genius, you see. If I were in the corporate world, I'd have been tempted to hire the boy for his genius, thinking I could control his sociopathy. That might not have been such a good idea."

When everyone laughed, the mood lightened. "Del, what about the break-ins around town?" Maddie asked. "Were they connected with Trevor's murder? And the rumors in Binnie's blog, what about those?"

Del took a sip of champagne. "Given Howie's lack of cooperation, we're still working on those questions. It's our hypothesis that Howie was trying to create the impression that a violent criminal was preying on Chatterley Heights businesses to throw suspicion off himself. Sort of a fall-back plan, if you will. It's interesting that he used a hammer to damage Lady Chatterley's safe and a different hammer to kill Trevor Lane."

"So Howie is a thematic sort of killer," Olivia said.

Del grinned at her. "Nicely put. Howie wasn't as smart as he thought he was, or he would have realized he should use Wade's hammer for both crimes. Also, Howie shouldn't have left the murder weapon in the band shell while Wade was in jail."

"I find it curious that Howie chose to attack the head teller at the very bank where he works," Olivia said.

Del toasted her. "That happens to be one of our best leads. The head teller was hard on Howie, for good reason. Choosing him to attack looks a lot like revenge."

"At least Wade Harald has been cleared, and Struts gave him back his job at the garage," Jason said. "I'm sure glad about that, especially because I was doing all the work. I mean, I love my job but jeez . . ."

"Stacey and the kids are back home, too," Olivia said. "So far, Binnie has left them alone. I hope she's ashamed of herself for hounding them, but I doubt it."

"And speaking of Binnie," Maddie said, "I hope she's under indictment for something. Where did she get those nasty rumors for her blog?"

With a laugh, Del said, "Probably from Howie, but she claims to be protecting her sources. Not much I can do about that until I hear from a judge. Although Binnie still seems to be conducting a determined vendetta against Livie and me." Del slid his chair closer to Olivia and wrapped a protective arm around her shoulders. "Lucas told me that he and Maddie have moved up their honeymoon to start tomorrow. So now I think we should toast the bride and groom one more time before they disappear to an undisclosed location."

Allan refilled their champagne glasses. It might be a Monday, but no one at the gathering had any intention of going to work, not even Olivia's brother.

To Olivia's surprise, Jason stood to give a toast. He looked handsome in his new blue suit. He'd even gotten his dark hair trimmed so it no longer fell over his eyes. He held his champagne glass aloft, and said, "Maddie, I gotta tell you, I will never forget seeing you take down that jerk. Wow. And in a dress, too. Lucas, you are one lucky dude. If and when I ever find someone I want to marry, I want her to be just like Maddie."

"Olivia was great, too," Maddie said. "The way she pulled everything together."

"Yeah, but she didn't save the day," Jason said.

"It was a cooperative effort," Ellie pointed out. "Del did the investigating, Livie figured out the connections, and Maddie —"

"And Maddie," Jason said, raising his glass to her, "was the muscle."

Olivia raised her own glass to her circle of loved ones. "I want to propose a toast, too," she said. "To each of you, my dear family and friends. You are the best of the best." When Olivia's breath caught in her throat, she stopped and said the rest in her heart.

RECIPES

ELLIE'S LEMON CHICKEN

6–8 boned, skinned chicken breasts
1/2 cup onion, finely chopped
1/4 cup olive oil
1/4 cup fresh lemon juice
1 tablespoon dried oregano leaves (or to taste)
1/2 teaspoon salt (or to taste)
2 cloves garlic, chopped
1 tablespoon finely chopped lemon zest
lemon-pepper seasoning

Place chicken in ungreased oblong pan, 13 × 9 × 2 inches. Mix remaining ingredients and pour over chicken. Sprinkle lemon-pepper seasoning over chicken mixture.

Cook uncovered in 375°F oven for 20 minutes. Turn and spoon sauce over chicken. Cook until thickest pieces are done, about 20–30 minutes longer.

Rose Wedding Cutout Cookies

2 1/2 cups flour
1 teaspoon baking soda
1 teaspoon cream of tartar
1/4 teaspoon salt
1 cup butter, softened
1 1/2 cups powdered sugar
1 egg
1 1/2 teaspoon rosewater
1/2 teaspoon vanilla emulsion (or extract)

Note: For a milder flavor, try one teaspoon each of rosewater and vanilla.

Using a sifter or a whisk, mix together the flour, baking soda, cream of tartar, and salt. Set the bowl aside.

Cream together the softened butter and powdered sugar until light and fluffy. (Use the paddle attachment, if your mixer has one.) Add the unbeaten egg, rosewater, and vanilla. Mix well.

Gradually add the flour mixture to the butter mixture. Use the low setting if you are using a mixer. Mix until thoroughly blended, but try not to overmix the dough. Wrap the dough and chill for about thirty minutes.

Preheat oven to 375° F.

Using powdered sugar (rather than flour)

on your rolling surface, roll the dough to a thickness of about 1/4 inch or less. (Powdered sugar keeps the cookies sweet tasting and more moist, especially if you reroll the remaining dough.) Use a round cookie or biscuit cutter if you wish to use the cookies for a cookie cake. Place the cookies about one inch apart on ungreased baking sheets. If you wish, sprinkle the unbaked cookies with sparkling sugar, in place of icing. Bake for about 7 to 9 minutes, or until they brown slightly on the edges.

Makes about 3–4 dozen cookies, depending on the size of the cookie cutter.

*If you wish to make a cookie cake, you might try using sparkling sugar before baking. If you want an iced cake, spread royal icing on cooled, baked cookies, and allow the icing to dry thoroughly before assembling the cake. Use a dab of royal icing to hold the cookies together as you arrange them in a pyramid. A dab of royal icing can be used, as well, to attach other decorations, such as organic or candied rose petals. Use your imagination and have fun!

The employees of Thorndike Press hope you have enjoyed this Large Print book. All our Thorndike, Wheeler, and Kennebec Large Print titles are designed for easy reading, and all our books are made to last. Other Thorndike Press Large Print books are available at your library, through selected bookstores, or directly from us.

For information about titles, please call:
(800) 223-1244

or visit our Web site at:
http://gale.cengage.com/thorndike

To share your comments, please write:
Publisher
Thorndike Press
10 Water St., Suite 310
Waterville, ME 04901